Hunter Steele was born in Edinburgh in 1949. He was educated at Daniel Stewart's College, and at the Universities of Edinburgh, London and Cambridge. He is based in Scotland, and from 1986 to 1987 he was Creative Writing Fellow at the Universities of Glasgow and Strathclyde. He has contributed to *Mind*, the *British Journal of Aesthetics* and *Penthouse*, and his other published novels are *McCandy*, *The Wishdoctor's Song*, and *Lord Hamlet's Castle*. In progress is a monstrous saga of intrigue, copulation and death in 16th-century France.

D1097617

HUNTER STEELE

Chasing the Gilded Shadow

A tale of the time of James IV of Scotland

PALADIN
GRAFTON BOOKS
A Division of the Collins Publishing Group

LONDON GLASGOW
TORONTO SYDNEY AUCKLAND

Paladin
Grafton Books
A Division of the Collins Publishing Group
8 Grafton Street, London W1X 3LA

Published in Paladin Books 1987

First published in Great Britain by
André Deutsch Ltd 1986

ISBN 0-586-08625-0

Printed and bound in Great Britain by
Collins, Glasgow

Set in Ehrhardt

This quasi-historical novel was inspired by, and is substantially indebted to, James Hogg's *Bridal of Polmood* account of the original scandal.

Less obvious debts I owe to William Shakespeare and Arthur Schopenhauer. From them I have learned most of whatever I know about the magic of language, the nature of fiction, and the craft of story-telling. For further interest on these two debts, see 'Character Maps', etc., in my forthcoming *Schopenhauer's Ethical Advice*.

Special thanks to my former agent and present editor, Sheila McIlwraith. Without her sustained creative enthusiasm for these pages, you might not be reading them today. Any pet armadillos still in the text are mine alone.

Last and most, a debt to my parents, who have given me a love of Scottish border country, a playground in the precincts of Crawmelt Castle, an education unfit for kings, and more good things than I have ever deserved. This book is dedicated to Mungo and Katharine Steele.

H.S., Provence, 1985

Contents

O, how this spring of love resembleth
    The uncertain glory of an April day,
Which now shows all the beauty of the sun,
    And by and by a cloud takes all away.

        Proteus in *Two Gentlemen of Verona*

The dramatic or epic poet should know that he is fate, and therefore should be, like this, inexorable; likewise that he is the mirror of the human race, and ought therefore to represent very many bad and sometimes wicked characters, as well as many fools, eccentrics, and simpletons; now and again a person who is reasonable, prudent, honest, or good, and only as the rarest exception someone magnanimous.

        Schopenhauer, *World as Will and Representation*

The fairer she is legged and faced,
The brighter jewelled, and richer laced,
And more in high position placed,
The faster must a maiden haste
To keep the gilded shadow chased.

        Thirteenth-century Iranian Lovesong

But pleasures are like poppies spread –
Seize the flow'r, its bloom is shed.

        Robert Burns, *Tam o' Shanter*

You aren't free, no matter what you say. Your freedom is only a phantom that travels the world in a cloak of fog. You try to grab hold of it, but it will always slip away. All you'll have left is a dampness on your fingers.

        Luis Bunuel, *My Last Breath*

PART ONE
Summer of 1506
Crawmelt

1

THE BETROTHAL

MIAOW, MIAOW
'It's a wonder what people see in some people!' remarked the beautiful Lady Ann Gray.

'Indeed!' her companion agreed. 'Some people there are, in this world, who are good for nothing but making a flash.' Lady Elinor Hume, small and waspish with the sting of the inadequately husbanded, gave a sniffing toss to her sharp-featured head.

'And others there are', said Lady Ann, 'who are good for nothing but admiring those people. Look out for that ditch, will you not?'

'Thank you, Mistress Gray, but I had observed it,' said Lady Hume, who had not. Lengthening her tight mincing step the few inches necessary to clear the sedge-screened treachery of the ditch, the wife of the Lord Chamberlain of Scotland added:

'It is doubtless the luckiest occurrence that could have befallen her.'

'It is hardly uncharitable to suggest that there was little time to lose.'

'Indeed not! If Polmood had not fallen for her so utterly, quite possibly no other would. And she might very soon have been obliged to leave our society *in some other way*!'

Tall and dark, Lady Ann sighed her sorrowful assent.

The two ladies reluctantly concluded that there were some who knew and some who just did not know about such things, and, as the late-afternoon sun began to yield its strength to the purply-brown heights of the distant watershed, they turned their walk around and headed eastwardly home, along the north bank of the meandering Meggat Water, towards the angular grey mass of Crawmelt Castle.

CRAWMELT CASTLE
It was not really a castle but rather a hunting tower, owned by the Crown and customarily visited by the King and his nobles during

the harvest months, when great sports were enjoyed and much merriment made. While the King and his lusty gallants enjoyed the chase and the slaughter of stags on Meggat-dale and the mountains of the Lowes, the Queen and her attendant ladies would usually remain at the larger and more comfortably appointed Castle of Nidpath, near Peebles, where the terrain was less intractable and the climate less severe. But when the weather was fine and the mountains of the forest clear, the Queen and her maidens would sometimes make excursions to the hunting quarters and here spend a few days in diversions with their menfolk.

And it was during one of these excursions that the laird of Polmood fell very desperately in love with one of the Queen's maidens, a very young lady, so freshly ripened in her outstanding beauties that the previous year her charms had passed unnoticed.

Elizabeth Manners was her name.

Of English extraction, and orphaned in early childhood, she had followed Queen Margaret from her native London three years earlier, in 1503, when Margaret, herself barely nubile, was banished north for politic marriage to the grizzly-red and already middle-aged King of Scots. Also in the wedding entourage had been the minx-minded Lady Ann Gray. Daughter of the Countess of Surrey and the same age as Queen Margaret, Madam Gray, raven-locked and as slim of waist as she was full of breast, had until recently reigned unrivalled as the foremost beauty of all Scotland.

But now the public eyes blinked wide for Elizabeth.

And yet, though many of the younger courtiers admired the glow of her opening attractions and not a few had begun to flatter her, with all the niggling silliness of the sexually captivated male, it was noticed that none had yet the purity of motive to ask for her hand in marriage. For, she being an orphan from a strange country and dependent on the bounty of the Queen, by whom she was greatly beloved, her prospects were severely hampered by her destitution of title and inheritance.

Until she came to Crawmelt in the summer of 1506.

POLMOOD PROPOSES

Norman Hunter of Polmood, the ninth of that name, and chief forester to the King of Scotland in all those parts, was a man of surpassing courage, physical endowment and sporting accomplishment, and hence was much respected by his Majesty and all the nobles of the court who frequented the forests of Frood and Meggat-dale for the purpose of hunting. He had often entertained the King himself at his own Castle of Polmood, and while James remained at Crawmelt, some six miles to the south-east, Norman of Polmood was seldom absent from the royal side. For, besides the other qualifications that endeared him to the King, Polmood was far and away the best marksman then in Scotland: so sharp was his eye that even when the deer was running at full speed, and the arrows of all others had fired and failed, whenever Polmood's shaft was unleashed the quarry was seen to founder.

'Your Majesty,' Polmood had requested, the morning after the hunt convened at Crawmelt, 'may I have a word?'

'Yes, indeed, great old friend,' said James, whose waggishness was noted. 'Our entire vocabulary is at your disposal.'

But Polmood was a man whom waggishness largely lost.

'It is yonder fair maid, Sire,' he confessed, earnestly direct and gruffly deep. 'She with the flowers in her hair, that is never apart from the Queen.'

'Mmmm?'

'Her name, Sire . . .'

'Is Elizabeth, Elizabeth Manners. A most polite and refined little name, for a most polite and refined young lady. Is it not?' James scratched his straggling gingery beard and gazed amusedly from Polmood's shuffling discomfiture to the far end of the Great Hall, where the court ladies were closely grouped round the Queen in their customary gaggle of giggle and gossip.

'I have in mind, Sire, to ask for her hand. If she is not promised, that is. And if your Majesty permits.'

'She is very young, Polmood!'

'I ken that, Sire. But . . .'

'Very young indeed.'

'No younger, Sire, if your Majesty will allow me to say, than the Queen Margaret herself when she was wed.'

'Quite possibly true, Polmood. Yet. . .'

'Yet what, Sire?'

'Polmood, sir! You do forget yourself!' But there was affection to cushion the King's rebuke.

'Forgive me, Sire.'

'Think nothing of it, Polmood,' breezed James, pricked by guilt at his readiness to put Authority to pranking advantage. 'The fault was entirely ours. As to the girl, she is comely, it is true. But an orphan, Polmood. An orphan. She has no dowry, you know.'

'I'll want no dowry, Sire, but her beauty and . . .' Polmood swallowed unsurely, for pretty words felt seasick on his simple tongue. 'And her virtuous honesty.'

'Quite so. Quite so. In these she is rich indeed. Incomparably richer than her Majesty's father!' The King's passing frown reflected his inability to forgive the meanness with which Henry VII of England had endowered the wedding of his daughter, Margaret, to Scotland.

'Very well, Polmood,' he then pronounced. 'As she is our valued ward and you our staunchest henchman, so we do consent. But only that you court her, Polmood. Not talk of weddings until the girl herself agrees. And even then the Queen will miss her sorely – as will we,' he added absently, his eye brightening as it passed from Elizabeth to the mischievous charade being enacted by Lady Ann for the titillation of the onlooking ladies.

'You Majesty is most gracious,' growled Polmood, his rustic mind already wrestling for fine phrases and tender endearments to enhance his suit.

'Eh?' murmured the King. 'Ah yes. If you say so, Polmood. Most of our subjects do – not all, mark you. *Et alors! Bonne chance pour votre amour.*'

So it was that the madly enamoured forester, having successfully started his game with the King's approval, lost no time in the chase, and by the most determined perseverance, to use his own expression, he ran her down in the course of just one week.

'Mistress Elizabeth!' he called, on the fifth morning of his campaign.

'Yes, kind sir,' she returned, politely cool. 'Good morning to you.' She paused and waited for her lumbering wooer to catch up. The Crawmelt Burn was fast and foaming, following heavy rains the previous day, and Elizabeth had gone strolling up the bracken-decked east bank of its lower reaches, to enjoy the pure primitive pleasure of singing with abandon in the privacy of the wild waters roaring.

Polmood's intrustion was far from unexpected, as for the past few days he had dogged her every footstep with the devotion of a lovesick spaniel.

Yet how irksome to have one's song cut short!

'It is clement once more, my lady,' observed Polmood.

'I suppose it is,' murmured Elizabeth. Being only fourteen and as yet sensibly more visual than lexical, she was unimpressed by the phrasy finery for which Polmood's recent sleep had paid so dear.

'May I walk with you, lady?'

'I pray you do.'

Polmood did.

Three silence-stretched minutes later he blurted:

'Mistress Elizabeth!'

'Y . . . e . . . s?'

'I . . . have you yet considered my offer, my lady?'

'Which offer would that be, my lord? You have made me so many of late.' Elizabeth's clear blue eyes smiled in innocence of a barely believable profundity – not for nothing had she spent long hours in close company with the ladies of the court.

Polmood shuddered in frustration, his smouldering dark green eyes glued helplessly to the lightly cotton-clad slender shoulders and lissom limbs that led him at a gentle girly pace towards a solitary full-berried rowan tree by the water's edge.

'My offer, lady,' he rasped, 'to make you my wife. To make you Dame Elizabeth Hunter of Polmood. Mistress of my house, my servants and all my lands. And mother of my children,' he urged in a sob of almost desperation.

Elizabeth reached up, plucked a fine-boned dainty handful of the rich-red berries and began to toss them, slowly, one by one, into the muddied turbulence that was normally a still crystal-clear pool of lurking brown trout.

When she had first cast an interested eye over Polmood, having been quietly advised by Queen Margaret of the giant forester's impending suit, she treated the whole idea as a joke. 'Hmm!' she had scoffed. 'That hairy old monster!'

But the hairy old monster had persisted, no other offered, and

Elizabeth remained without a dowry: a fact with which her galloping court-bred mind was firmly saddled.

And which sorely chafed.

'Well?' coaxed Polmood, as she bent to wipe her berry-stained hands on the soft mottled moss of the riverbank. 'I can promise you a wedding, my lady, for the whole world to envy. With the ceremony in the Chapel of Saint Mary, and the celebrations at Nidpath. The King has promised it!'

A *wedding*!

Elizabeth straightened slowly, delicately rubbing dry hands. 'And when, sir,' she asked, 'would this wedding take place?'

'Doubtless within the week, it would be. For the King is an impatient man.'

A wedding *within the week*!

'Very like this Saturday,' Polmood surmised, unconscious of the trump he played.

'Sir,' said Elizabeth in only moderate excitement, as though requesting her favourite dish for dinner, 'if it is truly your wish to marry me, I shall be most honoured to make you a loyal and faithful wife.'

Polmood staggered as if stricken. 'Oh Lord!' he cried, throwing wide his huge leather-jerkined arms and addressing the wisped blue sky. 'NOBLE LORD! PRAISE BE TO HEAVEN!'

Elizabeth smiled in youthful pleasure at triggering such explosive happiness.

'Oh, my *lady*!' gulped Polmood, half-choked by his joy. 'May we seal our pact . . . with a kiss?'

'Indeed we may, my lord.' Unaware both of the tears in Polmood's eyes and of his wish that their lips should meet, Elizabeth held out her courtly maiden's hand.

Polmood sank to his knees, pressed her little fingers against his thick grey-whiskered lips and for a moment tasted, through the running brine of his own ecstasy, the dry tender fragrance of her soft smooth skin.

Two hours later the betrothal was announced by the King himself – he being a man who delighted in all forms of revel and pageantry – amid the brassy blasting of trumpets and bugles and the several draining of copious bumpers, and hence it was, that same afternoon, that the Ladies Hume and Gray took their carping consitutionals along the bank of the Meggat.

WOOF, WOOF

The Crawmelt Burn gathers and grows in the time-hewn crags and gulleys of some of the highest and most inaccessible mountains in the south of Scotland, where, some hundred and fifty years later, the miserable remnants of the fugitive Covenanters were to find themselves burrowing in the peat hags for shelter and scrabbling with the foxes to burgle the nests of the grouse and the curlew. In drought a trickle, in flood a devouring torrent, the Burn flows about five miles approximately south to join, at right-angles, the larger and lazier Meggat Water, which in turn rolls sedately east to offer itself in eternal sacrifice to the deep blue womb of Saint Mary's Loch.*

The Castle of Crawmelt stood very close by the Burn, perhaps a quarter of a mile before the Meggat, and it was on the green to the south of the Castle, on the evening of the betrothal of Elizabeth Manners to Norman of Polmood, that the following conversation took place.

'Bogger these ferking midges to hell!' exclaimed Donald, Laird of Lamington. With tipsy vigour he slapped his brow and scratched around his sandy-curled crown.

'It is less likely the midges, Donald, than the wine,' opined his friend, the thin and tubercular Sir Patrick Hepburn. 'What say you, my Lord Hume?'

'What say I?' said the slight but pugnacious Lord Chamberlain 'What say I? Why, I say this.' And, after pausing to belch a long loud wet confession of protracted overindulgence, he said:

'I say that is seems Carmichael's mind is away with the brownies. And I also say this loss is the more regrettable as it is now CARMICHAEL'S TURN to throw, while my own throw can scarce be beat. This say I!'

'Well, said, my lord!' slurred Lamington, lunging for his pewter goblet and almost upsetting it.

'Your pardon, my lord,' said Carmichael, jolted by Lord Hume's pointed loudness. 'I was thinking.'

* Here, alas, man's damming endeavours have overtaken literary eternity.

'A dangerous habit!' gurgled Lamington.

'It saps one's manhood,' wheezed Sir Patrick, whose quips were as thin and tubercular as himself.

Carmichael reached forward and gave the dice a desultory throw.

'Ha!' crew Hume. 'My win! My win!' He scooped eagerly at the pool of silver coin in the middle of the spread hide whereon the four men played. 'Will not the King join us?' he added greedily, thinking his luck to be in and knowing James for a punter of peerless prodigality. He squinted through the upper flickers of the large log fire that lit the green. 'Polmood has had his ear for as long as I can remember!'

'About an hour, my lord!' Lamington tittered.

'It is the wedding, my lord,' explained Hepburn. 'They discuss the wedding.'

'The wedding!' cheered Lamington. 'Oh, the *wedding*! A pretty piece!'

'The *wedding*?' Hume acidly inquired. 'The wedding is a pretty piece? I pray you, Lamington, inform us how that may be. That the wedding is a pretty piece, when the wedding is by no means yet come to pass? I ask you! What say you?'

'He means the *wench*!' said Hepburn. 'Elizabeth. He means that the wench is a pretty piece, and that there is nothing he would like more than to . . .'

'I mean no such thing, Patrick,' grunted Lamington. 'Bogger your boobles!'

'Then why . . .'

'I mean that it is a pretty piece of play on the part of the King. To have kept her dowry a secret until she was already bespoke – bogger me! Had I but kenned, but kenned!'

'Indeed?' said Hume. 'And what if you had but kenned, but *kenned*?'

'Why, my lord, is it not plain as the harvest moon yonder. If I had but kenned what the lass would bring with her, I would myself have tried for her hand. And all her other parts forby! For she is indeed a pretty piece – as pretty as ever a man could broozle.'

'Ach, Donald!' scoffed Hepburn, his voice thin and damp as a strand of green slime. 'But she would not suit you.'

'And why should she not suit him?' asked Hume. 'Is he leprous?'

–

'No, my lord. Not leprous, precisely. But he has the most monstrous muckle quhillelillie upon him, and the girl is such a meatless child, that I fear they would not fit.'

'*Indeed?*' thrilled Hume. 'So Lamington has a monster broozler, has he? Excellent! Well done, Donald!'

'Like a horse,' added the phthisic Hepburn. 'Or even . . .'

'Come now, Lamington,' Lord Hume tartly chided. 'Our curiosity is fully cocked. Is it not, Carmichael? Yes, indeed it is. And so we pray you, Lamington, bring your muckle wonder forth. Produce! Our eyes would feast.'

'No doubt they would, my lord. But I fear the ladies might not like it.' Lamington cast a glance round the fire to where the Queen and her ladies, spectred in the additional illumination of several lackey-lofted flambeaux, were raptly tuned to the ballad wealth of Old Curry, the King's own harper and sometime clown.

'I should say,' wheedled Hepburn, 'that the ladies would *love* it!'

'There may be indeed be those that might,' conceded Lamington. 'Those, perhaps, that know not what they miss.' He studiously avoided the Lord Chamberlain's gaze. 'But the Queen would not like it. And if the Queen did not like it then the King could not like it. And if the King . . .'

'Enough, Lamington. Enough. Your point is made,' rapped Hume. 'Hey! Hey, boy! You there – more wine. More wine!' From his shameless slumped squat he held up his goblet to the panicking kitchen varlet who materialized out of the umbral gloom with a large earthenware jug.

'And here,' said Lamington.

'Here too,' said Hepburn. 'Carmichael?'

No response.

'*Carmichael!*' Hepburn insisted. 'More wine, sir?'

Baron John Carmichael of Hyndford morosely stirred the elbow-propped hulk of his long loose frame. 'Thank you no, Sir Patrick,' he replied, his strong voice tremoring. 'I have sufficient.'

'Then hurrah for Carmichael!' cried Hume, wiping wine-slopped whiskers on his sleeve. 'And hurrah for Elizabeth and Polmood too. Hurrah, hurrah! HURRAH!'

'Why so, my lord?' asked Hepburn, wondering if the spiced and flame-warmed wine had unhorsed the Lord Chamberlain's reason, this being a not infrequent occurrence in those days.

'Why so?' returned the unabashed cheerer. 'Why so what, pray?'

'He means, my lord,' quipped Lamington, 'why hurrah, hurrah, HURRAH for Elizabeth and Polmood too? Sir? Indeed!'

'And I mean, sir,' snorted Hume, his hot little eyes reflecting yellow from the fire. 'Hurrah for Polmood, as he has sufficient. As has Carmichael sufficient. For Carmichael has sufficient wine, and Polmood has the person of the beauteous Elizabeth and now the dowry lands of Fingland, Glenbreck and Kingledores as well. The conjunction of which he cannot but deem sufficient in the ... what ails Carmichael? Carmichael, sir, what ails? You did groan, did you not?'

'Groan?' groaned Carmichael. '*Groan*, my lord? I may ... perhaps ... this evening's meat, my lord ... a trifle ... red ...'

'And Elizabeth?' prompted Hepburn, whose lack of interest in Carmichael's intestines was enormous. 'How, my lord, has Elizabeth sufficient – she who is promised to a plodding old brute three times her age?'

'More!' said Lamington. 'They say he is now in his forty-fourth year.'

Lord Hume took a further quaff from his goblet and regarded the Laird of Lamington for a thoughtful moment. Then he said:

'His is in fact forty-two – one year younger than myself. And my meaning is. That Elizabeth will have sufficient in Polmood's *person*. In his *quhillelillie*, his battered old broozler. For it is sufficient indeed, my lords, and will take a lot of beating.'

'If he still can salute it,' sniffed Lamington.

'There is yet no man can throw him in a wrestle,' remarked Hume.

'You have *seen* it, my lord?' inquired Hepburn, who would have liked to.

'Indeed ... I have,' said Hume. His speech was slowing as his downed wine mounted and his eyes and mind went journeying. 'Many years ago. I saw him swim a race. Across the Tweed, it was. Which he won. Of course. A most ... remarkable man. He is. Albeit ... slow. In speech and wit. Yet honest. *Honest!*'

A brief lull in the lordly disclosure bore tribute to the cardinal quality and disclosed the background larking levity of the ladies retiring for the night.

'Will you not kiss your beloved, Elizabeth?' piped Lady Elinor

Hume, gaily unaware of the nearby wineful wince on her husband's face.

'Or bring him with you?' purred Lady Ann Gray. 'For the Castle is cold past midnight, and the bedding – '

'Time enough for that in days to come,' decreed Queen Margaret, of necessity precociously mature for her seventeen years. 'Let the girl be.'

As the ladies trooped out of earshot into the Castle, Donald of Lamington resumed:

'His first wife . . .'

'Was a goodly woman,' continued the reminiscing Hume. 'God rest her soul. And the child . . . he has no heirs, you see. He has no heirs, and sore must it grieve him. His bed is lonely, his nights are long, and with the happy sounds of children playing his hall rings not. So great must be his love for the girl!'

'Love, my lord?' said Lamington. '*Love*, you say? I ask you, sir, if it is love of the *wench* that drives the man. Or rather passion to serve his *line*? His blood and breed?'

'Hark at you, Donald!' sneered Hepburn. 'Are you not waxing quite the philosopher? Blood and breed, indeed! And would you not give all my Lord Hume's silver winnings to blood the girl yourself? As would I. For doubtless the Queen has kept her yet pure, that she is now ripe to burst and yield like a bumper plum. And her towdie too, I'll wager, is small and trim and burning to juice . . .'

'I'LL THANK YOU, SIR, TO MIND YOUR FERKING TONGUE. As you speak of a lady you are not fit to even gaze upon!' Unsane rage quivered in Sir John Carmichael's voice as it lashed from his shadowy corner.

A hush of amusement puffed up from the various other huddles of male intrigue and inebriation that dotted the green like a ragged necklace around the fire.

'Bravo!' called King James, from his Tête-à-tête with Polmood. 'Hardly could we disagree with the noble lord less. Our national speech is indeed in dire need of refinement, as he so nicely demonstrates.'

Raucous chuckles and odd echoes of the Kingly 'Bravo!' then signified the drunken insouciance to which the collective interest in Carmichael's eruption subsided.

'I ask your pardon, Sir John,' muttered Sir Patrick, acidly nervous, being mindful of Carmichael's great size and physical strength. 'I had not previously noted such delicacy in your sensibilities.' Stiff with indignation, he contrived to inch his posterior cautiously closer to the large and powerful Lamington.

'Come, come, Carmichael!' tutted Lord Hume, far the most senior man present, both in years and authority. 'Sir Patrick meant no harm. Did you, Sir Patrick? No, indeed! And if a certain doggy licence is not allowed us in our cups, when there are no ladies present, then is not the world the poorer by half? Come, come!'

'Excuse me, my lord,' growled Carmichael, jumping to his feet and hovering at the outside edge of the remaining three-man huddle like a vulture by a corpse. 'I am . . . irritable with my grumbling belly.'

'And will you not also crave pardon of the good Sir Patrick?'

'I – forgive me, sirs. I fear my gorge rises.' So saying, Carmichael's silhouette turned and swiftly plunged into the bushes that jungled thickly between the green and the Crawmelt Burn.

'Myself I found nothing amiss with this evening's meat,' Lord Hume in a puzzled tone remarked.

'I wonder if Carmichael may not be jealous,' said Lamington.

'Who would not be?' said Hepburn.

'Why should he be jealous?' inquired Hume. 'He has had time in plenty to stake his claim. Nor is he lacking in credentials, being greatly Polmood's inferior in years and hugely his superior in estate. He even shares blood with the King: how could he be jealous?'

'The Duke of Rothesay', rejoined Lamington, 'is the King's own brother, and yet would be quite mad with jealousy . . .'

'And will be when he hears!' nodded Hepburn.

'If he were not away a-mounting all the foolish young nannies in gay Paree.'

'What *is* jealousy?' the Lord Chamberlain suddenly wondered. For his own part, he was no longer able (he would himself have said *inclined*) to service the spritely Lady Elinor upwards of twice a fortnight. In a good month. Yet the sinking suspicion that she sought solace from the loins of others was constantly with him. 'Is it perhaps', he pondered blackly, 'a foretaste of the Good Lord's justice to come?'

–

'It is wanting', opined the burly Lamington, a cart-horse among men, 'to shove your quhillelillie – '

'Where another man's is shoving already!' agreed Hepburn, who knew the feeling well.

'Ah!' murmured Lord Hume.

For several moments a skin of silence formed across the conversation, like surface tension on a stagnant pool, inviting stray splinters of sound from the crackling fire and the rushing stream to skate across it with the evanescence of insects newly hatched.

To see which, the several senses of the three jealous lords were too dull by far.

'The King retires,' whined Hepburn.

'Then so shall we,' rumbled Lamington, initiating the leaden shifting of large limbs.

'Not so, gentlemen!' Lord Hume protested with the thinly veiled alarm of one for whom night, insufficiently sedated, means nightmare. 'Not so! Another throw, I pray you.' He reached to cup the dice. 'And one last drink to cap the night! Agreed? I thank you. Hey, boy! Bring us wine. More *wine*!'

2
THE NEXT TWO DAYS

GILDING THE SHADOW

The day following the betrothal was the second Wednesday in August. By the middle of the morning the light but clinging Scotch mist has lifted and vanished into the shimmering heavens, like a mood of grey uncertainty dispelled by the King's announcement that the wedding had been fixed for the Saturday.

A wedding, *her* wedding, only three days away!

Now that the time and place were fixed, the person of her prospective life-partner was of all things the least in Elizabeth's mind. She thought of nothing but the gaiety and splendour of her approaching nuptials, of the deference and respect that would be paid by all ranks to the lovely bride. And, most of all, she pictured in fantastic detail the envious glances, gestures and wistful frowns that would signify her mighty conquest over all her titled associates, every one of whom, the Queen assured her, would have stooped to great lengths for the sake of Polmood's hand.

Elizabeth had teethed on court splendour, and hence had learned to emulate with passionate fondness every ornament of dress and decorum and every groomable personal quality that ladies had which ladies envied and men admired. Her heart as yet was a stranger to the tender passion. Certainly she had known times when life seemed empty and her future foreshortened and flat, but these she attributed to precisely her own total lack of such finery, estate and position as were possessed and enjoyed, apparently without qualification, by all the greatest ladies she had grown to model herself upon.

Who can blame her?

Her bridal regalia, the brilliant appearance she would make, the honour of leading the dance in the Hall and on the green – of course these sparkling phantoms wrought powerful on the youthful Elizabeth, and any tiny bubbles of warning arising from her instinctive depths churned instantly to faery foam on the surface of her excited awareness, which pulled like a moon-drawn tide toward the magic shore of Saturday's celebration.

And it is surprising that these tingling anticipations of envious homage and gallant compliments paid should have had a warming, cheering effect upon Elizabeth's perceptions of herself? No longer did her little glass portray, as previously it often had, the doubtful pout of a newly arrived stranger to womanhood, undesired and undesirable. Now, she found, her large steady eyes communed with those of a maiden so beautiful that all questions of doubt and envy fell abjectly before her, like sinners reaching out for redemption! And duly she redeemed them, with her full oval countenance so full of grace, her tall slender form so elegantly perfect, her demurely small high breasts so pertly appealing, and her matchless colour to outvie the lily and the damask rose.

What a wonderous piece of work, this woman!

By sharing these impressions, Polmood greatly strengthened them. He had got himself a wife, he believed (and tirelessly repeated to such gentlemen as would listen, and even to his horse and hounds), who was the very original of everything lovely and desirable in Woman. Who played upon the lute and sang so exquisitely that she ravished the hearts of all who heard her, and who even was said to charm the wild beasts and birds of the forest to gather around her at eventide.

With the wedding so close, it might be conjectured that the bride so smiting and the groom so smitten would fill such short conversations as they could snatch together, or rather which Polmood could snatch from the bustle which naturally centred round Elizabeth, with tender exchange of fond endearments, perhaps alternating with moments of sober reflection on the mode of life they were to lead together in the future both near and far. Yet whenever Polmood's remarks veered serious he would find that Elizabeth instantly teased him back to prattle of such and such articles of dress or necessary equipage, or with proposals for future festivities and social pleasure such as never before had even knocked at the forester's mind.

But smitten he was and smitten he everywhere yielded, telling her with cheerful complacency that, as she had been bred at court and understood such matters, everything would be arranged and provided according to her direction. He would then seize and kiss in the most affectionate manner her daintily offered virgin's hand; she in return would take her leave with a courtesy and smile so bewitching that Polmood felt his heart must melt with the overpowering heat of his soft delight.

And he congratulated himself as the happiest of men.

Only once, towards noon on the Thursday, did he, dizzily drunk on the fumes of his ardour, actually attempt to kiss his beloved on the lips. So astonished was he at seeing her shrink involuntarily from his embrace, as from some foul-fanged beast of prey, and so immediately did she recover her gaiety and amiable banter, that the incident passed unmentioned and within moments might never have occurred at all.

And everything went on as before.

CARMICHAEL PLEADS

By late on the Thursday afternoon Sir John Carmichael of Hyndford had tightened into such a tortured clench of physical and nervous tension as might have induced some fatal attack in a man of frailer constitution and longer tooth. The meat gripe he had feigned on the Tuesday night, to scape the lewd attentions of his fellow dicers, had now actualized, his heartbeat he found irregularly racing, and his grinning mask of manners had fled him utterly, like a pageant of rats from a breaking barge, so that not a few of the sporting lords could be heard to mutter such ominous diagnoses as:

'Carmichael is not himself of late!'

And:

'It is surely the loss of his father that grieves him.'

Whereas in fact it was the prospective loss of the incomparable Elizabeth that ate so greedily into Carmichael's bowels, and the raging jealousy that in him now blazed, compared with the trivial sexual pique so lately and loosely characterized by my lords Lamington and Hepburn, was as the midday equatorial sun to the light of a cold winter's moon.

Now that Elizabeth was promised to Polmood, together with the jointure lands of Fingland, Glenbreck and Kingledores (lands which bordered his own estate of Hyndford!), Carmichael found that he admired and loved her with all his heart, that he had long intended to ask the King for her hand when the time was ripe, and that this pre-emption by Polmood could only be blamed on his own foolish chivalry, in that the girl was in years still tender and barely ready for the ardours and rigours of the marital state. It was thus not diffidence or want of opportunity that had previously prevented Carmichael from acquainting Elizabeth with the sweet depth and eternal nobility of his sentiments (other than by his pointed smiles and virile glances, which he fancied had always returned bespeaking great congeniality of feeling and reciprocity of ultimate intention).

Rather was it his considerateness and concern for Elizabeth's welfare.

Ooooooooh!

How cruel, then, for young Carmichael to find his fair flower plucked, or marked for plucking, as one might say? And how natural that his shuddering anxiety should drive him repeatedly to the thickest, most private tangle in the heart of the Crawmelt wood, there to form and abandon and re-form and re-abandon a thousand desperate schemes to prevent the scheduled marriage and to win Elizabeth back to his rightful self?

But misfortunes are incurably gregarious, as Carmichael discovered to his further turmoil when fianlly he mustered resolve to address Elizabeth's person. She was with the Queen, debating marriage. Or with the ladies, sewing dresses for the wedding. Or with the King, entertaining him with her luted song. Or she was pursued by Polmood, whose unjust right it now was to pursue her – unjust because Polmood owned no place in her heart. This Carmichael knew as, spying upon them from the bushes, he had observed (with a surge of wild glee that almost caused his betrayal) the fleeting moment wherein Elizabeth shrank in fright from Polmood's labial advance.

'*Hallelujah*!' Carmichael's soul had then cried out. 'It is myself the lady loves!' Which laced with hope the crazed diligence with which he thereafter monitored Elizabeth's every movement.

His opportunity arose towards evening on the Thursday.

Elizabeth, seeking a short spell of privacy and refreshment from the uncommon heat and excitement of the day, stole quietly to bathe her hands and feet in the Crawmelt Linn, a deeply still pool, which, a hundred paces upstream from the wood, soothes back to its own cool tranquillity the anguished white froth of a waterfall some two men tall.

Perturbation trembling his every member, Sir John Carmichael followed.

'Good day to you, Mistress Elizabeth!' he blurted, walking up behind her.

'Good day to *you*, Sir John!' she replied, looking round day-dreamingly. She was sitting on the dry brown grass on the bank of the stream, with her plain olive dress pulled up past the knee and her long pale legs flirting freely with the pool. 'I had thought I was alone.'

'I crave your pardon, my lady, for my rude intrusion.' Carmichael squatted beside her, close as he dared. 'But . . .'

'Why, Sir John! I do believe there are tears in your eyes. Indeed there are! How so, Sir John? Can there be some tragedy afoot? On such a glorious day?'

'The tragedy is . . .' said he, his clear voice frogging, 'that I love you, my Lady Elizabeth. I *love* you, more than all the world! And am driven by my love to speak.'

'How kind of you, Sir John, to say so,' she laughed, splashing lightly in the water with her toes. 'I find today that *everyone* loves me – except a few of the ladies, perhaps. For I am to be *married*!' She made her pause express due awe. 'I am to be married on Saturday, and all the world loves a wedding, does it not?'

'Well it may, my lady. But such is not my meaning.'

'Indeed, Sir John? Then I fear I understand your meaning not.'

'My meaning is *plain*, my lady!' Carmichael, drily hoarse, was almost angry with the girl. Blinded by his own obsession, he failed to see hers, and hence interpreted her lack of comprehension as merely a mischievous front. 'My meaning is just that without you it is no longer possible that I enjoy such comforts as this world is pleased to offer.'

'Really, Sir John! They why – '

'That my life itself is quite impossible. Without you. Without *you*, my . . . dearest Elizabeth, as my *wife*! I ask you, lady, to be my wife.'

Elizabeth pulled her dabbling toes from the brook, demurely smoothed her long green skirts to cover her ankles, and shifted round in not a little alarm to fully face this new importuner from the blue. Until a moment ago Carmichael had been nothing to her but a large, quietly sullen young man, darkly handsome yet apparently more devoted to the hunt than to the company of courtly ladies. Now, shading her eyes fron the sun's westing streaks, she perceived in his pleading gaze and crouching intent a passion whose force she found oppressive.

Why did gentlemen take things so vainly *personally*?

'I regret, Sir John,' she said with vehemence, 'that what you propose is quite out of the question. For I am *already* to be married. To Polmood. On Saturday!' Possessively she hugged her Polmood-promised knees. 'As you must surely know.'

Sorely surely Carmichael knew, and furiously could he have roared with rage: why must women be so perversely *conservative*?

Instead he said:

'Oh, Elizabeth, but can Polmood truly *love* you? A man whose years outnumber your own not twice but thrice?'

'What a question, Sir John! Certainly Polmood loves me – hc is to be my husband!'

'And you, lady? Do you love him?' Carmichael coaxed, thinking to play his ace.

'Most certainly I do love him.' Elizabeth tossed her head emphatically, causing two petals of pink to flutter from the baby rose woven into the locks of her light-golden crown. 'For he is to by my husband!'

Were all men so obtusc?

Carmichael sprang to his distracted feet and beat his chest with the plumed vclvct bonnet he had respectfully removed before his opening blurt. Facing into the soft breeze wafting from the undulating upper reaches of the glen, he cried:

'Oh *Lord*! Is my life to end this way?'

Elizabeth looked up at him in astonishment. How could such silly things be seriously said? And yet there seemed no bottom to the sincerity of Carmichael's distress. 'My lord,' she implored him uncomfortably, 'I pray you, do not jest so. My heart . . .'

'*Jest*!' he raged. 'Jest? Ha! Lady, how can you be so cruel? To treat my love as a clown's charade. Ooooooh! May Heaven forgive you. And Heaven *save* you, lady! Heaven save you. For it is not love that Polmood feels for you, but sordid stinking *lust*! He seeks your body only. Craves your beauteous youthful flesh with the sick desperation of an old man's final flicker.'

'I beg you, Sir – '

'And where shall you be when the flicker dwindles and the old candle snuffs? A cold and lonely widow, so young! In Polmood's dark and cheerless halls – so soon! For Polmood is old, my lady. Old! And I do swear you love him not – it is not love but pity, *pity*, that he with his oafish attentions and creaking promises has won from your most generous heart.'

Elizabeth said nothing, but behind the amazement that troubled her eyes a clamouring rookery of questions soared in fright. *Pity*? It could not be pity she felt for Polmood, as she had only the remotest idea of how the word felt. Yet was it love? And if Carmichael did love her as fiercely as he claimed ... he was a much more attractive man that Polmood, there was no denying that. What were Polmood's gapped yellow stumps to Carmichael's flashing white rows of even strong teeth? Polmood's thinning wiry grizzle to Carmichael's full black mane of waves? The forester's greasy hides and leathers to the courtier's velvets and satins?

But did she love Carmichael?

Elizabeth's perplexity rocked her forward. She rested a dimpled chin on hugging knees and sucked for comfort from her thumb.

Kneeling beseechingly, Carmichael gently took her unsucked hand from her knee and pressed it urgently between his own, like a tiny filly betwixt two burly stallions.

'Oh, Elizabeth!' he chided her. 'Consider! Will you spend the rest of your days as plain Dame Hunter of Polmood, immured in a forester's hut? Or ensure your own eternal joy, and mine, as Lady Elizabeth Carmichael, Baroness of Hyndford? And cousin to the King!'

If distantly, he prudently did not add.

Slowly, Elizabeth said:

'Very well, Sir John. If you can obtain the King's consent and will marry me tomorrow, I shall be most honoured to make you a loyal and faithful wife.' Her eyes flashed as her memory rang with an echo of some memory scrap, and she added:

'Or it you choose to carry me off privately this very night, then to Paris shall I gladly follow you! That we may wed in splendour there.'

Carmichael groaned:

'Either of these modes, my dear Elizabeth, is quite utterly impossible. The King cannot and will not revoke his agreement with Polmood, and were it possible to carry you away privately tonight – which it absolutely is not – to do so would infallibly procure me the distinguished honour of losing my head in a very few days.

'But you have everything in your power! Cannot you on some pretext or other delay the wedding? As I promise to make you my own wife, and lady of my extensive domains, just as soon as circumstances will permit?'

Elizabeth tugged her hand free from Carmichael's pressing, and abruptly stood up. Restlessly she turned and took several paces towards the tireless white spume cascading from the waterfall to the linn. Up turned her flawless blue eyes, distantly due west, seeking counsel from the darkly bald summit of the high Clockmore.

Carmichael rose and followed, bonnet crushed in anxious hands, awaiting her decision with breathless impatience.

Suddenly she turned to face him again, though her eyes looked past him, back to the Castle.

'Yes?' he begged.

'I wish', said she, with considerable emphasis, 'that you had either spoken of this sooner or not at all!' She pushed dismissively past him and hurried along the narrow path through the bracken, down the gentle slope to where the company would soon be gathering to dine.

And Carmichael was left standing alone by the linn like a statue abandoned, regret preying relentlessly on his harshly pounding heart.

Foolish man!

How could he fail to see the utmost odiousness with which that *permission of circumstances* would ring in the ear of Elizabeth's youthful impetuosity? For a moment, it must be said, Carmichael's ardent manner and manly beauty had striven for a share in the movements of her heart, but the mention of *the wedding* had at once restored the ascendancy of all the associated train of cherished images and delightful anticipations. Which Elizabeth simply could not reconcile with that hated *delay* – are not the serried forces of our vocabulary at a loss to furnish another word so utterly repugnant to every sense of Woman?

The wedding could not be delayed!

All was in readiness, and such an opportunity of attracting notice and admiration might never again occur – it was a most repulsive idea: the wedding *could not be delayed*! Such were the fancies that had glanced on Elizabeth's mind as she looked up to the sombre peak of the distant mountain.

Carmichael's posture of sculpted desolation stired as her retreating figure was lost to his view.

'Oh Lord!' he moaned between clenched teeth. 'Blessed Lord, how can this *be*? She loves not Polmood – no maiden could. Oooooooh!' Boiling with thwarted incomprehension, he turned and stalked up the glen at a cursing pace which few men living could match. Every thirty or forty paces he would pause and mutter:

'Sooner. Sooner! Or not at all. *Ooooooooh*!'

Far into the late evening Carmichael roamed the heedless hills, frenziedly muttering, besmirching the name and issue of Fortune, and wildly petitioning the darkling heavens for guidance. As to whether the Hand of Heaven may be discerned behind the hasty and desperate resolutions to which Carmichael in due course came, the reader must appeal to the sequel.

But what will not love urge a man to encounter?

HOW DOES IT FEEL?

The voice of mirth at dinner, and the bustle of wedding wardrobery for an hour thereafter, abeyed in Elizabeth's mind the anxieties that her conversation with Carmichael had excited, but once the sun had set and the nobles clustered for drinking and gaming, and nothing remained for the ladies but chortle and tattle until it was time to retire, she found herself disturbed anew by the strident passion he had avowed.

What was it about her that got the men so exercised?

What exactly did they *want*?

It was vague and general questions such as these, jostled by a pregnant dialogue between Lady Elinor Hume and Countess Katherine of Mar on the mixed blessings attaching to the damming

34

of a numerous family, which eventually siphoned Elizabeth's reluctant attention into the physical dimension of the relations between the sexes. It occurred to her that Polmood's wife would be called upon at some point to attempt the production of Polmood's heir, which prompted more soberly specific reflection on how the process might be initiated.

The mechanics of the thing were no mystery to her, as how could they be in an earthy age when mixed bathing (even mixed natural functioning) were still not uncommon? But such general knowledge threw little light on details of personal intricacy and propriety of response, and so it was that, while barbed debate continued to fly between Lady Elinor and Countess Katherine, Elizabeth shyly consulted the experience of her beloved guardian and mentor, the youthful Queen Margaret.

'My lady,' she said, kneeling beside the Queen's wooden throne, 'may I ask you something?'

'But of course, Elizabeth!' Margaret smiled fondly. 'What about?'

'About men, my lady.'

'About men! Then well may you ask, Elizabeth, and right royally shall I endeavour to answer. Though I fear there may be others present more entitled that I to pronounce.' The Queen spoke quietly, her glance flitting ambivalently amid the bevy of some fifteen ladies sitting with her by the vast log fire at the north end of the Great Hall. Some on stools and benches from the dining table, some on long cushion-sacks filled fat with dry rushes, the ladies aged from Elizabeth up to the shrewish mid-thirties of Lady Hume. Not a few were of considerable beauty, and several had at one time figured in rumours co-featuring the King.

For James was an ardent and copious lover, and Lord of all Scotland.

While Margaret's budding cynicism blossomed.

'Concerning what part of men, exactly,' she murmured, 'do you wish to hear?'

Elizabeth rested her chin on the crudely carved arm of Margaret's throne. 'I understand my body, my lady,' she explained. 'I think. And what will be required of me. But . . .'

'Yes?' urged Margaret, her interest hooked. 'But?'

'But Polmood is truly a giant among men, and I am very slight and . . . narrow. And possibly it is wrong of me to say so, my lady,'

Elizabeth confessed now all in a rush, 'but I do fear I never shall be able to support the weight of his embrace!' Pale face hotly blushing, she averted her innocent shame.

'There, there, Elizabeth!' Margaret soothed, stroking the silky flax of the younger girl's worried crown. Had she not herself been wracked by identical anxieties just three years past? 'Have no fear. For you are young, and growing still. As I will inform the King. And his Majesty will counsel Polmood, I assure you, that he upon pain of our royal displeasure will respectfully suspend the full exercise of his marriage rights for one year hence. Wherefore, worry not.'

'Oh, my lady!' Elizabeth's gratitude gasped, a shallow film of tears across her eyes. 'Is it possible?'

'Why should it not be? It is no larger a favour than his Majesty accorded myself.' Margaret's small green-flecked eyes narrowed above her pinkly plump cheeks, suggesting the unwelcome adulteration of some pleasant reflection – though she was far from plain, in the harsher sense, it was no secret that looks alone would never have made her Queen. 'And besides,' she frowned, 'Polmood is most fortunate to have won such a treasure, and must not mind waiting: it will do him good! It will heighten his respect for you, and his appreciation of your qualities.'

'Oh, my lady, will it really? You are so kind – how ever can I thank you?'

Margaret's answering sigh was nearly despondent:

'Thank me, Elizabeth? No, no! No need of that. Already your cheerful company has thanked me ten-fold for any service I might do you. I shall miss you. Dearly.' Not least, she forbore to add, in the interminable unManned coldness of winter, when the King was so often 'elsewhere'.

A ripple of audience titter arose round the heat of the family-size polemic. 'Answer that, Lady Mar, if you can!' cried the fat but notoriously lewd and lustful Lady Annabelle, sister to the Duke of Hamilton.

Lady Ann Gray stirred restlessly from her perch of bolstered rush. Ineligible to discourse on family life, and unable to overhear more than the isolated peaks of Elizabeth's talk with the Queen, she had for more minutes than she could comfortably bear been sitting out on the sidelines of the proceedings, idly tickling the twitching ears of a nightmaring deerhound. Now she seized two logs from the pile on the floor and hurled them on the already adequate blaze. This achieved her joint aims of restoring a moment's envy to the flawless cleavage curving daringly from her lowcut lace and of enabling her to reseat unobstrusively closer to the Queen's conversation.

For who could know what might be said about whom?

Elizabeth allowed the brief lull to reinforce her appreciation of Margaret's bounty, then said:

'There is one other thing, my lady.'

'Yes?'

'About men, my lady.'

'Who else?' quipped the Queen, in a manner she had caught from the King. 'Forgive me, Elizabeth,' her better nature recovered. 'What other thing about men?'

'When a gentleman . . . puts his quhillelillie into a lady's towdie and broozles her, my lady,' rushed out in a monotone torrent, 'how does it *feel*? My question is whether it be at all pleasant, as sometimes one hears said, or unspeakably painful and unpleasant, as one cannot help but imagine!'

It was perhaps unfortunate than an unheralded falter in the general hubbub should have coincided with Elizabeth's inquiry soon enough for all the other ladies to catch its drift, yet too late for her to check and change its course.

So scarlet did her pretty ears burn, scorched in the beam of some thirty fascinated eyes.

'Oooh, Elizabeth!' chirped Lady Ann. 'Have you not heard? It is the most divine sensation! Depending, of course, upon the man. It is as if the earth exploded beneath one, and carried one to Heaven, with cherubs adoring every smallest corner of one's body. Is it not, ladies? Oooh, Elizabeth! How can you be not impatient? When – '

'And how, pray, Mistress Gray, might you know these things?' hissed Queen Margaret in a venomous temper. 'You who are still single and chaste?'

Lady Ann's sloe eyes cast contritely down. 'I crave your pardon, my lady,' she simpered to her bosom, 'if I spoke out of place. I was of course repeating what I have heard. From Mistress Hume, my lady. Whose wisdom and experience of marriage are famed. Are they not, Lady Hume?'

'We thank you, Mistress Gray, for your contribution. You may retire.'

'My – '

'Madam, you may *retire*!' snapped Margaret, insinuous poison in her glare.

Lady Ann's voice was small and tight when, rising, she said:

'Your Majesty is most gracious to perceive my weariness and so excuse me.' And with a minimal courtesy she departed.

Gypsy triumph hinting in her flounce.

Margaret was left with telltale little blotches of fury afire on the plumps of her cheeks. To the innocent bride she said:

'Come closer, Elizabeth. And we shall continue our conversation without interruption.'

Her other ladies she gestured back to their various niggles and natters and debates on the morrow.

3

THE DAY BEFORE THE WEDDING?

MANLY STRIVINGS

The Thursday, after the strong dry heat of the body of the day, had fallen unseasonably chill in the evening. This was followed by a recurrence of heavy rain in the small hours of the night, dwindling to a sullen overcast wetness on the Friday morning. Many a sleep-cured spirit thus woke and leapt up to encounter only a drizzling disappointment.

'Bogger this ferking contrary weather!' grumbled the young men.

'How will the young men pass the day now?' wondered the young ladies.

For the Friday had been fixtured by King James for performance before the ladies of celebratory sporting competition among the men – events over which Elizabeth, as bride in hand, would preside with all the carnival power of a Queen of the May.

Or wouldn't!

Depending entirely upon the weather, which not even James could command. Was it not then natural that by ten o'clock, when the soggy depression showed no glimmer of abatement, a mood of irritable moping should be rife, and Elizabeth's lovely eyes rubbed red?

And all for nothing.

Round about eleven the sun burned a trapdoor through the carpet of gloom, and by noon the skies had balded to a deep wispless blue, floating like a careless dream on the steamy haze arising from the countryside all around.

Before a further hour could pass, the lush green contest field, a small distance east of the Castle, was thronging and yelling with squirely preparation, and the Queen and her ladies were making their way to the vantage from which they could spectate. The rest of the ladies, and such nobles as would not engage in violent exertion, were obliged to sit rough on the still damp heather of the bank below, but the Queen and the privileged Elizabeth enjoyed the comfort and superior perspective of a small straw-filled sack spread flat on the long smooth grey stone which, to this very day, is known to local folk as Queen Margaret's Stone.

First on the programme was a round of tilting at the ring (or jousting, as we might say), an event in which a man's attainment is necessarily bound to the calibre of his charger. It was thus to be expected that King James would emerge the victor here, mounted on his magnificent milkwhite stallion Pegasus (presented to him the previous year by the present king of France).

But it was also noted in the eliminations that, in Polmood's engagement with Carmichael, the latter unhorsed him in a very rough and ungracious manner. Polmood rolled to his feet immediately and claimed to be nothing hurt, but his deepset eyes and bristly cheeks flamed with a furious vexation clearly visible to all. Nevertheless, if Carmichael had hopes of approbation from the onlookers, he was disappointed – it being obvious that the triumph resided solely in the edge possessed by Carmichael's purpose-bred mare over Polmood's intractably unsuitable mountain pony, the general feeling was quietly expressed that the younger man had acted a shade unhandsomely.

'Not the fairest of matches,' as Margaret murmured, lest Elizabeth require consolation.

'No, my lady.'

'And let us only hope they may conclude this dangerous foolishness with no blood shed!'

Which they did.

Next came the race, consisting of ten laps of the perimeter of the field, fought hard between nine of the younger stalwart lords. Here, though furiously chased by the impetuous Earl of Mar (twenty-four and father of five), Carmichael took the first prize fairly, finishing the final lap with a superhuman burst of speed.

As though his very life were at stake.

Still sobbing painfully for breath, a sleeveless jerkin of purple velvet thrown carelessly about his shoulders, he bounded up the heather bank to the grey stone, there to receive his prize from Elizabeth.

She, handling gingerly the jewel-encrusted dagger that was his trophy, rose to present him.

All eyes followed.

Elizabeth was dressed in a light, flowing cote-hardie of sheerest maidenly white. Cut wide across her shoulders, it allowed the gentle golden halfcurls of her hair to whisper suggestively against the slender delicacy of her ivory neck. Unlike the Queenly starch of Margaret's padded-roll head-dress, Elizabeth's hallmark rose was all her crown, held in place by a silver pin with a great pearl head. From where the striving nobles watched in the arena below, she appeared, through the intervening heat haze, like the wraith of a virgin goddess from some long-lost paradise of chased grails and vanquished dragons.

And her gracious poise seemed to sense it.

'We congratulate you, Sir John,' she said, 'on your great speed.'

Carmichael seized the fair hand that bestowed his dagger. He fell urgently to a single kneel, pressed and protractedly kissed the captive hand. Then, eyes dilate with desperate meaning, he intimated over his shoulder to the southbound pass that cleaves between the buttock-splayed hills of Craigdilly and Drowning Dubs. And croakily whispered:

'*Tonight*!'

Elizabeth courtesied daintily, but the enraptured beatitude of her smile continued to radiate undented, and Carmichael feared she had not comprehended his proposal.

'Hurry now, Sir John!' she urged. 'The King beckons you back to the field.'

More distraught than ever, he rejoined his athletic fellows and found a number already stripped to throw the mall. These included his enthusiastic Majesty, who had recalled Carmichael as he valued his opponency. Each candidate was to have three throws, and when the rounds were almost exhausted King James lay leader by a foot.

'Our prize!' crowed the playful King, gleefully rubbing the ginger mat on his handsome heaving chest. 'Our prize. Unless Carmichael can take it from us, and we wager he cannot. Can you, sir?'

Carmichael avowed that no-one should attribute his failure to want of effort, though he refrained from publicizing his principal motive: his desire to win Elizabeth's heart by the demonstration of his unmatched manhood, and once again to receive his prize from her, that renewed intimations of subversive elopement might pass between them.

He seized the doughty mall, swung it wildly, faster and faster, till the blood vessels knotted obscenely on his arms and neck, then, with a sobbing shriek of ultimate effort, he let it fly to whistle like a cannonball down the valley.

'The best yet!' cried an excited squire, from where the throws were measured. 'This beats his Majesty by a full ten inch.'

'Ha!' scoffed James. 'We are bested, are we? Very well, very well – what it is to be young! Carmichael wins again, it seems. So be it: more treasure to his coffer. Or will some seasoned trusty even now step forth? To save the name of age? No? Very – '

'With your blessing, Sire, I will venture an old man's throw,' growled Polmood. Stepping forward, he removed his shortsleeved doublet of leather and waited for the hammer to return.

A feather of pleasure tickled around the company at this spice on the general interest. For it had been noticed that, since taking some umbrage at Carmichael's use of him in the tilting, the bridegroom of the morrow had kept his profile sullenly low and tersely declined to engage either in the race or in the present hammer tossing.

Was he now to be revenged?

'Consider, Elizabeth,' said the Lady Annabelle Hamilton in a voice that rang far, 'that if all Polmood's muscles are in keeping with his arms, you shall not require to await his death in order to be amply provided for!'

Elizabeth blushed as the ladies sniggered.

But the Queen spoke no rebuke, for the age was permissive and the sally well formed.

And Polmood was ready to throw.

Standing at tense unease by the footing post, he flexed his massy shoulders as though to dislodge the vicarious speculation that rested upon them. Then suddenly, jerkily, swinging only twice, he threw with great violence.

But:

'Hoo, hoo, hoo!' hooted some of the ladies, to Elizabeth's hot annoyance.

And:

'Lord save us, Polmood!' chortled the King. 'If we measured you for altitude, mind, you would surely win. Rise up, will you not?'

Polmood's hasty throw had flown at a right angle from the line he intended. Over the heads of several spectators, at an immense but useless height, it plummeted into a shallow pool of the river, leaving its foot-lost thrower spreadeagled face-flat on the squelchy muddy ground, while the sides of the valley thrilled loud with the laughter and shouted delight of the onlookers.

All but one.

What was it, fretted Elizabeth, that Carmichael had said? '*Tonight!*' But why?

Polmood's heavy features flushed crimson. 'I beg you, Sire, a second throw?' his tortured voice grated when the mall was retrieved.

'Take a dozen, sir!' crackled the King. 'A hundred! If each can amuse us as the last.'

Polmood stepped again to the post and commenced a slow, deliberate, scowling swing.

Much breath bated as the whirling hammer sliced the air.

Then, just when it seemed that the fury of the movement must accelerate into invisibility and lift the incensed forester into the azure heavens, he released it with such enormous force that, to the howled astonishment of many beholders, it buried itself with a trimphant splat in a boggy patch one third as far again as any previous throw.

'Bravo!' clapped King James, above the mingled congratulations of the multitude. 'Bravo, indeed! A sterling blow for the elder statemen. Polmood's prize, do we all agree? No man will beat that this day. Polmood, sir, your prize. Your bride awaits you. Indeed, noble lords, let us all attend the presentation, and take some refreshment with the ladies.'

The noble lords were nothing loth.

And how ferocious was the exultation that broiled in Polmood's breast as he led them up the sloping heather to the Queen's grey stone!

CLOSER ENCOUNTERS

It so happened that the prize for the champion of the mall was a loveknot of scarlet ribbon, together with two beautiful bonnet plumes which branched out like the horns of a deer. When Polmood approached her, speechless with worship, Elizabeth, in a most becoming manner, took his respectfully clutched blue bonnet from his hand, and, fixing the knot and plumes upon it, in a most elegant and tasteful fashion, lodged it back on his obediently bowed head. Polmood, in the most gallant and courtly style of which he was master, then kissed her hand, bowed to the Queen, and placed Elizabeth back by her side.

But when he turned and faced about from the privileged ladies, the appearance he unwittingly made struck everyone so forcibly that the entire company burst out in an echoing volley of uproarious laughter.

And Carmichael, his heart grudge still gaining, seeming to value himself upon his wit, cried out:

'It is rather a singular coincidence, Polmood, that you should place Elizabeth upon the straw, and she a pair of horns upon your head, all at the same instant!'

The general mirth redoubled.

Carmichael smirked with pleasure at the success of his jibe.

Elizabeth frowned, and Polmood's cheek, for the second time in half an hour, burned visibly to the bone. He could not for shame tear off the ornaments with which his darling had so lovingly bedecked him, but he was unable to keep his itching hand from giving his troublesome headpiece a twist of dismissive adjustment. This made him look like an angry old stag with both antlers growing out of its left ear.

The level of hilarity roared to the pitch of helpless tears.

Fertilizing in Polmood that hatred of Carmichael which was duly to wreak so fateful.

The next trial of skill was that of shooting at a mark, and here the competition was utterly fruitless. Polmood, naturally greeding to succour his mangled pride, struck the bull's-eye with such unerring exactness that all were amazed afresh at his arch dexterity, and unanimously accorded him the prize. This was a large and handsome brooch in the form of a silver arrow, which he again received from Elizabeth, she pinning it admiringly to his leathered bosom.

Carmichael, still warm from the triumph of his former philippic, saw fit then to break some further jests premised on the symbolism of the silver shaft, which, though not in those wholesome days considered any breach of good manners, were nevertheless extremely coarse. But the laughter he triggered on this occasion was sheeplike and ragged, and hardly worth the swelling animosity it assured him in the belly of Polmood's passions.

Sixteen of the gentlemen then stripped to try their skill in wrestling, and, his Majesty having whimmed it a law of the day that the winner of any one contest must begin the next, Polmood was obliged to take part. They all engaged at once, two by two, and how many more magnificent spectacles can the history of the valley have scened, than this furious tussle of man against man: pride against pride, glistening rippling torso against rippling torso glistening?

Some of the nobles were so expert at the exercise, and opposed to others so equal in strength and agility, that several of the contests were exceedingly equal and amusing, and only eventually decided on the strength of stamina. But in due course the weaker half of the original number were overthrown, the remaining eight regrouped according to the King's direction (he having abstained to save his subjects the possible discomfort of laying victorious hands on his Majesty), and, four of these soon being cast, only the final two couples were left.

'Polmood against Lamington,' King James deftly seeded. 'The giants together!' Donald of Lamington being the only man present to equal Polmood in breadth of build and bulge of muscle. 'But first let us see Carmichael and Mar. Gentlemen?'

Mar, however, soon proved no match for Carmichael, being too hot of head and light of limb.

The second semi-final was also a disappointment, as, muscles notwithstanding, it immediately became apparent that Lamington had neither the effective strength not the experience and skilled killer instinct of his older opponent, and Polmood easily strangleheld him into the indignity of having to cry for mercy.

This produced precisely the playoff the wily King had hoped for.

'Polmood fights Carmichael for the prize!' he proclaimed. 'Ready, sir?' he asked Polmood. 'Or shall you rest?'

'I thank you, Sire,' Polmood grunted ominously and deferred his head, 'but I need no rest.'

'Very well. Then let us press on. Carmichael? We offer you, sir, the spurring knowledge that our money is on Polmood's back. Gentlemen? Will any man dispute our hundred merks?'

'Indeed, Majesty! That will I.' The Earl of Hume, unable to resist even the diciest wager, arose from his non-combatant heather perch and tripped down to the gladiatorial circle on the field. 'A hundred merks on Carmichael, Majesty? Agreed. Two hundred if you will.'

'Delighted!' James accepted. 'Gentlemen,' he said to Polmood and Carmichael, 'behold the great investment in your bout, and be aware that he who is triumphant here shall be announced the champion of the day and shall this night lead out the dance with the beauteous Elizabeth upon his arm. Shall he not, my lady?' he called, bowing gallantly to the ladies. 'Hence, with a blast of brass to start, we pray you, commence!'

Two bugles leapt to ruffled squirely lips and blew a sharp snort.

The nobles on the field formed round the contestants in a human horse-shoe, its open heel for the benefit of the viewers on the hillside.

The wrestlers closed.

'Come, sir,' snarled Polmood, braced in bearlike balance, his arms half-raised in open-handed menace. 'What have you to fear?'

Carmichael did not reply. Tensely tightlipped, he continued to circle and feint for a grip. The fight would be decided by any combination of a knockout, a submission, or two clear throws from a standing position. Carmichael, despite being the tallest man in the company by a handsome inch, was thus obliged to manoeuvre in the light of Polmood's extraordinary weight and strength.

Suddenly Polmood lunged.

Carmichael saw the move coming and danced back, but slipped and almost fell on a heel-scooped mud-skid.

'Ha!' growled Polmood. 'The – '

Carmichael darted forward, ducked, cupped his hands behind Polmood's left knee and heaved with all his might.

'First throw! First throw!' cheered Lord Hume. 'Majesty, I do believe my man shall win. He has the speed.'

'We shall see,' sniffed James. 'Come, Polmood. Our entire exchequer is in your hands!'

But the regal quip and the polite titter that courted it were lost on Polmood. Bounding back to his feet with the speed of half his age, he crowded Carmichael south to the closed toe of the horse-shoe. The grass-stranded mud that patched his scalp and shoulder-blades objectified his blotted pride, and his green eyes were crazed with a dark foreshadow of violent death.

Whose?

When?

This time when he lunged Polmood anticipated Carmichael's anticipation, and, following through with the mad rush of a viking berserker, he pinned his adversary against the ring of spectators before they could break and scatter.

Carmichael wriggled sideways, knowing he must at any cost avoid the pulverizing power of Polmood's hug.

But Polmood had no hug in mind. With his massed right fist he unleashed a blow at the other's solar plexus which would have been fatal if it had connected with its target. As it was, due to Carmichael's attempted dodge sideways, it was the right side of his rib-cage that received the full force of Polmood's assault, and, the blow coming at an upward angle, he was lifted visibly clear of the ground and deposited on his back by the feet of the passively exulting Sir Patrick Hepburn.

'His ribs!' Queen Margaret gasped. 'I swear I did hear his breastbone break. Oh! Surely now they will cease this madness.'

'Second throw to Polmood,' observed her Husband, with the smiling unconcern of one who has many times seen men die howling, in the thick of bloody battle. 'But is it the last? Carmichael, sir? Can you continue? Or will you concede? Your bosom, we warrant, will smart awhile!'

'Sire,' Carmichael panted, 'I am nothing hurt. And will continue.' But the sick sweat of agony was dribbling from his brow and beading into his handsome dark eyes to blend with tears of rage. If Polmood were to win the bout, *he would be champion of the day*!

What would Elizabeth care for the loser?

Despairing, Carmichael rushed, lusting wildly for the pain, the blood, the pulped humiliation and decisive death of Polmood.

'HAAAAARGH!' roared Polmood as the advantage literally flew into his arms. Weaving under Carmichael's flailing fists, he wrapped his gargantuan forearms around the younger man's waist and locked them behind his back. 'Submit, puppy!' he hissed as he lifted and viciously squeezed. 'Ye prissy wee gelding! Submit, or your spine shall crack.'

'Never!' moaned Carmichael, attempting to hammer his elbows down on Polmood's thick skull.

'SUBMIT!'

'NEVER!'

Polmood shook his victim and squeezed yet tighter, and it was evident from Carmichael's purpling countenance that his situation was fast growing perilous.

'Enough, Polmood!' breezed the King. 'We would not have your wedding delayed by a funeral, and therefore in Carmichael's place do we submit. With my Lord Hume's blessing, of course?'

'Majesty, I – '

'Most gracious of you, sir. And so, Polmood, *enough*! Release the man, we pray you. Bravely fought, Sir John. A notable feat it is, to throw Polmood even once. We do congratulate you. Trumpets, boys! And all hail Norman of Polmood: CHAMPION OF THE DAY!'

The bugles brayed their twin cacophony.

Polmood released Carmichael with a contemptuous toss, landing him in a panting crumple upon the mire.

'Come, Polmood,' James directed. 'Receive your final prize before we dine. Your admiring bride awaits you.'

Not only did Elizabeth await him, she was already standing, impatient to make the presentation for the wrestle. Polmood's triumph in three of the five contested events had pleased her greatly, and now that he was champion of the day he was fast coming to seem to her a superior character: one whom others must value and whom she herself had underestimated hitherto.

'Your achievements are wondrous impressive, my lord.' Elizabeth handed Polmood his prize with a smile so bewitchingly adulatory that his eyes brimmed with tears and his hands shook with joy as they received it.

A joy that was almost a frenzy.

'He loves too hard,' Queen Margaret murmured disquietly to herself.

'Put it on now, Polmood,' urged the King. 'Wear it in to dinner.'

He referred to the prize just bestowed: a fine leather belt with seven silver buckles in crafted shapes of bird and animal heads.

Polmood immediately wrapped the belt around his waist, but his enamoured fingers were too full of thumbs to fasten it.

'I pray you, my lord, allow me.' Elizabeth stepped forward and took over with wifely efficiency, then held up a dainty hand for Polmood to kiss in gallant thanks.

All of which was magnificent entertainment for the cheering court.

But not for Carmichael.

Having limped up from the field, nursing hs bruises and inwardly bewailing his misfortune, he now stood, neglected, at the rear of the crowd assembled below Queen Margaret's Stone. Though he was not naturally given to malice, the flood of tenderness and endearment apparently surging between Polmood and Elizabeth was so intolerable as to lead him to cry from his isolation:

'Better, Polmood, that you get a belt around you both! And once you get her buckled in, be wise to keep her there, else you never may become one flesh!'

'Heed him not! Heed him not!' King James adroitly smoothed Polmood's rising hackles. 'He means no harm, we warrant. This is but the chagrin of a young man's defeat. No so, Carmichael? And now, sweet ladies and noble lords, it surely is time to dine.'

4

THE WEDDING'S EVE?

AFTER EIGHT

When dinner in the Great Hall was done, washed down by plentiful goblets of the red wine that arrived from France so rough and raw that sprinkles of spice and lashings of honey were necessary to render it palatable, the company adjourned outdoors once more to close the evening with a dance upon the green. A rippled curtain of colourless cloud had drawn across the sky, sealing down warm echoes of the heat of the day, and a huge fire blazed in the centre of the lawn, to bright the wide eyes of revelry and keep at bay the hovering cold of the spirit of darkness. The King's own throne was carried out from the Hall, and thereon sat Old Curry, the dwarfish harping clown. Hard did he strum and loud did he sing, and sweeter than ever before were his lilting strains to the well-wined ears of the insatiable frolickers.

'*O'er the Boggy*!' called James.

'I've just done that one!' objected Old Curry.

'*Cutty's Wedding*, then.'

'We've had that too.'

'Then play it again, Curry! Play them both again.'

He did.

They danced.

And one cannot but wonder how many a journeying eye, roving causally over the present-day sheep-dotted desert of a valley that is Meggat-dale, can believe that once a king and queen and all the lords and ladies of a court did drink and dance there, and laugh and sing. Yet the facts are well established, and it is known that such royal disportment continued there until the days of the notorious and unfortunate Queen Mary, the last Head of Scotland to slumber in Crawmelt's stark tower.

This night was rightfully Polmood's, yet the figure he made in the dance was scarcely indifferent. The field on which he appeared to advantage was overpast, whereas that of Elizabeth's excellence was only now commencing.

As her graceful movements and shining eyes showed.

And the heavier steps and vinegar looks of certain other ladies confirmed.

Doggedly did Polmood his duty, in the opening double octave, but his vast booted feet were so clumsy, and his lurching unease so excruciating, especially beside the flitting fairy movements of Elizabeth, that both were greatly relieved when King James stepped in to request of Polmood the pleasure of partnering his lovely lady in the coming reel.

Polmood replied that he would be most honoured, provided, of course, that Elizabeth consented, which he was confident she would.

And which she did, with discreet enthusiasm.

Polmood bowed himself away and headed for the steps of the pavilion, in quest of more wine (lots of it) and possibly some sprawling bawling game of chance, among whose cheerfully slurred and foul-mouthed transactions he might feel less out of place.

James was a jigger of great accomplishment, and continued to pair Elizabeth during the remainder of the dancing, thus further cementing her command over the assembled (if scattered) forces of male admiration and female envy.

'She makes a dazzling spectacle, my dear, does she not?' asked Lord Hume of his good lady. 'A man might almost swear the grass bends not beneath her fair young toe!'

'No doubt a man might, my lord!' carped Lady Elinor, roughly steering her poorly co-ordinated spouse away from collision with a neighbouring couple. 'And much would this tell us of his passion for Truth and his devotion to the Grape.'

'My dear Elinor! I – '

'And furthermore, my lord, on the matter of toes: if you could so control your own that they trod upon mine one quarter as lightly as hers tread the grass, my gratitude would know no bounds, I'm sure.'

But evidently Lord Hume could not, as only minutes later that couple was seen to retire from the green in the middle of the square dance, discordantly clashing in their habitual frowning harangue.

Although Elizabeth was the banquet of beauty whereof the general eye of this night feasted, it was remarked by some (though not, apparently, by Queen Margaret) that the jailors holding captive the gaze of the King were the dark flashing charms of Lady Ann Gray, and in particular the twinly revealed provocation of her magnificent bosom.

'You Majesty is most generous,' ventured Elizabeth, when her Partner's distraction had grown so blatant as to irk, 'to have honoured me so long. But I am now content to rest, to catch my breath, so please you, and feel sure my Lady Gray would be most happy to take my place.'

'Your pardon, Elizabeth!' said James, hurriedly recalling his scrutiny from Lady Ann's teasing lips and neckline of plunging maroon. 'A thousand pardons! More. Where have our manners flown? We were of course merely commiserating with Mistress Gray in her misfortune. Her misfortune, we mean, in having to bear with the ungainly cavortions of the Earl of Mar. But if you would rest then all shall rest, and we shall propose a toast.'

'My Lord! I did not mean . . .'

'No matter. No matter. It is our wish. TRUSTY LORDS AND GALLANT LADIES, A TOAST! HOLD OFF THERE, CURRY! We thank you. Let us drink a toast, ladies and gentlemen, to the bride of the morrow, wherefore gather you with us before the pavilion. BOYS! Attend the wine. Each glass to the brim.'

Thus, with the sun set and the midges rising, the dancing feet calmed, the splinter sprawls of manly gambling abeyed, and the entire company sat down together in a promiscuous circle between the fire and the pavilion (an unfortified dormitory overflow for the Castle, whose single storey fronted on the east border of the green).

The music resumed quietly in the background, commingling with occasional snorts and whinnies from the stabled horses and the periodic screech of a low-flying owl to ring with a halo of unheard night noise the foetal throb of mirth and social glee that echoed the numerous toasts. To Elizabeth. To Polmood. To Polmood and Elizabeth. And to as many other worthy subjects as the King deemed appropriate.

Only Carmichael appeared absent and thoughtful, which was simply attributed, by the few that noticed, to the defeats he had received in the sports. Yet his intents toward Polmood were evil and dangerous, and there was nothing he desired more than to challenge and do him down. But, as the bumpers proliferated and the rosebush of ebrious hilarity blossomed louder, no opportunity looked likely to arise.

Hence it was, shortly after eleven o'clock, that Baron John Carmichael slipped away from the rear of the circle and made his tormented way to his little chamber in the Castle.

Without being missed.

And it is arguably only now that our story really begins.

AND SO TO BED
The Castle of Crawmclt was fitted up to accommodate a considerable number of lodgers. In the third and uppermost storey, each with its own door off a small circular hall, were some twenty tiny chambers, all equipped alike with a narrow bed laid with rushes and mattressed with a bag filled with a light feathery bent, which could be gathered in abundance from the lower slopes of the summer hills, and which made a bed as soft as any down.

When the Queen and her attendants came over from Nidpath, the top floor of the Castle was wholly given up by the gentlemen, most of whom then settled for a communal doss on the floor of the pavilion. Thus each lady retained the comfort of a room to herself, though she had no curtain to her bed, nor any covering save one pair of sheets and a rug. The rushes were placed on the floor between a small wooden stool and the wall, and this was all the permanent furniture that these chambers contained, the beds being only intended for single individuals on short-term stay.

On the second floor was the King's bedchamber, spacious, and warmly luxurious with its tapestried four-poster bed and large open fire. Also on this flat were five smaller rooms, customarily allocated to other members of the royal family, and thereafter, according to rank and seniority, to such peers and dignitaries of the realm as might be present.

Due to his distant kinship with the King, it was one of these rooms on the second floor that Carmichael now occupied.

With his bosom in a fearful ferment, and sorely bruised withal.

He lay on his bed, dressed as he was, and gave himself up to the most poignant and wracking reflections.

Had not Polmood put him to shame in the sports?

Must not this have lost him his foothold on Elizabeth's affections?

Yet who could deny that the marriage so imminent was a nonsense? That the girl felt nothing for Polmood? How could she, whose heart was still too light and young to have known the awful burden of true love's pangs!

Carmichael groaned.

In his solitary slit-windowed darkness the sweet pungency of desperation in his perspiration fluttered round his nostrils like a taunting moth.

He tossed violently on his mattress; groaned again.

Was not the night cruelly short?

Was it not the last on which the girl was free?

Before she would be *lost to him for ever*!

Love, pride, envy, hatred, and all their most virulent neighbours took flight at this thought, in startling fear at the violence of its explosion into Carmichael's quivering resolve to act now, risk all, and rather die than suffer Polmood, drooling obscenely like the smelly old mountain goat he was, to carry Elizabeth away to an eternity of spiritless tedium.

But no sooner had he leapt to his feet than his quivering quaked.

For there were female voices ascending the stair to the second-floor landing.

And among them, Elizabeth's.

Shortly after Carmichael's retreat from the toasts, Queen Margaret, judging from the volume and content of garble which the wine had excited in the men that the time was now proper for herself and her ladies to retire, had arisen with her flock and bidden the rollicking party of noising stags a fond goodnight. King James, his Lord Chamberlain Hume, and one or two others having chivalrously conveyed the ladies to the foot of the staircase, her majesty thanked them kindly but urged them to return forthwith to the rout on the green, where she was sure their company would be much missed.

King James disclaimed but agreed to comply, then added:

'However, my lady, we do beseech you to keep the torch lit. For hardly a grain shall fall in the glass before we repose by your side once more!'

Margaret allowed that she would, and led her bevy up the stair, giggling freely and speaking most openly about the gentlemen they had just left.

'It is well, Lady Elinor, is it not,' suggested Lady Ann, her sloe eyes teasing darts, 'that your husband is a peer of renown?'

Lady Elinor frowned a swaying frown. 'It is true it is well, Lady Ann,' said she. 'But I fain would know the way it may be well to you!'

'Why! If he were not then how could he ever be rid of all those oceans of wine he has drunk?'

'Hoo, hoo, hoo!' hooted some of the others.

And thus Carmichael heard them.

When they reached the second-floor landing they clustered for several minutes around the entrance to the King's apartment, apparently unwilling to part from the Queen, but secretly reluctant to abort such a glorious orgy of scandal and innuendo.

Carmichael's door was two along from the King's, on the far side of the landing. He eased it open a breathless inch and peeped out.

As the ladies brandished their flickering, smoking night torches, their noses lengthened, their flushed eyes goggled, and their rasping voices cackled harsher.

But where was Elizabeth?

'Come!' he heard Queen Margaret say at length. 'Since his Majesty inclines to enjoy himself with his lords, we shall leave him to occupy his chamber alone this night, that he may not be restrained in his mirth. Nor have the opportunity of disturbing us.'

Lady Annabelle's face leered fatter. 'Oooh, my lady! You are too kind. There are many present, I am sure, whose disposal of such a privilege would be hardly so charitable! What say you, Elizabeth?'

Several titters, slightly nervous.

Lady Ann flushed; her eyelids hooded.

Queen Margaret frowned.

And Carmichael head Elizabeth say:

'I say nothing, Lady Annabelle, so please you. For I understand you not.'

Lady Annabelle began: 'My meaning is plain – '

'Quite so!' snapped the Queen to the company at large. 'As are the best of her features. Well said, Elizabeth. For there is nothing to understand, but that Mistress Hamilton is in love with her own frustrations. And now, ladies, to bed! We divine you need rest.'

Margaret turned with stiff dignity and led the way up the narrow spiral stair to the attic.

The wing-clipped hen party fluttered meekly after.

Carmichael strained his ears through seeming eternity before he heard the closing click of the attic door. He then removed his boots, tip-toed out to the landing, and, his heart racing faster with every step, crept noiselessly up through the spiralling darkness.

Into dire danger of discovery and disgrace.

He pressed his ear to the small wooden door at the head of the stair.

Silence, except for distant scufflings.

Did this mean the ladies had already retreated to their own little burrows?

This did seem likely, in view of the Queen's displeasure.

But what if some restlessly grooming dame were to venture forth again, to borrow some suddenly indispensable toiletry of her neighbour?

Carmichael knew he would find Elizabeth in the fifth room to the left as he entered the flat. This he had established, also at considerable risk, in the course of his demented fury at the news of Elizabeth's betrothal to the despicable Polmood. Why else did he spy up at her turret window in the gilded solitude of Thursday dawn, in the feverish hope that she might miraculously there appear to smile confidingly down at him?

Yet what were his chances of stealing to her door unheard and unseen?

And how would she receive him?

Might she not faint, or hysterically yell?

Only the certainty, that if he lost Elizabeth now, by bowing to his trembling fears, however rational, he would be quite unable to live with himself another week, was sufficient to lift Carmichael's hand to the latch.

Praise be to the Lord: the door did not creak!

All at first seemed dark in the lobby. Not until he moved some way round the wide circular chimney in the middle (which carried up to the sky the collected flues of all the Castle and thus provided the attic flat with a pristine central heating) did Carmichael perceive that perhaps a quarter of the chamber doors still had thin strips of candle glimmer peeping beneath them.

Elizabeth's included.

Carmichael padded towards it and listened.

Were not those measured silky whispers of golden locks acombing!

Somewhere behind him he heard the frantic quickness of a ratting scurry – doubly hateful now, as his feet were naked.

Then, all in one desperate sudden flurry, he tapped lightly, seized the crude latch, and burst in.

'Heaven save us, Sir John! Are you *mad*?' Elizabeth's protest was husky with the pleasure of anticipating sleep. Her raised hands froze for a moment in their attitude of scrupulous curl taming, but there was surely more in her high-browed frown of intrigued self-righteousness than of hysterical outrage.

Clad only in a knee-length night rail of thin and much laundered white, she sat on her bare wooden stool, facing a dressing mirror and stumpy tallow candle set up on the improverished table of her modest leather travelling trunk.

Carmichael had never imagined a prospect so unutterably lovely. He rushed forward and sank on his knees before her, pressing his clenched fists together and shaking them in imprecation.

His breaking whisper urging:

'Oh, my Lady Elizabeth! I pray you by all that is holy, *do not cry out*! Or I am for ever undone.'

Elizabeth's nose wrinkled prettily in puzzlement. Slowly, with impaired efficiency, she resumed her combing.

'Rest assured, Sir John,' she said, 'that cry out I shall not. So long, at least, as your extraordinary temerity goes no further. For to do so would displease her majesty greatly, and she is already near as out of temper as ever I have seen her. Therefore, for all our sakes, I pray you retreat this instant, return whence you came, that we both may consider this affair at an end.'

As she continued to tease out the ringlets she had so painstakingly teased in just a few hours before, the firm high promontories of Elizabeth's small but perfect breasts, thrusting hard through their almost transparent covering, carried on a sotto peeking conversation of their own that would have been tantalizing beyond endurance to any young man in his right mind.

Which Carmichael was anything but.

'Ooooh, Elizabeth!' he wailed. Yearning forward, he clutched her combing wrist and repeatedly pressed it to his brimming eyes and imploring mouth.

And continued to do so for the next ten minutes, as he beseeched her by all the endearments of love and tenderness at his command (and by several that were not), and for the sake of one who adored her beyond power of expression and who was willing to sacrifice his happiness and even life itself for the privilege of calling her his, to elope with him instantly, to gallop off *now* under cover of darkness, and to unite with him in fortune and spirit (he did not mention flesh), for better or for worse, for ever and ever, in life both here and hereafter.

'This is the last possible moment,' he concluded. 'The ladies are sleeping. The King and his nobles are drinking themselves unconscious. I know all the passes of the forest. We shall easily elude them tonight. If indeed we are once missed, which I do not for a moment believe. And tomorrow we shall be over the border, to safety.'

Elizabeth's listening lips parted, she drew breath to reply.

But Carmichael hurried on:

'And consider, my dearest Elizabeth, before you answer me finally – consider that Polmood is nowise worthy of you. His years outnumber your own three times. His manners are crude and uncourtly, and his breath abominable. And is it not known by all that his estates, honours and titles cannot once be compared with mine own? I beg you, consider!'

Elizabeth did.

And were not these adducements of much weight? Especially the point about Polmood's breath, which, ever since his ill-advised attempt on her lips, had been niggling the back of her mind like the simmering hint of a molar abcess. How should she shrink from his halitose mouth when he was become her lawful lord and master?

And Carmichael was *handsome*!

He was tall, well formed, his noble brow high and unwrinkled, his wide dark eyes were clear and steady yet still burned urgent

58

with health and ardour of youth, his generous mouth and strong white teeth ... altogether, he was a pleasure to look upon, especially when one's look returned so immediately charged with slavish worship of oneself! Whereas Polmood, though in his way as passionate, was ...

Elizabeth sighed; tensed to speak.

Carmichael's breath caught.

She hesitated for a moment, looked him full in the eye, and a flickering ray of joyful anticipation appeared to play upon her lovely countenance. Then she said:

'It will make a great noise, I suppose. The ladies will be terribly astonished.'

'Yes, my dear Elizabeth. Oh *yes*! They will all be astounded as never before. And some, without doubt, will be highly displeased. But if we can escape to the court of England, or to France, until the first fury of the blast is overblown, your kind and loving godmother, the Queen, will soon be happy to receive you again into her arms and household. As Lady Hyndford.'

That title sounded charmingly in Elizabeth's ears. She mouthed it several times to herself, then beamed with the pleasure of one whose new garment not only fits but flatters as well.

Carmichael perceived the pleasure, and rushed to pursue the theme.

'I ask you,' he asked her, 'which of the two titles is most likely to command respect at court? The plain, common, vulgar designation: Dame Elizabeth Hunter of Polmood? Or Lady Elizabeth Carmichael of Hyndford? The right honourable *Countess* of Hyndford!'

In that moment it was all over with Polmood.

Elizabeth tutted impatiently, savoured the *Countess* several times on her tongue, and forthwith inquired of Carmichael what immediate action he proposed.

'Come directly to my chamnber,' said he. 'I have a suit of clothes in which you may pass for my squire, and two good horses in the stable. We shall cross the steps of Glendearg before the rising of the sun, and be well into England by noon. And thus frustrate Polmood and all the court of their precious wedding for once!'

Wedding?

Frustrate the court of a *wedding*! Oh, rash and unfortunate expression!

The utterance of *wedding* alone would have been too much. It glanced on Elizabeth's mind like a flash of lightning, illumining the crucial image of the ceremony, and all its attendant ecstasies of limelight and homage.

'We shall have no wedding, then?' she murmured, distant with renewed indecision.

'Not tomorrow, of course,' breezed Carmichael, still unaware of his folly. 'But certainly we shall contrive to have a wedding by and by. Perhaps in Paris!'

Elizabeth freed her hand from Carmichael's pressing, folded her arms protectively across her bosom, anchoring her fingers on the points of her shoulders, and buried the slight dimpled rose of her cheek in the valley created by her forearms.

But on whose side the troubled balance of her cogitations might have settled will never be known, for at that moment the door to the stair was thrown brashly open, and the King's ringing tones suggested:

'Now, Polmood, be so good as to carry the torch, and we shall place upon ourself the burden of discreet inquiry.'

Knock, knock, knock: the royal knuckles rapped on a nearby door.

'Elizabeth?' James called in a carrying whisper. 'Is the fair Elizabeth within? It is *Elizabeth* we seek.'

Imagine, then, the cornered horror of Carmichael's panic.

RUE FOR WHO?

When the party that accompanied King James in escorting the Queen and her ladies from the pavilion to the Castle had returned to the rout on the green, they found several of the nobles already succumbed in varying measure. In particular, it was noted that the Lord James Douglas of Dalkeith (a small and ineffectual man, whose bane was to equate virility with capacity for liquor) had already fallen prone and was only known to be still with the living by the volume of his stertorous snore.

With afforded great merriment to his larger and more virile confrères.

But despite the blatant excess, King James, himself notoriously strong-headed and given to mischief, proceeded to insist on further toasts, in which all still conscious were required to join.

A bumper to the bride, proposed the King.

A second to the land's most gracious Queen, insisted Polmood.

Nor was the incomparable beauty of the Lady Ann Gray allowed to pass uncelebrated.

On and on it went, until several more lordly heads has fallen back to the state of Douglas of Dalkeith, many others were severely addled in their speech and demeanour, and even the stoutest topers were considerably simplified in their loftiest faculties.

The battles of bygone days were fought again, the sports of the day just passed were re-enacted, and, miraculous to relate, it soon emerged that every man was stronger and swifter and more courageous than any of his companions. Many bets were offered, readily accepted, and never more thought of. Even the Lord Chamberlain Hume, a relative wasting midget, at one point proffered to wrestle with Polmood for a purse of a thousand merks.

But the latter paid little attention to the raging rodomontade around him, having entered into a close and one-sidedly humorous argument with his Majesty, who was rallying him unmercifully on his relations with his young wife-to-be, and who at length, draining yet another bumper dead, turned to him a countenance down-mouthed in earnest concern, and said:

'Indeed, Polmood! But there is one particularly necessary ceremony you have quite forgot. A ceremony which has never been dispensed with in this realm. Never!'

Polmood wiped his wet lips uneasily, and slurred:

'Yooour Ma—'

'It is the custom of asking the bride, at parting with her on the wedding's eve, if she has not *rued*.'

'But Si—'

'Many a bridegroom has had to travel far for that purpose, Polmood. Therefore, why should you neglect it now, when living under the same roof as the girl? Eh?'

Polmood stirred uncomfortably in his cross-legged squat. He straightened his back and shook his head, as if to quash its rising clamour to go spinning to the ground. Haltingly he acknowledged that the custom of rue was indeed still current. But, he added:

'If Elizabeth had repented, Sire, she has had oppor ...' he stalled in a belching hiccup, 'tunity in plenty to say so.'

But his Majesty insisted that Polmood's omission was most serious, leaving Elizabeth in full liberty to deny him in the morning even before the priest.

'Which would prove an awkward business, Polmood! Wherefore we do urge you to make way now, conform with the good old custom, and put the question to the lady, even though she be abed.'

Polmood reacted with gestures and movements that in a less mountainous man might be described as squirms and wriggles, and respectfully objected that:

'To visit the lady *now*, Sire, in her *bed* when she is very like even *asleep*, would surely be a much worse and unfor*giv*able breach of decoorum. Would it not? Sire?'

This only excited further raillery against him.

'He dares not! He dares not!' piped the indomitable Lord Hume. 'Polmood does not *dare*!'

'Is it so, Polmood?' James inquired solemnly. 'That you do not *dare*?'

Polmood was much nettled by this, and instantly growled:

'Very well, Sire. As your Majesty pleases. I shall be happy to approach the lady now, provided that your Majesty will accompany me as a witness.'

'Gladly, Polmood! With truly illimitable gladness! And let us delay no further,' the King urged, rising, and brushing blades of damp grass from his skintight parti-coloured hose and codpiece. 'As Elizabeth may be still awake but soon must sleep. BOYS! A torch. And more wine. Lord Hume requires more wine. Excuse us, gentlemen. We shall rejoin you shortly with our news.'

And off he went.

With Polmood lumbering unwillingly after.

Is not the mind of woman ever fruitful in expedient? Is it not wonderful to behold with what readiness they will avert the most sudden and fatal surprises? With regard to all affairs of love, in particular, if the woman cannot fall upon some shift to elude discovery, are not the exigencies desperate indeed?

'Oh, dear *Lord*!' gasped Carmichael, when he heard the tapping and calling of the Elizabeth-seeking King. Whirling from his kneel to a haunted crouch, he stared stricken at the door, as though at the broad unbending back of his executioner. 'I am *doomed*!'

'Hush, Sir John!' said Elizabeth. 'And hasten, I pray you. Stand there.' She firmly pushed his helpless bulk flat against the wall at the hinge side of the door.

'Oh, Elizabeth!' he nearly sobbed. 'How ever can I apol—'

'Hush!' All in one quick-winking flash, Elizabeth pulled her wispy night garment over her head and threw it on the bed, danced over to the travelling trunk, bent to blow out the candle, and skipped back in the total darkness to take her naked station by the door, not three feet from the blindly ogling incredulity of Baron John Carmichael.

To glimpse Elizabeth in such tomboyishly dimple-bottomed voluntary nudity! Yet how fiendishly cruel that the glimpse should come now, like *this*!

Hardly daring to shift his aching weight from one foot to the other, he lowly implored:

'Eliz—'

'*Sssssh*!' she scolded fiercely. Pressing her body against the door to muffle any noise, she unlatched and pulled it an inch ajar.

'A thousand pardons, madam!' they heard the King appease. 'A million. Two doors to the left, you say? Um, but whose? Never mind. Never mind. We shall seek and we shall find. So long as we . . . remain not blind! Ha! What you say, Polmood? A Kingly rhyme?'

'Sire . . .'

'Well, a rhyme at least. Come, man! As you are shy, we shall take the torch ourself.'

Their feet stepped closer.

Through the ajarness of Elizabeth's door came the oil-smoky flicker of the approaching flambeau.

Carmichael marvelled at the intrepid paleness of her unclad silhouette. How terribly much he burned to touch, yet no muscle dared move.

'Elizabeth?' cooed the King. 'Is Elizabeth within?' Knock, knock: he tapped. 'Aha! The door, Polmood, is unfastened. Elizabeth? No doubt the girl sleeps, and we had best enter, had we not?'

Polmood was too feal to question the logic of his Majesty's intention.

In his left hand James held up the low flame of his torch, at shoulder height. With his right hand he pushed gently at the door. 'Elizabeth?' he called again, in an impish singsong whisper. 'Is – '

Elizabeth's golden head and undraped shoulders bobbed into view in the doorway. She threw her arms protectively across her bosom, and from a perfect mask of aghast amazement cried:

'What can your Majesty *mean*? I am *undressed*!'

'A million pardons, my lady!' spluttered James. 'We – '

Elizabeth, impregnably aggressive in defence of her modesty, leaned out unexpectedly and blew hard at his torch, extinguishing it in two quick puffs. Darting back behind the door and slamming it shut, she called:

'Your Majesty will surely excuse me! For as I am not dressed you must not enter. But if you will allow me a minute, then shall I be ready and glad to attend your pleasure.'

The King made no immediate reply, instead devoting his breath to trying to fan back to light the stinking wick of the snuffed flambeau.

A moment later, coughing through its death fumes, he tetched:

'Confound the girl, Polmood! The devil refuses to rekindle. What shall we do now?'

'It it please your Majesty,' suggested Polmood's invisible gruffness, 'perhaps we had best just put the question in the dark. As we are.'

'No, no, Polmood. No, no, *no*! It pleases us not. For a No is all too easy in the dark, when the eyes may say what they will and not be heard. No! As is a Yes, mark you – it is all one in the dark. No. We must get our torch relit: some other dame must have her candle still alive and will oblige us. Come. Elizabeth?'

'Yes, my Lord?'

'We shall return in a minute.'

'Very well, my Lord. I shall be decent.'

But what would the King and his reluctant henchman have thought, as they stumbled away in the black, round the lobby to Elizabeth's left, has they known that the maiden outraged in her chamber was actually teeth-clenched and side-wracked by her spasms of barely controllable laughter?

Carmichael hissed his alarm:

'Elizabeth!'

'All is . . . well, Sir John,' she chortled. 'Fear not.'

'Oh, my lady, you have saved my life without a doubt! How ever may I repay you?'

'You may repay me, Sir John, and shall, by forsaking me this instant. Though the King seems now at the far side of the lobby, he will return at any moment.'

'But – '

'Go!'

Carmichael, knowing he must obey, fairly seethed in unanswered frustration: all his beloved's defences down, and yet he dare not press his suit.

'Come, Sir John. I *beg* you!' she urged, serious again on sensing his dither. 'I have the door open – be gone!'

He brushed past her, and, feeling the pressure of her soft young body against his protuberant cod, was unable to resist the ungracious impulse to seize her shoulders, swing her about, and savagely force to her tightly protesting lips a fleeting kissful of jumbled emotions.

'My love is thine for *ever*!' he vowed in a leaving whisper. 'Rest assured, I shall return.'

Elizabeth closed the door after him, quickly resumed the modesty of her night gown, sat down again in the dark to continue her combing, then surprised herself in a sudden eruption of muted giggles.

Did *all* men take themselves so seriously?

Meanwhile King James was still slowly groping his lap round the lobby, with Polmood in unvoiced questioning tow. Had his Majesty truly forgot the two men-at-arms that stood by the stair on the second-floor landing, with a flaming torch apiece? Or did he *choose* to forget?

Polmood, groggily aware that both his Sovereign and himself were variously the worse for drink, kept his mouth shut.

Tapping imperiously at every chamber door around the circle, the King inquired of each of the occupant ladies whether she yet had a light alive, as his own flambeau had fallen on an unhappy dark patch, and would be grateful for resurrection.

Several of the ladies denied having light, but at length James came to one door below which still trickled a promising glimmer. Here too he knocked and forwardly called, and was astonished to recognize, through her mumbled reply, the voice of the lady within.

It was the Queen!

For reasons best known to himself, James affected not to know. He lifted the latch, and, pretending a discreetness of manner quite absent from his previous calls, did not look into the chamber, but only held in the torch and requested of the resident that she relight it.

She did, without speaking, and handed it back to him.

The two question-bearing champions then returned in a blaze of triumph to Elizabeth's door. The King tapped on it with a newfound softness, and more quietly asked if she were undressed still.

Elizabeth begged a multitude of pardons for the trouble she had caused his Majesty, which had arisen solely from his having surprised her in deshabille. She was indeed now decent again, as promised, and of course his Majesty was welcome to enter her chamber and confide his Pleasure.

Motioning that Polmood should follow, James entered cautiously, keeping his flambeau away from Elizabeth, and began by commanding her forgiveness in respect of his former impoliteness.

'But seeing that your door was not altogether shut,' he explained, 'we judged tht you must be asleep. Did we not, Polmood? And thought it better to come on you quietly than rouse you with a din that might have waked the others. Such is our excuse, but now to our purpose. We are here, Elizabeth, at your lover's request. In order to witness a question he shall pose you. Polmood!'

That person stepped forward from his self-effacing slouch in the doorway. Much abashed, with the confusion of his wineful glaze inspecting every corner of the chamber but the curious points of Elizabeth's eyes, he bluntly said:

'It is just the question, my lady, that his Majesty insists that I ask you whether or not you have . . . repented of the promise you made to me to marry.'

Elizabeth laid down her comb and blankly regarded the two intruders. James she trusted as a father – he *was* the closest to a father she had ever known. But what was he after tonight, with his strong-fumed breath and penetrating yet mischief-laden eyes, whose colour had the peculiar quality of appearing to vary with his mood?

And Polmood?

In his vast, vulgar, dance-crushing boots, his carelessly creased and wine-stained leathers, with his drunken gaze of danger green, that now seemed shifty and fearful to follow the question he voiced.

And his odious breath!

Must she really be his until death did them part?

Elizabeth's puzzlement raised her right knee six inches from the floor. She clasped it with the locked fingers of both hands, and rocked on her stool in dynamic indecision. Her lips she found dry from the excitement of the past half hour, and with a hint of nervous impatience, she licked and sucked them back to comfortable moistness.

Why was Polmood so absorbed in the toes of his boots?

What was he ashamed of?

Then with clarion clearness it came to her. If Polmood *and* the King felt it necessary to knock her up in the middle of the night, hardly twelve hours before her wedding, to inquire if she had rued, then this must be because Polmood himself (doubtless for some diabolically silly reason that only men would understand) had repented of *his* choice and now was ignobly fishing to throw the blame for the last-minute cancellation on his discarded betrothed!

Who, in that case, had mettle in plenty to oblige with panache.

'Indeed, sir!' she cried, leaping to her feet and stamping with as much misused resentment as one may with bare feet on rough stone. 'Then I must inform you that I *have* rued our agreement. Most heartily I have. And humbly moreover do I beg his Majesty's permission, sir, this instant to wish you goodnight. Sir. As I am weary beyond endurance, sir, and fain would betake me to the comfort of my bed. Sir! In peace.

'My Lord, I do beseech you,' she added in a demurely different voice to King James, 'to forgive your foolish young servant for the rudeness of her outburst, but – '

'Bravo!' clapped the King. 'BRAVO! Come, Polmood. Our welcome is outstayed, and we may not put upon this lady further.' So saying, he about-turned and departed the chamber, pushing the flabbergasted forester before him by means of vigorous prods in the chest.

'BRAVO!' he yelled in glee again, and slammed Elizabeth's door behind him. Seconds later he was hurtling down the stairs and sweeping down the cobwebs of the Castle's peace with:

'HURRAH! The bride has *rued*! THE BRIDE HAS RUED! And POLMOOD IS UNDONE!' Wildly whooping and chanting thus, he shot past the startled men-at-arms on the first-floor landing, out of the Castle, and skipped gaily across the green to irrigate with yet more bumpers his relation of the delicious details to such of his waggish lords as still could follow.

And thank the heavens for their Monarch so merry.

IN THE DARK

So exuberant was the King's insistence when he bustled Polmood out of Elizabeth's chamber, and so limply staggered was Polmood's desolation, that not only did he fail to follow his Majesty's cavortions down the stairs, but he tripped over his heels and fell backwards on the lobby floor, banging the back of his head with sickening force against the central chimney.

Hence it was, a painful moment later, when Polmood pulled his bewilderment into an unsteady kneel, that he found himself utterly in the dark. King James had carried off the one flambeau, and now along the bottom of no damely door did any shriving glimpse of candle flicker.

What was he to do?

Pondering with the dull woodenness of a simple man stunned, he crawled forward and located with exploring hands the frame of the door whence he had been ejected. He bent his whiskery lips to the crack beneath it and hoarsely whispered:

'My lady? My lady Elizabeth?'

Throughout ten teeming seconds no answer came.

'My *lady*!' Polmood hissed. Though naturally given to diffident silence where courtly company and ladies were concerned, he was now driven by mounting desperation, not to mention his reeling intoxication. 'My Lady *Elizabeth*! I pray . . .'

'And I pray too, sir!' her pert young voice hissed back. 'For I am in bed – asleep! – and ardently implore you leave me thus.'

'But what you just now said, my lady: your change of heart most ... cruelly sudden! Surely you did not mean – '

'I mean what I say, sir, when I say that if you do not retire from the attic immediately, I shall call out for assistance in the defence of my virtue.'

'But *why* – '

'And any further account you require from me I shall render in the light of morning. In the presence of his Majesty. Goodnight to you, my Lord Polmood!'

Polmood groaned and cursed as he stood up.

Then groaned again three times as loud when his rising head slammed into the sharp stone lintel of the doorway recess. He rebounded a half pace, and, madly muttering the indelicate extent of his frustrated resentment, shuffled off to his left, in the direction of the door to the stair.

Not until he had taken more paces than he could remember did it occur to him that he had no means of identifying the stairway door, which in size and shape was exactly like all the others. He paused for a moment to ponder his predicament.

Might not the capering King have left the door open?

By touring the lobby full circle, with one hand feeling along the outside wall, Polmood established to his rioting consternation that all the doors were equally and anonymously shut. He could easily have opened any of them, as all were unbolted (a circumstance hardly surprising in the occasional sleeping quarters of a medieval hunting tower), but was fearful that in doing so he might chance upon some sleeping countess, or even the Queen, and thereby procure himself even more ridicule and disgrace than already seemed assured by the fickle retraction of Elizabeth's hand. Even encroaching upon that lady again for assistance was now out of the question, as his exploratory circuit had lost him track of which door was hers.

The expedient that Polmood at length hit upon may seem somewhat whimsical, but it must be remembered, in addition to the reason-scrambling of far too much wine, that the floundering forester was rent by violent emotional upheaving and confused in consequence of his two recent bonks on the head. Thus, to him, the notion appeared splendid, and no sooner struck him than he put it into practice.

It was to listen at the bottom of every door, for breathing beyond, and so by elimination locate the one door which screened the inanimate and hence unrespiring stairway.

The first stage posed little difficulty.

Soundlessly crawling, Polmood began his second tour of the lobby, pressing a straining ear to the draught beneath each door, and creeping always to the next as soon as he had certified that some snoutering madam was within. And as he progressed he kept count of the doors he vetted: his fuddlement failing to perceive that, since he left no landmark at the beginning of his lap, he would be eternally at a loss to determine its completion! Nevertheless, his tally was climbing the teens when suddenly it collapsed like a gusted house of cards.

As he froze in his crawl, on hearing a door softly open.

Close by.

No light appearing, Polmood judged that he had been overheard: that this was one of the ladies looking out of her chamber to investigate the disturbance. Then, on the point of his whispering out for pardon and assistance, he heard the pad of furtive steps approaching.

Heavy, booted steps!

As of a doughty knight.

No man on earth did Norman of Polmood fear by day, face to face. Yet such is the paralysing power of the phantoms of absolute darkness that now, in the added ignominy of being caught kneeling like some peeping knave by a sleeping lady's door, he felt his hearing almost overwhelmed by the palpitations of his heart.

He drew breath to roar a manly challenge.

But too late.

Suddenly the newcomer accelerated.

Bang!

'RRRRRAAAAAAH!' yelled Polmood as his nose crunched under the impact of an invisible oncoming knee. 'Bogger of HELL! I'll *slay* ye for this!' So vowing, he rose up like a human earthquake, lashing out and grabbing wildly at his unwitting assailant.

Who grunted:

'Grrroooof!' in astonished alarm, and desperately beat at the deadly huge hand that Polmood lunged at his throat.

'Who are ye, varlet?' Polmood raged. 'Speak now or ye di –

yeee – ' His opponent had dealt him an enormous blow to the solar plexus. 'Whoowoof . . . the boggery?' he gasped as the other danced away.

Seconds later there came a doory slam, immediately followed by the frantic clatter of boots descending stairs at breakneck speed.

Thinking he must have surprised some naughty courtier rooting for his mistress, Polmood, sobbing for wind, intending both his own escape and the come-uppance of the rogue who had noddled him, charged blindly after the sounds of flight.

Coming up with a bang against the door through which the wicked bird had presumably flown, he wrenched it open and thundered on, his ankles flexing to deal with steps.

Which, of course, they did not encounter.

Polmood hurtled across the floor with a momentum he could not check, but which was redirected for him by a low-lying shin-denting object in his path, and thus, to his infinitely sunken chagrin, he alighted all his prodigious weight diagonally across a lady's bed.

Who erupted like a razor-clawed wildcat and screamed out innumerable colours of murder, fire and ravishment, in a voice so shrilly loud and savagely eldritch that Polmood's ears were momentarily defeaned and his joints rendered utterly powerless.

'HELP!' bawled the injured fair, at crystal-shattering pitch. 'LADIES! GUARDS! YOUR MAJESTY! HELP! OH, BLESSED VIRGIN, I AM BROOZLED BY A VILLAIN IN THE DARK; WILL NOT SOMEBODY *HELP ME!*'

At least, since she called for the Queen, she could not *be* the Queen – but who was she, with her outraged wiry arms wrapped around his neck to impede his departure?

'Hush, lady!' Polmood rumbled. 'This is – '

'GUARDS! *HELLLLLL* – '

Polmood tried gently to push himself free, but the hysterical harpy beneath sank talons of the utmost fierceness into his hair and his left ear. And as he feared to disengage from her frantic violence through violence in return, he remained captive in that manner until rescued.

The other ladies had meanwhile awakened, set up one universal yell of MURDER, leapt from their beds, and in the ongoing darkness were endeavouring to escape – though from what they did not know. Thus the beauteous bevy of Scotland's leading ladies, some clad nightily and others not at all, were found careering round the lobby, bumping into each other and all the while escalating their volume of keening despair.

When the guards alarmed from the first-floor landing burst in with their light-throwing torches.

'Eeeeeek!' cried some, as their privates flashed.

'Ooooooh!' gasped others, in dread at appearing ungroomed.

And the whole circular apartment was like a rabbit warren, with distressed and undressed ladies skipping madly back to their holes like so many terrified bunnies.

A moment later King James arrived, supported by several nobles. All scowling and ominously armed.

The ill-chosen door, whence the deafening cries of 'HELP' came, was only two inches ajar, echoing the force of Polmood's entry.

With drawn sword the King approached, and threw the door wide.

'Merciful Heavens!' he cried, on beholding the worthy, the bold, the giant and invincible Norman Hunter of Polmood, held prisoner by the sheepish hairs of his head by the right honourable Lady Elinor of Hume, who denounced him all the while as a stinking libertine and incorrigible ravisher, her sharp features flushed apoplectic scarlet and her eyes goitre-wide.

'Polmood, sir!' barked James. 'Have you forgot yourself? Our trust – '

'AAAAAAAH!' wailed Lady Elinor. 'BLOOD! I AM DEAD! THE VILLAIN HAS STABBED – ' So convinced, she broke off in a shallow swoon.

Polmood seized the respite to jump up, as flustered a forester as ever there was.

'It is true!' exclaimed the Earl of Mar from over the King's shoulder. 'She bleeds!' His eyes fixed in fascinated horror on the slight breast of Lady Hume's lilac silk nightrobe, besmirched with the dark crimson gore that had made her faint.

'We think not,' said the King. 'No. It is Polmood who bleeds. Consider his unfortunate nose.'

'Your Majesty!' mumbled the owner of that swollen and still trickling organ. 'Sire, I can explain – '

'No doubt you can, Polmood,' scolded James, grave against the background mirthful abuse that poured from the Earl of Mar and the other supportive nobles who had twigged. 'And in the morning we shall require you so to do. For the present, however, it is time to retire, and we shall content ourself with your pledge of immaculate behaviour until such time as you can be got married. That we need not confine you in the keep, for the preserved intactness of the virtue of other men's wives! Your pledge, Polmood?'

'You have it, Sire. My pledge most solemn.'

'Very good, Polmood. And now, gentlemen, come. Our welcome here is outstayed.' The King turned to lead the males below.

Around the lobby hurriedly combed damely heads were peering, curiously agog for scandal, from their slit chamber doors.

'Ah, Lady Annabelle!' said James in a passing afterthought. 'Could you attend the Mistress Hume? She has come over a wee bit faint, we fear, and will draw great comfort from your ministrations.'

'But of *course*, my Lord!' Lady Annabelle's fat cheeks wreathed in a simper. 'I shall – '

'You there!' rapped the King to a flanking guard. 'That torch you have: leave it here with the good Lady Hamilton.'

MOST HORRIBLE!
One might be forgiven for expecting that the untoward happenings of that night must be over, yet such is far from the case. Indeed, the unlucky adventure which befell the Laird of Polmood was merely a prologue to further mistakes, profounder atrocities, and consequences more calamitous.

At least for some.

The King bid goodnight to his followers as they passed the second-floor landing, and retired to his chamber. The younger rakes who had accompanied him to the attic, their minatory scowls tranformed to merciless grins and jibes at Polmood's expense, now made a great show of conducting him back to the company before the pavilion, guarding him as a prisoner in jest and lewdly miming such reprehension as might befit a rapist caught red-handed.

Polmood, his head in a pounding whirl from its flurry of knocks both mental and physical, played along with his blattering captors in the bemused passivity of a sleepwalker. At one point, as they rattled down the Castle steps to the green, he haltingly began to relate the painful details of his encounter with the stranger knight in the dark. But at this the derision of his companions was tickled far beyond any possibility of sensible communication, one even suggesting that Polmood had better be quick in getting hold of the dog biting him, else he might soon find himself bit quite to death!

'Hoo, hoo, ha!' greeted this.

And:

'Hey, boy! A brimming stoup for the Laird of Polmood.'

'Ay! Where else in Scotland will you find a man can beat the Devil in a wrestle?'

'In the dark forby!'

'And tell us, Polmood – be honest now. Had you contact with the Evil One's broozler? They say – '

'But of course he had. Of *course* he had! *Consider his unfortunate nose!*'

'Hoo, hoo! Hoo, ha!'

So Polmood abandoned his attempt to spell out his sozzled suspicions, squatted broodily on the green with his back to the fire, drained in a single quaff the large bumper given him by an obedient squire, demanded an instant refill, and methodically set about the balmy business of drinking himself unconscious.

A state into which the Earl of Hume seemed destined soon to pass.

Twenty minutes earlier, when the alarm was given to the effect that the ladies required succour, the Lord Chamberlain had already achieved the single-minded intensity of extreme and fatuous drunkenness which men so unaccountably prize. He had fallen into a raging dispute, over some growingly vital detail of Border chivalry, with the comparably but more placidly diminished Donald of Lamington. And who could expect, in view of the paramount heights achieved by their debate, that these two gentlemen should have felt it their duty to break off and assist in the rescue of some dame being molested in the turrets?

But now the rescue party had returned.

Lamington had attained oblivion.

And Lord Hume loosely grasped, from the goaty embellishments of the Earl of Mar and his fellows, the most salacious and suggestive highlights of Polmood's intrusion upon his own Lady Elinor.

'WHAT, SIR?' he roared at Polmood, tottering to his feet from his patch on the pavilion steps. 'How DARE you?'

'My lord!' grumbled Polmood, looking up in startlement. 'It was al—'

'How DARE you?' ranted Hume, his narrow eyes crossing in fury. His long ceremonial gown of office, of deep-pleated gold-brocaded crimson and rich ermine trimming in wine-stained white, which it was his privilege and fetish to wear on almost all occasions, he now struggled out of and cast to the ground.

Tugged from his belt his cosmetic rapier.

Brandished it in front of Polmood's unfortunate nose, slicing the midge-thick night, and raving:

'What, sir? What, *what*! And is this the practice of a gentleman? I ask of you!' Swipe. Thrust. 'Because you cannot get you a wife of your own, this gives you the right to creep up there like – like some insolent cowardly donkey, sir, and take violent possession of mine? Does it now? Eh? and have you no tongue, sir, to bray out your craven denial? Ha! Well, I tell you, sir, it does not. Wherefore I command you: rise up and draw like a man. Draw out your sword, Polmood, like the treacherous jackass you are, and I shall give you to know the contrary. And carve you, sir, in a multitude of pieces and have you thus fed to the hounds for their breakfast. Sir, I *order* you, DRAW!' he jibbered.

And his performance was so convincing that all the other lords still able were absolutely knotted by it in rolling, sobbing fits of veritable stitches.

Except Polmood, who could only shrink in dismay from the dancing point of the Lord Hume's blade.

Who was his total superior in rank and power.

And equally his inferior in physique and martial skill.

And who hence could never be fought in a duel without risking the untold wrath and retribution of the King.

'My good Lord Hume,' Polmood faltered, leaning back uncomfortably close to the fire, to retain unslashed possession of his nose, 'the fair Lady Elinor and myself – '

'Shall soon be half in the grave, sir. For as you will not draw I shall CARVE YOU WHERE YOU LOLL!' The maddened earl drew back his sword to thrust in earnest.

But the nimble Mar, perceiving the red light of bloodlust in the aggressor's eye, leapt up and stayed his fatal lunge.

'My lord!' he hissed urgently in Hume's unwilling ear. 'You cannot, my lord. For Polmood has no sword! Look you, and see that his belt is bare. And forby, my lord, there is no need. There is no *blame*, my lord, and no dishonour. As *Polmood but mistook the bed*, that is all. He meant no harm.'

'Then why – '

'Yes, my good Lord Hume! Most truly. And forby you have cause for rejoicing. For the fair Lady Elinor, by taking him a prisoner, has surely merited immortal glory, has she not?'

Hume's champing eyes rolled round in a cusp reflection.

And moments later, such is the nature of a peer in his cups, he was so pleased with himself and his valiant spouse that he was never weary of shaking hands with Polmood, and drinking to him – though he did not forget to observe, at each toast, that it would in the future conduce to the general weal if no man in the world but his venerable self were to attempt the pruning of the brambly Lady Elinor.

And many more words to that effect.

And what might his brambly lady have given to hear them?

So besotted did the earl become with the resolute intrepidity of his wife's behaviour that, being at heart a sprightly and ingenious gentleman, he resheathed his sword and began to dance a little jig in her honour. And by and by as he danced he sang, a song that he swore was extempore, which was readily believed by his audience, as none had heard it before. It is still extant and may sometimes be heard during the later stages of shepherd stag parties in the wilds of Selkirkshire, and the chorus goes like this:

> I have a good wife of my own.
> With a tongue like a venomous weasel;
> But in bed, on her belly,
> She is soft, like a jelly,
> And no end of a pleasure to broozle!

'Bravo! came the chanting claque, when, after five capering verses and all-sung choruses, the creative statesman came to a panting pause. 'Bravo!'

And:

'More, my lord! More. Another verse.'

'Should not the song mention, my lord, the precise extent of the broozler the good lady pleasures?'

'The frequency with which she favours it!'

'And if, my lord, she is truly no end of a pleasure (on her bedded jellybelly, with all respect), then how come you are here on the green with us, and not up yonger no-ending your good lady in the turrets?'

'Doubtless she pines for you, my lord!'

Doubtless she did, his lordship assented.

'Then must you not fly there, and invest the remainder of this night in her company?'

Indeed he must, he shortly decided, encouraged by a flood of plausible arguments from his merry associates. Her chamber was singly tiny, it was true, yet how could she grudge him a share of it for one night? And was it not long since last their loins conjoined?

'I *have* a good *wife* of my own,' he happily hummed as he tripped across the lawn, struggling back into the smothering fur of his shoulder-boosting robe, 'with a *tongue* – '

'Like a dose of the pocks!' some anonymous wag behind him muttered.

The hard core remaining then drew together in continued toping and gleeful speculation on the brouhaha his lordship might ignite.

'Come, Polmood,' counselled Mar with more truth than he knew, 'take heart! For your own indiscretion shall soon be eclipsed and forgot.'

'Aaaah!' the Lord Chamberlain panted, as he crossed the first-floor landing to the low and narrow archway of the stair to the upper storeys.

The two men-at-arms, who had been stationed there since the ladies retired, started guiltily and stood to sluggish attention. Both were in their middle thirties, tall and well muscled for the day, even if lightweights compared to Lamington and Polmood, and their habit was thick soldierly leather, broadsworded at the belt. One supported the single torch remaining on the landing, while the other held his seven-foot halberd diagonally across the archway. Though not incapacitated, the two soldiers were jovially slow on the aftermath of the wine they had earlier filched, and still bedazed by images flashing from their insight into the unclad scurrying privates of Scotland's greatest ladies.

'Guard, guard,' puffed Hume, the points of his narrow cheeks purple from effort and drink. 'Well done, well *done*! Just what I need.' He reached imperiously for the torch.

'Your pardon, my lord?' With the nervousness of a rank insubordinate, Sergeant Torch withdrew his flambeau a subtle inch from his lordship's grasp.

'Why, man, you turkey-brained dolt, the *torch*! I would have your torch. And *will* have it. And will have it *now*!'

'May it please your lordship sir,' mumbled Sergeant Torch, 'but gladly though we would confirm to your lordship's wishes, sir, we may not. As we guard the King, my lord, and this is our only light: we have not another.'

'Indeed!' rapped Hume, his purple patches pulsing with the acidity of his easy anger. 'And have you not another?'

'No, good my lord, we have not another. This – '

'And *why*, pray, *gentlemen*, have you not another?'

Sergeant Torch shuffled as much as a soldier at attention can, and uneasily explained:

'We had a second light, my lord, but his Majesty commanded us to leave it with the good Lady Hamilton which we did. For her to attend to my good Lady Hume, my lord, in her distress. And – '

'Whose? *Whose* good Lady Hume, ninny? Eh? You insufferable pip-squeak, you: the morning shall see you flogged half to death! Rest assured.'

'So it please you, my lord. Though I meant no offence, I do swear.'

'Oh you do, do you?' sniffed the lordly terrier, relenting a fraction. 'I'll wager you do, by Saint Giles! And howling to Purgatory for eternity may it take you. Ha! You follow me not? No? Well, no matter – indeed it may be better so. But the torches, man. The *torches*! Why had you but two? Are the others all devoured by the rats, by the Lord?'

'No, my lord. It is not the rats, but the celebrations on the green. So please your lordship, the torches are mainly wanted there this night, for to light them. And so we have a shortage here.'

'Ah! Well, I suppose it may be so. No matter then: it matters not. I know the way and shall ascend unlit. You HEAR ME, FELLOW?'

the Lord Chamberlain suddenly roared at the unmoving vacancy of Sergeant Halberd, whose pike barred his way. 'Move aside there, I say.'

'Forgive me my lordship,' the unbudging Sergeant Halberd intoned laboriously to the gloom-wombed spiders in the shadows. 'But you may not pass.'

'*Whaaat?*' choked the bilious earl, whipping out his rapier and pressing its point dangerously hard against Sergeant Halberd's thick throat. 'I may not pass, you pig-livered minion, may I not? Know you not *who I am*? Then know at least, foul scum that you are, that your life's blood shall answer for it.'

'He means, my lord,' pleaded Sergeant Torch, 'that you may not pass *thus*. With your sword, my lord.' For the rule was, when royalty were in residence and gone to bed, that none but his Majesty might bear weapons beyond the first floor. 'We have to ask your lordship to leave your blade in our safekeeping till the morning.'

'Varlets, all! The dawn shall you never see!'

'My lord to slay us as we stand with the King's consent is your lordship's privilege but – '

'Grr . . .'

'We only attempt to enact his Majesty's wishes.'

'Indeed?'

'My lord, that is all. And his Majesty moreover commanded us, your lordship, before he retired, following the disturbance to the ladies, that if any man should wish to pass us tonight we must ask of him to state his purpose. Sir.'

'My purpose!' spluttered the infuriated earl, withdrawing his rapier from the neck of Halberd and brandishing it under the nose of the dutiful Torch. 'My *purpose*! Lord save us from the idiot knaves that serve us: is not my chamber upon the second floor, next door, indeed to his Majesty? Ah?'

'And do you now go there to retire my lord?'

'Why no, my dear man! As it chances, I do not. I go first to the attic, to see my wife. To ascertain her fitness, do not you know, following her ordeal, and subsequently to enjoy my rights in broozling her from the rear. Shall this satisfy you, dearest fellow? Or will it please you accompany me, observe, and rush to report to his Majesty the glory of my performance? Huh?'

'My lord, the ladies are all sleeping.'

'What marvellous spiritual powers the ruffian has! You whimpering bucket of pestpus, you! And if the ladies *are* all sleeping, then one at least has a treat beyond her dreams in store. The which to delay not, *step aside there*!'

'The attic chambers, my lord, are – '

'EXCREMENTS! TRY ME NOT FURTHER!'

'Over wee for two persons. And his Majesty – '

'Shall hear from his Lord Chamberlain in the morning,' snort, belch, 'of the summary execution of two sergeants of the guard caught committing acts of high treason against the state while drunk on their watch. If you dare delay me one moment more.'

'But your sword, your lordship! We cannot – '

'Then take the bogger!' snarled the earl, hurling his blade behind him. 'The thrusting I am bent on needs it not.'

Sergeant Torch stamped to renewed attention. 'Sergeant,' he instructed his fellow, 'hold back that pike there, and allow his honour, the Lord High Chamberlain of Scotland, to pass up the stair about his business.'

The pike drew back.

The scowling earl shot past.

The soldiers slumped at ease in a grumble of sweating relief. And a minute later the bellicose peer arrived in the circular lobby of the ladies' apartment, as blindly lightless as Polmood before him. He closed the stair door, turned right, and confidently felt his way round the wall to the third door along. Softly he lifted the latch, quickly entered, pulled the door to, and seductively cooed:

'Elinor! Elinor, my dear. Ooo, hoo: it is mee-hee! Your Archiba—'

But something was terribly wrong.

The bed corner issued frantic mutterings and scrabblings, as of desperation for covering garments.

'*Whaaaaaat?*' cried Hume. 'WHAAAAAAT? Who is here?'

The rustlings of desperation redoubled.

'POLMOOD!' roared the earl, instantly insane with drunken jealousy. 'Polmood? Is that you?' he yelled as he charged across the invisible floor and fumbled for the rapier that was not there.

Arriving with a crash by the bedside, his robe-hampered arms flailing before him, he found a large shaggy knight rising up from the bed and furiously struggling into his nightshirt. This appeared, however, to have hitched around his shoulders and left all the lower portions of his filthy fornicator's body acutely uncovered.

'FORNICATING FILTH!' screamed Hume. 'For this you both shall DIE!' His madly windmilling hands thumped into contact with a strongly muscled forearm. He gripped it viciously and gouged with his nails.

'Uuuuurgh!' said its owner, through teeth determinedly clenched.

Then an escaping elbow thrashed down into the left side of his lordship's neck. With the force of a cannonball landing, he later would allege.

Half stunned he fell, his features outraged further by tweaking with a meaty slap against the projecting of the unseen other's manhood.

On the floor he thudded, rolled, once more blindly grabbed, and this time secured the nakedness of a knobbly ankle. Heaving his aristocratic mouth against the other's skin, he closed his teeth around it.

And savagely bit.

'*Feeeeeerk*!' hissed the bitee.

Whose second foot came flying to the rescue of the first, its instep smashing the Lord Hume in the bridge of his nose and the sockets of his eyes.

Causing him to fall back, moaning.

Allowing the fornicator to skip away and make good his retreat.

Bang, slammed the chamber door behind him.

Bang, the stair door echoed.

'MISERABLE CAT-ERSED *TROLLOP*!' bellowed Hume. He rocked to his feet and threw himself across the bed, beating vengefully at the form of its occupant and vowing: 'SLIME-BREEDING SLATTERN, I'll throttle you NOW!'

And a non-stop torrent of similar threats.

'HEEELLP!' the threatened one yelled meanwhile, on apprehending the departure of her paramour. 'HELLLLLLLP! MUUUUUURRRDER!'

'SLUUUUUUUT! TAKE – '

'SOMEBODY, *SAAAAAVE* MEEEE!'

This caterwauling continued for about a minute, with Lord

Hume groping for the lady's throat with strangulous intent yet being thwarted by the vigour with which she, laying hold of the hood-like collar of his robe, forced down his head and smothered his smarting face in her writhing breast.

In the background the other ladies woke, took unseeing fright, and for the second and last time that night set up a hellraising soprano chorus of ravished distress.

Slam, banged the stair door open.

Slam, banged the door to the trouble.

'Bogger me with a sassenach!' Sergeant Torch ejaculated on seeing what he saw.

For it was not upon his own Lady Elinor that the errant earl had stumbled. No. The shrieking dame on whose bosom he battled was none other than the dusky Lady Gray!

Who collapsed in floods of tears and sobbed:

'Oh, woe is me! Woe, woe, *woe*! My virtue for ever stained! Oooooh!' Sob, sob.

Cementing on her side the wide-eyed sympathies of the onlookers.

'Madam!' the confounded gentleman grabbled. 'My dear Mistress Gray! I know not – '

'Ooooooooh! *Woe*!' Sob.

'What gives, what gives?' called the approaching voice of the troublerooting Earl of Mar. 'Tell us not that Lord Hume has mistook his lady's room! Is it possible?'

'What means this unearthly din?' Queen Margart's coldly disapproving figure appeared in the doorway to appraise the scene.

Followed by the avid redheadedness of Mar. 'Well, bogger *me*!' he whistled.

On the floor they saw the kneeling, handwringing horror of the Earl of Hume. While on the bed the violated Lady Gray lay full-length in all the trappings of hysteria, a protective elbow shielding her weeping eyes, her put-upon nakedness rendered barely decent by a corner of sheet across her loins.

Exhibiting to all the arresting heavings of her breasts.

'Mistress Gray!' snapped the Queen. 'You will cover yourself at once.'

'Oooooh! Ooooooo-hoooo!'

'*Mis*tress – '

'SILENCE!' roared King James, appearing from behind in his nightshirt and stockings. His long ginger hair in ruffled disarray, his habitually genial features black with Thunder, he pushed roughly through the gaggle in the doorway and strode forward.

'Oooooo . . .'

'Hold your peace, madam!'

Lady Ann held her peace.

The king bent down, took hold of her sheet, and draped her modest to the neck. The he turned on the kneeling peer, and in a voice thinly brittle with danger said:

'And now, Lord Hume, you will explain your conduct.'

'Majesty, I cannot – '

'Oh, but you can, sir. And you *will*. This *instant*.'

His humbled lordship swallowed anxiously. The purple on his cheek gone pale, he said:

'I came up, Majesty, to pay respects to my good lady wife. And seem – I know not how – to have mistook the door. And then, when I entered, I found within the bed one great hairy knight, who . . . set upon me, and brutalized me sore – '

'ENOUGH!' James raged. 'Dastardly poltroon that you are, is it not enough that you crawl like a drunken scullion upon a sleeping lady? Think you, in seriousness, to exculpate your own vile villainy by heaping smirches on a maiden's honour?'

'Majesty, it is the truth. I swear! Who else did beat me so about the eyes?' Right earnestly did the hapless Hume point out the swelling hues in question. 'And him did I also mark, I vow. His craven shin shall bear the evidence of my teeth for days. His '

'GUARD! This cliping knave has lost his honour with his reason. And with them his office and our trust. He seeks to crawl from the stage of his peccancy by lying his slimy path across a lady's virtue, wherefore arrest him. Convey him to the dungeon, till the morning shall determine if his head and shoulders may continue to commune.'

'Majesty! I beg – '

'Take him. And make no concessions.'

Sergeant Halberd and Sergeant Torch duly did and did not. Their job satisfaction sternly masked, they took their distinguished prisoner by the armpits and dragged him from the scene with no ceremony.

Still despairingly protesting.

Lady Ann proclaimed her attitude to the proceedings by pulling her sheet over her head, huddling miserably into the wall away from the door, and snivelling almost silently.

Queen Margaret frowned her ongoing disapproval.

The Earl of Mar and his mischievous retinue kept their faces a study in grave neutrality, cautioned by the King's extreme distemper.

Behind them (but not including the doubly humiliated Lady Elinor) had gathered a handful of nightrobed ladies, their pretty heads cocked curiously.

'To bed, ladies and gentlemen,' their Sovereign commanded them. 'The incident is closed, and it is almost morning: we would not deprive you further of your sleep.'

'Sire?'

'Yes, Lord Mar,' answered James, frowning at the reluctant dispersal of the ladies. 'What ails you?'

'Your Majesty is most wise . . .' Mar retreated respectfully from Lady Ann's chamber.

King James followed him out, pulled the door shut, leaned his shirted back against the lobby wall, and arched a quizzical eyebrow. 'Well?'

'It is just, Sire, that my Lord Hume is rightly famed for his honesty and honour – all across our nation and even into Europe. Even in England, Sire. And his lordship would not lightly lie, even when disadvantaged by drink, as he was.'

'Importing?'

'Sire, with no disrespect to my Lady Ann's eternal purity, is it not possible that there *was* some stranger knight within her chamber? Against the lady's will, of course.'

'In truth, sir, your loyalty and scrupulous fairness to the Lord Chamberlain are most laudable. However, if we postulate the Lord Hume's veracity, then, as no knight descending could pass the guard unnoticed, and as the only gentleman above the first-floor lobby was ourself – Ourself, mark you! – then the resulting implication is hardly favourable to the Earl of Hume. You follow, sir?'

'Majesty, I do,' said Mar, rattled but unflinching beneath the pressure of the King's innuendo. 'Yet I beg you consider that the possibilities are not exhausted by your Majesty's speculation.'

'Ummm?'

'It is possible, Sire, though of course we trust not, that the guards are bribed.'

'Possible – nothing is not, you may say. Save an honest sheep-thief. And so?'

'Majesty, if the sergeants on the landing are covering for some scaping knave, then his exit cannot have passed unnoted. It must have been remarked by the servants in the lower storeys, Sire, or by the attendants upon the green.'

'Um-hah?'

'The other possibility, Sire, if both the guards and the Lord Chamberlain are honest, and avoiding the implications that would aggravate my Lord Hume's case, is that there was a knight within the chamber – naturally without the Lady Gray's consent – and that the rogue is somewhere *still secreted* about the Castle. Above the guards' position, Sire. Perhaps even at this moment holding some other helpless lady in hostage terror!'

'You are most astute, sir, for the hours you have kept and the wine you have drained. But . . . yes, justice must prevail. Hence we do command you: take these other restless lords, scour the lower storeys and the green, and question every soul you find capable of speech.

'Should no villain thus emerge, you will search the second floor. Behind the drapes, beneath the beds, *everywhere*!

'Failing there, you shall report to ourself, who shall be stationed here – and we trouble you now for that torch, Lord Montrose: there are plenty by the pavilion – in case the monster, if monster there be, be preying still upon some speechless lady. Then and only then shall we ourself examine the ladies' chambers. And if, my Lord Mar, from all these measures no culprit comes, then to what conclusion shall we all be forced?'

The Earl of Mar scratched the flames of his curls in deference, and conceded:

'We should only infer, Sire, with the utmost regret, that the good Lord Hume has broke faith with the truth.'

'That is correct. Now proceed.'

SURPRISE, SURPRISE

Bristling curtly and glinting with the verve of youth endowed with mission, the Earl of Mar and his posse in due course unearthed the insomniac distraction of Sir John Carmichael: skulking in his chamber on the second floor, fully armed and dressed for flight, and seemingly pouring guilt.

King James was summoned down.

Carmichael turned a paler shade of white.

The King evinced his dumbfoundment by several silent openings and shuttings of his Mouth – like the final gasps of a landed trout. His composure recovered, her sternly inquired of Carmichael whether he had betrayed the Trust invested in him by stealing to some furtive tryst with a lady in the attic.

Carmichael, in a shaky stammer quite foreign to his normal self, allowed that he had been present on the top floor, but –

His Majesty commanded SILENCE and consigned Carmichael immediately to the dungeon, there to await his fate in the morning. All other lords were dismissed to the pavilion, on pain of death to remain without the Castle gate until such time as the King should please. A double guard was posted, the portcullis brought down, and James retired to bed for the final time that night.

Upon the green no doubt remained (with such as thought) that Carmichael was the perpetrator with regard to Madam Gray, especially when hesitant unravelling established tht he had been absent from the party since before the ladies withdrew. Satisfaction was reached that the two must be lovers and their rendezvous preconcerted, and comment also passed on the deftness with which their passion had hitherto kept secret from the public eye.

The whole affair now appeared perfectly obvious.

At the same time, the knowledge of their King's enormous displeasure slowly gathered and settled like a cold numbing mist on the spirits of the souls so recently hilarious. Their risibility completely quashed, they durst not even speak freely to one another, for nagging fear of having their remarks overhauled at the inquest in the morning. Hence it was only through the tangential insinuations of sporadic pregnant mutterings that the sombred lords, bedding down in the pavilion as the first hints of light whispered low in the east, recorded their general feeling that Sir John Carmichael was in a very unenviable predicament indeed.

Was not the Lady Ann a special favourite with the King?

In the stinking dank of the lightless dungeon, beneath the dropped portcullis, Carmichael too perused his pickle.

Why was the King so incensed?

How could he ever explain himself now, without compromising his darling Elizabeth?

Was his poor head doomed to roll?

And who was this other wretched fellow incarcerated beside him, who, to judge from the winnied agony of his snore, had had his face smashed in by a stallion hoof and his nostrils bunged with donkey dung?

5

THE MORNING
AFTER THE NIGHT BEFORE

COCK-A-DOODLE-DOO
Saturday, the third of September.

Fair and lovely rose that morning on the forest of Meggat-dale.
The dawning spread a wavy canopy of scarlet and blue all over the
eastern hemisphere, the young sun mounted behind the green hills
of Yarrow, and the faery curtain updrew into the viewless air while
the shadows of the mountains etched their ancient beauty on the
dazzling mirror of the Lake of Saint Mary, their clear and natural
tints lying softly cradled among the ripples of her flawless blue
complexion.

The Queen of Scotland and her ladies took their morning walk
among a glorious garnish of small and delicate mountain flowers,
balled as with the dews of very heaven, fragrance wafting at every
step, and bracing health in every tiny murmur that breezed across
the purple heath.

Yet their paces were silent, short, and sullen.

The King took his constitutional Aloofly Alone.

His nobles sauntered about a further slope in aimless pairs,
discoursing only to their hounds, whose panting gambols and
mimic hunts were harshly checked by the unwonted gloom on the
brows of their masters, and by the toes of their whimsically irascible
boots.

In the dismal keep, Carmichael's chagrin and foreboding continued to climb about his unslept helplessness like a poisonous ivy.
His alcoholically sleep-snorting colleague turned out to be Lord
Chamberlain Hume, and when that worthy eventually came round
it was not from any spontaneous blossoming of his appetite for
Life's endless banquet, but rather, so it appeared from the vicious
abruptness of his self-addressed periods, owing to the appalling

pains in the back of his head, about the base of his proboscis, and in the bulbs of his eyes.

These having proved no longer tolerable in the world of his nightmare.

Accordingly, such intercourse as did pass between the two captives was savagely minimal, and terminated in a splutter of glowering once sufficient information had exchanged for Humc to deduce that the unseen instrument of his present discomfort and disfigurement could only have been Carmichael.

Who now was possessed by the additional torment of knowing that he must be tried for impinging upon the favoured Lady Ann.

And not deny it.

JUDGEMENT

'Call Polmood,' ordered the King.

'Call Polmood.'

Polmood was called.

But before he had time to arrive in the Great Hall, at the head of whose long oaken table King James inscrutably sat, Queen Margaret bustled in.

Resplendent in a full flowing ceremonial mantle motifed in heraldic gold, she ignored the assembled nobles, who stood uncomfortably phalanxed on either side of the table, and made straight for the mandarin peacock plumes that curved extravagantly from her Husband's velvet bonnet.

'My Lord?' she courtesied.

'Yes, my lady?'

'I come, my Lord, to plead for the merciful release of the poor unfortunates in the keep.'

'Indeed, madam, you are an angel to the disadvantaged. Yet on what ground, we pray, do you plead?'

'Upon the ground, my Lord, that the only injuries inflicted in the night were sustained by themselves. And that they knew not what they did, my lord, being quite beside themselves with drink. As was many another man last night. My Lord.'

'And lady too, we trow!'

'I think not, my Lord.'

'Hrrrm!' The King surveyed with blandly colourless eyes the prettily flushing cheeks of the spouse he had not shared (in the fuller sense) for many more days than are conducive to the continued mellifluence of ideal marital melding. He was genuinely fond of her, that could not be denied, but what a pity she was not better endowed, both in physical person and appetitive imagination!

Polmood appeared behind Queen Margaret, cap in hand and stooping in nervous subservience.

In the background, between the table and the door, a colourful throng of ladies had gathered and was loitering. Doubtful of Jovial Reception, they were yet driven to struggle for presence by their ardour for spice.

James pushed back his heavy throne with a scrape of impatience.

'Madam!' he boomed. 'Ladies. You are done immense credit by your sympathetic concern for those accused. However, sympathy and justice are by no means one, and it is the latter we now must serve. Therefore do we beseech you withdraw a while, as the coming elucidations may light some details offensive to your gentle modesties.'

Ownerless mutters in the doorway gave testimony that their gentle modesties were more than willing to take the chance.

Queen Margaret said: 'My – '

Her Lord said: 'Go! We shall duly request your evidence, but, for the moment, go!'

They went.

The King slouched back in his seat.

The standing lords shuffled, scratched beards, cleared throats, inspected fingernails and booted toes.

Polmood's knotted hands wreaked crumple on the brim of his brown hide hat.

'Well now, Polmood,' mused James. 'Come forward, man.'

Polmood stepped closer.

'And you, Curry,' the King directed. 'Pay the closest heed to all that passes. And none of your nonsense, mind. The issue is serious.'

'Nonsense, Sire?' sneered the bright-eyed clown.

'That will do!'

The dwarfish jester, obeying the eloquent crook of his Master's finger, stepped out from his squat in the warming nook of the great fireplace and took up his position at his Majesty's left hand. The truth of the matter is:

That though the average nobleman at the beginning of the sixteenth century was dexterous enough with the spoken word, the general standard of writing and spelling in those days was at a drastic low, and literary proficiency was hence at a great premium. The King's own personal scribe and amanuensis, one Honourable Roderick Whitelaw, being grown too long in the tooth and sear on the pate to brook any longer the inevitable squalor and scrummage of hunting holidays, had for this occasion been left to his own transcribing devices in the palatial comforts of Edinburgh.

Old Curry's present brief, therefore, was to commit to his ballad-trained memory the minutiae of the morning's proceedings, that they might later be relayed to the copperplate competence of Whitelaw and posteritized on parchment.

King James lounged easily in his seat, scratching his aquiline nose and stroking his gingery beard.

And which noble could have thought, as his occasional squints took in the unruffled countenance that his Sovereign played upon Polmood's incongruous discomfiture, that his Majesty too was inwardly perturbed? That he too was paining with self-reproach over his contribution to the questionable antics of the night just past, and was not a little troubled by the piteous tomato discolour of Polmood's swollen nose, and by the gnawing possibility that his faithful forester's intended marriage and future happiness might now lie ruined?

'Polmood?'

'Sire?'

'We require satisfaction relating to your involvement in the embarrassments of yester evening. What say you?'

Polmood's coated tongue licked moisture around his drily grizzled lips. Besides the massive bruising of his almost broken nose, a nasty sty had ballooned in his sleep beneath the inner corner of his left eyelid, forcing that eye half-closed, as in conniving disingenuousness, and combining with his natural dearth of facial beauty to feature him now, on the brink of his scheduled nuptials, quite breathtakingly hideous.

The furrows in his heavy low brow tightened, the thick veins on his temples stood out, as he began, in his gruffly accented country falter, to say what he had laboriously rehearsed for the past two hours:

'Sire. My most gracious and Sovereign Lord, may it please you not believe of your own true servant and most faithful liegeman, Honest Hunter of Polmood, such sneckdrawing and demented pawkery as that he would sneak in the night, to plunder a loftful of snuftering queans, and to broozle a poor defenceless dame and another man's wife forby. Never, Sire! Never. My misfortune . . .'

And he went on to relate, in scrupulous (not to say ponderous) detail, his adventures in the dark and the manner in which he had suffered at the knee of a mysterious assailant. (The entirety of this account, incidentally, together with records of all the other judicial proceedings of that morning, as dictated by Old Curry to Roderick Whitelaw several week later, may still be found in a private collection of ancient Scottish manuscrips, belonging to Dr R. C. Brown of Richmond Street, Edinburgh.)

'Sire,' Polmood eventually concluded, 'this is the whole and loyal truth, as I do swear upon my hope for mercy by our Blessed Lady. God save your Majesty. Amen.' He bowed.

'Can you be certain, Polmood,' James wondered, 'that it was a *man* that stumbled upon you in the dark?'

'As certain, Sire, as that my nose does pain me.'

'How so?'

'Sire, he was bigger, and heavier, and stronger by far than any three women in the world. And I did feel his garb forby: it was a knight.'

'Hrrrm!' hummed the King, seemingly inclined yet not able to doubt this point. 'Very well, Polmood. We are happy that your actions stemmed not from devious roots. On condition that you do seek forgiveness of Mistress Hume, her Majesty, and all the ladies, for the pandemonium you inadvertently caused, you are hereby excused.'

'Thank you, Sire. Oh, *thank* you. Your Majesty is – '

'Not at all, Polmood. Give thanks only to Justice, whose mere unworthy vassal we attempt to be. You may resume your place among the nobles.' This was stressed by a lethargic dismissive flexing of the right royal fingers.

Polmood fell back, still bent in gratitude, and merged his identity with the disconsolate phalanx at the table, to the King's left.

'Call Lord Hume,' called the King.

'Call the Lord Hume.'

The Lord Chamberlain was ushered up from the dungeon.

It was now shortly after nine o'clock, and, as the ends of the Great Hall faced north and south, bright pencil beams of dust-laden sunshine came shafting through the deep and narrow head-high windows in the east wall, poignantly contrasting the cold solemnity of the investigation within and the warm flitting joys of the summer day without. The cheerless austerity of the Hall was enhanced by the flameless deadness in the unstoked fireplace, where only the stones of the grate retained an invisible echo of the past night's heat, and by the stark grey-green nudity of the undecorated walls: the Castle of Crawmelt being inhabited for only a few weeks of each year, no effort had been made to furbish it with the homely subtleties of permanent ornament and bright draught-baffling tapestry.

Such decor as was required had either to be transported seasonally, in one's personal luggage, or else, in the case of men, achieved through the ingestion of appropriate beverages.

But that was for later: not for now, when no-one had yet broken his fast by even an oatcake crumb. How vexing, then, for the attending nobles in their standing ordeal, with their too sluiced stomachs all growling and grumbling in unfed protest, to whiff from the basement kitchens oaty porridge bubbling and meaty bones of venison simmering!

'Ah. Lord Hume!' exclaimed James, not ungenially. He left off toying with the trailing foot of the heavy iron chain he customarily wore around his waist. Four guards marched the Lord Chamberlain to his Majesty's side.

Then hung diffidently back.

'Your Majesty!' his Lord Hume bowed deeply. He wore no hat and his mousy hair was crinkled and unkempt. His gorgeous robe was stained from the slimy filth on the floor of the keep, his fleshless cheeks and bloodless lips were pale as a terrified lily, and his twin black eyes, grotesquely enlarged, were all the colours of the rainbow except black.

He looked, in short, a ludicrous shambles.

Yet no-one ventured to chortle.

King James sat forward, looked earnest, and in a deeply confidential voice said:

'My dear Lord Hume, against you it is charged that, hardly a handful of hours ago, you did wilfully engender horendous racket among the ladies in the turret, and moreover did attempt by drunken violence a gruesome assault upon the maidenly body of the Lady Ann Gray. How plead you?'

The defendant's chastened eyes abjectly averted.

'Most merciful and Sovereign Majesty,' he purred beneath the weight of the great unction, 'I do most humbly beseech your royal pardon for my unforgivable folly and misdemeanour, and implore that the episode be attributed not to any foul and insidious design, but rather to coincidence, and to developments arising from the good-humoured and benevolent expedition in which your Majesty's own great liberality and wit had already been pleased to indulge.'

Pause.

'Go on,' said the King.

'Majesty, I have no further plea to urge. Only that, in the regrettable confusion of my enthusiasm, I did mistake the bed. Due, as – it shames me to say! – since I have divined, to my counting as the first door the stair door itself, thus undershooting my own lady's entrance by a margin of one. An error so crass that your Majesty would grant his penitent servant the most inestimable boon by accepting that it could only have been due to the lateness and blackness of the hour.'

'No doubt.'

'And then, Majesty, as I did endeavour, with all respect, to divulge at the time, the towering heat of my misplaced rage on finding rising up from the bed like a demon of Hell one huge hirsute knight with – '

'*Enough!*'

'But, Majesty! The marks of my teeth on his – '

'No more of that.' The King's eyes flashed all the colours of warning as he added:

'Lord Hume. Being satisfied of the absence of treason in your conduct, we do restore to you all office, title and prestige that we, in the heady heat of the night, may overhastily have confiscated.'

'Oh, most Merciful Majesty!'

'Three things there are, my lords,' the King issued a clarion general reminder, 'that come not back: the sped arrow, the squandered chance, and the utterance of a hasty word. None is perfect: all may err, as let us all reflect.'

A chorus of knowing sighs and unlipped murmurs betokened discreet applause for his Majesty's wisdom.

'Wherefore, good Hume, on condition that you solicit pardon of Madam Gray, the Queen and all her ladies, we hereby pronounce your blunder closed and direct you to resume your rightful place at our table.'

'Your Majesty is Mercy incarnate!' The worshipful depth of the Lord Chamberlain's retreating bow stopped just short of grovelling.

'Call Carmichael!' rapped the King.

'Call up Sir John Carmichael of Hyndford!'

While Carmichael was fetched to the Hall, all the other attendant lords, for reasons apparent to none but King James, were for the time dismissed. Their rumbling bellies notwithstanding, they were advised to enjoy the heavenly clime in a further saunter before breakfast, which is was hoped would be within the hour.

'Now, Carmichael,' said the King, when the escortive sergeants had withdrawn, 'on pain of your life tell us truly, were you at any point in some lady's chamber last night, or were you not?'

Carmichael's proud head bowed, his hands clasped crestfallen behind his back. His unchanged clothing was creased and smeared with the grime of his captivity, and his wide dark eyes, usually so alive with excitement and romance, were not inert in their unslept hollows, enlivened only by the occasional flicker of desperate uncertainty blinking in the bright light of day. And his swallowing voice was thick with featful determination, when he said:

'Your Majesty, I was.'

'And was it you that stumbled over Polmood and boggered the poor fellow's nose?'

'I . . . yes, Sire. It was indeed myself.'

'Then tell us, sir,' like a silent muscle of some great wild beast, the royal baritone rippled with menace, 'what, before God, was your business there?'

And the gallant issue of Carmichael's night of anguish was:

'Majesty, gladly will I yield my life for you – in battle, or any arena to which you please to command my service. And yet, Sire, I value at a price beyond my life the secret answer to your Majesty's question, and so must humbly remain silent.' He stressed the tightrope boldness of his chivalry by daring a moment to lock eyes with his frosty Sovereign.

Before looking abjectly away.

James sniffed in disdain, then said:

'Carmichael, we thank you. It – Curry! Lord save us, man, are you *listening*?'

'Indeed, Sire!' mimicked the drowse-shattered clown. 'I am *always* listening, am I not?' He forefingered the jutting exaggeration of his chin, and frowned a mirror image of the King's asperity.

'You are *always* listening, are you now? Always, eh? Then take off that farcical lice-ridden bonnet, in deference to our present gravity. At ONCE!'

Curry obeyed with promptness almost insulting.

'And tell us what last we said.'

'What last we said, Sire? Nothing simpler. What last we said!'

King James, who had not heard this quip before, in growing anger spluttered:

'Nuh?'

'What last we said: Sire, before we said "Nuh?", was "what last we said". Was it not, Sire?'

'YOU INTOLERABLE SCOUNDREL, SIR! Tell us now, this *instant*, at risk of your miserable neck, sir, what last we said before we did rupture your slumber. NOW!'

'Very well, Sire, did you then say: '"Carmichael, we thank you. It – Curry! Lord save us, man, are you *listening*?" Did you not, Sire?'

The King, who could not recall in any case, growled:

'Curry, you are fortunate – '

'That your Majesty, in his great Wisdom, did also say (not one page of the book of my cudgelled brain before): "Three things there are, my lords, that come not back: the arrow sped, the squandered chance, and the hasty word said. None is perfect, all may err: let us all reflect." Thus, Sire, does your poor old harper and unworthy fool petition your merciful forgiveness for his untimely impudence. He, Sire, whose shadow life depends from your Majesty's own, like an icicle from a winter willow.'

The King exhaled through lengthy pursed lips.

Carmichael squirmed in impotent agitation, fearful that the insolence of the clown would rebound on himself.

Old Curry stood back a quiet pace, his never-mentioned function well fulfilled.

'Very well, Curry,' said the King in even calm. 'Very sharp and fairly droll, and worth a hundred merks to your pension forby. But Heaven help you now if you do drop the thread!'

Curry bowed seriously.

'Carmichael.'

'Majesty?'

'We thank you, as we had begun to say, for your candour. We are glad that not *all* honour has deserted you. Had you but hinted at your motives for prowling in the tower . . . your brash young eyes would never have seen the noon of this day. You follow?'

'I do, Sire,' Carmichael muttered.

'As still they may not, as our inquiry continues. GUARD!'

Four sergeants entered and quick-marched to Carmichael's side.

'Return the prisoner to the dungeon, but remain hard by, for we soon shall require him again. You, sir!' James barked at Sergeant Halberd. 'Seek out the good Mistress Hume, and communicate our desire for her testimony. Which, you shall impress upon her, and any other ladies with her, we are pleased to hear in private. Is that plain?'

'Sire!'

'Good. Then quickly go, for we are fast famished.'

For the next half hour King James heroically surmounted his hunger gurgling to interview, one by one, a considerable number of ladies – including the Lady Ann Gray and Queen Margaret, but excusing the youthful Elizabeth.

Each was assured that none was required to divulge any intimate detail concerning herself, but only what had been heard passing with regard to others.

Then was it not predicable that such a flood of mystery and snide surmise should pour upon the King that he could not distinguish truth from fiction?

At least at first.

Great battles there had been! Great bodies of men a-cursing and swearing in murderous voice, and frequent volcanic thuddings upon the lobby floor, as if the very roof had fallen in! There were besides whisperings heard, and *certain noises*! These could be graphically described, to be sure, though of their nature they required the worldly comprehension of the Judge to fill out their interpretation!

Thus did it gradually appear, from the variegated versions of the fair enthusiasts, that *all* the nobles of the court had been rifely rooting in the attic that night, and that *every* lady in the Castle (always with the sole exception of the narrator) had been vigorously engaged with one paramour *at least*!

James would soon have been glad to put a stop to this torrent of insinuous scandal, but, like the sorcerer's apprentice of old, he found himself bound to continue what he had begun, as only so might he sieve some further glint of fact from its camouflage of wordly silt. In due course, however, he came upon a double gleam he could not ignore.

In that:

It was independently affirmed, with alarming consistency between the two accounts, by both the ladies whose chambers neighboured Elizabeth's, one of them the relatively unfanciful Lady Katherine of Mar, that the lady next door to them (they would not, naturally, be so ungenerous as to identify Elizabeth by name) *had* been in receipt of some manly visitor – and this some several minutes *before* his Majesty's own interrogative frolic had commenced. The two knowing neighbours were so eager to swear to their evidence, by all they held holy, and there was so clearly no calumnious complicity between them, that the King was extremely disturbed.

For Elizabeth must have been concealing her visitor within her chamber at the very time when she had (so artfully!) contrived to extinguish the royal flambeau.

And what did this mean?

It meant, since James had excellent reason for believing that it was not upon the later compromised Mistress Gray that Carmichael had perpetrated, that Elizabeth's secret visitant could only have been Carmichael.

Although:

How could Carmichael have escaped in the short time before James and Polmood had returned to Elizabeth with their torch relit?

Where had he escaped *to*?

Did his subsequent skirmish with Polmood imply that he had stolen back to attempt more mischief (and of what kind?) upon Elizabeth?

And had he in the meantime been holed up in yet another lady's chamber?

Whose?

Why?

James, having graciously dismissed the earnest Mistress Mar, leant his left elbow upon the table, wearily rested his brow against the palm of his long supple hand, and sighed a long sigh of puzzled concern. It was impossible, was it not, that Carmichael's intercourse with Elizabeth had been in any way carnal. The girl was too young, too pure, barely nubile! Had she not this very week confided to the Queen her fear of the physical consummation of her marriage? The delicate question of which he Himself had yet to broach with Polmood, *assuming* the wedding was still to take place.

No! Bodily infelicity in Elizabeth was unthinkable.

Yet, what else . . .

'Aaaach, Curry!' grunted the divinely right King of all Scotland and the Western Isles. 'What a niftering plowter of polecat shite!'

'Sire?'

'Not a word of it, mind. Not even to the trees of the forest.'

'Indeed not, Sire. They are not to be trusted!'

'GUARD!'

'Yes, Sire?'

'Bring back Carmichael.'

The prisoner was produced.

'Carmichael!' said James, Frown severe, Voice ominously grave.

'Majesty?'

'We are deeply shocked, Sir John Carmichael, at the behaviour of which you are guilty. We have trusted you in our court and near our person for many a year, and for what?'

Miserable floor-inspecting silence from Carmichael.

'To find that you have been incautious, ungrateful, and presumptious in the extreme! You are aware of that to which we refer?'

'I . . . yes, Sire.'

'That attempt you have made on a royal ward, on the very eve of her marriage to a man of honour and integrity, whom we esteem most highly, manifests a depravity of mind and a heart so dead to gratitude that it forces our judgement to ignominious shame at ever having admitted such an unworthy fellow to our household. If you have any desire to question the accuracy of our deductions, or the probity of our dudgeon, you may say so now, though we counsel you only do so with the utmost circumspection.'

Carmichael looked up to face the piercing gaze of his Judge and Juror. Such was the haunted desolation of his broken posture and haggard countenance that the malleable sympathies of a womanish heart must have warmed and melted to look upon them.

Not so King James, an unwavering study in cold stony grey.

'Your Majesty,' said Carmichael, 'your conclusions are admirably correct in the main, and your displeasure wholly natural. I would only please, Sire, that you believe – and may I burn in Hell for ever if here I lie – that the blame is all my own. And that no indecent act was committed: that the lady's honour remains – '

'No doubt it does, and fatal would be your plight, Carmichael, if we for a moment believed the contrary. Whatever were your motives for this disgraceful and clandestine procedure, whether the seduction of her person or her affections from the man who adores her – '

'Sire – '

'SILENCE! Whatever your motives, they must have been subversive, and absolutely opposed to that respect which, in return for our confidence, it was your duty to maintain.

'We therefore will that you immediately quit, for three full years, the society of which you have proved so unworthy. If at any time within that period you are found inside twenty miles of our residence, wherever that may be, then your life shall answer for it. You understand us?'

'I do, Sire.'

'Your sentence we shall have proclaimed to the country at large – though not the nature of your crime, which will remain secret. Meanwhile, you have not a minute past a score to make your departure, during which time we require to hear from you no excuse nor entreaty. Nor shall you converse with any of the courtiers: lords and ladies both.'

'Sire, I shall obey.'

'Then be gone.'

Carmichael backed away, bowing, then turned and rushed from the Hall, brittle with agony of mind and heart.

Might he look upon his coveted Elizabeth *never again*?

'GUARD!' bellowed the ravenous King.

'Sire?'

'Summon up the porridge from the kitchens, and request of our noble lords and gentle ladies the pleasure of their assisting in the belated breaking of our fast. QUICKLY NOW!'

ELIZABETH HAS NOTHING TO SAY!

Though it is doubtless understood, it may not be improper to confirm here what exactly transpired with Carmichael after he had escaped from Elizabeth's chamber in the dark and slunk quietly down to his own. Minutes later he had heard his Majesty rampaging down the stairs, laughing uproariously and crowing that THE BRIDE HAD RUED. Never suspecting that Polmood would remain aloft among the ladies, Carmichael assumed his rival must have descended with the King, albeit less loudly.

And what could have restored him to a greater ecstasy of hope than hearing the King proclaim that Elizabeth had broken off her pledge to Polmood? Carmichael, attributing Elizabeth's retraction to the impassioned conversation she had so recently with himself, and thinking to strengthen her resolution and again prevail upon her to elope with him that very night, had stolen once more to his beloved's apartment, before such steps should be precluded by any further irruption into the Castle of the revellers on the green.

How close must he then have come to a thunderstruck failure of heart, when he stumbled with such sudden violence into the invisible sprawling Polmood, whose murderous voice and Herculean grasp he knew so well!

'Such a stinking, brainless old *plough horse*!' moaned Carmichael. 'How ever could she wish it?'

'Beg pardon, my lord?' said Ronald, his fifteen-year-old groom and only attendant – a blotch-featured boy, whose veneration of his master was outstripped only by the enormity of his credulity.

'Nothing, lad,' the banished master muttered. 'Nothing that concerns you. Mount up now.'

Ronald did.

They were outside the stables, travel bags strapped to the saddles of Carmichael's two horses. Above them the sun continued to ascend without cloudy impediment, while the air around was warmly pungent with the excretions of the horses and of the hounds kennelled up in the bothy close by. Horseflies and large bluebottles buzzed in the vanguard of the morning's insect onslaught like mercenaries commissioned to salt with their thousand small goads the freshly raw pain of Carmichael's disgrace.

He tugged savagely at his reins, nosed his mount forward, out of the rough-cobbled stableyard, and led the way round the back of the Castle. East they headed, across the crystal babble of the Crawmelt Burn and towards the distant heights of the Meggat watershed, with the dismal prospect of Carmichael's own unwived estates ten leagues beyond.

At the shallow ford that took the crude bridleway across the Linghope Burn, Carmichael paused and said:

'Tell me, Ronald.'

'Yes, my lord?'

'If you loved a young lassie – someone in my own household, say. Old Kenneth's wee Nancy, maybe. She's – '

'My lord, I *never* – '

'Listen, lad. Listen and just *imagine*, will you? Suppose you loved her more than all the world – can you suppose that now?'

'Indeed I can, my lord!'

'And suppose that I commanded you – on pain of your life, mind – that you never ever must speak to her again.'

'But *why*, my lord?'

'As she was promised to be wed to another.'

'I am sure I cannot say, my lord.'

'To be wed to another man, fully three times the age of herself, and ugly as fiendish blasphemy forby.'

'Perish the thought, my lord. With all respect.'

'Whom she, your Nancy, loved *not at all*.'

'Imposs—'

'Imagine all that, Ronald. What then would you do?'

'My lord, what *could* I do?' Ronald squirmed, his blotches madly blushing.

'Would you, do you think, obey myself, your lawful lord and

master, and thereby lose for ever your one true love? Or might you risk life itself, by disobeying me in hope of converting her with one last desperate word? What think you?'

Ronald thought nothing, except how awfully weird it was that Carmichael had framed the puzzle around Nancy! Why *Nancy*, to whom he, Ronald, had never yet declared outwith the volcanic transports of his dream? Had Sir John the eldritch power of the Inner Eye? Hesitantly the youngster said:

'My lord, I think . . . if . . .'

'Yes? If what?'

'If you had only forbade me ever to *speak* to her again, so that it was only forbade, my lord, that *I* should *speak* to her. Then . . . it would not be disobedience if I did commission *another* to plead with her on my behalf. To do that, my lord, would not disobey your own command. Would it, my lord?'

'So it would be wrong of me, unjust, to punish you for so doing?'

'My lord! How could it be else?'

'How indeed?' Carmichael muttered grimly, then said:

'And suppose you did so court her through another. Yes?'

Ronald nodded.

'And suppose that other returned her word that she cared nowt for you. What then?'

'Then, my lord, I should quit this unhappy realm – with your own consent, of course! – and betake me to the Holy Wars.'

'Why so?'

'The sooner to lose my life, my lord! With Honour, and in the service of my Saviour.'

'You would?' Carmichael mused, his eyes full of distance. '*You* would!'

'Indeed I would!' the groom enthused. 'That my unloved blood might – '

'You see that heron yonder, Ronald? She that flaps above the Meggat, by the rushes.'

'Yes, my lord.'

'That bird, Ronald, with her hellish eyes and great blue wings, is a *witch*!'

'*Witch*? Oh, *dear God*.'

'Who hears all, sees all . . .'

'Art in Heaven, hallowed be . . .'

'Hush, lad. Hush. There is nowt to fear, for she cannot harm us. Unless, mind, we ever repeat the things she heard us say when she was passing near. For then she will come in the night, while we sleep, and tear our souls in strips to feed the fires of *Hell*!'

Ronald shivered, staring in horrified fascination at the tall spiky rushes in which the witch had vanished.

'Lord *save* us!' he begged.

'He will. But we must assist Him, by never again breathing a word of what passed between us just now. Will you remember that?'

'Oh, my lord! To my dying day!'

'Very good. Then long may the memory last you. Now, Ronald, I have – are you listening to me?'

'Yeeee-ees, my lord.'

'Think no more on the heron, I tell you. I have a commission, a *special* commission, which you must mark well and obey to the letter.'

The guillible Ronald heaved his mind away from sorcery and glued his senses to his master's will.

Which was that:

'You, Ronald, shall wait here a while. There is an urgent affair of state just crossed my mind, which his Majesty and I must discuss without delay. Hence will I return to the Castle now, alone, while you shall follow my progress from this vantage.

'When my audience with the King is concluded, I shall either return here to you, and we continue home, or! Or, Ronald, his Majesty shall have entrusted me with a brief of the highest importance, to be conveyed abroad. Concerning the conduct of the Holy Wars, no less! And this will you understand if you see me head south, cross the Meggat, and make my way up yonder valley, above the S-shaped wood.'

Ronald obediently gaped as Carmichael pointed to the winding cleavage between the hilly twins of Craigdilly and Drowning Dubs.

'Should you perceive that my destiny is so, you shall return home to Hyndford without me, instruct the household that I will be gone some months, and inform Old Kenneth at the Manor Farm that he is Factor to all the estates until my return – if I must be long away I shall send word before the New Year. You I charge with the communication of my order, and Kenneth shall I summon to answer for the condition of my property and lands. Is this plain?'

Ronald sniffed, nodded, tremulously assured Carmichael that it was plain, 'But . . .'

'But what?'

'If you do journey abroad, my lord, then . . . shall you not have need of my services?' the poor boy blabbed in a rush of weepy misery.

'You are a good lad, Ronald, and there is none I sooner would have by my side. But the issue is of the *utmost secrecy*! And hence, if go I must, then alone must I be. And think on your comely wee Nancy, forby. Whatever should become of her, if you deserted home to squire with me to foreign parts? Shame on you, lad! Dry your eyes now, and keep good watch. For I may be back within the quarter hour. Meanwhile, farewell.'

'Farewell, my lord.'

Carmichael rumpled the yearning youth's hair in a parting flourish of manly affection.

Then wheeled his whinnying mount about and cantered back east, by the foot of the steep white-bouldered shoulder of the purple Clockmore.

Towards the Castle.

When he clattered back into the stableyard and reared to a snorting halt, he regarded with accustomed authority the only personage in view, and rapped:

'Hey, boy!'

'Hey, boy, *what?*' the personage sneered back. In point of fact groom to the Earl of Hume (and therefore, in his own estimation, a cut or two above his fellows) he was slouched against the archway to the covered stalls, idle buttocks wallowing in the soft comfort of a sheaf of fresh hay. He was perhaps fourteen years old, with a faint incipience of bristle just beginning to discolour his upper lip, and a hint of sprouting curl on his callow pigeon chest. From the downward corner of his mouth he sucked on an insolent straw while, in his sunning omniscience, he flicked fried peas at the sparrows gleaning corn from the yard.

Carmichael gawked at him for a disbelieving moment. Then roared:

'ON YOUR FEET WHEN YOU TALK TO ME, BOY! *MOVE!*'

The groom, without stirring, condescendingly removed the straw from his mouth, and said:

'You are the Baron Carmichael, are you not?'

Carmichael simply stared.

'Him that is in disgrace with his Majesty and banished from the court! Why then should I move for *you*?'

Dizzy from his whirling rage, Carmichael apprehended his sword hand on its flight to the hilt of his rapier.

For what would that achieve?

'Very well, young sir,' he ground instead through a loathing smile. 'Move not, but tell me this.' He diverted his reach to the pouch on his belt. 'How does it suit you, sir, to enhance your worth in the world by the value of this fine gold crown?'

The sneer dissolved in greed, whose victim said:

'How so?'

'Through the investment, sir, of a few short instants for your most valuable time.'

'And what must I do?'

'You must hurry within the Castle, seek out a certain lady, and deliver to her a certain message.'

'Indeed! And which lady must I seek?'

'You accept the commission?'

The sneer clamoured for a comeback on the churlish face, but greed, being endless, said:

'*Two* crowns, my lord. And I am your man.'

Man? *Man!*

Carmichael, however, could not but accept. 'Very well,' he said. 'You will seek out the lady Elizabeth, the Mistress Elizabeth Manners, wherever she may be, and inquire of her if she wishes to confer the undeserved boon of a final word with Sir John Carmichael, on the brink of his departure for glory in the Holy Wars. Can you retain that much?'

'Retain that much!' scoffed the groom as he lazed to his feet. 'Can I retain – do I look like a bedwetter? I – '

'With speed!' snapped Carmichael, reluctantly adding: 'if you please.'

'Payment now, my lord.' A grimy hand reached out.

'Half now, half when you return.'

The gold coin flashed as it spun through the air.

Then deftly was it caught and insultingly bit.

Before the loutish messenger set off at his infuriating saunter.

'And a third!' Carmichael called after him, loathing searing through his straitened desperation. 'If you will *hasten*!'

In the Hall, the King and his courtiers were drawing to the close of their breakfast. Much hot porridge had been supped, sweetened by rich comb of honey and cooled by the cream of fresh cows' milk from the home farm of Pearce Cockburn, in the mouth of the Meggat Valley (the farm now known as Henderland). With newly baked oatcakes, dried apricots, and apples from the orchards of Lothian to follow, washed down by any amount of the thick strong brown beer from Traquair, the company was becoming understandably less nervous, more mellow, and here and there tingling with invoiced anticipation that the balance sheet of the day might yet show a profit of pleasure.

But on the rising hopes still sat a heavy silent dampness of jockeying dubiety. Baron John Carmichael had been *banished*! For an offence, so far as most could see, little more serious than stripping off for a lightning dip of cool relief in some ownerless mountain tarn. Yet the dipper had been banished! What might this augur, concerning the ongoing humour of the King? Who might be next to depart? And for what unwitting peccadillo? Then there was the wedding.

Was it on?

Or was it off?

No-one seemed to know where it stood, and no-one dared raise the matter, for might not his Majesty take umbrage and fly in the throes of a second rage? None could tell. Better then to keep one's peace, or restrict onself to only the most secure topics – the glorious weather, the luscious fragrance of the mountain flowers, the health and fitness of one's hounds and horses, and other themes of equal blandness.

And what of the bride and groom so vaunted yesterday?

Elizabeth sat in sullen silence, which, even had she not wished it, was guaranteed by her highly charged role in the web of prevailing uncertainty. How much perilously further from weather and mountain blossom could one venture than to inquire into the questionable marriage prospects of a teenage bride not an hour out of tears? Eschewing porridge, and picking without appetite at minuscule morsels of oatcake and apricot, she kept her head determindly bowed and willed her eyes to stray no further than her platter on the table. But the awareness forced itself upon her, nonetheless, that, several persons along on the far side of the table, sat the glowering mass of her (former?) betrothed.

With his mutilated nose and the still closing eye of his sty, Polmood looked further than ever from the paradigm manly beauty. Nor was his appearance enhanced by the unwiped fringe of cream on his moustache and the spawn of oatcrumb in his beard. As he had exchanged no syllable with Elizabeth since she (perhaps, on reflection, a shade haughtily) had commanded his drunkenness away from her in the attic, he may be forgiven the height of his fret as to whether his beloved might yet rescind on her King-goaded statement of rue. At the same time, one wonders whether such purposes may be better served by the suitor who contrives not to stare upon his dear one with the slavering intensity of a starving hound.

To an insensitive and superficial ear, however, the light bright chatter in the Hall, with the courteous interest in its interrogative inflexion, the exclaimed restraint of its appreciation and the well modulated pleasantness of its occasional tight-reined laughter, must have seemed little other than a windless haven of urbane good cheer.

Such an ear was produced in duplicate with the rushing in of the Earl of Hume's groom.

'Message for the Lady Elizabeth!' he gasped at the sergeant by the door. 'Most *urgent* it is!'

'That's her in the blue,' the stolid guard said, his voice almost infinite in boredom.

'Where?'

'There. Two along from her Majesty. With the tutties like a brace of pear.'

This definition being apparently adequate, the groom bustled round to Elizabeth's place.

'Mistress Elizabeth?' he inquired importantly, bending arrogantly close to her gold-screened ear.

Elizabeth sat up in startlement. 'Yes?'

'I have a message for you, my lady. An *urgent* message.'

'Indeed?' was the tone of Elizabeth's bewilderment. Were not all possible communicants already here at the table? 'From whom?'

'From the Baron Carmichael, my lady. His that is banished in disgrace. He ask to know if you have any last word to say to him before he departs for the Holy Wars.'

'Sir John Carmichael? The Holy Wars? But why?'

'I know not, my lady. Only that his impatience is great.'

'The Holy *Wars*!' Elizabeth marvelled in undertone admiring horror. 'But where is he now?'

'My lady, he awaits – '

'YOU, BOY!' came the petrifying boom from the Throne.

The light bright chatter dulled to death.

And the greedy groom froze in terror, as all eyes, following the icy intransigence of both Eyes, fixed upon his person. 'M-m-me, your M-m-m-majesty?' he jibberd.

'YOU, indeed. What business have you here?'

'I b-b-bear a message, your M-m-m – '

'To whom?'

'To the Lady Elilili – '

'FROM whom?'

'From the Baron Ca-ca-carmichael, your M-m-majesty.'

'Oh do you now?' mused the King.

A spider's egg falling at that moment would have deafened the breath-held company.

'And what', preyed the now quietly frosty Voice, 'might Carmichael's message import?'

'He-he-he – '

'Take your time, boy. Our ire falls not on you.'

'Your M-m-majesty is most merciful. My Lord Carmichael wishes to know, your Majesty, if the Lady Elizabeth has anything to say to him before he leaves for the Ho-ho-holy Wars.'

King James scratched the bridge of his nose with the pointed nail of a long blueblooded forefinger. His searching stare beamed from the pandering stablelad to Elizabeth, who, in the thoughtless unwisdom of her youthful generosity of heart, had already stood up to comply with Carmichael's request. And what, to a worldly and cynical turn of mind, of which there was no present lack, could be more damningly compromising?

Behind his façade of measured disapproval, James was coldly furious: why else had Carmichael been banished, if not for the protection of Elizabeth's honour in name? Yet the King was conscious that the punishment exceeded the crime: that the penance of the knight was in sacrifice to the lady's reputation. So how should Justice respond to the image of young Carmichael's broken-hearted body lying mangled in bloody death on the smoking, stinking aftermath of some battlefield afar? The troublemaker *could* be further punished now, in terms of his sentence he certainly *deserved* it, but . . .

The King indicated with a fractional flick of his head that Elizabeth was to be reseated.

With the timidity of a doe darting for cover, she obeyed.

'You, boy,' said James, 'will return forthwith to Sir John Carmichael and advise him that Mistress Elizabeth has nothing whatever to say to him. Have you, Elizabeth?'

'No, my Lord.'

'Of course not! Why should you? Boy, you will also convey to Baron Carmichael our compliments on his temerity, and inform him that any further delay in his departure will ineluctably multiply for him the distance between the fount of his passion and the seat of his reason. Have you that by rote?'

'Y-yes, your Majesty.'

'Then mouth it back.'

'I am to t-tell him, your Majesty, that if he does not leave immediately it will cost him the hacking off of his head, so please you.'

'Very sharp, lad! Do you mark that, ladies and gentlemen? The nuance is already a mite diffuse, but the boy shows commendable grasp of the gist, does he not? To which you may add, lad, that his Holy endeavours shall not go unsupported in our prayers. Hurry now to tell him so.'

The gangling groom beat a grateful retreat.

'As you were, ladies and gentlemen,' said the King's more Jovial voice. 'Continue breakfast at your leisure, but feel not obliged to dally when you are replete.'

Carmichael, still mounted in the stableyard, was white and tensely perspiring from his remorseless conflict of hope and dread. Even if

Elizabeth were to appear, might not soldiers come with her, to arrest his wilful disobedience? Should he then attempt to flee, or passively submit . . .

'Well?' he croaked, when the grunting groom hove round the wall. 'Speak, boy! Does she come? Does she *come*? *Speak*, God damn you!'

'My lord,' the commended gistbearer wheezed. 'The Lady Elizabeth has nothing to say to you.'

'Nothing to – ' Carmichael's lungs filled full of molten lead. Then he raged:

'Nothing to SAY! Was it *she* that told you this?'

'Yes, my lord,' gasped the groom, contorted by his stitch. 'And his Maj—'

'AAAAARRRRUH!' Carmichael bellowed like a wounded bull. '*Nothing to SAY*!' The reining and spurring he gave his horse was so violent that the poor beast nearly reared over backwards.

'But my lord!' cried the anguished groom as the huge animal thundered from the yard in great-hearted response to the furious lashings of it demented cargo. 'My money! My *payment*, my lord! MY TWO CROWNS!'

But he might as well have harangued the wind, if wind there had been.

Carmichael was already three furlongs distant, galloping south towards the Meggat at lunatic speed, and catatonically moaning again and again:

'Nothing to *say*, Elizabeth . . . has *nothing to say*!'

A mile to the west the patiently waiting Ronald screwed his eyes against the angling sun and looked long for a farewell wave from his border-bound master.

But looked in vain.

6

A GOODLY KING

A LITTLE BACKGROUND

James IV of Scotland is sometimes said to have been the most important, perhaps the most nationally and internationally conscious of the Stuart kings. Born in 1473, he was a robustly vigorous thirty-three in the year of our story. His father, James III, married to Margaret of Denmark in 1469, having been crowned at the princely age of nine in 1460, may possibly be titled the least successful Scottish James. Throughout his minority he had been fueded for by the most powerful and ambitious of the nobles, whom he later antagonized and alienated through his bent for appointing to lucrative sinecures his favourites from the lower orders – sycophantic arrivistes, as they must have seemed to the jealous nobility. This propensity contributed much to the end of James III, which followed his leading an army against a force of rebel barons in a battle near Stirling in June 1488 (sometimes called the Battle of Sauchieburn). The royal generalship was disastrous, on top of which his horse bolted, throwing and leaving him (so the story goes) to be assassinated at Beaton's Mill in the region of Bannockburn, by a rebel masquerading as a Samaritan priest.

The interest of all this, for our purpose, is that the army of rebels that overcame James III in 1488 was nominally led by his eldest son: the fifteen-year-old prince who was to be crowned James IV, at Scone, only a fortnight later. Now, whatever psychiatrists may say, it seems certain that the figurehead prince, which is all that James then was, had no undue desire to bring about his father's death, and it is indisputable that he was afterwards the victim of a haunting remorse which continued until his own tragic death on the fields of Flodden in 1513. And, as tangible token of his repentance at having accepted the Oedipal role thrust upon him, James ever after bore around his waist the pennant girdle of his heavy iron chain. This self-imposed burden he seems only to have shed for sleep, on Sundays, and in deference to especially Favoured ladies.

It will be appreciated that, insofar as he features in the fortunes of Elizabeth Manners, James IV must be characterized very partially: through a lens of selective introspection, and distorted a little by dictates opposed to those of history proper. Therefore, to multiply our perspective, and to enhance our appreciation of the divisions between fact and fictionalization and of the possibilities of fruitful intercourse between the two, let us quote for a moment from the admirable account of a recent historian (*A History of Scotland*, by J. D. Mackie):

His colourful personality appears in the stories of native chroniclers and in the reports of foreign observers like Pedro de Ayala, the Spaniard, and John Young, the Somerset Herald: but the best picture of all is that which is given in the *Accounts of the Lord High Treasurer of Scotland*, which reveal every aspect of the royal life, and present the portrait of a true renaissance king.

James was interested in everything, in ships, in guns, in tournaments, in clothes, in music; in surgery too – he bled a patient, he extracted a tooth, he seems to have set a broken leg – even in alchemy, for he financed the adventurer John Damian in his efforts to find the *quinta essencia* which would produce gold. There may be no truth in the story that he isolated a dumb woman with her children in order to see what language the bairns would speak ('some say they spoke good Hebrew'); but he certainly knew something of languages, including Gaelic, though he was not the polyglot marvel described by Ayala.

Yet what shines most clearly through the document is the king's love of good government and of his people. To the sick and the poor, whom he met upon his restless ridings, the King's face gave grace in a practical way. A single extract reveals the intimate detail of the evidence. Somerset Herald made one qualification to his admiration for the gallant figure of the King, – his beard was 'somethynge long'. Its length, perhaps, attracted unfavourable notice from the Countess of Surrey and her daughter, Lady Grey, who accompanied Princess Margaret to her marriage with James in 1503.

In the accounts for August of this year appears the entry: 'Item, the IX day of August, eftir the marriage, for XV elne claith of gold to the Countess of Surrey of England, quhen scho and hir dochtir Lady Gray clippit the Kingis berd, ilk elne XXIJ li., summa CCCXXX Li.'

Thus the exceptional King who, when breakfast in the Great Hall was over for all except the odd gluttonous noble, inquired of Elizabeth if she would accompany him to the balcony for a minute, to enjoy the view and the morning air, and as he had a slight problem to solve, concerning which he would be most grateful for her kind advice.

DIPLOMACY ON THE BALCONY

Elizabeth was delighted by his Majesty's solicitation, and many-faced was the envious glance that followed them, as James linked a gallant arm with (so many said) the most beautiful young woman then in Scotland, and led her at a stately pace to the second floor, where the balcony, reached via the royal bedchamber, looked out over the green and south across the Meggat.

The day was dewy clear and the scene romantic and warmly wild. The high mountains, the straggling woods, the distant lake, and the lazy limpidity of the river, with its hundred branches winding through valleys of brake and purple heath, whose spectral variety of light and shade the plough had never marred – animated, in the easterly distant pastures of the farm of Cockburn, but the brotherly gambolling of newborn goat kids and fleecy summer lambs, while on the freer heights of slopes untamed by fence or dyke an eagle eye might soon descry the twitching fellowship of the young deer and the leveret brood, feeding or sporting together in the peaceful harmony of the same green shady holt: when ever again shall Britons gaze upon the like?

'We shall have a sweet day for your wedding, Elizabeth,' said the King.

'Indeed, my lord?' Elizabeth replied doubtfully. 'I – who rides yonder, my Lord?' She pointed excitedly. 'Upon the brow of the further hill?'

James followed her indication and immediately discerned, by dint of gimlet sight and piercing Judgement, that the horseman was Carmichael, a tiny speck slowly plodding over the peaty heights of Craigdilly, heading for the Moffat valley and the border. So he said:

'It is no-one, child. No-one of importance. Merely a messenger bound for the southern towns, to spread the news of your wedding.'

'Oh,' said Elizabeth, unable to conceal her disappointment as the horseman sank from view beyond the peaked horizon. 'I thought, my Lord, that it might be . . .'

'It was a most effectual rub you gave the bridegroom last night!' exclaimed the King, in tones admiring. He gently wheeled Elizabeth about and walked her to the eastern end of the balcony, leading her gazing uncertainty away from the hills and towards the curving slice of brilliant blue that was their view of the lake.

'Was it, my Lord? I really did not intend it so.'

'Indeed it was! Our sides have not so quaked for many a day. We owe you a kiss for it,' which he promptly bestowed with great Liberality, 'and a frock of purple silk forby.'

'Your Majesty is most generous!' cried Elizabeth, her eyes a-sparkle for the first time that morning.

'Not at all. We would not have missed the jest for a hundred bonnet pieces, and as many merks to boot. You are a most exquisite girl!'

Elizabeth's pleasure at the compliment broke through in a welling smile, in which the tiny twin tips of her top front teeth rested, just girlishly visible, on the appealing outwards curve of her lower lip. Baby dimples twinkled for a moment by the up-curling corners of her mouth.

Then by modesty were banished.

'What a loss it is', continued the King, 'that we cannot push the jest a mite further. Do you suppose, Elizabeth, that we might so try?'

'By all means, my Lord! Why should we not? Let us indeed push the jest further.'

James rubbed his forehead with the back of his wrist, tipping to a jauntier angle the vast extravagance of his high-plumed hat. Pensive was the Frown that said:

'There is, of course, a certain *danger*.'

'Danger, my Lord? What danger, pray? Why so?'

'Polmood is in sad taking already, and were you to persist in your refusal any longer the poor man might very well hang himself.'

Elizabeth's dimples twinkled back.

'But the worst of it is that he will take it so heinously amiss. As, if our acquaintance with his proud heart is not deluded, we may be sure that all the world will not persuade him to ask you ever again. Following which, if the match should break off in the miscarriage of our further jest, we fear the consquence is irretrievable ruin to you.'

'Ruin to *me*! What can your Majesty *mean*?'

James tutted severely, looked fraught, and said:

'Yes indeed, Elizabeth: certain ruin to you! For the court and all the Kingdom will say he has slighted and refused you, and you know we cannot help what people say.'

Where were the dimples now?

'You know,' the Voice sank deeper as the Solemnity mounted, 'they will say it is all because Polmood and ourself surprised a man in your chamber at midnight. And much more than that will they say.'

Elizabeth's lips pressed tight to control their sudden trembling.

'They know that you would not, and could not, resist our will, and therefore they will infallibly regard you as an offcast. And you will be flouted and shunned by the whole court. It will almost break our heart to see those who now envy and imitate you turn up their noses and look the other way as they pass you by.'

'But I will *inform* them!' cried Elizabeth. 'I will *swear* to them that it was not so!' Eyes brimming, she tightened the possessive insecurity of her grip on her Guardian's arm.

Who shook his head in Worldly sadness, and said:

'Is that not the very best insurance of making them all believe that it *was* so? And shall we not lose a splendid wedding – the priest is already ordered to the chapel! – in which we had hoped to see you appear to unique advantage: the wonder and admiration of all ranks and degrees?'

Elizabeth flashed his Majesty a glance of restless and fearful impatience. The little tug she gave the royal sleeve was a tremulous plea for a word of reassuring reprief.

But the Tuggee appeared not to notice.

'Never mind!' he scoffed. 'It is no matter, the loss of a wedding. It is but a moment's bauble, is it not?'

'My Lord, could not – '

'Whereas a joke of such magnitude is an entity of great rarity: quite priceless, indeed. For which reason, Elizabeth, we do after all agree with you. That we *should* proceed to serve Polmood his final refusal. For the sake of the peerless jest.

'And what of worth is lost thereby? A ceremony of show that

lasts but an hour? A jangle of music, dancing and drinking, and a richness of feasting that palls within a week? And then a long lifetime of wifely security and comfort, with monies to supervise and servants to oversee!

'Meagre shadows, my sweetest Elizabeth, are they not? Hardly worth the burning of the candle that casts them. No! Often have we thought, even in thc worst of cases, that an old maid does better than many a well-married lady. She may boast no happiness, it is true, but what of her *un*happiness? Never can it fall to the dismal depths of the mismatched spouse. What think you?'

Elizabeth was fidgeting furiously with her bracelet. The seemingly careless reflections his Majesty had thrown out presented to her maiden mind a picture so repulsive that her naturally fluent amiability was choking in the grip of palpitations and burning breathlessness.

'Shall Polmood be refused again?' the artful Monarch hounded her.

She snatched a deep gulp of the heady morning air, and replied:

'I have often heard your Majesty say ... that ... we should never, knowingly, let the plough slay even the meanest mouse!'

'Yeeee-es?'

'The jest has surely been capital, my Lord. So much is true. But ... I never saw *long jokes* come to any good. My Lord? And therefore ...'

'Upon our soul!' declared the King, as though humbled by confrontation with the obvious. 'We do believe, Elizabeth, that a scrutiny more profound can only pronounce your reservations wise. You have more sense in your little finger than many ladies have in all!'

'Thank you, my Lord.'

'You suppose, then, that the wedding must go on?'

'I suppose it must, my Lord.'

'Hmmmmnn.'

Elizabeth masked with a frown of resignation the tingling thrill that Recognition of her acuteness and discernment had flushed. Myopic through her intense awareness of self, she allowed her gaze to wander again to the brow of the Craigdilly hill, where ...

But the King adroitly changed sides with her, linked his left arm in her right, and led her from the balcony at a spanking pace. All the way down to the Hall he never once let off commending her prudence and discretion as far beyond her years, expatiating on the envy and spleen of the other court ladies and the joy they would have manifest if the marriage agreement had been irrevocably dissolved.

What could Elizabeth do but concur?

Thence his Majesty proceeded to descant at vertiginous pitch on the celebrations and amusements in which they would soon be engaged, even on the fine dresses and exotic jewellery in which such-and-such ladies were likely to get themself up, until he hand winded Elizabeth's fancy to the summit of its capacity for bursting anticipation.

Nor was her manoeuvred decision allowed any reconsideration.

Back in the Great Hall, King James, in an irresistible flood of enthusing energy, summoned together the Queen and all her attendants and reproachfully inquired why they were so dilatory and behind.

'Make haste, my ladies. Make *haste*!' said he. 'How could you forget that we have this day – and soon – to ride to the Virgin's Chapel, and then the long way to the Castle of Nidpath? Where the preparations for the ensuing festival have been in progress for several days. Several days, ladies! Yet not one of you is dressed for the journey – why so?'

The ladies gawked at the unwonted fickleness of his Majesty's mood.

Who went on:

'Falseat is high, dear ladies. And the braes of the Hundleshope steep. Therefore make *haste* now, as we ride within the hour.'

DIPLOMACY BY THE CRAWMELT BURN

The suddenly urgent order of the day was not well comprehended by the ladies, but what did that matter? Once the King had expressed his will, in such good humour and with such verve, away tripped she, and away tripped she, each lady bustling gleefully to such equestrienne magnificence as her portable wardrobe could afford.

And who more gleefully than Elizabeth?

Meanwhile his Majesty ran down to the kitchens, where he ordered to be hampered for the journey a plentiful repast of sliced venison, honey, wholemeal bread, goats'-milk cheese, apples, and as many flasks of wine as the pack-horses could carry.

The victuals commissioned, James hurried out to the green, where he found the main body of nobles in lack-lustre congregation by the pavilion – some killing time by tumbling dice, some killing silence with low parabolic mutters on the disquieting unpredictability of recent events, and many already advancing the demise both of themselves and their throbbing ennui through conspicuous consumption of the afore-described murderous red wine.

'MY NOBLE LORDS!' boomed the King. 'You are tardy, are you not? While the ladies are all nearly set for the wedding march, which begins within the half hour. Therefore, gentlemen, make haste. Be *swift*! Ensure your grooms do have your mounts saddled: there is no moment to lose. And where, pray, is the foremost groom of all? Our honest Hunter of Polmood?'

The obsequious whine of Sir Patrick Hepburn recalled:

'Your Majesty, I believe I did see him head up the Burn to the Linn, possibly for to rinse his breakfast from his beard.'

'Thank you, Sir Patrick. We shall investigate ourself. In the meantime, my lords, forget not the magic word of the moment. Which is: *Speed*!'

Three minutes later to himself James said: 'Ha hum!'

From his crouching vantage behind a luxuriance of yellowing bracken, he with a grin espied the muttering distraction of Polmood pracing the bank of the pool below the waterfall. In his heavy buskin boots, with their unsummery turnover tops, and his sleeve-less doublet of oily leather, held captive by knotted thongs against the ursine nudity of his chest, poor Polmood epitomized the love-trussed picture of abjectly dejected rejection. At every second step his biceps bulged massively, his great fists clenched savagely, and he seemed to remonstrate in menacing undertones with phantoms dancing on the surface of the water.

All of which delighted the onlooking Eyes.

'Hey there!' James called at length, rising with a flourish of plumes from his cover. 'Polmood?'

The forester froze, then slowly turned. 'Sire?' he growled,

respectful duty labouring in vain to overcome the black misery of his scowl.

The King approached him, saying:

'You know, Polmood, loyal subject that you are, there are times when you amaze us. Did you know that?'

Polmood cleared his throat in a coarse barking retch. 'I do most solemnly beg pardon, your Majesty, if I have in some way offended.'

'Offended? Heaven save us, man! No, no! It is not that you have *offended*. Just that your conduct *astounds* us.'

'How so, Sire? If I may be so bold.'

'Why, Polmood, is it not plain? Here are you, taking your exercise by the stream, as if this were a normal day, with no uniqueness afoot. While not the flight of an arrow yonder, in the Castle and upon the green, all the company except ourselves is busily packing away and mounting up in readiness for the wedding procession!'

Polmood's non-sty eye flickered in unbelief. 'Procession, Sir? Wedding . . .'

'Indeed, Polmood. Wedding! And whose wedding, man, if not your own?'

'But . . .'

'And how will your lovely Elizabeth feel, if her lord and master and husband-to-be is the only one late to the chapel? Eh?'

The harsh promontories of Polmood's craggy features softened in a shower of comprehending joy, and in a voice still scrabbling for certainty he said:

'I had thought, Sire, that Elizabeth had changed – '

'The nonsense of yester evening, mean you? Polmood, Polmood! A jest is but a jest is but a jest in this world. And are you not doubly fortunate, in that Elizabeth, so tender and so young, has a sense of the humorous so enchantingly delicious? But you must not take life too seriously, my friend: fie on you! No. The girl is even at this moment in a paradise of preparation, and well advised will you be to join here there.'

Polmood's unwieldy body began to limber in a waltz of indecision. He flexed his knees, he rubbed his pulpy nose, and, scratching his scrub-grey crown, he knocked from it his flat-brimmed hat of hide, which fell backwards unheeded to the ground.

'Sire,' he said. 'I know not . . .' He bent towards the pool, as if in vague recollection of some previous purpose. But before his hands reached the water he jumped up again and rushed past the King toward the Castle. Ten paces later he shuddered to a halt as though transfixed by an oncoming thunderbolt, turned, and charged like a lumbersome puppy back to the stream. Hurling himself full-length upon the bank, he plunged his head into the water, like a smoking torch beyond trimming. Then up again he leapt, and made to dry his dripping face in the elbow of his doublet sleeve, the nonexistence of which appeared, for a moment, to restore him sufficiently to recognize the King, to whom he sheepishly confessed:

'Your pardon, Sire, I beg of you. But I'll be shot to dead with an arrow, so help me, if I know what I am doing.'

'Our pardon you have, Polmood. As this day is yours.' King James kept his countenance severely straight. 'Yet shall we be shot to dead with an arrow ourself, if we see any sense in that you are about. How can you idly saunter here, dabbling like a toddler in the water, when all the cavalcade is mounted and awaits you? Fie, man: be gone!'

Polmood bowed tersely, turned, and thundered off again, his breast of leather glistening with the trickles from his beard.

James, the stern line of his mouth in apparent difficulty, watching the other's attempted departure, then did something rather unexpected. He swooped to where Polmood's handsomely unassuming bonnet lay abandoned, snatched it up, elevated his own exorbitant headpiece a few inches above his head and popped Polmood's beneath it. Rising, and bending the velvet of his own brim down, to perfect the deception, he cupped his mouth at the retreating back of his bareheaded victim, and hallooed:

'Oh, POLMOOD!'

'Yes, Sire?'

'There is one point further, Polmood. If you would attend us there until we come abreast of you.'

'As your Majesty commands.' Polmood anchored his furious clenching fists behind his back. What could the King want *now*?

'The matter is this, Polmood,' James explained. 'You will have observed that Elizabeth, though already incomparably beautiful, is yet very *young*?'

'Indeed, Sire.'

'She is in many ways – not more so, perhaps, than in her *mind* – in many ways still a child.'

'Your Majesty is doubtless correct.'

'And her *body* – we trust it will not offend you, Polmood, if we, from the pure disinterest of our Guardian office, do venture to suggest that Elizabeth's fair body is fully as desirable, already, as any that a poet might imagine.'

Polmood, distrusting his voice, curtly nodded his absence of dissent.

'And yet, Polmood, she is desirable, is she not, in the manner of a blooming rose? Still a time from the sweetest and most perfect ripeness of her blossom?'

Silent licking of suddenly apprehensive lips.

'Who, Polmood . . . can we say . . . excuse us!' His Majesty indulged in a cough of discreet Embarrassment. 'If plucked before her rightful time, if the metaphor we may plumb, we . . . should hate to see her prematurely withered. Therefore, Polmood, must we ask you, as you do love your duty to ourself, which is to say, in a word, that her majesty has asked us to ask you, to defer . . .'

PART TWO
Over to Nidpath

7

THE FIRST PART OF THE JOURNEY

MIRTH BY THE CASTLE OF COCKBURN

Can there be any picture of life which more exhilarates the mind and buoys the spirits than that of a large party of men and women setting out on an expedition on horseback?

As the flower of the Scottish nation rode out that morning they were all once more in soaring humour. The lightness of the breeze, the abundance of fresh beauty and great nobility, further blessed by the presence of divinely endowed royalty, together with the joyous intent of the occasion, seemed to wipe from the windows of the collective mind the effects of the previous night's intemperance and motley misrule. Right freely did the nobles boast and the ladies prattle as they scoured down the links of the Meggat, so full of zest and jesting glee that every earthly care flung itself in shame upon the whispering wind, quietly busy as it also was with the debonair floating of many a lovely lock and streaming ribbon.

Upward of forty courtly souls were in the company, followed by grooms, pages and other attendants. Yet so little was King James afraid of any befalling harm that, beyond the venerable martial powers of the nobles themselves, the only armed security was a modest background dozen of his Majesty's own soldiers of horse.

Hardly three miles into their adventure had they trotted when the almost noble Pearce Cockburn galloped out in a tizzy from his homely little castle (really no more than a fortified manor house) and earnestly compelled them to dally a moment and do him the honour of taking some wine at his gate.

'Hold, hold!' the King exclaimed, when all who counted, still mounted, had taken their glasses and were gathered in a circle awaiting his Toast. 'For where is the man of the hour? Where, oh where, good lords and ladies, is our honest Hunter of Polmood?'

The good lords and ladies cast their eyes about and confessed their wondering ignorance.

'For how', complained the King, 'may we drink to the health of the bride and the groom when one of them is absent so starkly?'

All were quite at a loss. Was it really possible, they marvelled, that they should already have ridden so far, bound for Polmood's wedding, without even one of them – not even Elizabeth! – perceiving that the man himself was missing?

'There he is!' cried a voice at length.

And there he was.

Nigh to the rear he furtively lurked, among the untoasting attendants. In the flushing of a silent scowl he sat, head bowed beneath the humiliation of a greasy old slouch hat lately cast by some clothes-conscious groom. His horse was finely curried, his other raiment was, if not elegant, at least costly and colourful, being the finest he possessed, and the contrast between these details so fitting and the grimy bathos of his shapeless headgear, plus the circumstance that the wearer was a bare two miles from the ceremony of his wedding, together combined in a concatenation of incongruity so ludicrous as to trigger a volley of hooting hilarity that resounded several times across the mouth of the valley and rose up to fracture the lofty passage of a distant kestrel.

'HOO, HOO, HOO!'

'Was ever a bride groomed better?' chuckled the Earl of Hume.

Polmood kept his unsmiling position without a muscle moving, which greatly augmented the corporate mirth.

And the King, who had forgotten his Purloining of Polmood's bonnet, which even then reposed upon the back of the pack-horse bearing his Majesty's own wardrobe, was so much tickled by the incident that he was obliged to alight from his milky Pegasus and sit down upon a handy boulder, the better to clutch his sides and bellow his laughter.

'Polmood, Pol . . . mood!' he chortled. 'Heaven save us if you do favour that swill bucket to your own fine bonnet of this morning!'

'Sire, I do not,' growled Polmood, edging his mount forward into the glass-holding circle of courtiers. 'But I prefer it to an uncovered head.'

'How so?'

'I regret, Sire, that when I was ready to ride I found that my bonnet was somewhere lost – I know not how.'

'And did you not then commission research for its whereabouts?'

'Indeed, Sire, I did. For I then deduced it was mislaid by the linn, yet my groom found it nowhere there.'

His Majesty leapt to his feet, blinking tears from his twinkling eyes. Stepping forward affectionately to the unwitting butt of his jape, he said:

'Trouble not, honest Polmood, for it is no matter. But, as you cannot step forth at your nuptials in a cap such as that, therefore let the two of us change for the day.'

'Sire! You have . . .'

'No excuses, Polmood. The issue is decided.'

Polmood obediently donned the velvet magnificence of the royal Bonnet, its towering peacock plumes held in place about the crown by a band of gold braid inlaid with the glitter of myriad diamond dust. The unaccustomed honour reflected in his burning blush, yet Polmood, from the heart of his simple bluntness, did still make so bold as to conjecture that his Majesty was the mucklest wag in the entirety of his dominions.

The Mucklest Wag clowned his assent by bowing to a slouch-hatted doff.

The audience cheered.

The health of the bride and groom was toasted with surpassing gusto.

And the party moved on.

I DO!

Soon they reached the Virgin's Chapel, sat back a little way from the bank of the north neck of the deeply long loch. Waiting for them, in a gushing ferment of pinking pates and clerical beams, were the lonely prior and two monks of Saint Mary's, all crimson and white and gold in their robes of great pomp. Also present, arrayed in the yet more dazzling splendour of his eclipsing rank, was the Abbot of Inchafferie, the King's own personal chaplain, whose paunchly bulk and balding wisps had been summoned down from Nidpath by special messenger on the Thursday.

He it was, in solemnity beyond depiction, who married the humble forester, Norman Hunter of Polmood, to the courtly lady, the lovely Elizabeth Manners from England. So radiant was she, in her flowing long-trained houppelande in purest white satin, coloured only by a tasselled girdle of fine-spun gold beneath her breast, that even the frozen susceptibilities of the holy brothers warmed to the alarming degree of their open-mouthed astonishment.

That a mortal could live with such beauty and still emanate an effulgence of purity so transcendent!

Elizabeth's blonde-waved pulchritude, brooched by the scented bloom of a single blood-red rose above her left temple, was highlighted to the zenith of its perfection by her sole crafted ornament: a necklace of clustered rubies, given her that very morning by Queen Margaret, from which there dangled a tiny crucifix of unalloyed gold, glistering yellow against her flawless bosom pale to proclaim her felicity beyond earthly compare.

The normal capacity of the little chapel was exceeded by a dozen that morning, owing to outraged insistence by the Queen and *all* her ladies that *none* of them could miss a single moment of the spectacle. Hence it was only a handful of the lesser nobles who were left to kick their heels and listen from the churchyard without, having only a premature bumper to console them, as the King gave away the bride in marriage.

'I do!' said she.

'I do!' said Polmood.

'I therefore declare you man and wife,' droned the unctious Abbot. 'You now may kiss the bride.'

Polmood, his eyes full of shameless joy, immediately did so, though due to immaculate mouth-manoeuvring on Elizabeth's part his thick hairy lips met only for a chastely short moment with her prettily presented cheek.

Abbot Graham, for so he was named, puce-jowled from unexercised excess of good living, found occasion several times in his address to return to the problem of the ravishing magnetism of Elizabeth's *personal charms*! The white of his eyes were sickly yellow from their lifetime of disapproving impotence, and the heavy crow's-feet all around them contracted in Heavenly apprehension as God through his unworthy servant, as in a prophetic spirit, prayed right fervently:

'That the peerless beauty which now outvies the dawn of

morning, and stuns the perceptions of all who behold her, may never come to prove a source of uneasiness, either to her husband or to her own fair breast.'

The King and Queen smiled proudly.

Polmood trembled in the clutch of his emotions.

Elizabeth kept her eyes cast down in faintly blushing demurity.

'May that lovely bloom', the Abbott petitioned, 'dwell long on the faced that it now so well becomes. And may it blossom again, and again, and again, on many and many a future stem. May it never be regarded by the present possessor as cause for exultation, or for self-esteem, but only as a transient engaging varnish over the more precious beauties of the mind and soul. And . . .'

At the back of the chapel the Earl of Mar stirred restlessly and smothered a contemptuous yawn.

For which he received from his diligent Countess Katherine, her mask of rapt attention unfluttering, a sharp intimation, in the form of pincing fingernails gouging skin from the back of his hand, that it was his duty to continue still and strain for edification from the sermon.

Which went on:

'May her personal and mental charms be so blended that her husband may never perceive the decay of the one, save only through the growing beauties of the other. For thine is the Kingdom, the Power, and the Glory. World without ending. Amen.'

Polmood's taut hulk relaxed in a grateful sob. The unfurred portions of his cheek were wet as windows swept by rain as he turned and feasted the passionate green of his ageing eyes on the paragon of the nation's womanhood, *whose worldly overlord was now himself*!

And Elizabeth?

Did she draw wisdom from the Abbot's petition?

Or was the meticulous ordering of her rigid posture, downcast gaze and modest blushes a mere opaqueness of baffling screen across her enjoyment of the enduring compliment to her beauty?

ON TOP OF THE WORLD

Shortly the party were on horseback once more, and trekking north towards Peebles and Nidpath. By three o'clock their meandering took them round the shoulder of the high hill of

Falseat, which, according to the King's decision, arrived at with the gracious blessing of the ladies, they ascended to the summit, there to dine by the tinkling side of a tiny crystal spring, whose offering trickles in tributary of the Quair Water, thence to the rolling Tweed, and thus to the salty gratitude of the ocean.

And from that elevated spot they enjoyed a prospect both varied and immense, on all hands intercepted by the shimmery blue of the hotting haze that even on the clearest day will rise for ever, a jealous husband to shroud the alluring mysteries of the distance. All the southern part of the Kingdom did they view, from sea to sea, spread around them as upon an endless map, where, in the bard's immortal words:

> The oceans rolled and the rivers ran,
> To bound the aims of sinful man,
> Who never looked on scene so fair
> As Scotland from the ambient air.
> O'er valleys clouds of vapour strolled,
> While others gleamed their burning gold,
> And stretching far and wide between
> Lay countless shades of fairy green.
> The glossy sea that carves her rocks,
> Her thousand isles and thousand lochs,
> Her mountains frowning o'er the main,
> Her waving fields of golden grain:
> When ever will the eyes of men
> Regard such unspoiled peace again?

Not Shakespeare, perhaps, but who would gainsay the sentiment?

In any case, it would be a crass romantic travesty to suggest that all the picnicking party took equal delight in the natural wonders around them.

Elizabeth's eyes, for example, saw little, as the audience of her mind gave rapturous encore to the tireless images that feasted, toasted, and merrily danced on the limelit cape of its stage.

Polmood's eyes saw Elizabeth, and little else. Why did the glances of the priding husband, so laden with adoration, go unreturned by the worshipped wife?

Almost as if unnoticed!

The custom, when such large mixed companies went abroad on horse, was for the King and his high-ranking intimates to lead, followed by the ladies, with the remaining nobles next and the attendants in the rear. The rationale behind this (that the least offence be given to the most exalted noses, by the abundant windbreaking of the many horses and gentlemen) was understandable, but the pragmatic result for Polmood that afternoon had been his inability to exchange even a syllable with Elizabeth since leaving the Virgin's Chapel.

And now?

Picking daintily at choicely lean slivers of venison, she was more inaccessible than ever, cordoned off by an impenetrable squadron of gabbling females, their admiration as effusive as it would be short-lived.

What was a man to do?

Polmood ate well, drank deeply, and cut dead the occasional invitation from his manly fellows to join in their goaty jollity.

Queen Margaret, aside from her genteel presiding, kept half an eye on Elizabeth's introspective enchantment, while also noting the thwarted devotion with which Polmood ogled his flighty spouse. What boded the total lack of loving intercourse between their eyes?

Her majesty was much disturbed by the sharpening teeth of her suckling apprehensions.

And through all the gorging, toping and gossip, the King sat distantly apart. Though the vales and leafy frith of Lothian lay stretched like a variegated carpet below his feet to the north, while the purple hills and wild green woods of Ettrick Forest formed a contrast so perfect to the south, yet did his Majesty's boundless aspirations return his roving gaze again and again to the far-off fells of Cheviot and the eastern border with England.

Did he even then premeditate invasion of that country?

Or was it some Invisible Power, hovering like a puppet master over the mortal mysteries of sympathy and elicitation, that drew his eyes and cogitations irresistibly away to that very Flodden Field where his goodly Form so soon would lie untimely slain?

8

ENTER WILLIAM MORAY

THE RAGGED GUIDE

Though not ideal from the point of view of unfounded fiction, the facts of our story require that several important characters have still to be introduced. The first of these found himself drawn into the action, much against his will, towards evening on the day of Elizabeth's wedding.

The sun was past its prime, but the company had descended from the breezy heights of Falseat, to file through the still humid heat of the lower slopes and glens of Hundleshope. Consequently, though the day had aged, the propensity of the party to perspire from the exertion and to snap in vexation at minor irritations, like the shying of a neighbour's horse from the startled slither of a basking adder, was in no degree diminished – if anything the reverse, a partial consequence, no doubt, of the irksome fading of the lunchtime wine.

But whatever the etiology, the feeling was poignantly expressed, by all but the fittest young nobles, that, when their beaten track dissolved in an unforeseen expanse of soggy morass in a dead hollow somewhere between Hundleshope and Crookston, the risk of dress-soiling foundering in the uncertain squelchy mire was so odious that, so please his Majesty, might they not discover a detour on firmer footing?

How could a true King say no?

To the clothes-conscious clamour of *all* his ladies!

Hence they diverted, and thus they got lost.

'It grieves us to remark', King James remarked, as they toiled through a labyrinth of shallow valleys unknown to anyone present, in hope that a downstream direction must eventually return them to familiar terrain, 'that we might now be clear of the bog, and even in sight of Peebles. Had we but ventured the traditional trail.'

'We might indeed, my Lord,' rejoined Queen Margaret, riding behind him. 'Or we might be stranded there still! With our steeds broken-legged, and the slime all over our wedding attire!'

'True,' James wearily acknowledged. 'How true, oh Queen!'

Several plodding moments later:

'Your Majesty!' cried a proud-eyed voice from the rear. 'Up yonder, to the right: beyond the grazing sheep, a shepherd!'

Sure enough, a recumbent herding figure there was, lying in a crucifixion posture in the springy dry heather, with his dreamy gaze apparently lost in the orange-tinged blues of the descending sky.

'Very good!' cried the King. 'Our thanks to that man. Rest here, we pray you all, while we ourself shall canter up and sue for yon fellow's assistance. Perhaps a good moment to breach a fresh flagon of . . .'

His concluding 'wine' was lost as, ever eager for anonymous intercourse with his subjects, he spurred his snorting stallion in a cavalier leap across the stream and up the further slope.

Now William Moray, the shepherd lad, was alarmed from his contemplative solitude by these voices below, and especially by the hooves coming drumming up the heath. Leaping from the leisurely care of his father's flock to his frighted feet, and seeing galloping towards him at tempestuous speed a stranger horseman with a great flashing sword by his side and a sinister slouch hat on his head, the boy judged instantly that he was pursued for his life by a rustling forager, of whom there were several in the south of Scotland in those days.

'Dear *Jeeesus!*' he wailed. Heedless of the meeping scattering of his ewes and lambs, he threw off the heavy tweed plaid from his shoulder and the sturdy brogues from his feet, and sprinted barefoot up the heather, clutching only his horn-handled baton.

'Hey there!' shouted his Majesty, surprised and annoyed. 'You, boy! HALT! Have no fear, boy: it is only information we seek.'

The terrified youth fled only the faster.

'Heaven save us!' muttered James. 'Can the realm be truly so rife with the horror of treachery?'

The Earl of Mar, impatient as ever, brandished high his sabre, and called out:

'WE FOLLOW, SIRE! AND SHALL HEAD HIM TO THE GULLEY OF SCREE.'

'HOLD STILL, SIR!' the King yelled back. 'THE MATTER IS IN HAND.'

The fleeting William, who knew the locality better than any man living, soon scrambled round the hump of the hill and struggled in a stumbling running crawl up a steep narrow gulch of loose jagged rocks.

Which had the intended effect of taking the pursuing horseman out of sight of his followers and forcing him to forsake his mount, for fear of a neck-breaking fall.

'Bogger the impudent scoundrel!' gasped his Majesty, as his toes were bruised in their boots and his knees sorely grazed by the flinty edges of the scree. 'HOLD THERE, BOY, CONFOUND YOU!' he roared, as, advantaged by having broken the back of the chase on horse, he gained on his frantic quarry. 'We require from you nothing ... but GUIDANCE! For the which ... you shall be *paid* ...'

The Earnest aborted when William, realizing his lungs would burst before he could ever escape, suddenly whirled and leapt on his tormentor from above.

'MURDERING FILTH, I'LL SEE YOU IN *HELL*!' he shrieked. And commenced to belabour his Sovereign Lord about the shoulders with his stout willow baton.

'Grooouf!' The winded King recoiled.

'And this too!' hissed William, angling a lethal swipe at the now hatless Head, with the heavy curved ram horn that handled his stick.

Had the blow connected, that nation would doubtless have been plunged into Kingless disunity.

But James IV was a nimble dolphin in the waters of close combat.

'It is well for you, lad,' he muttered, jerking his face two inches clear of the swishing baton, 'that you know not what you do. But NO MATTER!' he bellowed. Then at blinding speed drew from his belt the sword that there hung.

'Dear God in *Heaven*!' sobbed William. Deeming confrontation with his Maker only a moment away, he mustered for a last desperate assault.

'Not this time, young friend,' murmured the King.

William's trusty staff came singing down.

James feinted gracefully to his right. Then with both hands on the haft of his sword he slashed upwards with extraordinary force, so that the blunt back of his blade met William's descending stick some fifteen inches from where the youth gripped it.

'Aaaaaaah!' cried the latter.

'Ha!' exclaimed the gratified King.

As the shepherd boy's baton described a harmless arc against the sky, before falling to rest a furlong down the gulley.

William sank to his knees, closed his eyes, and clasped the stinging numbness of his hands in garbled prayer.

James stepped back a pace. His humorous spirit and merciful propensity were somewhat cooled by the smarting weals coming up against the muscles of his arms, and he kept his sword at the ready as he perused the miserable, flinching salvation-seeking of the grovelling youth. Perhaps fifteen, the King supposed, though William's sixteenth birthday had in fact just passed. He was a shade above medium height for the time, and still filling out, though already sturdy in the wiry fashion of the people of the mountains. His unkempt hair was lankly blond, and his ragged short-sleeved jacket was of coarse woollen cloth and faded brown colour, gathered at the waist by a length of knotted leather, from which hung a pouch large enough to carry a small loaf of bread and a hunk of cheese. Tattered hose ran in patchy blue from his cod to his ankles, and the soles of his feet were oozing blood from their furious ascent of the rocks.

The detail restored a degree of the King's natural warmth.

'Hey, boy,' he gently said.

'And pray God let my mother believe I died . . .'

'Open your eyes, boy! There is no-one here will do you harm.'

William's eyes unclenched and blinked their steely-grey incredulity.

'Your exhibition transcends the rational,' James informed him. 'All we required of you was the way to Peebles. For we have entirely lost our path.'

'Us?' said the boy, sitting back from his kneel to a fearful squat. 'And who is we?'

'And who is we?' the King echoed in wonder. 'Why, boy? What affair of yours may it be who is we?'

'It is my affair,' William insisted, 'as it is my town.'

'Importing?'

'Eh?'

'Meaning what, young friend? Meaning: expand, if it please you.'

'My meaning is that before I direct ye I must ken who you are.'

'Why so?'

'I fear ye can have no good design on Peebles, and Peebles is my town.'

'Ah! Most loyal, lad. What a fortunate town, to be shielded by valour so trenchant!'

'Importing?'

'Importing, boy, that clearly you are an insolent fellow. That your confidence grows as you see we have need of you, yet rest assured that when information is required of a treasonous captive . . . there are ways, and there are ways!'

'Peebles . . .'

'But since we march with no dishonour, so shall you be enlightened. We are but a humble wedding party, bound for Peebles to make merry. And so, we pray you, rise up and walk down to our horse, and you shall ride behind us.' James beckoned, then slid down the scree, recovering Polmood's hat as he went.

William followed, tender-footed, his suspicion voicing:

'We? And who is us?'

James swung into his saddle. 'Saw you not many many ladies in our company?'

William recovered his stick, plaid and shoes before he grudgingly allowed:

'Ay. But . . .'

'And think you seriously that such ladies ride forth to rustle your handful of lambs? Are the times indeed so dire?'

'Maybe not,' sniffed William. Hobbling to the side of his highly mounted captor, he made a bleeding attempt to squeeze his swelling feet back into their brogues.

'Leave the footwear, boy!' scoffed the King. 'Else your injuries shall redouble. Spring up here and ride with – me, pilot us in safety to Peebles, and I shall see your brogues replaced fourfold.'

So saying, James reached down, took William's wrist, and lifted him up to straddle the great white stallion behind its saddle.

Moments later the incongruous couple were trotting quietly down the slope to rejoin the waiting party. (And it may be of interest to some that the glen where the shepherd boy William was found is known as the Weddinger's Hope to this very day.)

CAT AND MOUSE

When the King and his youthful passenger came in hailing distance of the others, James, rather than ride up to his followers and regale them with his adventure, chose instead to cross the stream several furlongs in advance, and, waving them forward with a twirl of his scruffy slouch hat, he rode on ahead.

To allow conversation between himself and William Moray to continue uncramped by his own true identity.

'So you see,' he explained to the unwitting William, 'we are, as I said, a peaceful procession from wedding ceremony to wedding celebration. The King and Queen are to meet us in Peebles, they say, and will honour us with their company. And as you come with us and point our way, you too shall be our guest, and shall see the King and all his court!'

William appeared not impressed, saying:

'Very fine it all sounds, I am sure. But I can see plenty of fancy-dressed fools without going the length of Peebles. I shall see the King, ye say? Huh! Well I account that no great favour.'

'Indeed?'

'Indeed not!'

'Why so, pray?'

'Because I have often seen the King. Turn right here, ye must, by yonder gorse. There is a sheep track runs down the side of the burn.'

'So you have often seen the King?' mused James, nosing his horse according to the direction.

'Near as often as my father has sheep,' William blithely lied. There was in him a budding poet, and his greed to tamper the literal was insatiable. Often had his childhood ears been boxed out of maternal despair at this gilding trait.

'And you would know him well, I suppose?' said James.

'Och ay! I could ken the King among a thousand men.'

'With the sharpness of your shepherd's eye!'

'But tell me,' William queried, 'are you folks indeed Scotsmen?'

'Scotsmen? My dear young friend! The bridegroom yonder is the great Norman Hunter of Polmood, of whom you have surely heard.'

'Ay. And yourself now?'

'I? Why ask you?'

'I ask,' retorted William, brazen with the confidence of youth, 'as who the devil ever saw a Scotsman wear a filthy old bonnet like yours?'

'Aha!' hummed the King. 'How cruelly the children see! My bonnet is mean,' he said over his jogging shoulder, 'as Heaven's punishment to me.'

'Importing?'

'Importing, lad, that I did gamble my last month's wage on a throw of the dice. And lose! And lose all! Therefore take warning from me, Duncan Laidlaw, head keeper of Norman of Polmood, and your servant humbler than a month ago. And gamble never, what your honest labour earns.'

'Gamble never!' William snorted. 'I see, friend Duncan, that ye are in sooth a simple fellow.'

'How so?'

'To stake a month's wage on a single throw! And to imagine a shepherd would ever do likewise.'

'Ah!'

'But as ye seem honest forby, and as ye did promise me four brace of new shoon, so shall I, William Moray of Crookston, guide ye well into Peebles. Therefore, cross the water there, where the three ewes drink, then skirt the side of yon blueberry bank.'

The route they then followed was extremely intricate. It wound among the woods of Grevington in such a manner that, beneath the swelling gloom of dusk, if it had not been for William's navigation, the royal party would never have reached the Castle of Nidpath that night. All continued well, however, thanks to the shepherd's familiarity with the locality, and, as James took care to remain out in front, the air was clear for further freedom of discourse between the bumptious youngster and the simple Duncan Laidlaw.

Who is due course harped:

'So you know the King well *by sight*, you say?'

'Perfectly well.'

'And what is he like, pray?'

William took a breath of deep gratification at the deference paid him, and in a disapproving voice pronounced:

'Ah, Duncan! He is a black-looking, thief-like chap. About your size – though with a muckle belly on him. And somewhat like you – but a great deal uglier.'

This produced a short trotting pause.

Then his Majesty murmured:

'I should like, of all things, to lay eyes on such a king. And to hear him speak.'

'Ye would like to see him and hear him speak, would ye?' sneered William. 'Well, if ye do chance to see him, I shall answer for it, ye shall soon hear him speak.'

'I shall?'

'Ye shall, and that in abundance. For there is nothing in all the world that more delights him than *to hear himself speak*!'

'Quite the loquacious pedant, you would say?'

'Ay. That too. If ye get near him, it will be a miracle if ye hear owt else. And if ye do not *see* him, it will not be his blame. For he takes every opportunity to show his *goodly person* to the world.'

'So you have no great opinion of your King, I perceive.'

'I have a great opinion that he is a silly fellow. A great rascal, and a bad man at heart forby.'

'I am sorry to hear that!' said the King with muted feeling. 'The more so from a young man who knows him so well. For I have heard, on the contrary, that King James is everywhere accounted generous, brave, and virtuous *par excellence*.'

'Ay. But his generosity is all ostentation, his bravery has never yet been tried, and as for his virtue – God mend it!'

'Well, shepherd, you know we may here speak the sentiments of our hearts freely, and whatever you say . . .'

'Whatever *I* say!' exclaimed the high-riding William. 'Mercy me! I have said nothing to you, Duncan Laidlaw of Polmood, that I would not repeat if the King himself were standing right next to me. I only said that his courage has not yet been tried, and I say so still. And I said, for his virture, God mend it. Was that wrong? The truth is, honest Duncan, that I like James Stuart well enough as my King, and would fight for him to my last breath against the Englishman, but I am unco angry at him for all that, and would just as soon fight *with* him.'

'Indeed!'

'I would! Why, if I had got the King among my feet as I had you lately – mercy! – how I would have chastised the man!'

'The devil you would!'

'Ay. Take your mount across yon ridge above the peat hags, and ye will see Peebles in the valley before ye.'

King James nudged his steed accordingly. The feelings on his face were sharply mixed, and William, had he seen his interlocutor's eye, might not have pressed so ardently the arrogant sedition of his warble.

Saying:

'But by the by, Duncan Laidlaw, what is it makes you wear an iron chain there about your waist? Ye have not murdered your poor father too, have ye now?'

'Murdered my poor father?'

'Ay. Murder, filthy murder! Or is it only for to carry your master's money?'

'No more,' rumbled the growing edge of the horseman's Baritone. 'But a safeguard for my master's silver.'

'Good enough. And it is hardly one sixth of the chain Himself wears. Man! Was not that a terrible business?'

'Was not *what* a terrible business?'

'How', declaimed William, 'can we expect any blessings to attend a king who dethrones and murders his own father? For ye ken it was the same as if he did the filthy deed with his own treasonous young hand.'

'It is well known that his father was much to blame. And I believe the King was innocent of his murder, and is forby most deeply sorry for it.'

'Though his blame be as long as a donkey's broozler, he was still the man's *father*! There's no argument can go against that. And as to him being sorry, it is easy for him to say so, and wear a bit chain about his belly, yet who deep down can disbelieve that if the same temptation and the same opportunity came together once more, he would do the same over again? A man's character, my good friend Duncan, is as a dark mole on his breast: it precedes his first baby bawl, and it outlives the rattle of his death!'

'So Life has instructed you?'

'That is has. And then, what a wicked man he is with the ladies!'

'Truly?'

'Ay! The lecher *par excellence*, James Stuart is.'

'And how know you this? You, a country shepherd lad?'

'Why, Duncan Laidlaw! It is all across the nation.'

'And what does the nation say?'

'That he has a very good queen of his own, even though she be an Englishwoman – which is certainly a very extraordinary and wonderful unification of qualities – nevertheless, she's a very good queen.'

'To be sure.'

'Yet he is so indifferent to her as barely to be civil . . .'

'Not possible!'

'And delights only in a witching young minx that they call Gray: Gray by name and Gray by nature, I would reckon. What a terrible shame and sin it is to gallaunt as they do. I wonder that the two of them never brood on Purgatory, and Hell!'

'We must allow our King a little liberty in that way, must we not? He who bears great pressures, for all our sakes?'

'Ay! And then he must allow such liberty in others, and they in others again? No, friend Duncan: Not a bit of it: it is clear you little think what a wicked prince has to answer for.'

Friend Duncan did not rise to this, having just become thankfully engrossed in the dusk-softened prospect of the little town of Peebles, nestling comfortably in its greenwood dell a mile downhill to the north, on the far side of the east-rolling Tweed. A mile west of the town the grey angularity of the Castle of Nidpath rose like a monster crouching in the growing gloom, its flickering eyes the torches on the battlements.

King James half-turned his horse and called back to his followers:

'BUGLES!'

Instantly two buglers blew a greeting lilt.

A few moments later, from the direction of the town, the salute returned. And thenceforth the bugling call and reply repeated constantly, like a homing discourse between an anxious sheep and her prodigal lamb, causing the outspoken shepherd to inquire:

'What signify these horns?'

'A warning, Master Moray,' replied the incognito King. 'To the steward and the revellers. That they be ready to receive us, and to conduct us into the town.'

'And will the King be there in sooth?'

'In sooth the King will be there.'

'Well,' sighed William, with the resignations of one accustomed to hand-me-down clothing, 'I wish I had on my brogues, and my Sunday hose. But it is all one, I suppose. Nobody will mind me.'

King James forbore to comment on this supposition, but shortly fished:

'And is it really true what you say, William Moray? That the common folk report such deeds of their King?'

'Och ay! Such words are in the mouths of all. Fy, fy: what a shame it is. Myself, if I were in James Stuart's place, I would "shoo the Herone away", as the old song says. Pray ye now, Duncan Laidlaw, did ye never hear the song of *The Herone*, which one of our shepherds did compose? A strange old fellow his is.'

'Not a word, I do confess.'

'Well, it is the sweetest thing ye never heard, and I will sing it to ye, when I have time.'

'You are most gracious, Master William.'

'Ay. And I would give the best wedder in my father's flock that King James might hear it too. I am sure he would love our dear old shepherd, who well deserves his love, for there is no man in Scotland that loves his King and nation so well as he.'

'Then, much should we give to encounter such a worthy.'

'We, Duncan? Again ye say *we*. Who is this *we*?'

'I spoke merely in general, my friend. Importing that any true Scotsman should give much to find a fellow subject so loyal and true.'

'Ah well, ye may hope your desire shall be sated, for I trow the fellow will never again depart the shire,' chuckled William, pleased with his invention of the ancient herdbard, and glad to have duped the gullible Duncan by housing in a carapace of elder pedigree the balled of *The Herone*: in fact a production of his own contriving.

Then, not wishing to be drawn on the exact whereabouts of the fictitious author, he said:

'But to return to the faults of our King – '

'Y . . . e . . . s?' drawled that faulty Personage.

'The worst is his negligence of the rights of the common people.'

'My good young friend, you little know how greatly you amaze me. Yet tell me more, as I have been . . . a while away from the chatter of lowly folk.'

'That will I gladly, honest Duncan. For plainly ye require instruction.'

'None more needy!'

'The pity is, that while it is allowed that James is a good-natured and merciful prince . . .'

'Not to say a silly fellow, a great rascal, and forby a bad man at heart?'

'Ay! All that too, by turns – as each of us contains us all, and none more constantly so than a king. Yet, while his fine intentions are acknowledged, the atrocities of injustice and cruelty which every petty laird and tyrant freely commits throughout the realm are gone beyond all sufferance. If his Majesty kenned but half that I ken, he would no more enjoy his humours and pleasures so gaily, till once he had rectified these foul abuses, which it is the chief study of his nobles to conceal from his sight.'

'In short, friend William, it appears his Majesty could hardly pass an hour in your company without that he should emerge appalled and ashamed at his transgressions of negligence?'

'Ah, friend Duncan, ye ken not how truly ye speak!'

'For what is knowledge?'

'Scenes there are not ten miles distant that I could show King James, to convince him what kind of king he is. But these must be your revellers walking out, are they not?'

'It so would seem,' said James, regarding the torch-bearing multitude of the townsfolk of Peebles, who had already crossed the Tweed and now, some four hundred paces down the slope of grazing green, were marching in an ululating tumult of jostling gabble, to welcome the wedding party and pay homage to the King.

(A short time previously his Majesty had conferred on the township of Peebles, on account of its great attachment and good will towards him, a grant of the lush lands of Caidmoor, to the south of the river, to be employed in perpetuity as common pasture.

Hence the zeal of the beneficiaries thronging to express their gratitude.)

Yet where was the King?

Not for a moment did the townsfolk imagine that the solitary horseman out in front, with the abominable bonnet and the ragamuffin riding behind him, could be their Sovereign Lord.

Rather did they presume that the King must be in the body of the company to come, a misapprehension that James was pleased to compound. Nonchalantly riding by the oncoming clamour of burgesses, women and wondering children, he kept his head unroyally bowed and then, wheeling about his horse, made a halt as if waiting for his superiors to come abreast.

Which a minute later they did.

The crowd stood still and gaped.

Where was his Majesty?

In the latter part of the journey, Queen Margaret, freed by her Husband's jaunt with young William, had required of Polmood that he ride with her, that she might counsel him on the conditions most conducive to Elizabeth's future welfare and happiness. Thus it was that Polmood rode still by her majesty's side, and in view of the glorious crowning plumage lent him by the King, it was natural that the simple people should mistake the bridegroom for the Monarch, even if a few among them nursed privately the uneasy impression that his Majesty was much transformed.

Five hundred heads were bared and a thousand bodies lowly bowed.

To the astonishment of all the horsemen and the surpassing amazement of Norman of Polmood.

William Moray was also perplexed, having expected the King and Queen to be with the welcoming sortie, rather than already among the travelling weddingers. Nevertheless, vaguely understanding some great affair to be going on, and possessing no bonnet himself, he projected his anxiety to comport aright on the straight strong back of his companion Duncan.

Hissing:

'For God's sake, neighbour! Take off that filthy old bonnet, man!'

His Neighbour did not stir.

'Duncan Laidlaw, have ye no *respect*?'

Silence.

Horrified at this unmoving insolence, the shepherd lad reached up and tipped the offending headpiece from the horseman's head.

King James deftly caught it by its falling brim, stood high in his stirrups and, in an even voice that carried far across the moor, inquired:

'To whom, young sir, shall I take it off? To you, *I* suppose?' And with a deliberate Flourish he recapped.

But not before his clarion voice and famous ginger locks had discovered his presence to the multitude.

'HURRAH!' they cried, as five hundred jubliant bonnets scaled the evening firmament.

And:

'GOD SAVE THE KING!'

'PRAISE BE TO KING JAMES!'

'LORD SAVE OUR GOOD KING JAMES!'

All of which combined to flash the dreadful truth like a lightning bolt across the youthful shepherd's errant mind. The great white horse, the flowing ginger beard and hair, the iron chain about . . .

As the marten of the Grampians springs from his hold when he sniffs the heather burning, so William Moray leapt in awful fear from his bareback seat, tumbled to the grassy ground, darted through an opening in the milling circle, and sprinted away across the moor in a terror-struck burst of inconceivable swiftness.

'HOLD THAT TREASONOUS RASCAL!' came the royal command. 'Bring down the villain but harm him not, that he may hang on Monday morn.'

THE KING'S REVENGE

The initial desperate speed of William's flight proved short-lived, tethered by his scree-cut feet, and soon a rabbling posse of lusties from the town had run him down and returned him, a bundle of forlorn hysteria, to the implacable presence of Him he had wronged.

'Take him to the Tolbooth,' King James decreed. 'And ready the scaffold in the market-place, for duty on Monday at noon.'

Their Majesties, followed closely by the beauteous bride and the starry-eyed groom (briefly side-by-side for the first time since their bonding in the chapel) and thereafter by the remainder of the mounted entourage, strung out in handsome pairs, then clattered across the crude wooden bridge and, amid a ringing night ambience of shouting allegiance and joyous acclamation, made formal their entrance to the town.

Meanwhile the unfortunate shepherd was brought up a prisoner in the rear by four of his Majesty's horse guard, and mightily amused they were by the myriad passions tussling in their captive's breast. One moment he would accuse himself bitterly for his folly. The next he would laugh, a bravado laugh, and proclaim to his jailors that though the King might stretch his neck two days hence it would not be for nothing, as executions often were. And, by his Maker, there was comfort in the thought that the wicked Sovereign had never before received such a hearty loundering and dadding of his pitiless Person, from the hands of a subject pure in conscience, whose one true Judgement would soon resound in the Mansions of Him That Ruled All!

The escortive officers chuckled as they locked him away.

And soon the royal company were gone to feasting, dancing, music and wine, and all the other laid-on carnivalities that the well-appointed Castle of Nidpath could provide. Leaving poor William abandoned in the black isolation of the Tolbooth cell, his heart like to burst when he wildly muttered to himself about his parents, his brothers, and sweet younger sister: how stricken would his passing leave them?

While the town was a riot of raucous carousing, the making of much merry, and a hive of tasteless jesting concerning the calamity wherein the presumptuous shepherd boy had fallen.

The next day, Sunday, after morning mass, the King, whose curiosity had been aroused, initiated covert inquiry into the circumstances and qualities of the incarcerated youth. He learned again that the boy's name was Moray. That he fancied himself a great scholar, but was, in fact, an idle and useless fellow! That the old Abbot had learned him to sing, for which there were a few witless souls that did value him – but that, unfortunately, he, the Abbot, had also imparted to him, young William, the unprofitable arts of reading and writing, the pursuit of which was all his joy. And hence, it was conjectured, he would most likely end a practitioner of the Evil Arts, and possibly a Warlock forby!

Now James IV was a not inconsiderable scholar himself, and, though the scope and profundity of his studies were bounded by his Affairs of State, he knew well the cardinal value of education, and how to estimate it in others. He was therefore desirous of testing the boy's bruited literacy, and so, not averse to being thereby avenged for the merciless galling he had received during the wedding ride, on the Sunday afternoon he sent a messenger to the Tolbooth, to inform the prisoner that though no power on earth could save him from the scaffold, yet if he had any message to send his people, his Majesty would graciously despatch a courier with it.

Gone was the steely twinkle from William's eye and the country bloom from his clean-pored skin. Wanly he replied that if the King would send someone with the letter who could read it to his family, then he would certainly write one instantly, but that the exercise was otherwise futile, since no-one but he in his family could read.

The King's messenger, knowing that his Majesty was keen to inspect the writing and composition of a shepherd, and to compare it with those of his clerks, immediately promised that such a courier would be sent.

William then set to with the fervour of the doomed, taking the messenger's quill and covering his parchment scroll in a frantic rapidity of jerky scratches. This letter still survives (in Dr Brown's collection of ancient manuscripts), though apparently only in a copy, as it seems to have been written considerably later than the reign of James IV – judging by the relative modernity of the spelling and the lesser yellowing of the ink. We have little reason to suppose, however, that Dr Brown's copy should break faith with William Moray's original, and, that being so, the following is what the wretched shepherd wrote:

Dr faythir, im to be hangit the morn, for daddinge of the kingis hate; for miskaing him to his fes ahynt his bak; for devering his whors, and layinge on hime with an grit stick. i hope el no be vext, for im no theefe; it was a sair battil, an a bete him doune wis dran sorde; for I miskent him. if it hadna bin krystis merse, ad kild him, me murthr I be wae, but ye men pleis her, an il be gled to see ye in at the deth, for i wonte er blissying. im

147

no ferit, but yit its an asom thynge; its no deth it feirs me, but the efitr-kum garis my hert girle. if kryste an his muthr dinna do sumthin for me there, i maye be ill – im er lukles sonne, Villem mora – to Villem mora of kreusten.

This crude but touching note was whisked by the messenger to the King, who perused it after dinner in the company of those of his courtiers that made pretension to literacy and learning. And it may horrify the modern reader to hear that, instead of roaring with scornful laughter at the imperfections of William's missive, the King and his companions admired it greatly, and wondered at the profundity of the shepherd's erudition: a further proof that education in the Scotland of those days was very much an orphan in the wilderness.

The messenger was sent on to read the letter to William's father, and the old man and his wife, on digesting the news beyond the choking of their first bewilderment, then repaired to Peebles in the utmost consternation.

But were flatly denied access to their son.

By eleven o'clock the following morning, Monday, a great crowd had assembled in the market-place. Besides the court and the townspeople, many hundreds had journeyed in from the outlying countryside, drawn like ravenous flies to the sweet vicariousness of seeing poor William hang.

Hard was the jostling in the ring around the scaffold, and loud the bickering, as the hanging buffs all jockeyed to better their vantage.

Here and there among the swaying crowd a thumbsucking toddler sat aloft on his father's shoulder.

And staggering was the stench of their rustic economy of personal hygiene.

Fifteen minutes before midday the Tolbooth gate flew open with an ominous clang. William emerged, blinking and purple-eyed in his delirium of sleep starvation, and was propelled without tenderness the twenty paces across the cobbles to the foot of the gallows. By the executioner, a redly beefy blacksmith named Pordage Lyall.

A great roar of approval rose up from the body of the crowd as William's bare feet, still raw from their flight from the King, plodded painfully up the dozen wooden steps to the platform. His shoulders hunched as in a shiver, his wrists were tightly bound against the base of his spine, and his young head, bowed in the dullness of misery, caused the fresh bright sunlight to glint yellow in the sheening wildness of his hair.

Yet the prepondering sentiments of the masses were:

'STRIP HIM NAKED!'

'YES, YES! HANG THE BOGGER BARE!'

'KILL HIM NOW, FAT LYALL! IT IS LONG GONE NOON.'

And, which would have wounded William most, had it penetrated his detached confusion:

'HEY, HEY, WILLIAM MORRAY, LET'S HAVE A SONG!'

'A SONG, INDEED, OH SHEPHERD BARD! LET'S HEAR A VERSE TO MARK THY PARTING!'

In fact the dread hour was still minutes away, and William's mother and father, simple old greyheads that they were, climbed up the steps in an agony of trembling, to exchange a few last words with their dear one.

William's right hand was freed, as a terminal privilege, and he shook each of them by the hand, kissed his mother's wrinkled brow, and yet, though it appeared from his expression that he was anxious to console them, his well of words had dried to dust, and his gaze was lost for focus.

Perceiving this, the old folks broke out in a discord of flagrant wailing. William's mother dropped to her knees on the gallows platform in a virulent incoherence of petitionary prayer, while his mild old father, wrung to an eloquence hitherto unknown in him, declaimed from the rail on the iniquities of a Justice that would bring a valuable and educated youth to the shame of a public execution for no more a crime than a boastful blunder, and on the unholy cruelty of any man, be he King or no, who would ordain it so with no leeway for intercession.

'And may the Almighty have mercy', he cried, tears streaming down his cheeks to the flowing of his silver beard, 'on the simple folk of such a land. For they are sailors all at sea, and *their Helmsman cares not where they sail*. GOD SAVE US ALL! Amen.'

'Amen!' came the fragmented echo from the crowd, whose worried frown and several sniffing exhibited the vacillation of its passion.

Only the courtiers remained unmoved. Mounted, for better viewing and speedier departure, they had gathered in a whinnying cluster before the entrance to the Guild Hall, a stone's throw upwind from the exudings of the rabble.

'What cold hard hearts these great folks have,' the locals softly muttered.

The Guild Hall bell, in slow and solemn depth, tolled noon.

'And where may his Majesty be?' complained the eye-darting Lady Annabelle Hamilton. 'There the hour strikes, yet he is nowhere to be seen.'

'Pray what is his Majesty's absence to you, Lady Annabelle?' murmured Lady Ann Gray, on a fidgeting palfrey beside her.

'It is to me, Lady Ann, that the execution may not proceed without his presence, and my inner person is ablaze with hunger.'

'But surely it is many a moon, is it not, Mistress Hamilton, since his Majesty's presence can have succoured the blazing of *your* inner hunger?'

'Forgive me, Mistress Gray, if I answer you not directly, but I am beside myself with commiseration at the pocks upon your tongue. His Majesty . . .'

'Ladies, ladies, I *pray* you!' hissed the Lord Chamberlain Hume, behind them on a brown-dappled mare. 'The King, rest assured, will appear forthwith, and would praise your patience. The which you will be most gracious to deserve.'

'But of course, my lord!' simpered Lady Ann, her animosity muzzled as if by magic. 'And is the King delayed by deeds of state, could it be?'

The sharp-featured earl warmed to the coy beauty of the deference paid him. Explaining:

'Not at all, Mistress Gray. His Majesty rides out hawking with Hunter of Polmood and my good Lord Mar. And as we see, is not returned. As is his privilege.'

'But of *course*, my lord!'

'But of *course*, as you so rightly say. And it may be that they have called at the Castle, for to escort her majesty hither. And young Mistress Elizabeth – Dame Polmood, I now should say. Though the change comes groaning on an old man's tongue.'

'Ah no, my lord. I think not.' Lady Annabelle swivelled on her well-covered rear, and in a rosy welter of ambiguous beaming declared:

'The Queen, my lord, has little stomach for a hanging. And so has gone a strolling by the Tweed . . .'

'With a basket,' chimed Lady Ann.

'To pick the bramble berries.'

'And Elizabeth . . .'

'Goes with her . . .'

'For company', butted Lady Ann in a determined rush, 'and to take instruction regarding the duties and transports of marriage.'

'Aha?' hummed the bludgeoned Hume. 'So say you? Um. Then possibly . . .'

It was now twenty past the appointed hour, and the crowd, like an untended rat bite, had begun to fester. Infants howled, hysterical women screamed and were smartly slapped, the odd bout of adolescent scrapping broke out, and here and there the occasional breakfast made a surprise return at the invitiation of the conspiring heat and foetor.

The tortured William, alone with the executioner on the gallows, could no longer stand unsupported, and had been propped against the rail with a beefy arm about his shoulders. Suddenly a shudder erupted from the boiling of his empty belly and exploded out of his mouth in a prolonged eruction that resounded across the square like the barking of a wounded seal. A meagre trickle of yellow slime dribbled out between his lips and down to foul his chin, his sight forsook him in a grotesqueness of rolling white eyeball, his ankles dissolved beneath him, and were it not for the blacksmith brawn that held him, he would certainly have fallen prone in the penultimate humiliation of a swoon.

'Hey, lad! *Hey*!' the hangman hissed. 'Ye cannot go a-fainting now, by the Lord. For ye would not wish old Lyall to get a beating. Would ye now? Eh? For neglecting of his duty. So come now, lad. We'll put the bag on ye, take courage to stand firm, and it soon will be over. Eh?'

William's body convulsed and barked again.

The solicitous executioner, holding the boy upright with his right arm, fastened about his neck, with the nimble fingers of a practised left hand, the nugatory blind of the black hood of death.

And urged:

'Fret not, my friend. Old Lyall will see ye right all right. No more shall ye feel . . .'

'THE KING!'

'HARK, HARK! THE KING APPROACHES!'

Sure enough, on the timbers of the old wooden bridge (out of sight behind the Guild Hall) there came a great cantering of hooves. Three horsemen swept into view and at dangerous speed cut a swathe through the scattering crowd.

Which nevertheless managed a hearty:

'GOD SAVE THE KING!'

'GOD SAVE OUR GOOD – '

'Not done? Not done?' breezed the good King, leaping from his steaming stallion in a chafing of leathers and a jangle of sabre and chain. A large hooded falcon on his left wrist flapped furiously at the ruffling impact of his Feet upon the cobbles, while on either side of his saddle pommel dangled a bloody brace of mountain hare. The hawking had been capital and King James was astride creation, as were his companions, Polmood and Mar, who looked on from where they remained mounted, their smouldering gaze a veil across the smugness of having excelled at that which men must do.

'Begging p-pardon, your M-majesty,' the hanging blacksmith stuttered. 'But . . .'

'Tut, fellow! Tut!' the King tutted. 'Have you no feeling for a jest? Mnnmmmm?'

So pent was the breath-held hush of the multitude that these quietly spoken Words carried throughout the market square and echoed back off the rough stone walls of the rambling grey buildings.

Fat Lyall swallowed in discomfort.

His Majesty removed his hunting cap and smoothed a long ginger straggle across his brow to behind his ear.

A mouse would have been embarrassed by the din of his scurrying.

The blacksmith lipped a phrase of clumsy exculpation.

King James clicked his tongue and impatiently ordered:

'No more delay, we *beg* you! For we have ridden far and ache for meat. The cord about the villain's neck, at once!'

The hangman nearly fell over his feet in haste to grab the

dangling noose and drape it over William's head. He pulled the knot tight, positioned the boy nicely in the centre of the platform, then moved to his station by the level to trigger the trapdoor release.

Anxiously he waited for the fatal Nod.

About the crowd odd pockets of premature culmination moaned.

The unseeing William drooped piteously where he stood, and remained upright thanks only to the choking tension of the rope beneath his chin.

Lyall yearned, but no Nod came.

Instead the King frowned pensively and said:

'Hold there a moment, hangman. Hold!'

The hangman held. All but his rivering perspiration.

'This fellow,' the King boomed, gesturing rhetorically to his subjects, 'traitor that he is, has yet behaved himself throughout with some degree of spirit. Has he not?'

Not a demurmur dared.

'Therefore shall he die not as the commonest felon. No!' his Majesty declaimed in an access of vibrance. Drawing the razor flash of his sabre and leaping lightly up the scaffold steps, he vowed:

'No, indeed! Rather shall he die by the hand of a King. Unrope the villain, you, and have him kneel.'

In frantic panic the burly Lyall complied. The hair that curled like a werewolf fleece between the fastenings of his black leather jerkin were slick with sweat, and his great horny hands palsied furiously as he ripped the noose from William's neck, moulded the catatonic youth to a decapitational kneel, and tore away the collar of his singlet, to render bare his long pale neck.

The King stepped into a chopping stance, his sabre gleaming high and his falcon fluttering irritably on his left wrist.

Across the crowd gasped a wave of further climax.

Like a woodman aligning his axe for the cut, King James touched the keenness of his blade against the nape of William's neck. Then raised it high once more and called:

'Rise up, rise up, Sir William Moray! We hereby create you a knight of the realm, and give you, and yours, the crown estates of Crookston and of Newby, to hold of us for – '

But his Majesty's 'ever in perpetuity' was engulfed in a pandemonium of ear-splitting passion.

'HURRAH FOR KING JAMES!' roared the crowd when it twigged.

'LONG LIVE OUR GRACIOUS KING!'

'SCOTLAND FOR EVER!'

'SCOTLAND AND KING JAMES!'

The furore spumed beyond control for several minutes, reverberating from the walls of the buildings nearby to the slopes of the circling hills behind. Hurled hats flew high in the air, wild huggings and kissing of promiscuous rejoicing swept across the population like a wind-fanned forest fire, and great abandon was unleashed upon the thousand bottles, flasks and jugs of liquor that had been brought to celebrate a death.

Meanwhile:

By the gallows-foot old William Moray the elder and his worthy dumpy spouse collapsed helpless in each other's arms, convulsed in a surfeit of weeping at once incredulous and joyful beyond bearing.

So that none but the executioner and the King were privy to the unexpected drama on the platform. For when James had laid his cold sword against William's skin, the boy's demented senses had perceived the first stoke in the agony of his beheading, and had blessed him accordingly with the natural mercy of a true dead faint. So, when the hangman freed his hands and uncovered his head, and the King desired him to rise, he neither answered nor even an eyelash flickered. James, suddenly fearful of having overplayed his jape, then threw himself upon the inert figure, and it was only through the most vigorous slapping of his face, blowing into his mouth and beating against his heart that the harrowed lad was at length restored to the semblances of the living.

And even then, so strongly was his fancy imbued with the certainty of his dissolution that it was several hours before he could be fully convinced that he was not adrift in a world of spirits and taunted by spiteful ghosts in human shape. When he did revive sufficiently to comprehend his real situation, and to appreciate the honours and estates conferred upon him by the King, he was seen to weep plentifully in token of his gratitude.

While by contrast, not a day had passed thereafter before

William (such was his character) was heard to impart the sage observation:

'That they who honour Truth are best rewarded in the end!'

His Majesty was elsewhere at the time, however, and thus not privileged to profit by Sir William's sagacity.

9

THE END OF THE SEASON

ROSAY RETURNS

The two weeks following the wedding were the happiest Elizabeth had ever known. And though it would be tedious to relate all the feasts, dances, carousing revels, tournaments and sundry other entertainments which prevailed in the town of Peebles and the Castle of Nidpath during the stay of the royal party, it should be borne in mind that they were so numerous as to be virtually continuous, that no mercy tempered the carefree ruthlessness with which the national exchequer was squeezed into making these celebrations the most lavish in the south of Scotland's history, and that Elizabeth shone through them all with the light bright joy of a newborn star still rising.

Her vanity, meeting no whisper of resistance during the continuing carnival of her nuptials, combined with her beauty and charm to blossom in a dignity of demeanour and discourse that, though considered perilously premature by caucus highborn ladies, was nevertheless acclaimed by all the gentlemen, and by the commoners in the town, as a living picture of womanly purity and perfection more consummate than any the world had painted hitherto.

And was this not the most sterling earnest that God was in His Heaven, Civilization was waxing strong, in the best of all possible Hands, and that Christianity would shortly wipe the Infidel scum off the face of the earth and ever after rule the globe in the bliss of the peace which passeth all understanding?

Such were the sentiments the halcyon days of that fortnight heard bandied constantly, across the groaning dinner table, along the grassy banks of the ambling Tweed, and into the magic gurgling privacy of innumerable crystal goblets.

All, in short, was much as many imagine the leafy glades and marble halls of Paradise must be, and, though no extravagance of lacy frippery could render the Lady Annabelle slender, nor no assault upon his liver expand the stature of my Lord James Douglas of Dalkeith by even the diameter of a grain of sand, still it was perceived, by those percipient, that all who were privileged to play a part in the festivities of those balmy summer days at Nidpath appeared at least as content as they ever had or ever would.

Everyone, that is, but the newly-wed Norman of Polmood.

Polmood had netted his lovely butterfly, yet the butterfly was not to be tamed and pressed! She talked with the Queen. She danced with the King. She laughed with the ladies and joked with the servants. And for Polmood? For him she reserved a unique prerogative: to lightly kiss his sacrificially upturned cheek twice daily – once in the freshly woken morning, and again in the dusty shadows of evening, before she retired to the inviolate maidenhood of her single chamber on the third storey.

So what had marriage changed?

The glowering husband could not see.

And worse!

Not only did Polmood's conjugal devotions go unenacted, but they went *seen to be unenacted*, by all the court. Elizabeth slept in solitude, on a level with the various single ladies, while Polmood couched two floors below in a dormitory with the single gentlemen. As Queen Margaret had contrived.

So Polmood durst not complain.

Yet what can be more poisonously galling for an ordinary man, whatever the strength of pride in his enormity of virile dimension, than to burn in the public knowledge that his wife's virginity remains intact?

And worse still:

The Friday following Sir William's preferment saw and heard the buzzing commotion that heralded the flamboyant return to court of the one man in all Scotland whom Polmood's churning jealousy could least have wished to see.

Alexander, Duke of Rothesay, more commonly known as Rosay, was younger brother to King James. His character has already been touched upon, when Donald of Lamington (while dicing on the Crawmelt green with the Earl of Hume, following the passionate outburst and withdrawal of the secretly distraught Sir John

Carmichael) had occasion to agree with his resistible friend, the sparrow-chested Sir Patrick Hepburn, that the self-same Alexander of Rothesay would be mad with jealousy at the prospect of the marriage of Elizabeth to Polmood, 'if he were not away a-mounting all the foolish young nannies in gay Paree'.

Rosay was now returned from just such activities in precisely that location (in company with his hulking buddy, and Duke of Hamilton, brother to the ample Lady Annabelle), and, sure enough, when he learned of Elizabeth's marriage, and saw how tantalizingly her womanhood had burgeoned in a slender span of months, the self-inflating bladder of his pique ballooned to pinch painfully against the swollen membrane of his inordinately preposterous ego.

'And tell me, sir,' said Rosay to Hamilton, 'do you think she'd have wed him had *I* been to hand?'

'Doubtless not, my lord,' came the sneer in the chuckling reply. 'For surely you would have found some means to disqualify the groom, or sabotage the bride.'

'You are cynical, sir.'

'Who is not, my lord?'

It was the morning of the Saturday, and the raking pair were strolling the winding mile between the Castle and the town. Normally they would have ridden, but their parts were all tender and aching from weeks in the saddle – from Paris to Calais, Dover to London, London to Edinburgh, and, only the previous day, from Edinburgh to Nidpath.

'Christ, but my erse is afire!' griped Hamilton, massaging the afflicted area, and deriving no mote of pleasure from the dry background chirping of a hundred happy crickets.

'So would the girl's erse be afire,' bragged Rosay, 'if I could but get her alone for a fly half-hour.'

'And where would you stand, my lord, if the King were to hear of it? For her place in his affections is secure, and all the world knows she is loved by the Queen.'

'Ferk them all!' grumbled Rosay, acknowledging the problem without humour and spitefully shattering a mud clod with the pointed toe of an elegant boot. He was short for a man of blue blood in those days – in bare feet he would have stood taller than Elizabeth by less than an inch – but the compensations of his elevated heels and high-crowned hats had grown into second nature, and his self-image was so bloated, his arrogant confidence in the height of his birth so profound, that he genuinely perceived those of his several dimensions that may touch a man's pride as exceeding their actual realities by a generously handsome fraction.

Likewise with his hair: brown but rapidly balding, and hence almost never on show. He never took part in a sporting event, outdoors was hatted constantly, and while in France he had taken to wig-wearing, so that even the silly young nannies he mounted would be lucky (or unlucky, depending on how they viewed it) to catch a pallid glimpse of his spreading pate. His eyes were dark and grasping, his nose prominent and thickly sensual, while the arrogant jut of his chin was accentuated by a spruce goatee beard of crinkly bristle in chocolate brown. It may assist in the estimation of his character if we remark that, whereas his brother, King James, was an indefatigable practitioner of the hoax wherein the nasty surprise turns out to be not true, the Duke of Rothesay would delight in nothing more than to present his poor Cinderella with her magic *pantouffle en vair*, in a flourish of utmost ostentation, and then slyly wait for her to discover the scorpion in its toe.

'And forby, my lord,' said the large, strong, but dissolutely indolent Malcolm, Duke of Hamilton, 'you have the pocks, have you not? Her Majesty . . .'

'It is *not* the pocks!' snapped Rosay. 'It is but a passing inflammation. And I'll thank you, sir, to keep your mouth closed on the matter.'

Hamilton sniggered. He was twenty-four, two years Rosay's junior, and though still conventionally handsome, with long straight hair once blond but now mousy at the roots, the classical regularity of his features was beginning to fade beneath the blubber of loose living and aristocratic lack of purpose. His birth and upbringing had left him cultivated, as far as cultivation then went, but never had he had to strive, lacking even the empire-building goad of inferior physique to drive him to some minor excellence, and he saw no point in any activity save feasting, toping, and the diminishing number of changes he might still ring on the themes of fornication.

'Very well, my lord,' he allowed with a shrug. 'So it is not the pocks. Yet there is many a towdie in France, I will wager, that soon will sorely burn for her inability to discriminate the distinction. And *I* shall thank *you*, my lord, to keep myself informed of any field that you have ploughed. That my own share may keep awhile from rusting!'

Rosay scowled a brooding wince as his new neurosis alighted screeching, like a great black carrion fowl, and sank its septic talons deep in the ghastly spectre of his imminent rotting. Lashing at the ogre with the irrationality of transmuted terror, he said:

'It is but a bauble, and will be long gone ere I run the girl to bed.'

'Elizabeth?'

'The *Lady* Elizabeth to you, if you please. Who else? It seems very like his Majesty had taken special pains to get the wench wed behind my back, think you not? The which being so . . .'

Now it so happened that morning that the Queen and her ladies had ridden the ten miles south-east to Traquair, to partake of a genteel luncheon with the Earl and Countess, and to admire the far-famed rose garden and make music in the afternoon. The King and his nobles being not so inclined, many meandering in the wooden mind-detachment that ever follows a prolonged alcoholic indulgence, it came about that the slopes of the hills and the banks of the Tweed in the vicinity of Nidpath were dotted with bilious barons in twos and threes, aimlessly mooching away the hours before their lunchtime tipple should sheath the claws of their self-induced gloom.

Aimless mooching, for Norman of Polmood, translated to a solitary sullen thrashing of the waters of the Tweed with a fisherman's rod and line. Having apprehended at breakfast that he must again survive the day without his lady wife, he had stomped away immediately the meal finished, for fear he might disgrace himself if called upon to talk. Almost the length of Peebles he had stalked in a muttering fury, before forcing on himself the ancient therapy of casting upstream in the pitting of his wits against the wiles of the darting trout. By eleven the rage of his thwarting had cooled to an evenly simmering savagery. He had three good fish in his basket, had thrown two babies back to the river, and was just swinging in to the bank his fourth goodly catch when he espied the two men coming towards him on the bridleway above.

One large and looming, like a bear.

The other short and slight, like a paunching weasel.

The Dukes of Hamilton and Rothesay, respectively.

In fact.

But it was under the misapprehension that the forms he descried belonged to Donald of Lamington and Sir Patrick Hepburn that Polmood curtailed his angling, dehooked his rod and secured his haul, and began a loping scramble up the steeply banked coppice of sycamore striplings, all pungent with the tingle of wet wood and green sap, that rose from the river to the bridleway.

Lamington and Hepburn were heading for the town, Polmood reasoned, and no doubt would be calling at a tavern there, for the slaking of their thirst. In which womanless company he, Polmood, would be pleased to join. Hepburn was a spineless worm, it was true, but Lamington was a stout enough fellow with whom to bend one's elbow, and . . .

Such were the lonely thoughts that thickened the furrows of Polmood's brow as he puffed up the wooded slope to intercept the walkers on the track. Imagine, then, the hollow depth of his dismay, and the resurgence of his impotent fury, when he heard:

Beginning with the nearing Duke of Hamilton's lip-lopping drawl:

'The *Lady* Elizabeth? My *lord*!' And since when did a lady wear swaddling clothes? She is – '

Polmood hurled himself face-flat on the ascending mud bank. Just in time to remain concealed, senses stunned and pulse galloping, he ripped off his bonnet, crushed it beneath his chest, and heard the Duke of Rothesay snap:

'She is a lady in tutties and towdie! Which are all that matter.'

'In these affairs!'

'And a ripely juicy one to boot, I'll warrant. As sweet a fig as ever I have sucked upon.'

'As sweet a fig as ever has sucked upon *you*, my lord, is surely what you mean. For the figure to be apt.'

'I care not a pig shit for *the* figure,' said Rosay in his cloying baritone, which sounded as if his Majesty's voice had been stripped of its muscle and coated in rancid syrup. 'I am drawn to one figure only, and that is the unclad body of the wench herself.'

'Of the *lady*, you surely must mean!'

'With her buds pressed firm against my breast, and her thighs astride my person.'

'Dear Lord, my lord! You are too modest by half.'

'Doubtless I am, sir. Yet I fain would know what aspect of my exceeding modesty it is that pains you so.'

'Why, my lord! You swear you care not a pig shit for *the* figure.'

'Yes?'

'But the figure you fashion, in the dumbshow you portray, is so pretty, my lord, and so exquisitely desirable, that here it has awoken my broozler from his slumbers. Look you upon him!'

'I *implore* you, sir,' said Rosay, whose wit fed only on the weary unsmiling humour of habitual cynicism, 'return your monster to his den. For while he is a fine wee fellow, I grant you, and beats the average by a nose, yet there are thousands could put him to shame without their so much as saluting.'

'Such as Polmood's?' the Duke of Hamilton sniggered nastily, as he rekennelled his straining diversion.

'Eh?'

'I mean, my lord, that I have heard it said, that Hunter of Polmood has the largest haft of any forester in the kingdom. And how the little wench – that is to say, *lady*! – Elizabeth is to accommodate it all is a mystery.'

'Fie, man!' exclaimed Rosay dismissively. 'Think you seriously that the old greybeard can still perform? Why, you have only to look at them together! She cares not a fig for him.'

'Nor a pig shit, my lord?'

'And that there has been no broozling afoot is as clear to the world as a pillar of fire on a moonless night. Why else do they sleep every night apart, and that at two floors' distance? Polmood, devil take the dullard's doltish scowl, and his filthy stinking breath, may hang full as long as his Majesty's stallion, yet I swear he never yet has saluted within an ell of the lady's cherry, and I wager he never will.'

'Unlike yourself, my lord?'

'Time will decide,' said Rosay, complacently immodest. 'But it is already clear she has an eye for myself. And who is there else among the gentlemen can talk to her of all she enjoys and admires: of embroidery, music, new fashions in dress, and the steps they dance abroad? Huh? When last did her elegant husband shower praise upon the sweetness of her luting? Or the care with which she chose the rose upon her hair to enhance the swimming azure of her eye? Or . . .'

'Pifflc, or piffle?' snorted Hamilton.

'Granted, sir. Granted absolutely! Yet such are the feathery fingers to nudge apart a maiden's legs.'

'Granted, my lord. Granted absolutely!'

'And so shall you see.'

'See what, my lord?'

'That Elizabeth's legs shall part for *me*.'

'Hmmmmm!' Hamilton hummed to a thoughtful pause and the two debauched young Dukes idled on. Slowly, dawdly, as befitted their natures and their saddle-sore members, they were now some twenty paces past where Polmood choked silently in his concealment.

Should he charge forth and carve the intending adulterer in several pieces?

But he had no sword with him.

Wring the puppies by thc neck and squeeze the world free of the plague of their existence?

But the Duke of Hamilton was first cousin to the King, and Rosay was his Majesty's own brother, and also his *next in line*! At least until Queen Margaret could produce an heir with the strength to survive its birth.

Polmood feared no man alive, and yet there was a sheepdog strain in his character, which made it impossible for him, even in the torment of the provocation he had chanced to overhear, to raise his arm in violence against his Sovereign's next-of-kin.

Accordingly, he continued to writhe where he lay, his jaw clenched so tight as to grate his few remaining teeth against his gums until they bled.

Nor was his ordeal yet over.

As:

'HEY THERE, MY LORDS!' came hallooing down from the slopes above the bridleway, in a breezy tenor voice.

The dallying Dukes stopped dead in their tracks.

'Who calls?' inquired Rosay of his companion. Irritably, for his own sight was short.

'It is the Earl of Mar, my lord,' drawled Hamilton. 'And the other, methinks, to judge by his gnomish magnitude, is the ludicrous Dalkeith.'

'Walking down to join us here?'

'It so would seem.'

'And you have about you, sir, have you not, your flask of eau-de-vie?'

'Indeed I have.'

'Then let us breach the spirit now, sir. Before our worthy fellows arrive with a thirst to drain it for us.'

'Let us drink by all means, my lord,' agreed Hamilton, rummaging for the flask beneath the mustard yellow of his beltless Parisian demi-gown. 'And will you do me the honour of accepting first swallow?'

Rosay would, it appeared.

THE DARK, THE FAIR, AND THE PLUMPLY MOUSY

'But does your husband *wish* to sleep with you, Elizabeth?' inquired the Lady Ann Gray in a murmur of sultry intimacy.

'I . . . suppose he must,' was Elizabeth's dreamy conjecture.

'Then why', demanded the Lady Annabelle Hamilton, 'does he not? Can he have the pocks, perhaps?'

'Your pardon, Lady Annabelle,' said Elizabeth tartly, 'but I fear I understand you not.'

'She means', explained Lady Ann, 'that, as Polmood sleeps never with you, nor ever spirits you away by day, it follows that he never yet has broozled you.'

'Y . . . e . . . s?'

'Well, Dame Polmood! I ask you!'

'Well, Mistress Gray!' returned Elizabeth. 'And *I* ask *you*!'

'Ask me what, pray?'

'Ask you why you are asking me!'

'As you what, pray?' crowed Lady Ann, with a chuckle of throaty merriment.

'She means, Elizabeth,' said Lady Annabelle, unsmiling and vicariously earnest, 'that it is plain as today that Polmood has not yet broozled you.'

'Indeed, Mistress Hamilton. So much, though I fail to see how it concerns yourself, has already been admitted. But what of it, I pray you?'

'Hark, hark,' mocked Lady Ann. 'The pretty maiden has a tongue!'

'My curiosity is aroused,' confided Lady Annabelle, 'and with it my concern for your own sweet happiness . . .'

'*Sweet* happiness!' jeered Lady Ann. 'Sweet *happiness*! Take warning, Elizabeth. She – '

'Requires no translation from yourself, Mistress Gray. Thank you *kindly*.'

'A thousand pardons, madam!' hammed Lady Ann, in the manner of the King. 'A thousand thousand!'

'Because, Elizabeth, it appears evident that as Polmood has wed you, and as you are youthful and not unpleasing to regard . . .'

'You are *too* kind, Mistress Hamilton.'

'It cannot be a million leagues from the man's mind that one day he may broozle his youthful and not unpleasing lady wife, as is his right.'

'Y . . . e . . . s.'

'And yet, it seems, his right goes unexercised?'

Elizabeth hummed distant assent.

'And it is this absence of exercise which, in the circumstances, we find so perplexing. Do we not, Mistress Gray?'

'Oh, indeed we do, Mistress Hamilton! In*deed* we do.'

'Another way of considering the matter, Elizabeth,' said Lady Annabelle in frowning kindness, 'is this. Are you absolutely sure that you husband is . . . a *normal man*? My meaning is . . .'

'Your meaning is extremely snide, Lady Annabelle!' Elizabeth sat up angrily. 'Of *course* my husband is a normal man! Of *course* he is. More so than most, I dare say.'

'You must forgive me, Elizabeth, if I seemed – '

'And the reason he does not sleep with me, and has not broozled me, though I am bound to say it strikes me as none of your concern, is that he is a kind and considerate gentleman, whereas I am extremely young and innocent still, and so desire to remain for a few months more. That is all.'

'Elizabeth . . .'

'And I trust, Lady Annabelle, that it will meet with your approval. For it is the truth.'

'Well spoken, Elizabeth!' Lady Ann clapped. 'For now you are a married woman, you must tolerate no foolish tittle from poor single maids such as we.'

Lady Annabelle pulled a moue at Lady Ann, clasped hands behind her head of wet mousy curls, and lay back upon the grass in a silent huff.

Elizabeth gently rubbed her shoulders to ensure that the skin had not begun to burn in the scorching heat, tuned a half-inquisitive ear to the shouts and laughter drifting across the water, then fell to meditative plucking of the giant daisies from the grass, and arranging them in rows between her toes.

Lady Ann looked across to the large-breasted but fleshing contours of Lady Annabelle's stretched-out nakedness. With her inner eye fixed upon the roving propensities of the King, she lit a private candle to the continuing lissom firmness of her own immaculate physique.

For now, with Elizabeth safely wed, who else was there to fear?

It was the Tuesday of the second week at Nidpath, and so unseasonably hot that the ladies had ridden out in the afternoon to cool their dress-hampered discomfort in the icy Tweed and bathe their shivering bodies in the steaming sunlight – all, that is, excepting Queen Margaret and the Lady Elinor Hume, for whom the time was uncongenial. The spot they had come to lay two miles west of Nidpath, directly south of the Edston Hill, on the north bank of a sharply curving elbow in the river. Known as the Virgins' Bower, the place was a natural suntrap and had been cultivated for bathing purposes a century earlier. The original jungle had been fought back from the water's edge, the bank levelled and scattered with flowers, and a protective half-moon of lilac, hawthorn and rose-hip grown up to screen the patch completely, from chilling breeze and prying gaze alike. Thus, though the soldiers and attendants who had accompanied the ladies hither were not fifty paces distant, at the further end of the dog-leg path through the thicket, their presence posed no obstacle to nudity.

Or freedom of expression.

The River Tweed at that elbow bend was wide, slow-moving and deep, and divided in its middle by a tiny island (about a powerful stone-throw from the bower) which flourished an ancient yew tree – twisted, gnarled, and leaning at an angle south, in tribute to the centuries of raging flood it had withstood. And it was there, to the miniature mossy shore beneath the shading yew, that the other ladies had swum out: those whose laughing cries had tickled Elizabeth's curiosity.

And drew her flitting thoughts.

Why were the stretch marks on Lady Katherine's belly so purply hideous?

Must they not have caused *great pain*?

Was it *always* painful?

'Elizabeth?' Lady Ann's intrusion lilted.

'Yes?' said she, annoyed.

'You say that Polmood is a kind and considerate gentleman.'

'And so he is!' Elizabeth rejoined sharply, combing fingers back through the dampness of her hair. 'Why else should I inform you so?'

'Why else, to be sure? Though I could not but wonder . . .'

'Yes, Mistress Gray? Wonder *what*?'

'Would a truly kind and considerate gentleman have absented himself without notice from the company last Saturday?'

'And not returned till late on Sunday evening?' chimed Lady Annabelle.

'Looking', Lady Ann continued, 'as though he had ridden a thousand miles and fought ten wars in the time between!'

'And managing barely a grudging smile for *you*, Elizabeth. For you, his *wife*! And a smile, I swear, that never knew his heart nor touched his eye. That was strange, was it not?'

'Indeed, Mistress Hamilton, it was surely not strange at all!' But Elizabeth, ever since the stormy silence of Polmood's return on the Sunday, had been troubled by this very reflection.

'Not strange! My dear . . .'

'Not strange in the least, madam. My husband was called away suddenly.'

'Why so, pray?'

'By the illness of his housekeeper, at Polmood. Who has served him many years.'

Lady Ann sat up and daintily flexed her arms, thus peaking her notable bosom. With studied nonchalance she said:

'And you heard this, Elizabeth, from the messenger who brought the news? Did you not?'

Elizabeth's eyes narrowed as she perfected the alignment of her daisies.

'Aaaaah!' trilled Lady Annabelle. 'You heard it not from the messenger, whom no-one, it seems, did espy? But from Polmood himself, upon his return?'

This was so.

But:

Elizabeth, being at once a woman and not long out of infancy, had still a brimming arsenal of easy tears to drown aggression from without, and a salvo streamed to aid her sob:

'I *do* wish, Lady Annabelle, that you would not *torment* me, with such *horrid* ... imputations. My husband is a good and *honest* man. He *never* would – '

'Of course, Elizabeth. Of course Polmood is an honest man,' Lady Ann purred reassuringly, not anxious to answer to Queen Margaret for corrupting Elizabeth's faith in her husband. 'And Lady Annabelle means no harm – it is but an ache of simple envy that disturbs her. Am I right, Mistress Hamilton?'

Lady Annabelle heaved upright, completing a sitting semi-circle of unclad nubility, and frowning above her doubling chin returned:

'Envy, Mistress Gray? *Envy*! I confess I am at a loss to follow your discourse. For I know nothing of envy. And certainly there is nothing that I do envy Elizabeth.'

'She means, Elizabeth, that while she admires your determination to preserve your ... *unsullied purity*, a quality that neither she not I shall ever covet more, God willing, yet would she give much to follow your footsteps down the aisle – '

'That would I *not*!' scoffed Lady Annabelle.

Elizabeth's tears were miraculously dammed by her earthquaking curiosity. 'What mean you, Lady Ann?' she asked.

Lady Ann shook the dry-curling ringlets of her raven mane, flashed a treacherous smirk at Lady Annabelle, then leant confidingly towards Elizabeth and whispered:

'Lady Annabelle has taken a lover!'

'Oh!' Elizabeth, sitting between her two seniors, knees hugged primly against her breast, gazed at Lady Ann in disappointment. What, in Heaven's name, was so gossipworthy about Lady Annabelle taking a lover?

'A lover whom she thought merely to groom as a boon to

himself, and as a service to the court. But who since has proved such a comely boy as to *steal her heart away*!'

'Is this so, Lady Annabelle?' Elizabeth inquired.

Lady Annabelle's long lashes fluttered. She avoided Elizabeth's eager gaze, massaged with the palms of her hands the wide dark points of her pendulous breasts, and helplessly blushed. Yes, on the smooth pink curve of her plumply pretty cheek, the Lady Annabelle Hamilton did definitely *blush*!

Elizabeth was shocked.

'Hoo, hoo, hoo!' wafted from where the other ladies had stirred from their mossy island haven and begun splashing in the river once more.

'Who is it that calls?' asked Lady Annabelle, shading her eyes and peering diversely at the balneal frolic across the water.

But Lady Ann was mooded not to spare her blushes. Saying:

'You see, Elizabeth? How piteous we poor women are!'

'How so?'

'For there you have Lady Annabelle, who thought to while a clutch of days in the arms of a stripling youth, and mould him to her whim – a trivial dalliance it was to be – but what should happen?'

'I know not, Lady Ann. What *should* happen?'

'Now! Now she is fallen so besotted with the lad that all her dowry would she cast away if he could but kneel with her at the altar. And yet, alas, it *may not be*!'

'May not be!' Elizabeth gasped. How could Life wreak circumstance so fiendishly unfair? 'Why ever not?'

'Because she is highborn!' crowed Lady Ann. 'And he is low. So never may they marry. *Never.*'

'Never?' echoed Elizabeth, in undertone horrified wonder. Then, her heart moved to righteous compassion by the mask of miserable longing into which Lady Annabelle's earthy lewdity had crumpled, she impeached:

'Lady Ann! How heartless you are, to gloat so over another's misfortune. Have you no shame?'

'No less than she,' said Lady Ann with a careless, insinuous gesture.

'Take heart, Lady Annabelle,' Elizabeth urged. 'And all may yet be well. For nothing is impossible when one is *in love*.'

The wisting one sniffed with much feeling.

'Come along IN, ladies!' a cackling soprano screeched across from the island. 'The water is WARM!'

'And how, Elizabeth,' asked Lady Ann, sweetly silky, 'should *you* know?'

'And how should *I* know what?'

'That nothing is impossible with one is *in love*?'

'And why should *I* not?'

'For when, may one ask, have ever *you* been in love?'

'I? Been in love? Of course I have!' cried Elizabeth. 'And *am* in love, indeed!'

'Indeed? And with whom, pray?'

'With my husband, of course. With my Lord Polmood.'

'Ah!' said Lady Ann eloquently.

'But if you *love* Polmood, Elizabeth,' said Lady Annabelle, perked by this savoury drift, 'then why, in the name of all that is pleasurable, do you wish him not *to broozle you*?'

Elizabeth's gaze fell.

Lady Ann grinned.

'Eh?' Lady Annabelle insisted.

Elizabeth's lips parted for a doubtful moment, before saying:

'Is it really . . . so wonderful?'

'Is *what* so wonderful?' Lady Ann.

'Broozling.'

'Broozling!' Lady Annabelle.

'*Being* broozled, I mean.'

'Ah!'

'Well, Elizabeth,' said Lady Annabelle. 'Let us fashion the question in the following form. Imagine the most delicious sensation you have ever experienced.'

'Yes?'

'What is it?'

'I . . . to have another scratch my back at night before I sleep, when sometimes it does tickle me nigh to distraction!'

'Then multiply that pleasure a hundred times, and there you have the sweet delight that being broozled brings.'

'Indeed?' But Elizabeth's mind was less sceptical than her guarded voice.

'Indeed!' concurred Lady Ann.

'But with the broozler of one's choice, as we hardly need add,' Lady Annabelle added.

'Performed with forceful tenderness.'

'And brutal skill.'

'Not to mention repeated vigour.'

'And in any case,' inquired Lady Annabelle, with a wave of languid finality, 'what else is there?'

'Exactly!' affirmed Lady Ann. 'What else?'

Elizabeth forbore to presume. After a brief lull of divagating ponder she asked:

'And the lowborn boy that broozles you, Lady Annabelle? Is it permissible to know his name?'

Lady Annabelle blushed again. Furiously.

'Come, come, Mistress Hamilton!' Lady Ann cajoled. 'He is no secret! Is he?'

Flustered silence.

Lady Ann dispelled it with:

'The Lady Annabelle Hamilton is privileged to inform you, Dame Polmood, that the newfound lord of all her heart, and person, is none other than the King's own youthful favourite: Sir William Moray, Laird of Crookston and Newby!'

'Sir William Moray?' Elizabeth was astonished. 'But he has barely left his cradle!' And surely was no more, she did not add, than an arrogant bundle of bumptious pretension.

'I shall thank you, Dame Polmood, to *mind your language*! As Sir William is the most ardent and gifted of lovers that ever I have known.'

'*Ever?*' quipped Lady Ann.

'Perhaps with One Exception.'

Elizabeth, repelled and fascinated, asked: 'And in what aspect does he so excel?'

'He worships my person so devoutly . . .'

'And so frequently!'

'Thank you kindly, Mistress Gray, for your interruption, the which, this once, is pertinent to the hilt. So frequently and so devoutly does Sir William pay his homage to my charms that by morning I am quite bemused, and feel I have spent a thousand years in Paradise.' Flushed with vehement loyalty, Lady Annabelle glowered at her companions – the one incredulous, the other impishly taunting.

Who said:

'And is the craftsman fitly tooled, that executes his task so well?'

'As it may appease your prurience, Mistress Gray, Sir William is quite consummately equipped.'

'Importing?'

'My meaning is: that when he is at rest he is quaintly trim, like a cherub. Yet when he salutes he is lavish – indeed, cornucopian! – as ever a lady could wish for. And beautiful to behold.'

'And to hold! Shall you say?'

'You must forgive the Mistress Gray her tongue, Elizabeth. It is a blight has troubled her from birth.'

'And . . .'

'Yes, Elizabeth?' wheedled Lady Ann. 'Hold not back. You have but to inquire, and the Mistress Hamilton will gladly requite you. Will you not, Mistress Hamilton?'

'I may.'

Elizabeth was normally the very epitome of demure discretion, yet hovering over her now was the shadow of a brooding ignorance that was quite unbearable. So, tracing a tear trail down her cheek with a tentative fingernail, she blurted:

'I wondered merely, Lady Annabelle, with Sir William being lowborn and all if you do allow him to lay his body atop your person.' White scarlet her embarrassment burned.

Then a breath of silence, until:

'Hooo, hooo, *hooo*!' howled Lady Ann, helpless in a sprawl of breast-heaving mirth. 'Atop her person? Hooo, *hooo*!'

'Atop my person?' Lady Annabelle marvelled, her redding cheeks betraying the indignant boiling of her blood.

'I meant not to pry, Lady Annabelle,' Elizabeth mumbled.

'Pry, madam? Huh! And as you inquire, so I will inform. That yes, Sir William does indeed lay him down atop my person. When it pleases me, and, more importantly, when it also pleases him.'

'Hooo, hooo . . .'

'Shut your maw, Lady Gray, I implore you. And highly pleasing it is too, Elizabeth. Profoundly gratifying. But since you ask, and because I feel the burden of instruction heavy atop me, I must relate to you that being broozled by Sir William is never more ecstatically fulfilling than when it is done *like this*!' Lady Annabelle rolled out of her squat and into a practised posture of blatant bucking lewdity.

'Lady *Annabelle*!' Elizabeth screamed, stricken with nausea as the gaping cleft bulge of the other's pelted gender protruded aggressively between her contorted thighs.

Lady Ann hooed on.

'What troubles you, Elizabeth?' asked Lady Annabelle, jouncing with the utmost provocation and looking round at Elizabeth with the bulbous eyes of a ruminating cow. 'You surely are not offended?'

'I . . . but not *people*!' wailed Elizabeth.

'Eh?'

'Surely it cannot be that *people* broozle so? In that . . . manner?'

Now it was Lady Annabelle's turn to collapse in a heapy flop of laughter on the grass. 'Not *people*?' she gurgled. 'Not *people*! Oh my . . .'

Elizabeth, spirited back to the brink of weepy misery, sucked hard on her thumb to quell the trembling of her chin.

'And why not people, Elizabeth?' asked Lady Ann, crawling up to the younger girl and draping a lithe arm around her in a squeeze of sisterly comfort. 'And Kings and Queens atop! Mm? Is pleasure ever wrong?'

Elizabeth sniffled.

'And you should know that Polmood will in due course broozle you just so . . .'

'And right soon too!' confirmed Lady Annabelle. 'If he truly is a *normal man*.'

'And so would the Duke of Rothesay have you,' purred Lady Ann, cradling Elizabeth's perturbed silky head to the warm yielding comfort of her own opulent bosom. 'In the winking of an eye! If you but dropped your guard.'

'No!' Elizabeth's breast-muffled voice protested. 'My Lord Rosay is a honourable man!'

'Honourable as a squirting tom-cat!' piped Lady Annabelle.

'Certainly, Elizabeth, Rosay will woo you handsomely, if you but let him.'

'And has his eye upon you.'

'Upon *me*?' But to what end?'

'To *your* end, Dame Polmood!' Lady Annabelle exulted.

'First he will prate to you of your skill on the lute, of the fashions of Paris . . .'

'Of the delicate ease of your graceful dancing!'

'But soon', warned Lady Ann, in a soft seductive murmur, 'he will be nuzzling in your neck. Like so. Then toying with your tutties. Thus. Till they rise up and grow hard with pleasure. Like so. There! Feel you no pleasure now?'

Elizabeth did, but *why* should the Lady Ann be kissing her so and stroking about her breast? Was it not wrong? Unnatural! Then why did she find it so agreeable, soothing, like a friendly tickle on an itchy shoulder? And the perfume of the dark one's glowing body: not heavy and sourly musk, as she might have imagined, but light and sweetly evocative, like the scent of a freshly picked apple. It was all . . .

'And then!' Lady Ann exclaimed, her wild eyes rolling. 'Then, Elizabeth, before you know it the honourable Rosay will have you laid upon your back. Like so!'

'No! I pray . . .'

'Nnnnnnnuh!' the raven beauty growled, holding Elizabeth's struggling head against the giving down of the daisied grass, pressing her mouth hard upon the protesting tightness of the young one's novice lips, and stabbing with a knowing tongue against their prim refusal.

Elizabeth, panicked by this swoop from mild caress to overt arousal, lashed out with her arms and scraped with her fingernails at Lady Ann's rippling back.

But the older girl was stronger, and pinned her down.

And Lady Annabelle rolled across the grass in a heavy twist, like a circus seal, anchoring the broad weight of her body across Elizabeth's flailing legs, and saying:

'And should you answer my Lord Rosay with such mettle, Elizabeth, it will only please him the more. He will take it, in the infinity of his vanity, as proof of your desire for his ministrations. He will paw with all your privacies. Like this. And call you his 'Pretty Kitty! Pretty Kitty!', and all the while will creep his little mole toward your tussock, to burrow through your treasure. Like . . .'

'HELP ME!' Elizabeth screamed, ripping her mouth free from Lady Ann's duress. Her eyes an unseeing frenzy of tears, sunlight,

174

and dangling locks of tormenting hair, her whole body knotting and retching with revulsion, she snatched a further breath for:

'PLEASE . . .'

But proselytizing duress descended again, in the form of a gagging palm.

'WHAT GIVES ASHORE?' a scandal-cocked bather called out from the island. 'Can there be RAVISHMENT abroad?'

Then a billow of fruity giggle.

But before the inquiry could be answered it was blown to oblivion by a gust of alarum.

As:

Two brassy bugles blew long and loud on the far side of the screening crescent thicket.

And attendant voices cried:

'HIS MAJESTY, KING JAMES!'

'GOD SAVE THE KING!'

Ladies Ann and Annabelle broke off their baiting and looked up in puzzled disquiet.

The King? Here? But why?

Elizabeth, feeling the shift of their oppressive weight, tore from under them and leapt to her feet. Gripped by vengeful humiliation, following her molestation, and by affright of being caught in daylight deshabille by the approaching King, she yet managed to stamp a fillip to her wrath, and scold:

'Ladies, you are *cruel*. Most cruel! It is not for me to say that you are *evil*, but I dare say it may be many a day before her majesty will forgive you this.'

The scolded ones had no reply.

Elizabeth cast about in indecision, then rushed in a jitter of gooseflesh to the jumbled wealth of colour and frill where the ladies' dresses lay piled in the shade of a hawthorn tree, beside the mouth of the dog-leg path.

'Oh, how *vexing*!' she muttered, her own clothes being not to hand.

Down the path came his Majesty's chinking chain, and the brushing of his sword against the bushes.

Elizabeth turned again, dashed in a flash of sylphine limb the fifteen paces to the river's edge, hastily dived in and struck out for the island.

'What ails Elizabeth?' Lady Annabelle wondered. For segregated bathing was only just peeping into vogue, and the shame of nudity among one's peers was barely in its infancy.

Lady Ann shrugged. 'It is doubtless ourselves she flees at root,' she opined. 'And not his Majesty.'

'And what of us, Mistress Gray? Shall we too follow England in modesty, and drape ourselves in water?'

'You, Mistress Hamilton, may act as you wish. For my own part I should deem it treason to nurture secrets from his Majesty.' Lady Ann yawned, and rolled over on her front, to face the coming King.

Lady Annabelle, seldom outflaunted, did likewise.

'Ah, ladies!' boomed King James as he burst upon the scene. 'We had thought our announcement should allow you time to array yourselves as best you might wish to receive us. But now it appears we are o'erhasty in our arrival, we do entreat you: cry out freely if you wish us to withdraw.' He beamed upon the buxom recumbents a feasting gaze of Proprietorial pride.

Which Lady Ann returned with a spritely gleam of pleasure in the gallant dash he cut, with his long red hair flowing free beneath his trophy turban, the long cool sleeves of his crimson silk chemise, and the belling legs of his green pantaloons. Her eye briefly dwelling on the sweat-trapping bite of his chain against the red fabric about his waist, she said:

'It is no matter, my Lord. Although, so please you, we shall not rise.'

James chuckled at the cheeky innuendo. 'So be it. So be it. And now, we warrant, you hazard at our purpose?'

'My Lord?'

'It is to inform you that today we dine early, as we have arranged entertainment for the evening, the which, if this fine weather holds, it will be most pleasant to stage upon the slope below the Castle. What say you to that, Lady Annabelle?'

'I say, my Lord, that it sounds a most splended notion.'

'And may we inquire, my Lord,' Lady Ann inquired, 'what content the entertainment shall have?'

'Indeed you may, Mistress Gray! Ha! And we shall have music, and we shall have song. And we shall have merriment all the night long! A cunning rhyme, no? Well, no . . .'

'Most wily, my – '

'Matter. No matter. And we shall have Sir William Moray singing ballads he wagers none shall have heard before: so brash the confidence of youth! In particular, he finally has been prevailed upon to regale us with the ancient ballad of *The Herone*, which once he did mention but since has been surpassing reluctant to recite. And Curry shall harp, Elizabeth tinkle upon the lute, and all shall drink wine, and the night shall be fine!' he exclaimed, his aesthetics overcome by sheer exuberance.

'And how, my Lord,' Lady Annabelle asked, thoughtfully, 'did you at length prevail upon Sir William to perform?'

'Aha! And how think you?'

'I know not, my Lord.'

'Well,' said James, smugly grinning. 'It is no secret. That we did play upon his greed to learn the art of the mounted falcon. The which we have been imparting to him all this fiery day, indeed. HAVE WE NOT, SIR WILLIAM?' he called suddenly, to the path. 'STEP FORTH, SIR!'

'Sire, I *cannot*!' Sir William's voice muffled through the rose thorns. 'Not if the ladies are *bathing*!'

'It is no matter, lad,' his Majesty breezed. 'The ladies care not – do you now, ladies? No. They care not. Therefore step out, bow to them, and be a man.'

No response.

'SIR, we do COMMAND you!' roared the King. 'Forgive the boy his blushes, ladies,' he added. 'He is yet diffident in the exercise of his station.'

Lady Ann looked a shade pale, and her smitten heart was pounding beneath a heavy weight of dread.

Sir William shuffled blinking from the thicket, uneasy in the rustling splendour of his knightly silks: purple and cream, in contrast to the green and crimson of the King.

And what the ladies saw, while the King did not, when the newcomer's eyes had narrowed against the dazzle and ogled wildly over their reposeful nakedness, caused a spasm of jubilant mirth to the one, and to the other?

The sickening first slide down the long, painful pit to despair.

For it was harshly clear, from the magnetized enlargement of Sir

William's glazed pupils, that he had fallen crazily, hopelessly, head-over-heels in love.

With Lady Ann.

THE HERONE

Neidpath Castle (as it now is spelt), the property of Lord Wemyss' Trust, unlike most of the other medieval tower houses of the Tweed Valley, still stands today (and can be visited by the public) where it has withstood the changing fortunes that the elements and the hands of men have wrought upon it since its stolid life began, probably in the early fourteenth century. The following is extracted from a pamphlet published by Lord Wemyss' Trust, to edify the visitor's exploration of the Castle:

The Castle is an L-shaped tower rising from a rocky outcrop eighty feet above the left bank of the River Tweed one mile west of Peebles. It stands at the west end of a courtyard enclosed on the north by a much reduced curtain wall, on the east by the main gateway bearing the family crest of the Hays of Yester, and on the south by a modern cottage built on the ruins of domestic buildings once adjoining the Castle. The Castle wall rises some sixty feet above the courtyard to the corners of the main block. The slated roof rises another twelve feet from the wall-top to a north-south ridge. The attic apartments were once lighted by dormers in the roof. The original chimneys rose through the north wall of the main block.

The walls consist of whinstone rubble, an igneous stone of peculiar hardness bound with exceptionally tenacious lime mortar, with sparsely used yellow sandstone dressings. They have an average thickness of ten feet but thicken to twelve feet in the east wall plinth, which continues partially around the north and south walls. A shaft to serve the garderobes (latrines) exists in the remaining portion of the south wall of the west wing, and the garderobes themselves may be seen in the wall of the pit prison and the room directly above it. Spiral stairs rise in the south west corner of the main block from ground floor to cap house, and in the north west corner from the great hall (first floor) to the cap house.

The present arrangement provides six storeys in the main block, the topmost being without flooring, and formerly provided the same number in the west wing where only the lower two still survive intact. The original architecture provided the main block with three vaults, one above the other, of which the upper and the lower were divided by intermediate timber floors. The west wing had the same number of main vaults, with an additional one over the ground floor prison.

Such then was the formidable towering structure the courtiers gaily left behind them, after dinner on that unusually warm evening in the late summer of 1506, when, in flamboyantly hosed twos and threes, and trippingly petticoated threes and fours, they jibed and jested down the gorse-dotted many-greened slope from the west wall of the Castle to the mingling silver reflections and cloudy brown troubles of the purling waters beneath.

There was a natural amphitheatre where the river suddenly curls from north to east, and there they gathered and seated comfortably on convenient ridges of soft dry turf, ringed in a sheltered gallery the shape of half an oval, facing down to where the lush green flatness of the riverbank provided the perfect open stage.

And when King James and Queen Margaret had arrived, affectionately Arm-in-arm as never for many a month, the invisible curtain lifted and the entertainments began.

Old Curry harped and ballads sang.

The company politely applauded.

He told lewd tales, and mimed incorrigible antics.

Thus earning the shibboleth plaudit of cynical laughter.

He mimicked barbed lampoons on the innate traits and dispositional propensities of *certain persons present*! Most notably not sparing the thunderous glowering and lumbering fidgets to which Polmood, in his sullen solitude, had lately been given.

Which won him the howling delight of the unshied many, together with the fuming ire of the excoriated few. Most notably Polmood.

Then Elizabeth sang some sweet refrains, to her own accomplished luting.

And was engagingly embarrassed by the tumultuous applause of the admiring majority.

Among them his Majesty, who next was required down to join Elizabeth and sing with her, in harmonious duet, some poignant verses, composed in the ever-lost ardour and leisure of his Younger Days, on the rending themes of Love.

Whose rapturous reception can well be imagined.

But there is nothing more attractive, from a distance, than the wholly novel, which is why, although the renditions of the clown, the King, and the beauteous songstress went heartily acclaimed, the burden of the evening's anticipation rested upon the squirming shoulders of the metamorphosed Sir William Moray. In the few days since being installed in the court according to his new title, all suitably robed and plumed, at the Crown's expense, he had frequently astonished the courtiers, and plunged not a few out of countenance, by the ready versatility of his bluntly incisive remarks.

Which were, along with his poetic pretensions and literate attainments, the essence of his appeal to the King.

Was it surprising, therefore, that behind the expectant tingle that awaited his debut recital, there festered odd pustules of poisonous hope? That the cocky young upstart should crack beneath the strain of his performance, and be obliged to slink cringing from the site of his audacity.

Much of this Sir William felt, and when at length King James called him down, averring that the time was high for him to recompense the company for their courteous patience, the young man blushed like a beetroot ablaze, gripped with the fury of helpless disinclination on the long silken liripoop that trailed over his shoulder from the brooch on his velvet chaperon, and protested that he was not fit. That his powers were too lowly by leagues to amuse for one moment any gallery of such grandeur and discrimination.

But his Majesty was not to be thwarted, reminding Sir William in tones of jocularity and severity interlaced, of their pact to swap songs for the lore of the falcon.

Sir William replied, close to yapping desperation, that though it was true he had promised to recite to his Majesty the ballad of *The Herone*, in exchange for his initiation into falconry, there was yet no clause in the bargain to say that he must perform to a vast congregation.

His Majesty scoffed.

The pustules clamoured.

Then Queen Margaret laid the ultimate straw upon the tortured hump of Sir William's resistance, by confiding that he had it in his power to confer an inestimable boon *upon her personally*! If he would but be so good as to nourish their assembled ears with *just one* choice morsel from his treasure store of song.

'*The Herone*!' decreed the King.

'*THE HERONE*!' chorused all, their blood fully as up for the poor boy's ballad as it had been a week before for the stretching of his neck.

180

Hence *The Herone* it had to be, despite its overwhelming unsuitedness to the occasion, the embarrassment of which will shortly unfold.

Knees melting, Sir William arose from Lady Annabelle's vainly adoring side, minced his way among the cheering bodies, down to where Elizabeth and the King held the stage, and wordlessly borrowed the lady's pearl-embossed rosewood lute – a Gift commissioned three years before from a refugee Italian artisan.

Elizabeth and his Majesty, warmly clapping, withdrew to the side and sat down.

Sir William hugged the lute to his heaving breast and tried its strings with a stroking chord. As the unseen ringdoves wooed themselves to sleep in the trees across the tinkling river, he threw back his head and chanted in a wild eerie voice, as if entranced, to the gloaming summer sky:

> Leash the hound on the tasselled moor!
>> Green grows the birch in the coomb so mellow!
> Strew the thyme in the greenwood bower;
>> For the dew falls sweet in the moonbeam yellow!

> For our good King's to the greenwood gone,
> And bonny Queen Jeanie lies left on her own,
> And deep might she sigh for she knows full well
> He sleeps *on his own* in the greenwood dell!
> Alack and alu! For our good King!
> He sleeps on the fog and he drinks from the spring!
> And no lord with him, to be his guide,
> But a bonny young page to lie by his side:
> And oh! That page's waist is slim,
> And his eye would make the day look dim.
> And oh! His breast is round and fair,
> And the demon lurks in his raven hair
> That curls above his brow so sweet
> And his ivory neck so pale and neat.
> Yet must he sleep all *alone* on the ling!
> Alack and alu, for our good King!
> And well Queen Jeanie may moan and sigh,
> For *she* sleeps alone, and the days fly by.
> The croaking crane cries o'er the flood,
> The capercailzie clucks in the wood;

The ringdove sings her song in the firs
And ever the moorcock bickers and burrs;
And aye the burden of their song:
'What ails our King: he lies so long?'

Go hunt the cuckoo another mile,
It's never her thieving red-eyed guile,
Nor never the white swan, lithe as the morn,
Nor the wounded deer with her broken horn:
And neither the hunt not the mountain scene
That has taken our King so far from his Queen;
Nor the twilight chill, nor the dawning dew:
As he goes for to capture the *Herone* blue.
The *Herone* with whom no bird can compare:
Her neck so tapered, so tall and fair!
Her breast so soft, and her eye so *gray*
Have stolen our good King's heart away.
And the *Herone* flew east; the *Herone* flew west,
The *Herone* flew to the fair forest!
And there she spied a goodly bower
That was all clad o'er with the lily flower:
And in that bower there was a bed
With silken sheets and wild down spread;
And in this bed there lay a knight
Whose ...

'HOLD OFF THERE, SIR!' the King suddenly roared, jumping up in erupting rage. 'And desist forthwith, as your song *offends*.' He had for some time been gesturing and balefully grimacing at his errant prodigy, but to no avail, the prodigious eyes being bent on the vacancy where Lady Ann had sat, between the Dukes of Rosay and Hamilton, until both the transparency of the allegory and the intensity of Sir William's doting eyes upon her as he sang became too much. After the line that sang of the roundness of the page's breast, perceiving that none present were to be distracted by her flippant asides, she had risen up in a haughty bustle, announced pointedly that the allusions of the ballad were overly parabolic and obscure for her taste, and flounced off downstream on a solitary saunter. Patting the midges from her raven curls and humming a raucous lullaby.

'Your pardon, Sire,' Sir William appeased, his complexion paling before the flush of his Majesty's dander, and his apprehension foaming, as it struck him only now that the ringing devotion of his declaiming to Lady Ann *in particular* might be construed as intent to underscore the *innuendo* in the tale.

Which had indeed been composed on just the theme of his Majesty's amatory digressions, had it not?

Sir William knew well that it had, and if his knees were melting when he began they were now ripe to pour him in a jibbering puddle on the riverbank where he stammered:

'So p-please your Majesty, there is no offence . . .'

'There is *much* offence, sir! And sore shall you regret it.' A challenging Eye cast about the company.

Who, for the most part, were silently absorbed in the fading hues of the sunset and the industrious plucking of blades of grass from the turf whereon they sat.

Only Queen Margaret dared the Eye. Saying:

'I do pray, my Lord, that you allow Sir William to continue his song.'

'It is not decent, madam!' growled the King. 'Not fit for the ears of a lady.'

'Once, my Lord, I do recall, your Majesty said that there is nothing indecent but thinking so makes it.'

'Importing, madam?'

'Why, my Lord? My meaning is that to *me*, and hence, you may be sure, to my ladies, there is nothing indecent in the song. Indeed, it ranks with the sweetest and most inoffensive of songs that ever I have heard. Does it not, ladies?'

The ladies murmured invisible solidarity.

Queen Margaret continued her plea:

'The melody is wild, it is true. But sublimely so. And ravishing to the ear. While the tale is doubtless a fable of the utmost morality, of the triumph of virtue and truth over weakness and wandering, whose conclusion we must surely hear, if best we are to profit by its precept.'

The King sniffed darkly at his Queen.

Who added with an eye-fluttering smile, full of homely dignity and righteous estrangement:

'So I, for once, *beseech* your Majesty. That our young friend may, for the edification of my ladies and myself, be permitted to go on.'

His Majesty took a breath that would refloat a stranded galleon. 'You, sir!'

'Sire?' gasped the hapless Sir William.

'You shall continue your tale, for her Majesty's pleasure. Though with caution, we do counsel you.'

'Shire,' Sir William garbled, 'if I have been so foolish . . .'

'Sir, we do COMMAND you! You will commence where you left off.'

'Sire, I . . . fear I cannot.'

'*Cannot?*'

'My memory fails me, Sire. I cannot recall . . .'

'"And in this bed there lay a knight",' Old Curry chirped from the sidelines where he crouched, a mildly vindictive leer at home on his flappy lips. 'Was the line where he stopped. "There lay a knight, whose". "Whose" was the final word, Sire.'

'Very fine, Curry. Our gratitude is boundless.'

'Your Majesty is *too* . . .'

'Though times there are, sir, when we wonder if your memory is entirely human.'

As the dread word 'witch' sat silently astride the King's remark, so the redoubtable clown subsided and held his peace.

His Majesty nodded curtly to Sir William, then sat stiffly beside Elizabeth.

Sir William retched and swallowed several times, and proceeded to sing himself through the second-most harrowing experience of his life:

> The *Herone* flew east; the *Herone* flew west,
> The *Herone* flew to the fair forest!
> And there she spied a goodly bower
> That was all clad o'er with the lily flower:
> And in that bower there was a bed
> With silken sheets and wild down spread;
> And in this bed there lay a knight
> Whose wounds did bleed both day and night;
> And by the bed, in white arrayed,
> There sat a loyal and patient maid,
> With silver needle and silken thread,
> Who stemmed his wounds whene'er they bled.
> And the *Herone* she flapped her every hour
> By the silken bed in the lily bower,

And aye she turned her bosom fair
And the knight he loved to see her there,
For oh! Her white and comely breast
Was soft as the down of the wild goose nest.
But the maiden that watched him night and day,
She shooed and shooed the *Herone* away;
But the *Herone* she flapped and the *Herone* she flew,
And she pecked the fair maid black and blue,
Till the knight he could not bear to see
The maiden that wanted his maid to be,
And the vanquished maid lay down to die
And the cruel *Herone* picked out her eye.

Away, *Herone*! And hide your shame.
Diana knows you are to blame!
Her bow is bent with a silken string,
And her arrow fledged with a *Herone*'s wing!
Oh, but who will prevent the woeful day?
Oh, who will shoo the *Herone* away?

Now the black cock ponders in his lonely keep,
The rowan tree rocks the raven to sleep,
While amidst the mists and the rains of Heaven
The eagle may shiver in his hermit riven;
And the swan may smooth her breast of milk,
But the *Herone* she sleeps in her bed of silk.
And the knight who kissed her bill so fair?
His wits are fled away on the air,
His torments grow with every breath
And aye he begs for the peace of death;
Yet he spurned the Virtue and lay with Vice
And now his soul must pay the price.
As the threads from his every wound she drew,
So aye his red blood runs anew;
As the adder has lain in the lion's lair,
So that blood shall flow for evermore.

Now, loose the hound on the tasselled moor,
    As green grows the birch in the coomb so mellow!
And bed with *rue* the greenwood bower,
    When the dew falls soft in the moonbeam yellow.

AFTERMATH

For several days after Sir William had wrinkled the King's composure, and hence the integrated amity of the court, with the sermonizing impassion of his rambling allegory, it was feared by some (and hoped by others) that his temerity had banished him for ever from the cloisters of Favour. His Majesty consistently ignored the beknighted boy, stared past him at the dinner table, and lifted no finger to mollify the harshness with which he was hounded and torn by the various court jackals – those whose resentment at the shepherd lad's advancement had hitherto festered in secret captivity.

To Queen Margaret, on the other hand, Sir William was a hero *par excellence*. She gave him a great diamond ring set in gold, and many other rich presents, and even caused the young balladeer not a little discomfiture by pressing him to reveal the identity and exact whereabouts of the ancient shepherd who had composed *The Herone*, that he might be duly rewarded and a pension of one hundred merks per year, to be funded from the rents of her own dowry lands.

What was the perfidious Sir William to do?

If he now admitted that the 'ancient' poem was in fact his own, and premised solely on rustic rumour, then how much higher might his Majesty's dudgeon rise – especially in the light of the common knowledge of the poet's own unchaste liaison with Lady Annabelle, not to mention the muttering speculation on his drooling adoration of Lady Ann? (Who, ever since the blushogenic recital, had returned the importunity of his longing glance with only the occasional glimpse of victorious black savagery.) Yet, if he persisted with his ancient-shepherd fiction, then how much worse might he fare if the hoax came to light in the future?

The descent from his dilemma which Sir William shortly contrived was to advise Queen Margaret that, as the author of *The Herone* was in sooth very old *indeed*, having but months remaining upon this earth, and since the excitement of introduction to royalty might only hasten the approach of his end, then, if her majesty should please to sweeten the old bard's twilight days with a lump settlement of perhaps two hundred merks, her most loyal and humble servant, Sir William Moray, would see to it personally that the benefaction was appropriate received.

Her majesty did so please.

Sir William quietly pocketed the two hundred merks.

And no-one was any the wiser until the end of the eighteenth century, when certain of Sir William Moray's papers and manu-scrips were unearthed in a long-forgotten cellar in the Castle of Drumlanrig, in Dumfriesshire.

As regard Sir William's reconciliation with the King, it was not until the morning of that Friday, after breakfast, that he received a summons to appear in his Majesty's closet on the fourth floor.

Where, after the initial urbane superficialities, unsourced by any suggestion of previous Displeasure, Sir William's twitching abated sufficiently for the following conversation to be had.

'This afternoon, Sir William, we gentlemen return to Crawmelt for the final hunt of the season.'

'Indeed, Sire.'

'And will it, sir, afford you pleasure?'

Sir William gazed for a thoughtful moment through the narrow window behind the King's seated head. In the distance gust-driven rain intersected a thin plane of sunlight before drumming on the roofs of Peebles in staccato promise of centuries of whimsical weather to come.

Why would the King not invite him to sit?

What answer would most certainly please?

'Sire, I am most honoured . . .'

'Yet would you rather tarry here at Nidpath, in the comforting arms of Mistress Hamilton!'

'I – your Majesty! Never – '

'Never, sir? Never! Quite the contrary, we have heard. *Often*, it has been suggested. Not to say *frequently*. Bordering *incessantly*!'

Sir William coloured vividly.

The King's inscrutable muse broke into a pithy smile. 'Aha! The young lusty has still the grace to blush. That is well, sir. It augurs redemption may yet be yours.'

Sir William nodded foolishly, causing his overlarge bonnet to slip forward over his eyes.

His Majesty chuckled. Then brushed to one side the rolls and scrolls on his table, leant forward, rested his chin on bridged fingers, and said:

'But doubtless you have divined that it was not concerning the ardours of your private life that we desired you to draw hither.'

'No, Sire. That is, I presumed . . .'

'A dangerous habit, young sir! But, to the point. On the morrow the season closes with the hunt.'

'Yes, Sire.'

'Thereafter all must wend their sundry ways awhile, and those with business to transact, duties to fulfil, Justice to see done, and especially those whose boon and bane it is to quarry for perfection amid the rubble of the world – which is to say, collectively, all *men* worth the name – shall leave the frisking frivolities of the summer behind them and return to the cold quotidian yoke of *work*!'

Sir William looked more knowing that he knew.

The King tapped his table and said emphatically:

'England desires us to break faith with France. France desires the use of one half of our navy. And why? The better to further her invasion of England! As always. Eh? How else could history be?'

Sir William mouthed his modest uncertainty.

'Bah! And here! Now. This morning. We learn that the Western Isles are revolting. Again! And so, sir, we ask you: Would *you* be a King? If the Lord God call you?'

'Sire, I *could* not.'

'And why, sir, *could* you not?'

Fingering a curl of blond hair free from the tight collar of his purple velvet doublet, Sir William said:

'Because, Sire, I have not feeling for Justice in the round.'

'Importing?'

'A King, Sire, must sacrifice his friend to save an army, whereas I would gladly sacrifice the army to save a single friend.'

'Ha! Well spoken, sir: a commendable confession from one so young. Yet think you upon this. Does the King – the good King, that is, for many are wicked as weasels – does he sacrifice his friend to save his *army*? Or is it not rather his *people* for whom the sacrifice must sometimes be made? His *people. Including* every lowly foot soldier in his army, yes. But also the simple souls who tend his sheep and plough his fields, who roast his beef and stitch his boots. Eh? Is it not for *all* of them that a single friendship may necessarily, and with untold regret, be sacrificed?'

Sir William could see the logic in this, yet also hankered to inquire of his Majesty what was to be gained for His people by the promiscuous despatch of Scottish weapons and troops to the far-distant bloodbaths of the Holy Wars. But, as his courtly circumspection was daily maturing, he merely nodded sagely.

'However,' said the King, dismounting from his Fervour, 'though this is not the matter of our interivew, yet does it happily bring us to its crux.'

'Sire?'

'Concerning the *people* of our nation, ingenious young friend. You will remember that, upon the day of our first acquaintance, coming in to Peebles, you did hint in the broadest terms, in innocence of our Identity, of great injuries: great wrongs that are suffered by the common folk?'

'Indeed, Sire.'

'Much injustice prevails, you did say, and that despite our government. Our chieftains and feudal barons, it appears, are frequently among the worst offenders. Fy, fy! Doubtless you did exaggerate . . .'

'Sire, I did not!'

'Yet these disclosures, freely made in the candour of your ignorance, ever since that day have preyed like angry bees about the smile that fain our heart would wear. Some there always are, Sir William, who sneer in doubt, but truly there is nothing so much concerns us as the welfare and happiness of our people.'

'Ay, Sire.' Sir William winced, recalling Lady Annabelle's admonition that gentlemen did not say 'ay' but 'yes'.

'Accordingly we have resolved, for the purpose of gleaning fresh evidences, that, immediately our affairs in Edinburgh be transacted, we shall ourself go journeying awhile throughout the realm. In disguise, Sir William! Mark you that. The better to witness in the unvarnished raw such grievances as truly exist and drive a humble shepherd lad to gripe so bitter against his King. What think you, sir?'

'It is a most capital scheme, Sire! Although . . .'

'Nor will it be our first venture upon such an excursion.' His Majesty leant back, looked out of the window, and moodily surveyed his rainy realm through eyes already hollowing dark in readiness for months of strain and insufficient sleep. 'Indeed not, Sir William,' he stressed. 'Several times have we so adventured, unbeknown to any of the courtiers, and even to the Queen. And though it appears that many, on these occasions, have been so ungrateful as to entertain suspicions that we were otherwise – and less honourably! – employed, yet the consciousness of our own good intention, and the interest and value of the experiences we did undergo, afforded us some compensation for the slanders buzzers puffed upon the wind like careless thistledown.'

'A splended simile, Sire!' Sir William applauded in flowering enthusiasm. His thirst for fancy phrase was endless, and any gem would echo to and fro across his mind until its rattled form and glinting facets fell spent to sink as greedy seeds in the topsoil of his memory floor.

'Passable,' his Majesty gruffly allowed. 'But not of the first water.'

'Sire, I – '

'And let us not be seduced from our purpose by the fawning wiles of Poesy.'

'Indeed not, Sire.'

'You little know, Sir William,' his Majesty informed him, from the confidence height of a lofty hobby-horse, 'how diabolically the actions of a Sovereign are wrested from their rightful perspective by the gabbling tongues of the discontended, and by the treasonous deliberations of the maliciously disaffected.'

Sir William's eyebrows framed a corporate question.

'The insidious imputations thrown out so glib, to take an instance, in your old bard's song of *The Herone*!'

'Yes, Sire.' Sir William felt a clenching in the knuckles of his toes.

'A palace of perfidy! A glorious feast of salacious insinuation, founded only, *perhaps*, on a single dry crumb of reality!'

'Indeed, Sire. And I repent . . .'

'Enough of that! It is long beneath the bridge.'

Sir William bowed in salutary gratitude.

King James picked a lurking shred of breakfast meat from between two enviable teeth. Scouring his youthful protégé as if vetting for insincerity, he said:

'But doubtless, sir, you still are inwardly asking why we confide in yourself? Well, partly it is that you evidently are concerned about the welfare of the commonality. Mmmmm?'

'Ay, Sire.'

'And are conversant with their habits and manners?'

Sir William did not dissent.

'Wherefore do we purpose to take you with us on our forth-coming expedition, as our only attendant and companion.'

'*Me*? Sire!'

'Who else?' The King chuckled. 'Together shall we visit the halls of the great and the huts of the poor, and freely converse with every rank of man. Unknown! We were a short while puzzled in devising what character to assume, but in the light of your own accomplishments, Sir William, the solution shines apparent.'

'Sire?'

'Cannot you hazard, sir?'

'Your pardon, Sire. I fear my brain still sleeps.'

'Between Lady Annabelle's . . . hoh, hoh! But enough of them! And may it rouse your slumbering brain, young sir, to know that we go as travelling bards and minstrels?'

Sir William blinked, then hastened to assure King James that:

'As I can touch the harp and lute, and sing a pleasing melody, while your Majesty's harmonies excel, therefore no other disguise could fit us quite so well. Except unless we became fortune tellers, which role we can in any case assume, as we find circumstances to accord.'

The King grinned in delight at the speed of his conspirator's warming to the ruse. 'And do you hereby swear', he counselled, 'to all necessary device of diligence, secrecy, and silence?'

'Sire, I swear.'

'No syllable even to the fair Mistress Hamilton?'

'Your Majesty may be *assured*!'

'Very well. And now, Sir William, you are excused. The time is nigh to mount for Crawmelt, and another there surely is who craves more than we the pleasure of your company in the slender hour betwixt!'

Sir William bowed, but, before departing, asked: 'Sire?'

'Mmmmm?'

'Shall we ride still, Sire? Today. If the rain continues so?'

'But of course!' yawned the King dismissively. 'Why ever not?'

AN ALTERED MAN!

In the final days of that second week at Nidpath, in all the feasting and dancing in the Castle, and the carefree strolls and revels about the banks of the Tweed, it was observed that Norman of Polmood was something of an odd-man-out in the endless whirl of polished irony and dilettante allusion that was the starch in the courtly staple. Like something borrowed from a poor man's wardrobe, Polmood seemed – a great shabby cloak that hung forgotten on the wall, rather than the dashing priding groom who gave the entertainments (or, at least, on whose account the entertainments were given).

When every lady had her lord or lover by her side, Elizabeth, in those latter days, instead of walking arm-in-arm with Polmood, as would have been most fitting, was always to be seen dangling and toying with Alexander, Duke of Rosay. Well could the King's brother flatter, trifle, and conjure great gleaming pearls of earnest conversation around points of worthless dross. He could speak of jewels and rings, of their colour and polish, of silks and laces, and of their styles and degrees of value. While Polmood cared not a jot for those things, nor knew no mote about them. What company for Elizabeth, in a circle where every lady was vying with every other in ornament and dress, was a man who could not tell an emerald from a jade, nor distinguish a ring of purest gold from another merely gilt?

And flattery?

To this poor Polmood was alien utterly, and never had one sentence savouring of that ingredient survived the passing of his lips. Alas. While Rosay was a connoisseur in music! So far did he comprehend its history and theory that he was able to skate like a brilliant dragonfly upon its shimmering skin, and would flourish the quaint borrowed phrases (even to *andante, grazioso*, and *affetuoso*!) like white rabbits appearing with mirculous fluency from the folds of his cloaking tongue.

Elizabeth would sing.

Rosay would hang upon her every quaver, declaiming the raptures of his delight in the most impassioned guff he knew. Sigh, he would, and shake his head, and lay his hands upon his breast at each thrilling climax and every dying fall. Whereas Polmood loved a song that told a tale and had a tune: a melody easy to the ear and kind to the simple memory. Further perceptions of music had he none.

Alas!

What partner was this to Elizabeth's maturing beauty and fining sensibility?

Here was the honeymoon nearly over, and Polmood not only remained as distant from his wife's virginity as any other man, but also languished unnourished by any smile to cheer his heart in retrospect. For the forester had wit enough to realize (only now!) that what he hitherto construed as affection for himself had really been no more than the glowing warmth of a young girl's pleasure at the slavish attentions heaped upon her.

But worse!

On the afternoon of the Thursday before the final hunt, Polmood, once more at a loss to occupy the hours before dinner, betook himself to the towering parapets of Nidpath Castle, there to hone his incomparable marksmanship yet keener by bringing down the unsuspecting rooks that floated past on the currents rising from the river: a feat of accuracy which, as Polmood derived feral satisfaction from knowing, few other men in the world would even bother to attempt.

By about four of the clock, according to the position of the sun, his huge yew bow and hissing shafts had wiped the sky of several caws and were patrolling around the southern perimeter of the battlements in scanning alertness for their next.

When suddenly:

The forester's hawking eye was summoned down to the further bank across the river by a flash of lilac in the sun. There stood Elizabeth, breast heaving, catching her breath in a tiny clearing where the riverside path became briefly visible before vanishing again behind the massive trunks of elder evergreens.

Suddenly again:

The lilac was not alone.

There was Rosay, in a bell-sleeved jacket of shimmering orange and gold, a priapic lech of conquest-in-the-chase about his fleshy mouth.

So it seemed to Polmood, in his impotence two hundred paces distant. How his soul screamed when he saw, as in the horror of a silent nightmare, the dissipate Duke wrap confident arms about Elizabeth's waist and shoulders, draw her quickly to his breast and kiss her squarely on the mouth.

Polmood drew breath to roar, but choked instead.

Tears of blinding rage, jealousy and hatred poured madness across his vision, blurring his image of the outrage to a single promiscuous mingle of lilac, orange and gold, all adrift on a sea of forest green.

Thus did Polmood fail to perceive the protesting indignation of Elizabeth's maiden mouth closing firm against the lustful liberty of Rosay's uninvited advance, and the struggling vehemence with which she pushed herself free from the unwelcome embrace.

Alas!

And when, a moment later, the ranting husband cleared his sight of its blinding brine, there was nothing left for him to see. The fleeting taunt of the dumb-show was gone, vanished along the forest path, dissolved into the impervious opacity of the screening greenwood deep.

But vanished to where?

To the gasping spluttering consummation of pre-emptive adultery: all juice and blood and lust and loins intertwined in pumping nakedness upon the fragrant carpet of the needly green floor!

'Aaaaaauu*uunk*!' Polmood choked (never thinking for an instant that nothing could be further from the truth) as some frayed sinew in his crude rationality snapped irreversibly, henceforth allowing the malignant tumour of his paranoia to feed unchecked on its own increasingly distorted apprehensions, the direness of whose consquences must ineluctably unravel in the sequel.

Why had Elizabeth changed her mind again, after telling him so plain that she had rued the marriage?

Was it all the doing of the King, and if so, why?

Why had his Majesty been so eager to get the wench wed so speedily?

Clearly, it now struck him with shuddering violence, it was because *she was already defiled*! And hence no other would have her!

'Aaaa*rrr* . . .'

That evening and the following morning Norman of Polmood was hard put to conceal from the company the alarming and escalating scale of his derangement. To his lovely wife he did not (indeed, *could not*) speak, while to his Majesty's amiable banter he was unable to respond save in grunts so sullenly terse that it was marvelled at by many that King James should allow such insolence to pass unrebuked.

And when, at breakfast on the Friday, the forester's absence was remarked upon, there was an edge of concern in Queen Margaret's voice when she asked of Elizabeth whether her husband was not increasingly solitary of late, and might perhaps be urged afresh to play a greater part in the court's amusements, that his flagging spirits should be restored.

Elizabeth replied that, so please her majesty, for her own part she perceived no cause for alarm.

But others shared the view, afterwards discreetly aired by Lady Elinor of Hume, that *Polmood was become an altered man*!

THE FINAL HUNT, AND THE PARTING OF THE WAYS

The last great hunt of 1506 was held the following day in the forest of Meggatdale, the tinckell being raised at two in the morning, all the way from Blackdody to Glengaber, and from there to the Dollar Law. Upward of four hundred men were there that day, to drive the deer with horse and hound and horn, circling closer and closer still, until at last some hundreds of deers and roes were surrounded on the green hill behind the Castle of Crawmelt, which is named the Hunters' Hill to this very day.

Around the skirts of the hill the archers were placed at equal distances, with seventy leash of deerhounds and one hundred greyhounds. At ten in the morning, at a motion from his Majesty's finger, the commencement bugle sounded. The straining hounds yelped loose, and the bustling clamour that then ensued, the whishing of umpteen arrows and the red blood staining the bracken green purity of the dome of the hill, were such as never before witnessed in that region, nor ever since. By the close of the day some sixty deer had been brought in, twenty-four of them fine old stags while the rest were does and yearlings.

On the following Monday the gentlemen rode back to Nidpath, and the next day the royal party dispersed. The Queen retired to Holyrood House, being constrained to remain in privacy for some time. The lords and ladies first accompanied the King and Queen to Edinburgh, then betook them to their several abodes and estates. King James remained in Edinburgh for just over a week, whereafter he withdrew awhile from the public eye in order to enact the scheme he had hatched with his accomplice, Sir William Moray. The adventures shared by this intrepid and unlikely pair were romantic (sometimes hair-raising) in the extreme, but as they constitute no further part of this particular tale, and as they have been amply recorded in the curious traditions of Scottish folk lore, it is with regret that we must dwell on them no longer here.

But follow instead our lovely heroine, Elizabeth, now Dame Polmood, to her cold and lonely vigil in her husband's Castle.

Him to honour *and obey*!

PART THREE
Into 1507
Polmood

10
ELIZABETH'S WINTER

A WORD TO THE READER

So far in our tale no human blood (discounting the unpremeditated bleeding of Polmood's nose) has had to be shed. But the warm gay conviviality and carnival good cheer of our story are largely at an end. Bare creeping cold, the utter abjection of hopeless and loveless longing, the shivering terror of paranoiac jealousy unchained and slavering at large in the dark swirling mists of the unsane – all these are all but on us, and no promise of eternal cosiness in the ending can be given. Possibly, then, the unashamedly romantic and soppily tender-hearted should now take their bow, hopefully not uncontent with the bright fluffy flutter and chirpy cheeps of the chicks already hatched, before the darker forms of menace and disruption burst bloody and squalling from the eggs still in the basket.

Still with us?

Then on you we impose a further condition:

That in our further adventures you sustain a more formidable suspension of disbelief than has hitherto been demanded. As certain happenings yet to unfold may otherwise not scale the towering heights of your enlightened, cosmopolitan, and media-calloused credulity – happenings, that is, whose very unlikelihood would naturally preclude their relation were it not for their unassailable foundation in early sixteenth century fact:

When Europen man believed not only in the infinite existence and omnipotence of God, but also in The Devil, in demons, angels, witches, warlocks, ghosts, goblins, fairies (called brownies in the south of Scotland) – not to mention the total credence also vested in the petitionary power of prayer, resurrection of the dead, eternal life in the hereafter, the efficacy of magic and miracle in the material here and now.

And quite apart from the skeletal role this seething welter of superstition had to play in the body of society's mentality, we have further to bear in mind that the fleshing of the limbs was constantly disfigured by such additional bugbears as: paucity of education; virtual non-existence of communication (only in 1507, for instance, did James IV issue commission for a printing press to be acquired and set in operation in Edinburgh); the limitation of artifical lighting to candles, torches and the like (and how conducive to the thrift of fairies is the spritely dancing of a candle shadow?); and, often underestimated, the potentially catastrophic mutation of a man's rationality by dietary imbalance – long harsh winters in the bleakness of snowbound country castles being obviously inimical to the vitamin wealth afforded only by plentiful fresh fruit and vegetables, so that many a prosperous ghost in the stony halls of Scotland's wilds, it may be opined, would never have got out of the ground in the first place but for want of a firm-hearted cabbage.

Accordingly, if aught in the remainder stops short of the inflexible point to which a modern credulity can easily bend, the attempting bender may be redoubled by the recollection that it is rather the characters, the protagonists in the drama, whose relatively infantile subscription to the supernatural makes possible not only the completion of our saga, but also the historical reality of the events on which the saga rests.

COLD COMFORT CASTLE

If the fortnight at Nidpath had been her happiest ever, the months of the following winter in the Castle of Polmood were to be Elizabeth's most tearfully, hysterically, and despairingly miserable. By many a salty cry.

But had she any right to be surprised?

To hope for sympathy?

Here she was, moved *by her own consent*, away from the accustomed gaiety of crowding flatterers constantly testifying their admiration of her fine form, beautiful features and elegant accomplishments, to vegetate in a desolate wilderness, surrounded by sharp craggy rocks and lowering mountains beyond. In the company of a man three times her age, whose manners and habits of life were as far from her own as lust from grace, and to whose huge and plainly raw person she found herself responding at first

200

with the civility of natural indifference and then, alarmingly soon, with the desperate scrubbed politeness that flowers out of smothered detestation!

'More pottage, my lord?' she would lightly inquire, though Polmood owned no title to that rank of address.

'Thank you, no, madam,' he would grunt after his third or fourth helping, then belch his lardy repleteness through the gaping fringe of his soup-smeared whiskers.

Madam?

To be called *madam*! By one's *husband*!

Though she never behaved except with the utmost decorum, Elizabeth had neither the stamina nor the expertise to mask the true sentiments of her heart entirely, and it soon became apparent to the domestics that their master enjoyed none of the comforts, privileges or intimate delights of the happily married state.

Elizabeth took custody of the spacious master bedroom, on the third floor, with a fine open fire and a magnificent view of the Tweed valley, stretching miles both north and south.

Polmood, with the King's injunction to chastity still stinging in his ears, was obliged to bed alone in a cheerless single closet on the storey below. There to lie writhing of nights, taunted by spilling images of the consummation that could not yet be his.

Or could!

But at what risk?

And coursing below the coagulating seepage of this frustration, like a sewer beneath a drain, ran Polmood's conviction that his fair, fragile and bravely smiling young wife was already impure in spirit, and defiled in body.

By the King's own brother!

This added to the brave smile and the light inquiry the aspect of obscene hypocritical charade, aggravated tenfold by the slur, implicit in the hussy's apparent assumption that he, Polmood, had not the intelligence to perceive the foul deception! But perhaps the sharpest acidity of all, in the dementing forester's mental poison, was the capping confusion and infuriation of a distant whisper hymning praises to the girl's unsullied virtue and thereby chanting condemnation of himself, for the shame of his twisted projections.

Polmood's brain was inadequate, in the scale and sophistication of its architecture, to survive unscathed its prolonged inhabitation by this proliferating family of egregious complexity. His solution was to incarcerate the troublemakers in the darkest and deepest of his mansion's dungeons, where they bred like ravenous rats, grew fleshy and sleek on the slime pushing up through the floors, and in due course set to gnaw mazing tunnels through the walls.

Reflecting this decay below, such genuine love, or sublimated longing, as the husband had felt for his wife, soon turned to the comfortless vinegar bind of mere physical craving – and whereas in the beginning the tender caress and the lingering kiss were frequent guests in the conception Polmood had of his coming marriage, they now were banished for ever, their seats usurped by the urgent unwarming heat of erect command astride penitent bending, moaning penetration, pitiless thrusting, unilateral climax, and the ultimate gloating conquest: the humbled beauty, a rag of wet and weeping flesh, abandoned with no word to the just solitude of her humiliation.

But none of this was guessed at by Elizabeth, who noticed only that the initial stiffness of Polmood's attempts at gentlemanly considerateness had lapsed into blunt unconcern as to her welfare and comfort, which she might have interpreted as the active tip of an iceberg of misogynous cruelty, had she not first evolved the view that Polmood's incresingly abrupt and wounding incivilities were but the inevitable consequence of a bumpkin's crudity, ignorance, and lack of culture.

'What troubles you, madam?' he snarled down the dining table, one evening at the end of November, when the first heavy snows lay thick across the land.

'It is . . . nothing, my lord,' Elizabeth replied. A little wince of pain had stabbed through the curving surfaces of her smile at just the moment when Polmood chanced to look up from scraping the gravy off his platter.

'Then why, madam, do you pull faces, pray? At nothing?'

'I . . .' Then the torture poured through Elizabeth's proud resolve like a torrent through a fractured dam. 'It is my *toes*, my lord!' she wailed. 'They are so swollen and so *painful*! So very painful, my lord. With the cold. And my . . .'

'Then you had best go converse with the sheep, madam!' snapped Polmood, who had never suffered a chilblain in his life, and who in any case, behind the contemptuous thick skin of the muscular mountain man, had no sympathy to share with the victims of life's minor discomforts.

Elizabeth, bowed, sobbed helplessly.

'Ay, madam,' Polmood repeated, rising from table and sneering with pleasure at his boorish quip, 'go inquire of the sheep up at Stenhope, if the winter be not to your liking. Them that have no fancy clothes upon their backs, no blankets on their beds, and no great blaze of burning trees to warm their chambers! And yet they, madam, *do not complain*!'

Such, Elizabeth came to accept, were her husband's true colours glinting through, vindictively mean.

And no notion had she of the rodent boom in the man's foundation.

HIM TO OBEY!

'Then, my lord, on Christmas day itself, we all did stir to the sound of carols, sung in sweetest harmony.'

Polmood grunted.

Elizabeth continued:

'For the chapel clerks had risen early and were singing by the door of his Majesty's chamber. Thus began the day in happiness,' her sewing fingers paused from their struggle against the never-ending rents in Polmood's hose, 'and so it did continue. Later we all walked out together to attend High Mass, and that being done our gifts we did exchange.'

No grunt.

'Shall it please you, my lord, to hear what gifts his Majesty did bestow upon myself?'

Polmood sniffed, took a long greedy swallow from his pot of mulled wine, and, sluggishly acid with sarcasm and alcohol, replied:

'Shall it please *you*, madam, to inform me? If it shall, then will I please to hear,' he growled to the flickering ephemera of the dining-hall fire. 'For the night is young, and other entertainment have we none, to slay its heavy hours.'

Elizabeth's spirit shrank. But her needlework continued as, in the carefree tone of singsong chatter that camouflaged her leaden emotions, she reflected:

'First he did give me a most exquisite gown – the finest ever I have had. With a long, flowing train, a lining of silken white fur, and a bodice fastened at the back by lacing in braided gold. I have it upstairs, my lord, in my wardrobe, and must be sure to pack it well for Edinburgh, for the cold is parlous wicked in the chambers of the Palace.'

Polmood's glazed eyes narrowed at this enthusing mention of the capital, but he refrained from comment. It was the first Saturday evening of December. Dinner was over, and the laird and his lady, with no thronging company to visit, were variously pursuing their pretence of union by the ancient warmth of their own home hearth. Elizabeth, her lissom figure muffled in a long shapeless over-robe of coarse brown fur, rocked comfortably on a wooden rocking-chair that Martha, the housekeeper, had recovered for her from some far corner of attic disuse, while Polmood, on his stark unornamented throne of oak, hunched forward in baleful communion with his drink and the yellow-tonguing fire.

Between the beauty and the brute lay the beast: a massive shaggy mongrelization of many hounds (and not a few wolves, if one believed the local folk) called Grimus – a hunting machine of coursing muscle and rending tooth, whose only love was the abusive rasp of Polmood's voice, and whose only fear was the occasional rib-cracking correction from the toe of the lairdly boot.

Elizabeth's gaze, returning from its fruitless quest for some appreciation of his Majesty's Yuletide largesse, shivered in revulsion as it took in the heaving chest and enormous slobbering head of the animal that terrified her so; whimpering bassly, it was, as the heat from the fire brought its bad dreams to the boil. Must not its weight be double her own? And why did Polmood persist in having it rove the Castle, when she had especially requested that it be kept without, enkennelled with the other hounds? The only plaintive entreaty she yet had put to him!

Looking down again to her handiwork, she said:

'But then, my lord, at dinner, when the tables were so spread with meat and drink and silver that no wood could be seen beneath, when came I to my dish of goose what did I find?'

Polmood declined to guess, but instead picked his nose, rummaging his nostrils with the nail of an unwashed thumb.

Elizabeth's innards screamed.

Masked by:

'There, my lord, concealed beneath a slice of breast, I found a tiny package!'

Pause.

Polmood inspected his nasal gleanings, rolled them together in a ball and flicked it to the flames.

'And in the package was a chain. And on the chain there hung a heart – a heart, my lord, in purest solid gold! And when in my astonishment I did look up, I found his Majesty regarding me. And smiling in his pleasure, but with his finger across his lips, as if to say: "Hush now, Elizabeth! The heart is a secret, for only ourself and you to share." Then later, as he passed me, and I did turn to thank him, he whispered to me: "Silence, child! For the heart is a charm, and a charm works never better than when no words are spoken. And this charm must work its best, sweet Elizabeth, for its duty is to bring you fortune in love and marriage. Which may not lie far ahead now! Who knows?" All this, my lord, his Majesty whispered in a rush and then was gone, and ever since that day I have slept not a night without that heart beneath my pillow.'

'Indeed, madam! And has it brought you . . .' In a restless lunge Polmood knelt down to the hearth, to prod the blaze and refill his pot from a jug that stood there warming.

'Yes, my lord?'

'Uh?'

'You asked . . .'

'I asked *nothing*, madam.'

Elizabeth subsided in silence, suddenly seeing the significance of what had not been said.

Polmood blackly drank.

At the far end of the hall (a bare unfriendly rectangle some thirty paces by fifteen) the door opened to admit the tray-bearing person of the kitchen maid, come to clear the dinner remnants from the table. A winsome wrench, in an ample way, she had been promoted, on Elizabeth's arrival, to the additional office of lady-in-waiting to the mistress, an elevation she had at first responded to with flooding anxiety, then painstaking reticence, and thence with cheerful and talkative pride – her stanchless bubbling gossip having proved the only oasis in Elizabeth's wilderness so far.

So the mistress now smiled fondly at the maid, who hummed

the shapeless corpse of some country ditty as her cloth flapped crumbs from table to tray.

'Bogger of FERKING DOOM, WOMAN!' Polmood roared.

'Ooooh!' gasped Betty in chalk-faced horror, fumbling and almost dropping her tray. 'Master, I – oooh!'

'Cease your gabble, ye brainless besom, and SHUT IT!'

'My lord,' said Elizabeth, 'be not unkind to Betty, I pray you. She did but leave the door open that she might better manage the loaded tray upon her departure. Did you not, Betty?'

'Ooooh, I . . . yes, my lady. Yes, indeed!' the poor girl blubbed, her rosy efficiency turned to jelly by Polmood's wrath. 'Oh, Master! Your pardon, I beg you!'

Polmood returned to his wine in a huddle of gloomy disgust.

'Be not troubled, Betty,' Elizabeth mollified. 'The Master meant no harm, but was only concerned for myself and the torment of my blains. Were you not, my lord? But these have been much better since the thaw, thanks to God, and shall not trouble me this night, I trust. Finish, therefore, with your business about the table, and then you shall be free for tonight.'

'Oh, my lady!' Worshipful gratitude pumped the chalk from Betty's cheek. 'You are so *kind*!'

Elizabeth flashed her a boosting smile.

Betty finished clearing up and quietly departed.

Polmood's eyelids began to tug together, their lashes short and nearly colourless, like those of pigs. He had been drinking constantly since returning, at dusk, from a factorial tour of the estates of Fingland, Glenbreck and Kingledores: the jointure lands of Elizabeth's dowry and hence his to manage, maintain, improve and enjoy as the fancy took him. Now, after four hours of soaking wine and the clogging surfeit of a heavy dinner, the best of the landlordly resolves he had formed during the day had winged away, and the unleavened dulling of his faculties dragged down to disconnected fantasy.

Elizabeth watched him for several minutes as the tugging sealed across his eyes, his lolling head began to nod, and his nose and mouth appeared to join in battle somewhere at the top of his throat, in a loud and soggy rhythmic snore that beat like the fist of an evil ape on the drum of a sensitive ear.

How could she sleep with this?

Ever!

With a slight shake of her troubled head, whose locks of silvered gold had grown to their warming winter length, Elizabeth dislodged her disquiet and slotted in its place the ever-pleasing picture of the Christmas holidays now imminent. On parting with her at Nidpath, Queen Margaret had pressed Elizabeth to bring her husband to Holyrood during the season of the winter festivities – an invitation which, even then, she had been overjoyed to accept.

And during the past month this impending respite in her exile had loomed larger by the hour, its images dancing forward from memories of seasons past and reflecting back as warm and colourful hopes of joy from her anticipations of the party to come. Gay waltzing galore there would be, with magic raining everywhere from the starry clouds of Holyrood's chandeliers, and spirited reels, pipers piping, mummers mumming and guisers guising.

And happy laughter all abounding!

Such were the goading and beckoning phantoms that had hardened Elizabeth's resolve to prolong her stay in Edinburgh to the last possible moment, and which had caused her such bitter dismay when Polmood informed her, at the beginning of the week, that they could not make the journey to the capital by December 6th, as was customary, but would have to wait for the week of Christmas itself.

Why, she had begged, in an effort of tearlessness.

Because there was work needing done, he had snapped.

And that had been that.

But now the date of their revised departure had crept close enough to rekindle her expectations. Old Curry would strum on his harp, and would fool, and she herself would lute and sing, would so be admired, complimented, gallantly applauded. His Majesty would . . .

'Ssshnuurg!' sounded Polmood, coming round like a mill-wheel from immersion in a stagnant pond.

'Had you pleasant dreams, my lord?' Elizabeth inquired, her daydream glowing in the place of wifely affection.

'Eh?'

'I said: had you pleasant dreams, my lord?'

'Indeed, madam. I had,' said he sourly, rubbing bleary eyes with thickly grained knuckles.

'Of what, my lord?'

'I dreamed, madam, that my chamber was large and warm, as it used once to be. And that I did lie in comfort beside my wife.'

Elizabeth felt a spasm of panic. What if he . . .

But he didn't – contenting himself with yet more wine.

'Upon what day shall we leave, my lord?' she said too quickly.

'Leave, madam?'

'For Edinburgh, my lord.'

Polmood turned to inspect her. His eyes were sharp with shrewdness, tipped with snide suspicion, when he said:

'Doubtless, madam, we can expect great revelry there, great finery and rout?'

'Oh yes, my lord.'

'Much dancing, feasting, jesting, and the like?'

'Indeed.'

'And voluptuous courtiers forby! Bent only on their filthy and licentious dissipations and adulteries!'

'Oh no, my lord!' Elizabeth dropped her sewing in alarm. 'Indeed not! For Christmas . . .'

'Indeed *yes,* madam!' Polmood hissed, commanding silence with a forefinger raised like a righteous truncheon. 'Oh yes in*deed*! Adulteries will there be in plenty, as always there are when great lords and great ladies', these words he literally spat, 'come together in idle congregation.'

'No . . .'

'As there were, madam, at Crawmelt in the summer. Or did you not perceive?'

'Why no, my lord.'

'Then were you blind, and deaf forby.'

'My sight, my lord, is . . .'

'Or possibly, madam, you were yourself so engrossed in *alternative activities* that you did not observe the fornications buzzing all around you! Like flies in summer, madam, on the shites of hounds.'

Elizabeth's breath knotted in her throat. What did he mean? Why were the veins so corded in rage across his brow, hatched uglier in shadow by the sputtering whims of the firelight and the blowing of the hall's few candles? Was it just the wine that had addled him so?

'I . . . forgive me, my lord. If in some wise I have caused

offence. Yet truly, sir,' she courageously protested, swallowing cinders as the price, 'I do understand you not.'

'And Nidpath, madam?' Polmood ground. His fleshy lips, like those of a charging gorilla, were opened out in a vortex of chattering hate.

But for whom?

Elizabeth cowered miserably in her chair.

'Had you no notion, madam, of the filthy infidelities and stinking . . . *depravities*, madam, that there were enacted by the score?'

'*No*, my lord!' she sobbed. The reins on her tears had torn away and her finest of womanly features bolted with them, back to childhood woe. 'I . . . saw . . . *nothing* such!'

'Then your husband, madam, was not so fortunate. And it is in consequence of the shameless, animal . . . nay, *bestial* promiscuities he there did witness, along with his natural concern for the delicate modesty – and the *physical chastity*! – of his lady wife, that he has decided they neither shall journey to Edinburgh this Yule.'

Only in the hall of his own domain and on the throne of wine could Polmood wax so fluent, as Elizabeth might have reflected, were she not choking with hysteria. Her skin drained to the texture of sallow parchment, her mouth gaped beyond control, and she gasped to sound the agony of retching that convulsed the neck of her belly.

'Therefore, madam,' said Polmood, rubbing his nasal moistness on the back of a leathered wrist, 'shall you content yourself with a quiet and humble season in the country, as befits . . .'

'*Nooooooo*!' split the night like a soprano from hell.

Polmood was so jolted that he dropped his wine pot to the floor, where it shattered on a flagstone.

'*Noooooooooo*!' Elizabeth was so jack-knifed in frenzy that her forehead banged against her knees. Her arms pressed tight in a crucifix against her breast, and her eyes disappeared as her mouth strained to horn the bawling from her throat:

'*Ooooooooo* . . .'

'Shut your filthy row, woman!' snarled Polmood. Rolling from his perch, he booted the wondering Grimus out of his path and leant to minister the stricken one a rough slap on either cheek.

'*Aaaaaaaaah*!' she responded.

Polmood's vast left hand seized the folds of robing fur about her throat and hefted her aloft as if she were a straw. His right hand yanked a purchase of hair at the base of her neck, so that her eyes, when they opened, could not escape his glare. And he commanded:

'*Silence,* woman! SILENCE, I SAY!'

'Gnnnuuuur!' his hound rumbled, jumping up to lend its master the dribbling of its outsize jaws.

Polmood turned to bat the monster down.

Elizabeth's eyes blinked open, and, seeing only the foreshortened menace of bared fangs stabbing at her, she flashed to the appalling conclusion that Polmood had decided to set his abominable cur to do its jugular-sundering worst. She hiccuped violently, a thin dark string of vomiting bile gulped between her lips, her eyes rolled back in her head, and she passed from total terror to the protective mercy of a swoon.

'Lord in Heaven, Master!' cried Martha the housekeeper, flustering in seconds later with Betty quaking behind her. 'Whatever is the matter?'

'The mistress is not herself today.' The laird passed the slender limpness of his wife to the custody of the domestics. 'But soon will recover. Take her to her chamber now, and tend her till she mends.'

Thus was Elizabeth bundled away and fussed to bed, by the elderly Martha and the youthful Betty.

'Then quickly to the kitchen,' Polmood called after them, 'and fetch up a pot for my wine.'

OF OUR DISCONTENT

In bed, or at least, latterly, confined to her apartment, Elizabeth remained for the next three months. Her investment in the pleasures and excitements of Christmas at court had been so heavy that her litheness of spirit was sorely wounded when the project foundered on the bar of Polmood's obstinacy. In fact the journey could not have been undertaken in any case, for in the week following her collapse there fell a further belt of snows so heavy and snaring deep that all travel was impossible, and the winter muffling lay across the land, other-wordly, like an infinite weight of swan down: the severest season in Martha's memory, so she repeatedly maintained.

Such intending travellers as had already reached Edinburgh

were snowed in, and all others snowed out. Which, as Polmood later remarked, in tide of appeasement conditioned partly by concern for his wife's health and mainly by apprehension as to how King James and Queen Margaret might interpret her malaise, was simply one of those things.

Like chilblains.

Elizabeth, in her invalid cocoon, remained for many weeks oblivious not only to the expediency of her husband's fatalism, but even to his presence. When, in the nursing company of his housekeeper and kitchen maid, he would visit her with the waking day and again in the frostbitten drowsiness of the darkening afternoon, she would look at him with the curiously troubled yet innocently fearless wonder of an infant astray in the bustle of an uncaring market crowd.

Whereupon Polmood would smile paternally, pat her hand, and gruffly recite some formula of vague encouragement.

When he had gone his manly way the housekeeper would rub her hands in worship, and say:

'There you are, mum!' For so she addressed Elizabeth, just as once, for some long-forgotten reason, she had learned to address the first Dame Polmood. 'Soon again we shall have you well as a lark in summer – did not the Master say so?'

'Yes, Martha.' In her initial fever of withdrawal, Elizabeth was malleable as wet clay.

But then, one morning late in January, the shooting root strength of her constitution said:

'Martha?'

'Yes, mum?'

'What was the matter with you, pray? When you were unwell?'

'Me, mum?' exclaimed the short and thinly grey housekeeper. 'God bless you now, mum!' she imprecated in a mirthful cackle, as she flicked her feather duster at non-existent motes. 'But whenever on earth would the likes of poor old Martha have the time to be going unwell?'

Elizabeth frowned. 'In the summer, Martha! When the court was at Nidpath? You surely did fall ill, did you not?'

'Ill, mum? Martha? Not a bit of it!' Trucing for a moment in her lifelong war on grime, the House of Polmood's eldest retainer perched on the side of Elizabeth's four-poster repose and smiled at her with rheumy grey eyes and lips that though colourless were still firm with the energy of a total faith in simple values. 'God bless you now, mum. But wherever came such a notion as yon?'

'And the Master came to visit you? He rode from Nidpath specially, when word was sent?'

'Mercy, mum! But when might my illness have been?'

'On the Saturday, Martha. The Saturday following my wedding! Do you not recall?'

Martha beamed indulgently, as on the babblings of a child newly woken from a dream. 'Between you and me and the bedpost, mum,' she confined, proudly patting the bedcovers humped on Elizabeth's knees, 'but the last time old Martha was that poorly that she could not do her work was *thirty-eight years ago*! There! When she was carrying Thomas's father.'

(Thomas being Polmood's stableboy, more on whom anon.)

'But here comes Betty with the cordial. Late again!' the house-keeper tutted sternly. 'And now, mum, will it please you sit higher in your bed for to take your drink?'

Her chance discovery that Polmood had deceived her over his weekend absence from Nidpath proved, by loading her rationality with a puzzle worthy of its mettle, to be the ideal catalyst in Elizabeth's recovery.

Why had Polmood lied?

Where had he gone?

Was it his burning for the physical consummation of their marriage that had driven him away to seek relief in some house of ill repute?

This suspicion did not alarm Elizabeth (for was not the nature of a man just so?) but rather provided a foothold for her slowly remounting morale. If Polmood's fidelity was so feeble as hardly to survive a week of unclimaxed marriage, this surely argued that he, at least as much as herself, was to blame for failing to foresee that the gulf between them could never close! And moreover, if Polmood had indeed repaired so soon to the solace of some other's charms, then might he not be encouraged to do so again?

Repeatedly?

Thus sparing herself the dread ordeal of his eventual bodily attentions?

Perhaps for ever!

Or until his . . .

Even in the innermost chambers of her mind Elizabeth would not allow such heinous words as 'death, perhaps by accident' to sound. Yet the spark of wonderment at Polmood's falsehood, on her endless tinder solitude that winter, set raging a blaze of reflection whose clarity of heat reached far beyond her insight hitherto. Why, for example, had Polmood so cruelly frustrated her wish to pass Christmas at Edinburgh? Was it *really* the result of his moralistic disapproval of the lifestyle of the courtiers? Or did he secretly sense his inability to maintain any consequence among them (in any scene save the gallop of the mountain sports) and that though he was deemed a most gallant knight out here, among the savage inhabitants of the forest, yet in the polished circle of King James's court, and most especially in the city, he was viewed as little better than a savage himself?

Then what did that make her?

Through such amazing inquiry Elizabeth wandered interminably, unwittingly circling nearer that resignation to one's lot which is the hubbing heart of grace, and by the beginning of March, when the snowline had retreated to the shoulders of the mountains and the first bright clusters of snowdrops had thrust their brave white heads above the hibernating lawns of the gardens that descended in terraced steps from Polmood Castle to the bank of the Tweed, she had strength enough to walk abroad. To sniff the freshness of the warming frost as still it sat like fairy dust upon the bushes and the trees, but softer now, as the sun began his stoking ever earlier, and filled a longer day with glowing promise, and with happy memories too: a drifting fragrance of blossom in May; a dancing ring of summer smiles; the hot dry dusty thirst of thanksgiving days, weary yet fulfilled!

Though milder snows were yet to fall, and chill winds yet would howl awhile, the all-pervading numbness of eternity that had sat across the country, just as the sheeting ice had choked the river to its source, now cracked and daily crumbled, and soon would all be borne away on the tireless back of new life rippling. And as Elizabeth's good health and the world revived together, so the claims she made on them reduced: her expectations of life and hopes of future happiness shrank like a gradually dieting belly to a closer approximation to the forms and dimensions of the possible. And how could resignation be better defined?

Polmood expressed great joy at his wife's recovery.

Elizabeth thanked him kindly.

Martha and Betty looked askance and clucked their tongues when the young mistress took to the management of her household with all the instinctive ease of a grooming kitten.

Elizabeth put them kindly in their place.

Polmood applauded. Here was the unforeseen emergence and excellent exercise of the second-most-important function of a satisfactory wife! Who, therefore, would lay a wager against the sudden flowering of the first? Though undermining rats in Polmood's soul still throve, none had yet broken through to cross his cellar awareness, and it was almost as if the petrifying depth of that winter's freeze had cooled their hiving scrabble to a torpid dormancy. This hiatus was prolonged both by want of current visible fuel for Polmood's jealousy and by his sneaking feeling that the helpless terrified child that Elizabeth so clearly was, in the nadir months of her confinement, could never be guilty of the slobbering, dribbling, adulterous extremities that so often had paraded in the path of his sleep.

That grapple between Elizabeth and Rosay he had spied from the Nidpath parapet!

Had his eyes betrayed him?

And was it really Elizabeth in the cameo? Perhaps another lady similarly dressed? Perhaps . . .

Elizabeth's winter weakness combined with time to brush a wash of saintly white upon these flimsy screens across the hairy plague behind. Uxurious as never before was the mighty husband to the convalescent wife. Elizabeth wished to enliven the dining hall with gorgeous-coloured tapestries from Spain – then Spanish tapestries would she have. Again she hesitantly expressed her horror of the great dog Grimus – then out went Grimus to a lonely kennel of his own, where the other hounds he could not savage.

And so on.

And in return?

Once or twice, perhaps three times, Elizabeth did manifest a faint feeling, if not solid fondness, for her husband. But immediately he reciprocated, through the homely warmth of some halitoid endearment, she shrank from any closer familiarity, and her disgust, though strictly veiled, was absolutely unconquerable.

So, as a shadow which threw longer as her superficial normalcy grew higher, Elizabeth's solitude continued. And in this fertile soil there soon appeared, consonant with the general greening on April's palette, the first peeping blades of truly unselfish tenderness, and the deeper-rooted yearnings which only the mutual sympathies of mind and heart can ever allay. The source of these feelings Elizabeth had no philosophy to discover, yet they led her to bestow a wealth of kindness all around her, to every crippled wing she found, and every mouth turned down.

Even to Polmood.

But in the main to the orphans of dumbness: abandoned lambs and fledgling runts, that every spring blows down from nature's nest. One week she became attached with the most impatient fondness to a tame young doe which Thomas the groom had weaned through the winter's worst in a corner of the stable. Then her protective affections rallied trenchantly to the rescue of a spaniel pup with a twisted leg, on its way from one of the cottages adjoining the Castle to easeful drowning in the river.

'How *could* you?' she cried.

'Beg pardon, my lady,' mumbled the flabbergasted cottar, nothing loth to delegate away the laborious business of death.

But somehow, though Elizabeth's impulsive fosterings continued, the joy they drew barely covered the bed of her young woman's oceanic capacity, while the nobler sentiments that poured from her heart reverted always like uncaught light reflected.

Untenanted.

Unsatisfied.

Then, the Saturday after Easter, when the final snows had thawed from the valley for good, and only the topmost tips of gleaming white still sat like skullcaps on the peaks of the furthest mountains, and the countless thousands of daffodils blazed their yellow avenues from the Castle to the river, there came to the rocky equilibrium of the locale the first furtive whisper whose accumulating reverberations were eventually to bring the building down.

11
THE ARRIVAL OF RAT FUEL

A WHIMSICAL FELLOW

Polmood was not fond of gardening (as why should a stallion plod in the harness of a donkey!) and yet, from some progenitor perhaps four generations past, he had inherited with his Castle a wealth of cultivated bower and garden scape which, thriving colourfully on the rich damp soil of the valley floor, was most uncommon about those parts at that time. Reluctant, in keeping with his national character, to squander any asset that might be husbanded, Polmood had, despite his personal indifference to orchid lures and scented sprays, maintained the tonsure of his bushes and the unthrottled respiration of his pansies through the green-fingered services of a resident yokel named Edward.

Son of Martha, father of Thomas.

Edward, however, had succumbed to pneumonia the previous winter, and in the following summer the crocus petals had lost their purple, the rosebushes drooped for want of pruning, and the weeds proliferated hungrily: cow-parsley rearing where bluebells cowered, and hogweed towering above the pining of the tulips.

Consequently, when Polmood observed the eager industry with which Elizabeth culled the never-daunted daffodils and vased their brilliant freshness about the musty nooks of the Castle's hall and chambers, and her rapturous 'Look, Betty! *Look*!' which greeted the pioneer violets, his inclination to recruit a replacement gardener was much augmented.

Yet who on the Polmood estates had the knowledge and the delicate patience to restore the flowers to their former perfection of bloom?

Three days after Elizabeth's rejoicing over the violets, came the arrival of Connel.

An idle fellow he seemed, who hailed, he said, from the

region of Galloway in the south-west, and who spoke in a nigh incomprehensible drawling burr, from so deep in his throat that he sounded like a bullfrog with a tumour in his windpipe. His appearance was whimsical beyond the rustic norm, his garb voluminously shapeless in coarse russet cloth, while his hair and beard, in the uneven colouring of half-washed carrots, spilled their curly tangle down from his scalp and out from his cheeks and chin so thickly as to leave unnaturally small the area of his features still visible. Tall and burly, he nevertheless stood in a loutish stoop and walked in a shamble of feet so splayed as to ensure him many a knowing grin and private gibe from the established domestics. But they never ribbed him to his face, for his eyes, large and dark, were narrow and shifting in their focus, never meeting another's gaze for more than a flicker – restless and disturbing they were, like the haunted eyes of a cat who senses danger.

And hence might be dangerous.

Diffident and self-effacing, the newcome Connel inquired, at the cottages behind the Castle, if there might be any work in the area. He was directed to the servants' parlour in the Castle, where Polmood shortly happened upon him, lounging uncomfortably beside the dregs of a bowl of broth.

The laird put pointed questions to the vagrant.

Connel's cap-in-hand replies, though filled with loonish idiom and fidget, seemed reasonably pertinent and sensible, and Polmood duly took him on as probationary gardener, with three months to restore the lawns and bushes and intricacies of flower to their pinnacle luxuriance.

A MAID'S LAMENT

One evening in late June, an hour before dinner, Elizabeth was sitting alone by the window of her chamber. The day had been blustery and uneven, with short patches of blowy blue sky giving way to flurries of fast-scudding cloud, and scattered intervals of restless rain. This weather (unseasonably unwarm enough to require a shawl about her shoulders) seemed to her just typical of the mood that had banged against her enjoyment of the summer, like a distant door unfastened in a gale.

As with the weather, she reflected, gazing through the open casement to the windswept dark slopes of the mountains of Herston a few miles south, so with the season's events. Little, it appeared, was to be repeated of last year's indefinitely protracted bonanza of holiday divertissement and sport. King James, it had been reported, was fully engaged restoring order to the Highlands and Western Isles, where several boils of rebellion had erupted in the spring. Queen Margaret, meanwhile, was in her third pregnancy and confined in strict and unmoving sobriety to her apartment in the Palace of Holyrood.

And with her the permanent corps of her unmarried ladies-in-waiting.

Consequently, though a hunting expedition to the Borders was scheduled for the end of July, the probability was that it would be a foray for gentlemen only: austere and unsmiling, compulsive and narrow in purpose, with none of the unhurried, lingering delight in the magical beauty of the present that only a balanced mingling of the sexes can procure.

'Ah me!' Elizabeth sighed, pondering the distant movement on the mountain-side of several young deer breaking cover for a moment and silhouetting against the shifting sky before vanishing among the camouflage colours of the heather. Looking down with eyes that fell of their own weight of wist, she fingered the lute that lay cradled in her lap, and gave melody to one of the most exquisitely mournful old airs she knew, its first two verses as follows:

> You came to me
> On a summer's day.
> You came to me
> In sad array,
> With your battle clothes,
> Your uniform,
> All torn and deathly grey.
> I wish I could say more for you,
> But it's not a happy song.
>
> And I took you in,
> I bathed your wounds.
> I took your seed
> Into my womb.
> Lovingly

> I tended you
> All the summer long,
> I made you well and whole again,
> And by winter you were gone.

Here Elizabeth paused in her singing but continued to play, improvising on the melody in a fashion whose bare simplicity and sombre minor-key tone combined to refine the expression of her feeling to a point that must have been quite heart-rending to any listener.

Though it was not to any listener that she played.

Picture her astonishment, therefore, when her eyes, wandering from her fingers on the lute to the rosebeds three storeys below her window, descried the transfixed figure of Connel the gardener. Resting from his task of turning the soil and breaking the clods, he leaned on the handle of his spade and faced between south and west, into the cloud-marred beginnings of the sunset.

And his eyes swam glistening with tears.

Tears!

Elizabeth was so amazed that her fretting nearly foundered. Why ever should the ludicrous Connel be moved to weeping by her song? Him whose awkward, lumbering furtiveness put her somehow ill at ease? Whose industry she had approved from a distance, but to whose person she had addressed not a word since his advent two months since?

Tears!

Scarcely crediting that her rendition could harrow so simple a heart, Elizabeth, leaning back from the casement lest her watching be perceived, led into her final verse with a trickling arpeggio, and with muting passion sang:

> Now summer's come again
> And your child is born.
> He looks a lot like you
> And his clothes are torn.
> But one thing
> I do swear to you,
> I will see to as he grows:
> Any maid who may encounter him
> Will sing a happy song.

Any maid who may *encounter* him
Will sing . . . a happy song.

When Elizabeth stroked the song to sleep, with its final haunting chord, it seemed to her that never before had she understood and interpreted it so well; that only now had she fully inhabited and explored its gravity of pathos and richness in humility. And was this feeling not confirmed by the astounding response of her uninvited audience?

The closing of the song appeared to waken the gardener from the brimming immobility of his reverie, yet thrust him in a dither of overwrought agitation.

He wiped his nose.

He dabbed his eyes.

Flung down his spade and paced to and fro on the lawn beside the flowerbed.

Head bent and shoulders heaving.

With emotion?

Elizabeth's curiosity was furiously excited by these observations, and her long-languid spirits suddenly catapulted to a piquancy of interest and anticipation they never before had known within the walls of Polmood. Hurriedly she flung off her dowdy shawl and workaday household smock, slipped into the finely primrose flattery of an elegant dress from her wedding collection, and tripped down the stairs and out to the gardens, her heart fairly hammering with the tension of its resolve to have some conversation with the gawkish but evidently sensitive Connel.

'Good day to you, Connel,' she greeted him.

'Ooor, mur lidie,' he rumbled in his beard.

'You are working sorely hard today, are you not!'

For Connel was once again delving and slicing his clods with the utmost assiduity.

'Are you not tired?' Elizabeth inquired, when her previous question met only with a shrug.

'Naar, mur lidie,' the gardener grudgingly replied, hunching even deeper into his rough brown collar. The front entrance of the Castle of Polmood faced directly west, and here on the lawns the waning sunlight now glanced at an ever-closing angle, weak with weariness yet clean from the washing of the showers.

'Does the sun trouble you, Connel?' Dame Polmood went on.

'Naar, mur lidie,' he growled, surly, his back half-turned to her. 'It urz me nick, mur lidie, me nick it urz indeed, yur see. Begin purrdon, mur lidie. But it urz me nick at urz dump at noights and so urz stuff, yur see.' He turned even further away from her and stooped to grub for a lurking white root in the thorny shade of a rosebush.

Then he clammed up.

'Are you then not comfortable, Connel, in your loft above the stable?'

Shrug.

'We could perhaps find a place for you with one of the cottar families. Old Robert and Tibby . . .'

Negative shrug, almost savage.

Elizabeth, arms folded across her bosom, regarded the toiling silence of the other with a measure of put-out surprise. Though she had accosted him in the tone of easy familiarity which those in power reserve for their dependents, she had had to make some effort to do so, to drape a veil of confidence across the flutter in her breast. And now she found the veil was wearing thin. Something about the reticent gardener was unnerving, yet also intriguing. But what could it be? The clumsy, hulking form? The rasping bass croak of his voice? His clownish gait and yokel diction? All of these must count against him: lead one to feel that the hours should be more profitably invested than in fruitless soliloquy before this terse and ungainly buffoon, and yet . . .

Was there not something elusively solid and reassuring about the fellow? As even the ugliest landmark may command affection through its pointing to haven home?

Elizabeth tickled the pensive curve of her lower lips with the tip of a dubious forefinger, and said:

'Connel?'

No response.

'Are not the roses ready for picking? These ones here, I mean, on the higher stems?'

Connel nodded abruptly. Since rummaging for roots he had wiped his face with the back of his hand, and his brow, cheeks and beard were all smirched with black soil.

Elizabeth smothered her smile.

'Then could you . . . *would* you', she switched to the winning society voice she had not used for so long, 'possibly be so kind, Connel, as to pick a few for me – no, no! Not now!' she exclaimed, as the gardener moved to comply. 'But tomorrow, in the morning, after breakfast. If the weather is fine and the flowers dry? Could you? Two would be nice: one pink and one blood. And about this size, if you can.' She formed a circle with her thumb and second finger. 'I like to wear them in my hair, you see. And so they must not be too large. Could you, Connel? That really would be so very kind.'

'Ooor, mur lidie!' the assenter effused. And jerkily nodded.

'If you would give the flowers to Betty, in the kitchen, then she will bring them to me. But now, alas, I fear the rain is with us again, and I must run to dinner. Goodnight to you, Connel, and I thank you again.'

'Gudnoight, mur lidie,' he gruffed.

'And Connel?' Elizabeth called back, as she scurried through the rain, across the shadowed lawn.

'Ooor, mur lidie?'

'Tarry not too long at work, I pray you. Lest your neck suffer further from the damp.'

The gardener made no reply.

Except to dab a raindrop from his eye.

When his volatile young mistress had disappeared from view, swallowed up in the stark dark maw of the Castle gate, its fortified thickness so greyly grim in contrast to the blazing garden bloom without.

For the next fornight it appeared to the inmates of the Castle that the gardens had become their mistress's only home. And the doltish gardener her only companion. Several times each day she would seek him out, commending his skills and the magic touch of his fingers, his treatment of such-and-such plants, and the taste with which he chose her roses in the morning. And though he hardly spoke at all, except in low grunts intoning Ooor and Naar, she clearly drew great nourishment from his company, often prattling to him in lengthy rambles of aimless excitement, requiring no rejoinder beyond the nodding encouragement of having a scant proportion of her declamations understood.

And every evening at her window she would sing.

Not *for* Connel, for what could be more incongruous than to sing for a goopy peasant fellow? Yet it was strangely cheering to know that somewhere he would be listening, plodding about his weeding and pruning with the beauty of her music in his ears.

And often at night during this time, in the twilight blur that fades into sleep like the uneven advance of an incoming tide, she would find herself in the flow of a reverie that carried her with great power through a tunnel yet too dim to light the frescoes on its walls – and often with a twinge of perspiring alarm she would emerge rewoken, feeling as if she had striven for long exhausting hours in the pursuit of some fey remembrance that always in the end turned out no more than a figment of vanished illusion.

But through the day these darker echoes did not sound.

Elizabeth was, if not happy, at least happier.

Therefore Polmood, away most days about the business of his marriage-brought estates, was much pleased. Not least because the hunting visit of the King was looming closer, and the forester had long foreboded his Majesty's reaction to discovering his ward in misery: when might she not disclose in Wrath-stirring tears her husband's heartless ban on the Christmas expedition to Edinburgh?

Polmood, then, came as close to delight as his dourness allowed, upon perceiving this affinity between his lady and the gardener, his attitude being: whatever tiny bauble may amuse her, by Heaven let her have! Just as a Louis XIV could regard his courtiers as so infinitely inferior that he would happily defecate in the presence of them all, so Connel to Polmood was merely a sturdier and more productive replacement for the crippled spaniel pup that had died of some yelping ague only a week after its rescue from drowning.

Thus did Elizabeth's newfound pleasure measure well against the laird's approval, and hence his household minions, who benefited thereby, became better disposed to the secretive Connel – he whose wooden company and surly patience with the mistress's fanciful twittering were the key to this welcome upturn in the peace of their collective mind.

Connel reciprocated no warmth, but equally posed no problem. Sleeping alone in the stable loft, and taking his meals in a self-appointed shift to avoid the society of the Castle servants, he very soon faded into the background and was little more regarded than the baleful resentment of the giant old stag head above the dining-hall room.

But then the rat fuel arrived.

ANATHEMA!

'What?' hissed Polmood. 'WHAT?'

'Your pardon, Master!' mouthed Thomas, the lanky jug-eared stable-lad. 'I did not . . .'

'When?'

'Master?'

'I mean, ye miserable rockhead,' Polmood snarled plosively between his stumps, 'when did the man arrive? *How long has he been here?*'

Thomas swallowed nervously, his eyes rolling in the long thin triangularity of his face. Having anticipated that the Master would be just as pleased to learn of the unexpected arrival of the Duke of Rothesay as the mistress had clearly been, he was now dumb-founded by the boiling of Polmood's contrary fury.

How impossible it was, to keep abreast of these great folks' whimsicalities!

'Speak, ye miserable bogger!' Polmood menaced him, then leapt off his horse and crowded Thomas against the stable wall.

'About . . . two hours, Master. Maybe three. I was – '

'Shite of ferking BOGGERY!' Polmood roared, his clenched fists raised. 'Why *this*? Bogger of ferking HELL: why THIS? Uh?'

Thomas had no idea.

'And where is he now?' Polmood, tired and sweatily dirty from a long day supervising the digging of draining ditches on the farm at Glenbreck, made a staggering effort to cage his hatred of his Majesty's brother. 'Is he relaxing maybe, in his chamber?'

'Not at all, Master,' returned Thomas, stroking the nuzzling nostrils of Polmood's horse and encouraged by this apparent return of the lairdly self-control. 'He is gone along the riverbank, for to take his pleasure, I do believe, in the colours of the sunset.'

'Alone?'

'Master?'

'*Bogger* . . . is he gone to pleasure himself alone? On – his – own?'

'No, Master. He is gone with the mistress.'

Polmood took a deep, jagged breath. 'And tell me, Thomas, were you to hand when my Lord Rothesay did arrive? I mean, did you *see* him appear?'

'Ay, Master. That I did.'

'And did ye see ... my lady, Dame Polmood ... was she on hand to receive him?'

'Ay, Master. She was indeed.'

'And came he alone? No other gentlemen with him? The Duke of Hamilton, for example?'

'No, Master.'

'Eh?'

'I mean *yes*! Master. That my Lord Rosay did come alone. At least ...'

'At least *what*, ye glaikit ninny? The man was either alone or he was *not* alone! That is plain as the plukes on your nose! Uh?'

Thomas rubbed ruefully at the blemishes aspersed. He was hopelessly adrift in love, with the curvaceous charms of Betty the kitchen-maid, yet how could true requital ever be, between a lady's lady such as she and a mess of pitted pimples such as he?

'Your pardon, Master!' he begged. 'I meant just that he – my Lord Rosay – came with no other gentleman. But a page he did have: about a year below myself in age, I would say, but much smaller ...'

'And where is the page now?'

'He is departed, Master.'

'To where?'

'To Dumfries, I heard him say. To Drumlanrig. For to summon – '

Polmood's mighty back proclaimed his uninterest in the errand of Rosay's page. But what of the *reason* for the boy's despatch? That he should not witness the flagrant improprieties of his master's intended adultery! Lost in turbulent passion, Polmood paced the hay-streaked mud of the stableyard. His features heavy in a twisted eloquence of loathing, the palm of his left hand he struck repeatedly with the knuckle-tight fist of his right.

Grimus the hound padded massively from the trough where it had been drinking and sank into a custodial sit beside the uncomfortably waiting Thomas. Green slime from the horse water hung from its panting jowls, and the protruding pink tip of its large brutish maleness pointed up at the groom like a third warning eye.

Which Thomas obeyed.

Polmood ceased his prowling, and said:

'And did she – Dame Polmood – did she seem . . . upset, put out, would ye say? That he should arrive in this manner: unbidden and unannounced?'

'Not a bit of it!' Thomas replied brightly. 'Quite the contrary, indeed. My lady did seem delighted to see him.'

'Meaning . . . what . . . exactly?' Each of Polmood's words was like a figurine hacked out of marble. 'How did she show her *delight*?'

'Why, Master! As any lady will. She smiled, she clapped her hands, she laughed. She spoke of this, of that, of the other – and all at the speed of a swallow swooping, which was wondrous hard for a simple soul to follow. Such as I,' he modestly added. 'And then when my Lord Rosay stepped close from bowing to her hand and kissed her on the brow . . .'

'He *what*?'

'Ay, Master. But only as a gentleman may, ye ken. With great delicacy and . . . decoorum.' Thomas squinted uneasily between hound and laird, as between a lion and a wounded bear.

'And she?' groaned the bear. 'How did she receive the Duke's attentions?'

'Right prettily, Master. She pushed him away, giggled, she did, and blushed bright red, but prettily so, indeed. And said he was too gallant by half, and that he must be weary from his ride, and therefore would he see his chamber, that he might relax awhile and change to fresh attire.'

Receiving this information, Polmood's never lovely face contorted into the pallid slits and wrinkles of unbearable constipation.

'Is everything well?' Thomas gingerly trepidated. 'Master?'

'Now hear ye this, lad.'

'Ay.'

'Ye will first tend the mare.'

'Ay, Master! I have a fresh bale in the stall, just cut.'

'Then ye will seek out yon Connel fellow – ye ken where he is?'

'Ay.'

'Where?'

'He is up the burn a wee, a-doing with the crab-apples.'

'Very good. Then inform him that the laird requires his services in the armoury. To be there straight after dinner. And if I be delayed, he shall await my pleasure. Ye have that? As he values his position.'

'Master, be assured! This all is as plain as a moulting peafowl.'

'And ye will not forget, mind. Or your hide shall repent it for ye! Come, sir!' Polmood snapped at the exhibiting dog, and lent his command the reinforcement of a bruising boot in its barrel chest.

And vented a slapping gust of his stormy exasperation on the rump of his chestnut mare as he passed, his longbow stretched on his shoulder and arrows quivering in irritation against his greasy thigh, out of the stableyard and down the winding spinney path that led the hundred paces to the Castle.

'Dear Lord!' said Thomas to the wide-eyed rearing mare. 'Easy, lady! Easy now.'

AROUND THE HOLE OF THE ASP

'I *pray* you, my lord!' gasped Elizabeth. 'Truly you must *not*!' Indignant yet somehow excitedly distract, she pulled her mouth free of the pointed brown beard of the implacably importunate Rothesay.

And broke away from his uninvited embrace.

'For*give* me, dear lady!' His voice a bowl of fruity gravity, Rosay bowed his regret and doffed his high-crowned bonnet, taking practised care to conceal his pate extent.

'Yes, *truly*, my lord!' Elizabeth, turned away from him and, facing across the river towards the shepherd's delight on the western horizon, was trembling with confusion. 'If my husband were to *see* us so . . .'

'Yes, in*deed*, my lady. It was a most rash and unpardonable presumption, I do confess. And the fault solely mine.'

'And besides, my lord, you did *promise* me one afternoon at Nidpath that such . . . would never . . .'

'Occur again! That is true, and for it I do repent. I mean, of course,' the charmer smiled winningly in voice, 'that I do repent me of my breach in vow.'

Elizabeth nibbled fretfully at her lower lip.

Myriad fish food hummed busily above the water's dark smooth skin.

A bat darted by overhead.

Such was the gloaming hour.

Rosay grinned to himself, his dark eyes sharpening like the stink of a tom-cat at night. Stepping forward, he patted Elizabeth respectfully on the shoulder.

She flinched.

'There, there!' he cajoled. 'Sweetest lady, I do implore you. Must it sack and ashes be? For a slight imprudence, after all, which only a gentleman's most passionate admiration must have driven him to? For a lady's most inordinate beauty! Alas! Then shall I depart tomorrow at dawn, as propriety is all.' Quite the epitome of contrite resignation, the heir to Scotland moved up beside his troubled companion, to the outer edge of the great grey stone: a natural flat platform jutting six feet above the basin-black secrets of the Cleaker's Pool.

Ten paces downstream a trout mouth rose and snapped like the wink of a hungry eye.

And then was gone bar the ripple.

Like the passing of a life.

'N-noo!' Elizabeth slowly decided.

'No what, my lady?' Rosay purred.

'I feel, my lord, that you must not . . . that there is no *need* for you to depart. Tomorrow.'

'But my lady! If, weak and sorry spirit that I am, I cannot contain within my silence the bewitchment that my heart cries out and the singing in my soul, rejoicing their astonishment that your own fair beauty, already incomparable, could attain yet finer perfections – and all in so few months! – what can I do? I must be gone, it seems to me, lest my rapture break forth anew and discomfit all. Must I not?'

'No, my lord!' Elizabeth blurted helplessly. 'You must not.'

'But . . .'

'It is no wise needful that you *leave*, my lord. But only, so please you, that you confine your . . . admiration to *remarks*! And not . . . else my husband . . .'

'Sweet lady!' gushed the courtier's polish. 'As your every wish is my absolute command, so shall I stay. And stay discreetly, this I vow,' he promised breezily, flapping short thick arms about his chest and affecting to relish the clean-scented tang of the cool even air.

Elizabeth smiled at him in the warm gratitude of relief. Though far from her conception of the ideal man (although, again, in which fine hues and what dashing style was this conception really executed, when details were required?), Alexander of Rosay was undeniably a *gentleman*! In speech? Fluent and entertaining. In dress? Flamboyant and debonair. In culture, musical conversancy . . .

She stifled a sigh, and said:

'I thank you, my lord.'

'And *I* thank *you*, my dearest lady! For the graciousness of your leniency. For the pleasure of your beauty. And for the provender of your larder. Which shortly shall sustain me, may I hope?'

'Oh yes!' Elizabeth touched her mouth in horror. 'Dinner! My lord, you must be famished. My husband, you see, has been working . . .'

'Trouble not, dear lady. It is no matter. Though now, as the view has fallen from the sky, and the bugs are rising off the water, it seems meet that we return. So please you?'

'Indeed, my lord.'

'And shall this also please you? Accept the chastely devoted support of a humble admirer's arm, to assist you up the slope to yonder track?'

'My lord, it shall delight me.'

Thus Elizabeth, young and vulnerable, still a tentative guest in Life's mercurial hostelry, was foolish enough (it may be said) to allow physical contact to resume between herself and a known libertine in morals! And is not the maiden who ventures so, however forlorn and abandoned her room at the inn might seem, herself acutely guilty? Of toying with fire? Of thoughtlessly playing around the hole of the asp? Of laying her virgin hand upon the lion's very snout!

To amplify a trifle:

Is it not indisputably and eternally true that whatever freedoms a man has once taken with a member of the weaker sex, he will deem himself at liberty to forage to again, whenever occasion serves?

Then why did no such notion occur to Elizabeth? And how much wiser should she have been to say *Yes*, when the lecherous Rosay disingenuously sighed and suggested that perhaps he better had leave on the morrow?

Oh, *foolish* Elizabeth!

And should you not have disengaged demurely from the rakehell's escortive arm, when once he had obliged you up the short muddy slope to the even keel of the bridleway? And then, oh fair young beauty, when he took the dainty fingers that you rested so light and gracious upon his arm and pressed them warmly (*confidingly!*) with his own – what then? Why did you chide him not?

Reasonable questions, these, for the vicarious such as we, but to the heroine in the pickle, to the innocently warm-hearted young damsel in the unfulfilled heat of her quandry, not one of them occurred. Rather, as Rosay walked beside her in apparently effortless rhyme with her little lady's step, south down the leafy tunnel through the promiscuous overhanging of the big old chestnut trees that lined the bridleway, she quizzed him eagerly about the circumstances and well-being of the King and Queen, and all of her former associate ladies, whose prickly company and acid conversation she now missed more than would have seemed possible just a few months ago.

So she learned, through the suave and oily glair of Rosay's gossip, that the Lady Annabelle Hamilton, reacting violently with the heart that Sir William Moray's youthful callousness had broken, had responded with immediate assent to the mumbled proposal of wineful marriage made to her by the radiantly inferior (though hugely rich in land and gold) Lord James Douglas of Dalkeith.

And that the former tigress vamp was already greatening with child.

'No!'

'Yes!' Rosay confirmed.

And what of Christmas?

What dazzling gifts had been given by who to whom? What music had lilted, what dancing had reeled? On all these points and many more Elizabeth, flitting erratically from orchids of impatient pleasure to thistles of fretful envy, had shed the loquacious light of her companion's first-hand acquaintance. Of tragedy too, she heard, and death: how the fiery Lord Chamberlain Hume, on the

230

morning of the New Year's Day, had awoken in a speechless palsy, had responded by nary a blink to the anguished solicitude of all around, and rapidly passed through a short sharp fit of bone-dry rattling to the rigid peace of lifelessness.

'Lord rest his drunken soul!' said Rosay languidly. 'And then Old Curry . . .'

'Oh no!' cried Elizabeth. 'Not Curry too!' For the dear old clown had been a friend, had taught her countless songs and exercised her laughter.

'My lady, I do fear so.'

'How?' Her inquiry husky.

'Oooh, you know!' Rosay gestured expressively, then returned his paw to a comforting squeeze on Elizabeth's lodging fingers. 'There was some nonsense on the Boxing Day, upon the loch behind the Palace. I was not there myself, as the hour was heathen early, but it seems that Curry went a-capering on the ice: sliding, somersaults, tumbles and the like – to amuse the company on their walk. And then . . .'

'Yes?'

'Well! About the centre the ice was thin and could not bear his weight, when once he landed from a frolic in the air.'

'But could not . . .'

'And the poor fellow could not swim, you see, and though his Majesty rushed to his aid . . . well, in his struggles, he trapped himself below the ice, and was drowned ere he could be got rescued.'

'Oh.'

'God rest his impudent soul!' intoned Rosay, his scant regret for the passing of Curry well disguised by warmth of concern over Elizabeth's distress: what better excuse for a further lingering pat upon her grieving hand?

'Then', she slowly supposed, 'that leaves the King without a clown?'

'Only in name!' Rosay darkly riddled.

Elizabeth was disturbed by the humourless viciousness that lit his scowl. 'How mean you, my lord?' she asked.

'There is one, my lady, whose unbridled insolence and foolishness with words are fitting only for a clown, but who yet enjoys a greater rank, and, indeed, too often has first voice in the King's ear: a sad and far from wholesome state of affairs, I fear.'

'But who in the court, my lord, can answer this description?'

'A miserable yappy mongrel-pup of a fellow, dear lady! Still spouting rhyming drivel from his cradle, and not yet dry behind his filthy lugs. Cannot you guess?'

'Not Sir William?'

'The very same!' Rosay shook his head angrily. 'Where the King goes, he goes. When the King jests, he jests. And when the company is invited to retire, that his Majesty may the better expedite the business of the nation, there is but one of all the courtiers privileged to remain. Yes! Aged, wise and anciently noble Sir William Moray of Crookston: scribe and counsellor of the utmost sagacity, and bard of all the nation's sheep – a *despicable* specimen!'

'I am not sure, my lord, that I may agree with *despicable.*'

'*Insufferable* then, madam: I urge you to try it on him.'

'No, my lord. I did but think him extremely *young,* and unsure in society. A little tedious at times, to be sure, and arrogant, but perhaps only so in the disguise of his illness at ease.'

'His illness, my lady, is first and foremost in his *wit.* He is an adventurer without conscience and a hideous albino forby . . .'

'Oh no, my lord! He is fair, indeed. But not unpleasingly so, in his surly way. And his eyes are grey.'

'Are they, my lady? If you swear so, then of course I do retract. It is more than I can abide, I confess, to squander my vision on even the least offensive portion of his person, never mind the contamination of his eyes.'

'My lord!' Elizabeth giggled uncomfortably. 'Your case you surely overstate?'

'Not a whit, my lady. The varlet imagines, among his countless other delusions, that his person is a benison from Heaven itself, thrown down as the Lord's own tribute to the charms of womankind!'

This!

From *Rosay?*

But Elizabeth saw nothing amiss. Torn between puzzlement at the Duke of Rothesay's vehemence and the unquiet feeling that perhaps her former evaluation of Sir William had indeed been overgenerous, she maintained a respectful silence.

Till Rosay ominously added:

'And if ever the Throne shall fall to me . . .'

'Yes, my lord?'

'Nothing, my lady. Nothing! It was but an echo from my childhood, when I did dream that one day *I* might rule.'

'And yet you might, my lord. For you are young, and . . .'

'No, my lady! A thousand times *no*!'

'Why so, my lord? What more on earth might any man wish?'

'Aaaah!' Rosay exhaled benevolent sapience. 'Sweet Lady Elizabeth! How innocent, how pure. But what of my love of culture . . . poetry, music? The unhurried society of the world's most beautiful ladies, such as you!'

'You are too kind, my lord.' But pleasure rose red on Elizabeth's cheeks, as when last had such words set her ears afire?

'Not kind, dear lady. Merely truthful. And what ecstasy it is to laud beauty in truth unalloyed! And forby, we must recall that her majesty is soon to present us with an heir: a healthy boy, God willing, to take the burden of my heirdom from me.'

'God willing!' Elizabeth traced a cross upon her breast.

For a silent minute they sauntered on. It was almost night along their chestnut-roofed route, and whatever yawning of nature's voices they might otherwise have heard was swallowed in the rushing of a wide and shallow stretch of the river on their right.

How chivalrous, Elizabeth was reflecting, for Rosay not to wish to be King, when . . .

He said:

'We surely are close to the Castle now, my lady? My inner Duke, I fear, is girning for his sustenance!'

Elizabeth smiled, and lightly patted the yellow rose upon her crown. 'Around this turn, my lord, is a glade that looks across the water, and then we have five minutes' walk.'

'That is well!' guffed Rosay, as they stepped into the rabbit-paradise green of the clearing. 'My inner Duke rejoices!'

'Then how much louder, my lord, shall he rejoice when, melting in his mouth, the juicy roast . . . what was that?' she whispered urgently.

'What was what, sweet lady?'

'A heavy crashing noise, I swear. Among . . .'

'EEEEEEK!'

'Ooooh!' she cried.

'Dearest lady, be not startled!' Rosay boomed his unperturbed valour. 'It was but a screeching owl. Come, come. I pray you, permit me?' He helped himself to the intimacy of wrapping a comforting arm about her quivering shoulders. 'A shriek most hellish, yes, but an owl, no more. There . . .'

Just then from the matted thicket to their left burst the colossal intensity of Norman, Laird of Polmood. Unchanged from his labours, with his broadsword sheathed against his thigh, and the unsane glitter in his eye of the thwarted fornication-seeker.

'Ah, Polmood!' Rosay blandly greeted him. 'What a turn you there did give your wife!' Did he not, my lady? We truly thought there was a wolf about. But no matter. How do you, sir? In Trojan health, it seems. As ever.' Unobtrusively detaching his arm from Elizabeth, Rosay formally saluted his host with the slight clipped bow that badged his rank.

Polmood, thus addressed, was obliged to return the bow. No obligation in all the world, however, could wipe the snarl from his mouth and the jealous hatred from his eye. 'How do you, sir?' he managed in a growl that hissed.

'Well, thank you, Polmood,' Rosay jauntily returned, stepping to close the distance between them. 'Well, indeed. And better, may I say, for the delightful conversation of your own most beautiful lady! We – '

'I hear, my lord, that you are pleased to visit with us. For a day . . . or two?'

'Why yes, sir. So please you. His Majesty, who conveys his warmest greetings, will ride here a week today, and asks that you stage a hunting party on the morrow. His duties this year sit heavily upon him, and his holidays can be but short.'

'His Majesty's pleasure is my instruction,' rasped Polmood.

'Well said, sir! Fine . . .'

'Though the notice is muckle short, my lord. To find where the beasts are like to feed and get the tinckell set.'

'Tut, Polmood!' tutted Rosay. 'These surely are modest hurdles for a forester of your distinction. Not so?'

'If the King commands it, my lord, it shall be done. But . . .'

'The words of a subject most truly valiant! Just as his Majesty prophesied. "Somewhat of a rush, it may be," were his parting words to myself, in sooth, "but our honest Hunter of Polmood will see it done, be sure." A confidence, sir, that all the court did share.'

Polmood sniffed aggressively.

Elizabeth, hanging back, looked wordlessly between the confronting men. Why, oh *why*, would Polmood muster no *respect*!

The tortured husband suddenly switched his glare from the affing guest and raked the pent figure of his lady. Scouring for carnal clues: for rumpled skirts, for grassy stains, for . . . oooh! The light was failing, yes, but were there not dark patches in the . . .

'Now, Polmood,' Rosay, from his status, leant to gee the situation back to a dinner-bound trot. 'I fear we have detained you from your victuals over long. Therefore let us step resolutely to table. And perhaps, Polmood, your lovely wife could walk prettily between us: a perfect picture, if I so may say, betwixt two homely pillars! My lady?'

'Delighted, my lord!' Elizabeth gladly allowed herself to be escorted from the clearing, Polmood on her left and Rosay right. In a split, impulsive moment she made as if to intertwine her arm with Polmood's jerkily swinging ham, but the gesture aborted on the invisible white-hot halo of her husband's hostility.

So in prim and proper silence she continued up the lane.

While Rosay chummily chatted:

Commiserating grandly with all the nation on the bitter extremities of the winter past. Praying devoutly that nothing like it would recur in the lifetimes of them all. Thanking the Good Lord for the tender summer to soothe the winter's memory. Commending Polmood's splendid gardens. Regretting . . .

'I see, madam,' Polmood could hold in no more, as they rounded from the mouth of the bridleway to the gravelled path that skirted the Castle lawns, 'that you had lodged our . . . *guest* in the chamber next your own!'

'Why yes, my lord!' Elizabeth exclaimed. 'That is right, is it not? It is the most comfortable by far, excepting yours and mine.'

'Indeed, Polmood!' Rosay enthused. 'It is comfort – '

'That is correct, madam,' Polmood barked. 'The room is less

satisfactory than yours and my own. It is less warm and forby still damp from the winter.'

'Not at all, sir! I . . .'

'My lord, so please you, I have had the housekeeper exchange your accommodation with my own. Which is all aired at least, and shall trouble you with fewer steps from the hall.'

'No, Polmood. Really!' Rosay protested, furious at this spatial wedge between himself and Elizabeth. Looking at his obstreperous host, he felt frustrated anger itch in the pimples beneath his beard – why did they linger so?

Elizabeth was astonished to the brink of outrage by her husband's presumptuous discourtesy. There she objected:

'But my lord! the view – '

'SILENCE, MADAM!' Polmood thundered. 'He shall lodge on the second flat and there is an *end* to the matter.'

Her mouth bit shut, a gulping pained her throat, and the points of unseen tears pricked her eyes: how *humiliating*! But what more could she say?

Rosay too was stunned to silence. Did Polmood *always* treat his lady so? Call her *madam!* Shame her before guests? And allow (force?) her to bed in a chamber so removed from his own?

Uncomforted!

Unpenetrated?

Each walled in fruitless privacy, among wild scamperings of distorted perception, untested suspicion, and all their scurrying kindred, this unlikely trio crossed the north lawn and mounted the steps to the terrace below the Castle gate. The anguished forester in his dirty jerkin, the lascivious courtier in his cloak of tailored purple, and the virgin contentiously ravishing in her long flowing dress of primrose chastely pale.

While the rising moon outshone the stars.

12
RAMIFICATION

CONNEL'S VIGIL

The conversation and manners of Norman of Polmood were unrefined at best, but the temper into which he was plunged by the arrival and supercilious demeanour of the Duke of Rothesay compounded his natural roughness and germinating paranoia to a degree of asperity that was scarcely bearable.

To himself just as much as to his wife and guest.

Dinner on that first evening of Rosay's stay was a tasteless and gruelling affair, leavened by never a flicker of warmth and seasoned by no pinch of jest, no twist of repartee. In the days that followed, the society of the querulous laird was little courted by the affronted wife and the clearly (though smoothly immovably) unwanted visitor. Moreover, to ensure the success of the imminent King's expedition, it behoved the faithful forester to ride away every day: to ascertain the movement of the deer, to assess the numbers of the stags and does with kids, to plan the best route for the hunt to follow, and to visit the neighbouring farms and estates to muster beaters for the tinckell.

These swingeing considerations flayed his mind that night at dinner, drove him abruptly from table before his cheese, and hasted his weary tread round the corridor to the north-west wing.

Where Connel attended in the armoury.

'Connel?' rasped the laird.

'Oooor, mur loord?' the rustic uneasily mumbled, arising awkwardly from the stool where he had been carving the figure of a lady from a chunk of dry kindling.

With a dagger as sharp as a razor.

By the dimness of a single tallow candle.

'Ye have seen, Connel,' growled Polmood, slamming the door

and slotting his bright flambeau in a holder on the wall, 'that the Duke of Rothesay has arrived this day?'

'Ooor, mur loord.' Connel stood blinking at his feet, dazzled by the brilliance of Polmood's torch.

'And is to stay for the week.'

'Ooor . . .'

'Until his Majesty arrives ensemble for the hunt.'

Connel sniffed a wary acknowledgement.

Polmood paced furiously around the small square deathstore, unwindowed except for two forbidding loophole slits above head height in the wall opposite the door, with its longbows, arrows, broadswords, metal shields, leather targes, pole-axes, halberds, and all other manner of cleaving implementation, piled on the benches and hung from the racks like the books in a soldier's library.

'And ye ken,' he said, with ominous deliberation, 'that yon is a man with a mind like the shiteyard of a swine?'

Voiceless toe-scuffing from Connel.

'Though this opinion, my friend, ye shall keep between the two of us!' Polmood underlined his seriousness by lifting a gleaming sabre from its home and gently testing the bite of its edge against the ball of his thumb.

'Ooor, mur loord.'

'Very good, Connel. And likewise keep to yourself what now I tell ye. That there is nothing our *guest* . . .' he spat an eloquent globule of saliva on his sabre blade, 'nothing the Duke would better desire than to . . . *take advantage* of the Mistress. To lead her astray – who is so young and foolish yet – to lead her astray *in her morals!* Ye follow?'

'Ooor . . .'

'While she sees not the evil in the man, and the filth in his soul, but only the glamour, ye may say, of his fancy clothes and the like. His gawbling about music and lutterature, and his womanish squawking about the stinking bedhopping depravities of his fellows! To the truth of all this my wife is . . . blind. Ye ken? Like a chicken with a film across its eyes.'

Connel nodded in growing assent.

'Meanwhile I, in the commission of the hunt, must be away all week. And cannot safeguard ... Dame Polmood's virtue as I should like.' Polmood glowered challengingly at the gardener.

Who continued stolidly passive.

'Now, Connel. The Mistress has been much in your company of late.'

'Ooor, mur loord.'

'Following you about the garden, and suchlike. And this is well, Connel. It is something I commend, as it keeps her ... young thoughts from darker matters. To which she is unequal. And therefore, Connel, you are commanded to keep by her in the coming days.'

'Ooor ...'

'Be always at hand by day, wherever his *lordship* may lead her.'

Connel flexed his toes. His whole body gestured willing understanding.

'Stay not always in evidence, mind. But bide nigh. And Connel?'

'Mur loord?'

'See here: this blade?'

'Ooor?'

'Take it with ye, but keep it from view – here is its sleeve, and ye can wear it like so, inside your blouse and down your back.'

Connel took the weapon, his reach full of wonder.

'And if ye chance upon a situation where the Duke puts by his due respect for the Mistress's ... *honour*, then shall ye ken *what to do*!'

Silence.

'Shall ye not, Connel?'

'But mur loord!' the hireling protested.

Polmood prodded his man domineeringly in the chest, and hissed in a breath full of poorly digested meat:

'Ye shall run the bogger through like a dog! Like the craven beast he truly is. And no resistance shall ye meet, ye may be sure, for in arms the man is but a pansy and will wilt at a single puff.'

Connel squinted sideways at his conspiratorial master. Brooding uncertainty cried out from his stance.

'Ye are thinking, my friend,' surmised Polmood, in a rumble of low menace, 'of who should carry the blame, in such a circumstance?'

'Ooor ...'

'That shall I, man. So fear you not. But one thing, Connel, ye shall *never* do, what*ever* hideous lechery ye may see. And that is: ye shall never lay a finger on the Mistress.'

'Naar, mur loord! Uff coors . . .'

'But relate to myself, faithfully and in full detail, all intercourse between the Duke of Rothesay and my wife.'

Connel bowed in obedience.

'It is for *me* to decide', Polmood muttered to himself, 'what punishment the . . . *Mistress* merits.' Aloud he said:

'And you, Connel?'

'Mur loord?'

'All these things are in the utmost confidence. As ye value the renewal of your tenure here, but also as you prize the continuance of your breathing in this world! And every night of the week that comes, be you here when dinner is done, to report the events ye have perceived. Will ye not?'

Connel would, and painstakingly did.

For the next few days, at least.

As a shadow seemed the gardener to the courtier and the lady, while the laird rode away. Or a bad smell, as Rosay irately remarked one afternoon. Elizabeth disarmingly laughed and replied that, on the contrary, Connel was a perfectly agreeable and most industrious menial, to whom the estate was much indebted, for the consummate resurrection of its gardens. 'Which you yourself, my lord, have complimented much!'

When Rosay led Elizabeth to the rich-scented privacy of the butterfly bower, in the half-wild orchard that stretched behind the Castle about a quarter mile, there among the fruit trees would the sedulous gardener be, with a garnering basket on the ground, a pruning knife in his large black-nailed hand, and a veiled hive of gleaning in his sullen eyes and ears. Likewise when they went walking in the woods: who more apt to cross their path than the indefatigable Connel, collecting kindling or cutting birch rods to dress his garden and train his flowers to the sun?

And by the river?

Then who to the water would also repair, to angle trout for the Castle table?

'Good morrow, Connel!' Elizabeth would warmly greet him as they passed.

'Gud moorow, mur lidie,' he would mumble from the head-bowed intent of enworming his hook.

'Devil take the churlish ruffian!' Rosay would shortly grumble. 'It is almost, my lady, as if he means to *spy* upon us!'

'Oh, my lord!' Elizabeth exclaimed in making-light delight. 'Come, come! And besides, why should he not? What have we to hide?'

What indeed?

As Polmood's scalding jealousy required to know each night.

The laird was little soothed to gather, through the gardener's reticent hedging, that while Elizabeth remained spotlessly blameless, there were nevertheless certain improprieties, one could almost say importunate *irregularities*, in the Duke of Rothesay's deportment that would scarcely be dared in Polmood's presence. Was it right, for example, that Rosay so often should seize and kiss the Mistress's hand, should venture to encircle her waist in the course of their endless strolling conversations, should presume to inquire how such an outstanding beauty as Elizabeth could bear to bloom so unacclaimed, in such a stagnant backwater?

'Aaa*ach*, Connel!' Polmood groaned, and in galling hate inquired: 'So ye do not consider that the grand and noble Duke of Rothesay is of a character to improve the morals of a lady? Eh?'

'Naar, mur loord.'

'Stinking namby *toad* that he is – shite on his soul!' Polmood chewed with his upper stumps on a lower lip already raw from frottage.

But what could he do?

What possible expedient could separate the bloat satyr from the lamb, with the King's arrival so imminent? And in any case, how lamblike was the lamb? Was it not possible (probable!) that the eavesdropping gardener was moved by some ethnic chivalry of his own to gloss over his Mistress's contribution to Rosay's increasingly flagrant indiscretions? For she had previously showered childish kindnesses on him, had she not? While . . .

Higher and higher the rats pushed the debris from their incessant gnawings.

Until the eve of the coming of the King.

When a new and most horrendous discovery was effected, which would ignite the forester's piling passions into the most furious fatal flame.

TOO MUCH FOR ELIZABETH

The trouble had begun the previous day.

A Tuesday morning it was, warm and bright, with small white clouds peeking meekly above the furthest hills of the valley's horizon, enlivened by sporadic breaths of wind that seemed to come from nowhere to puff the butterflies off their course.

Polmood had ridden south, to instruct the beaters in their positioning along the edge of the Quarter Hill.

Rosay, sybarite to the gills, was still abed.

Leaving Elizabeth hungry for company: to luxuriate in the magical fragrances and lambencies that lurk in the lushness of such a day like mushrooms after rain! The presence of Rosay had reawakened in her that yearning for an admiring audience which grows greedier in proportion to its own consumption. She was like a kitten drinking salt-laced milk, and this morning the saucer was still locked away on the larder shelf.

So:

'Martha?' Elizabeth called up from the lawns.

'Yes, mum?' coughed that indomitable housekeeper, beating blankets on the terrace.

'Where is Connel, pray? Do you know?'

'That I do not, mum. I haven't set eyes – '

'Your pardon, my lady,' butted Thomas, who, with his beloved but uncourted Betty, was holding taut the blankets that Martha beat, 'but – '

'You, Thomas Rankin, shall hold your young tongue', scolded Martha, 'until it is called to wag!'

'Thank you, Martha,' said Elizabeth, ascending the dozen steps to where they laboured. 'But he may speak now. Thomas?'

'My lady,' the bottle-shouldered youth gargled squeakily, 'the fellow was going to the orchard this morning, for to scythe the long grass round the hedgerows.'

'Yes, my lady,' Betty seconded. 'From the parlour window I did see him head that way with his sickle in his hand.'

'And what might some folks be doing a-gazing from parlour

windows, I wonder?' muttered Martha. 'When there is so much *work* to be done!'

Elizabeth smiled. And gently reproved:

'There now, Martha! We do not live to work, I have heard it said, but rather we work to live. Do we not?'

'No, mum.'

'Pardon?'

'I mean: yes, mum.' Thwack, thwack.

'And Martha?'

'Yes, mum?'

'You must stop calling me Mum, you know.'

'Yes, mum.' Thwack.

Thomas and Betty broke out in a giggle, their eyes interlocked in a first light grapple of shared knowing and hinting promise.

Which neither other noticed.

Elizabeth saying:

'Seriously, Martha: has not Connel in these last few days seemed distant and distract?'

'I know not specially about these last few days, mum,' grunted Martha.

'Yes?'

'For to these old eyes, at least, yon fellow has ever been an eldritch fish.'

'It is true, my lady,' exclaimed Betty brightly. 'What you say. Connel is off his food, and finishes but a quarter of what he ate before.'

'Very like some malady within his belly!' pondered Thomas.

'Indeed?' said Elizabeth, thoughtfully patting her morning rose. 'Then it behoves us to ask after his health. And Martha?'

'Mum?'

'When it shall please the Duke of Rothesay to arise, you may advise him to find me in the orchard.'

'Very good, mum.' Thwack, thwack . . .

'Connel?'

'Ooor, mur lidie?'

'Are you not comfortable?'

'Mur lidie?'

'Well! Here the sunshine is flooding down, and you, toiling hard, have yet your heavy blouse upon your back!'

'Ooor, mur lidie.' The kneeling gardener stole a quick glance round at the pretty figure of his accoster, then returned to his rhythmic hacking at the grass.

'Oh, Connel! What an exquisite scent!' Elizabeth thrilled at the prickly-sweet perfume of the grass haying dry in the swathe already cut. 'What a world of memories: quite divine!'

Connel cleared his throat in tribute to her pleasure.

'Are you well, Connel?' she suddenly asked.

'Big purdon, mur lidie?'

'Betty tells me your appetite has greatly decreased of late.'

Speechless sickling.

'Is this so?'

'Ooor, mur lidie. If you sigh so, mur lidie.'

'But why, Connel? Is there something ails you?'

'Ooor, mur lidie.'

'But *what*? I pray you tell me!'

The gardener stopped scything, mopped his pouring red brow against a flapping sleeve, and confessed:

'Ize theenkeeng abowat my hoom, mur lidie.'

'And of your family?' kindly thought the maiden who herself had none.

'Ooor, mur lidie.'

'You once did tell me, Connel – or you allowed me to believe, through your absence of denial – that your parents were in circumstances not unfortunate?'

Connel nodded unhappily and returned to his hacking.

'Then why, pray, should you leave them?'

Several strokes of the long curved blade felled umpteen head of knee-high grass, rich green and bleeding sticky sap, before the sickler blurted:

'Urt wurz *lurv*, mur lidie, that wurz the caurze!'

'Why, Connel!' Elizabeth clapped her hands and laughed in delight at the ludicrous image of this great awkward yokel fleeing in heartbreak from some foundered romance. 'But you are not serious!'

'Ooor, mur lidie!' he rejoined almost savagely. 'Ize surious az niver befower.' His teeth snapped shut and his labours redoubled in vigour, if not efficiency.

Suddenly Elizabeth was unsure of herself. Had she poked unfeeling fun at the unsung grief of the lowly vassal? In precisely the needless and selfishly cruel fashion she so despised in others! Edging round behind the stooping figure, she angled for the reassurance of contact with his eyes. Then cried:

'Oh, Connel!'

His body shivered.

'I am so *sorry*! I did not *think*!'

For the gardener's ploddingly devious eyes were swollen with tears!

'Urt's orl roight, mur lidie. Urt's nothing.' But his nose-wiping and eye-dabbing belied him.

Perceiving the wetness of his sleeve, Elizabeth felt strongly that she should change the topic of their conversation.

Yet curiously:

'So truly, Connel,' she continued, 'you really have been seriously in love?'

'Ooor, mur lidie! And still I urm!' Swish, hack. Swish.

'Then why do you flee the one you love?'

'Ize . . .' Connel drew from a pocket in his blouse a carrot-shaped honing stone, and mutely set about the keening of his sickle.

Elizabeth expanded:

'If you did love with unalterable devotion – as any man must who loves *truly* – then how could you abandon hope of your affection being returned? For is not Time . . .'

'Bigging yowr purdon, mur lidie!'

'Y . . . e . . . s?'

'But hurv yow iver been in lurv? Mur lidie?'

'Why!' she gasped. 'Connel! What a question!'

'Mur lidie?'

'Consider my situation!'

Connel sniffed and wiped his nose, while continuing to hone.

'I am a married woman, after all!' Elizabeth declaimed, still not out of love with the concept. 'Am I not?'

'Inde-id yow ur, mur lidie!'

'And therefore, Connel, how can you ask me – how *dare* you, I might say – if ever I have been in love? Indeed!'

'Big purdon, mur lidie,' he mumbled abjectly. 'Mayhup I knowe nut whurt urt urz tow be in lurv.'

'Oh, Connel!' she exclaimed, instantly restored to kindly sympathy, and unaware of the furtive menial's gaze around the prettiness of her sandalled toes peeping tipsily beneath the hem of her summer-thin white kirtle.

Like berry buds at the base of a blossom.

He thought, through his hazing concentration.

'Love, Connel,' she expounded, pacing impulsively where she stood, 'between two young people of similar disposition . . . love is the most delightful of all sensations. And all the other generous feelings of the soul are not to be compared with it. It is . . . but no matter of me! It is of *your* love, Connel, that I do wish to hear. And in grave sincereness of heart will I listen.'

But Connel volunteered nothing for her grave sincereness of heart to listen to.

Whereupon, enterprising as any of her sex on such a trail, she seized the leading rein. Saying:

'I suppose you will claim, Connel, and well may I accept it, that she was the most sweet, the most lovely of womankind, but that Fate did so ordain that never could she be yours?'

Connel, gingerly testing the sharpness of his sickle on a stroking thumb, nodded vigorously.

'She showed herself not averse to you,' Elizabeth dreamily mused to the cream-speckled heavens, 'and soon might have been won to love you with all her heart. But that heart was . . . too young in experience at the time, and soon was over-ruled by power, was swayed by false arguments – and before your lady could get leisure to appraise her circumstances aright, she was *bestowed upon another*!'

'Ooor, mur lidie!' Hackhackhack.

'Truly, Connel? Was it so?'

Violent mane-waving nodding.

'Oh! Then tell me, Connel, if you will: do you love the lady still? Even though she be wed to another man?'

'*Ooor*, mur lidie!'

'But . . .'

'Inde-id I lurv mower darely than iver befower!'

'Now, Connel! You are making fun with me after all.'

'*Naar*, mur lidie. Ize *nut*!'

'Yes, Connel. I do believe you are. And next you will tell me that joy lives not for you in any thing with which your lady is not connected! That the only purpose of all your being is to hear her speak, to gaze upon her smile? That if only you could contribute to her happiness, there is no excrucation you would not submit to in exchange for the privilege?'

'Ut uz *trooo*, mur lidie!'

Elizabeth smiled in benevolent superiority at the broad exertion of the speaker's bent back. How could *he* know! Frivolously she scolded:

'It is a gallant prospect, Connel. Yet what you tell me is impossible, for nowhere in all the world exists such pure, disinterested and lasting love between the sexes as that which you pretend.'

'Mur lidie, yow ur *wrung*!'

Elizabeth blinked. And blinked again. To be contradicted by the gardener! 'I *beg* your pardon, Connel?'

'Uz yow shurl sooon belave!' The crouching labourer dropped his sickle, rummaged furiously in the cowling collar at the base of his neck, and turning, standing, apparently pulling his shaggy red head off, all in one shift flowing motion, there stood tall, straight and revealed.

'Sir John *Carmichael*! Oh no!'

'Oh yes, my lady!' he quietly confirmed, then further transformed from the shambling menial to the handsome, noble and accomplished young Baron of Hyndford, by tugging the turnip roundness from inside his cheeks, in the form of two thick pads of seasoned leather. 'I am myself, dear Lady Elizabeth. No more, no less. As you see.' Smiling sadly, he bowed as to a queen.

Elizabeth was singular, within the limits available to one so tender in years and gender, for her coolness of temper and presence of mind, but Carmichael's revelation was so benumbingly stunning that she stood stock still in the cast of a yearning statue for nearly a minute, her exquisite form leaning forward like an angel about to take leave of the dwellings of men. Her hands upraised in the shape of horror, yet her gaze smoothly devoid of expression.

Until:

Carmichael dropped to the ground his mummer's mask. His every gesture an unrehearsed pageant of hopeless longing, he knelt slavishly at Elizabeth's feet.

Beaming up at her with unwavering devotion.

She, reanimated, looked down. 'Carmichael!' she repeated disbelievingly.

'Elizabeth!'

'Oh, God of Heaven! Is it *possible?*'

'Dearest lady,' said he, rising, 'may I prove it to you beyond all doubt, by the humble kissing of your lovely hand? There! These lips are truly mine!'

His brushing caress transported the adulated lady back to the slings and arrows of outrageous reality.

'But Sir John, you are *mad*!' she cried, pulling away from him as though pricked by a thorn. 'Are you not *banished?*'

'Aaah, my lady!' he sighed. 'All the world does tell me so, wherefore must I believe it.'

'But you had journeyed to the Holy Wars! You so informed his Majesty, on the day of your departure!'

'And on that errand did I reach the port of Venice, when I realized that if die I must, so young and unfulfilled, and of death itself I truly have no fear . . .'

'Of course!'

'Then die I would, albeit unrecognized and unrewarded, in the nearness of my dearest and only love. Of whom your lowly gardener just now spoke so true.'

'Ooooh!' Elizabeth quietly wailed, her little hands tensing in panic. 'But surely, Sir John, you must see! This is impossible! I am a *married woman*!'

'Indeed, Elizabeth. And are you a happy one?'

'If my husband – '

Carmichael grinned the tight-lipped ironical grin of one who has toyed seriously with the notion that nothing in Life is Freely Done. 'Yes,' he said. 'If Polmood did discover us together, he would run me through like a rabid dog.'

'Ooh, dear Lord!'

'As he did order myself to despatch the Duke of Rothesay!'

'Oh *no*, Sir John!'

'If ever I find him in breach of your . . . purity, my lady.'

Elizabeth's astonishment and horror wed in trembling.

Carmichael reached down the back of his coarse baggy blouse and withdrew his gleaming sabre. 'You see, Elizabeth?' he gently remonstrated. 'So sorely does your husband fear for the chastity of his wife, in the company of his most exalted guest, that his gardener is instructed to keep watch on the intercourse between the two, and to execute the malefactor on the spot, if outrage should occur.'

Elizabeth's fingers pressed so hard into her cheeks that the lower lids of her eyes pulled down, in blemish of her beauty. Her knees at sea, her viscera squeamed in faintness as of hunger. Where, oh where, had stoic resignation flown? 'Oh, Sir John,' she huskily whispered, 'truly this cannot be! You must away forthwith, before some dreadful tragedy transpires.'

Carmichael lodged his sabre in the sward by its point.

How fine his large dark eyes: wide-set and steady, fearless yet imploring! His thick black hair and beard, cut short to accommodate his mask! The high sloping sincerity of his noble brow! His full firm lips and strong white teeth, and that nose with its gentle downward curve so well to the handsome of sensual!

'If such be your heartfelt wish, my lady,' he replied, smiling down at her in pain, 'then surely shall I obey. And pour my life away, like wine turned sour.'

Oh!

What was the short and balding Rosay compared to this, with his empty banter and his endless stream of babbling compliment?

And Polmood? Her *husband*!

'Ah, me!' Elizabeth quavered, to the tugging of harrowing heart-strings.

'Only would I ask, my dearest Elizabeth,' Carmichael acutely plucked, 'that you be irrevocably certain, before I . . . pour.'

'Sir John, there is – '

'*Bzzzzzzzzeeet*!'

'*Aaaaaaah*!' she shrieked.

Carmichael exclaimed: 'It is only a bumbling bee!'

But Elizabeth had already swooned.

Carmichael caught her as she crumpled and carried her to the shade of a flowering cherry tree, where he laid her down with loving care, shrugged out of his billowing blouse and rolled it in a pillow for her head.

Water!

The Polmood Burn flowed past the far side of the hedgerow that bordered the orchard, but with what could he sponge its coolness, to carry back to the fallen beauty's brow?

Tear strips off the lady's dress?

Unthinkable!

Yet ...

His agitated eye espied, in a modest inch of cleavage, a small corner of lilac-coloured cloth. Ever so tentatively, with the holy precision of a castaway sailor striking fire for his rescue beacon, the nipping nail tips of Carmichael's right thumb and forefinger teased from Elizabeth's firm high bosom the salvation of a scented linen handkerchief.

With it he rose and strode to the hedge.

But before he could vault it:

'Sir John!' she weakly called.

He looked round.

Elizabeth, though sickly ashen of complexion, was sitting up in returning consciousness, and fighting away the aftermath of her hysterical lapse by flooding her lungs with breath.

Carmichael rushed to kneel by her. 'My lady?' he solicited. 'I thought to fetch you – '

'No matter, Sir John,' she croaked. 'It is just the startlement of the insect in my hair, together with the shock ... all together ... too much, I fear. But now I am myself again. Your hand? I thank you.' Shaky but determined, she pulled herself upright on the strength of his gallant arm.

'And now, my lady ...'

'And now, Sir John, you must resume your mask immediately. *Immediately*! The Duke of Rothesay is likely already abroad and seeking my company, and what if he should find us thus?'

'Oh, but Elizabeth! May I not stay? Disguised as Connel? Allow me, at least, I *beg* you, the meagre alms that unsung worship of your person may afford, from the safety of my lowly pose!'

'Safety, Sir John?' she doubted, rustling grassy clingings from her dress. 'I know not of safety!'

'Then surely, my lady, the danger is mine. And gratefully, *ardently*, shall I embrace it!'

'I know not, Sir John.' She shook her head in worry. 'I must consider at leisure. And then the King . . . you know? Arrives . . .'

'I know it well. And yet, I swear, no-one shall discover me, and meanwhile shall I eke the pittance of my days within the sweetness of your own fair presence. My *loveliest* Elizabeth!'

How, in the face of this, could any young victim of a cold, loveless and unconsummated marriage be expected to enunciate the harsh expulsive dictates of her reason?

Carmichael raised her captive hand, pressed it first to his lips, then against the moistness of his eyes.

'Enough, Sir John!' she cried, pulling free. 'To your mask.'

'Sweet Lady ELIZabeth?' Rosay boomed self-importantly in the distance.

'*Now*, Sir John!'

'But . . .'

'My decision you shall learn this evening. An hour before dinner. At . . . at the stone by Cleaker's Pool.'

'As you command, my lady. I shall be – '

Elizabeth tripped away like a haunted sylph among the maze of fruit trees.

'Have mercy, dear Lord!' Carmichael prayed, then returned to the dirty-carrot persona of the shuffling yokel.

DITHERING

Poor Elizabeth.

What *was* she to do?

It was in a sense a morsel most sweet: to have *two* besotted admirers at hand, the one overtly brazen and the other clandestine!

But how immeasurably deranged was the risk?

And yet: who could tell what gruesome path Carmichael, if banished, might tread?

As she flitted tensely from the orchard, her inclination veered against Carmichael's staying: it would be *lunacy*! So she told herself a thousand times in the next two hours, drawing on her deepest wells of stamina to stage an entertaining hostess for the unctuous Rosay. After luncheon she excused herself on the pretext of having to oversee the grooming of the Castle for the reception of his

Majesty, and thus was free to dither aimlessly about the parlour and the kitchens (where her irritable anxiety put the domestics ill-at-ease), her resolution like a boat with no sail at the mercy of a squall-battered sea.

Then the King's steward arrived from Peebles with a dozen pack-horses bearing silverware, provender, and wine – much wine! And a handful of cheffing extras and slopping scullions to assist the smooth ordering of the Hunting Party's enjoyment.

'Oh, Martha!' Elizabeth panicked.

'Yes, mum?'

'I cannot see these people *now*!'

'Mercy, mum! Why ever not?'

'It is . . . I am not strong today, Martha. My uncongenial time, you understand? And the makings of a fever, I fear.'

'Then go you lie down, mum, and never mind the steward. Pompous fat rogue that he is! Begging your pardon, mum, but Martha shall keep him in his place.'

'Martha, you are so wonderful! What should I do without you?'

'Any honest body could do as well, mum,' the housekeeper blushed. 'Any body that did their *best*! Though many – '

'Thank you, Martha. I shall be myself again in an hour. Or two.'

'Very good, mum. Shall Betty then attend you with a cordial?'

'No, Martha. I feel it best to rest till I wake.'

But not before pacing miles across her chamber floor. Posturing. Pondering. Throwing herself down on the couch, then as hasily jumping up again. Peeping nervily from her window, though knowing not what she hoped to see. Gazing fearfully in her dressing mirror, trying a hundred facial falsehoods, trusting none. Then up again. To and fro. To and fro. Wrestling to unfankle the reality from the romance, to cream the heady sweetness off her dread, to weigh the competing ingredients distinctly and apart.

Impartially!

But of course she could not, and in the fourth hour of the afternoon she collapsed across her bed in a healing depth of sleep approaching coma.

At six the mother-henly Martha happened by, and softly called. Elizabeth slumbered on.

Not until nearly seven did her eyes blink open in a dreamy smile. She yawned prettily, like the enchanted princess at the end

252

of a thousand years, and realized that the squall had died: that her mind was made up.

In her dreams Carmichael had shone ideal, as all that was noble, just and generous in a man. He loved her purely, sought not base carnalities, but rather aspired to the exaltation of a union of kindred souls, to a bond that would soar like a seraph across the cruel divisive walls of monogamy, marriage, and oppressively Patriarchal Law! And how many ladies in all of history, so loved, could sever the bond and feed the desperate lover to the wilderness?

'*Hallelujah*!' Carmichael's tearful gratitude cried, on receipt of his permission to tarry.

'*Hush*, Sir John!' Dame Polmood scolded, as she plucked the petals from her rose and strewed them upon the stilling river. 'And never, Sir John, I *beseech* you, must you stray for an instant from the shelter of your mask.'

'Oh, Elizabeth!'

ROSAY'S CHAGRIN

At dinner that Tuesday evening Polmood was amazed and delighted to perceive that his wife, though still the epitome of charming politeness, seemed suddenly coldly estranged from the odious Rosay. Her inquiries were all directed to her husband! Would the tinckell be adequately manned, she was interested to know, and were the deer in pink condition for the sport of the King?

While:

'More cheese, my lord?' she distantly offered the blustering Rosay. As soon as the gout-bound gourmand accepted, she excused herself, recalling some exigent instruction for the gardener! Concerning the colours of roses to be picked on the morrow, and their tasteful distribution about the Castle's chambers.

Leaving Polmood and Rosay to cheese together: a blend so ripe as necessarily soon to disband. In silence.

And the following morning?

Elizabeth had flowers to examine. She had berries to pluck. Or topiary tonsure to supervise . . . always in the garden or about the orchard, and in the company of Connel.

Not Rosay.

As the shunned one found to his unbuttoned chagrin.

And as Polmood, not journeying today except for the exercise of his hounds on the adjacent slopes of the Polmood Hill, observed to his gledging glee.

'Shall it please you, my lord,' he grunted at Rosay, as the epilogue to luncheon, 'to stroll with myself up the hill awhile, and see the running of the dogs?'

'Thank you, no! Sir,' Rosay sharply declined.

Polmood feigned surprise.

The Duke disgruntled:

'Something of an allergy have I to the stench of hounds.'

'Oh, alas! My lord, you should . . .'

'Nothing malignant, mark you, Polmood. Nothing to deter me from the hunt itself.'

'My lord, I am so *relieved*!'

'You are kind, sir. Most kind. No, it is hardly mortal, my affliction. Yet disagreeable to the length of dissuading me from the company of hounds for its own sake, may we say?'

Polmood's sneer burned through its gossamer veil:

'You may say what you will, if and when it please you. My lord. As you are the King's brother, and as you are my *guest*!' The host pushed back his heavy chair. 'And now, my lord, if you will excuse me, I am obliged to labour awhile in the stench of hounds.'

'Oh, Polmood!' Rosay afterthought, freezing the forester's stomp in the doorway, beneath the great stag's head.

'Ay?'

'I had thought, Polmood . . . that is to say: it vaguely had occurred to me that I might occupy the early hours of the afternoon, before the King shall arrive, in the eximious society of your most accomplished and very lovely lady.'

Polmood hawked.

'Yet it appears, Polmood,' Rosay burbled, myopically squinting the fifteen paces from his seat to the door, and failing to affect unconcern, 'that the lady already has departed the precinct!'

'Ay!'

'Something she said, I believe, of gathering wood-rasps? To boil for a sweet preserve.'

'I do believe she did, my lord!'

'Then I wonder, sir, if you could be so very hospitable as to advise me of the route she is like to take in the pursuit of her rasps? That there I may follow and venture to assist.'

Polmood all but spat. Then said:

'My lord, as it please you. Though the wood-rasps are wicked in their niff!'

Rosay's lips drew into puzzlement.

'Their *stench*, my lord! They give out a muckle – '

'Really, Polmood!'

'But if you wish to brave the niff, my lord, you shall find the rasps cluster thickest round the mouth of the Herston Burn.'

'North?'

'South, my lord.'

'Far?'

'Some would consider it so.'

'Meaning?'

'That barely a mile from here does it lie, along the river bank.'

'I thank you, Polmood.'

'Where even a crippled child might walk! And *I* thank *you*, my lord, in advance. For your service to my kitchen. Though I warn you that, as she has the gardener already in her employ, the baskets may be filled ere you join them. But what of that? And now, my lord, if you will excuse me!' Polmood nodded the minimal nod into which his bow to Rosay's rank had shrunk.

Then clattered away.

LITTLE GOOD

Has not jealousy a thousand tireless eyes?

Rosay, of course, could not concede that Elizabeth might seriously prefer the company of the comical red-headed gardener to his own, but suspected that it was owing to some snide insinuation of Connel's (some odious calumny pertaining to the inflammation of his loins, perhaps!) that the maiden had so brusquely exchanged the Duke's repartee for the cloddish mumblings of the untouchable delver.

For this reason, when the heaviness of his luncheon had dispersed a little from his tailored paunch, he traversed the mile south that Polmood had depicted, following the east bank of the Tweed upstream, toward the west-flowing tribute of the Herston Burn.

To spy and hopefully eavesdrop on the pluckers of the rasps.

And this, after he had contoured laboriously round the lowermost slope of the Great Hill (which wedges like a giant's heel between the burns of Polmood and Herston) and crept close to his unsuspecting quarry, taking vantage behind a towering luxuriance of cow parsley that skirted the fertile flat wherein the wood-rasps thrived, is what he heard:

'And did you not find it hard, Sir John, to persuade the players to accept you?'

'Indeed, my lady!' Carmichael's voice carried strong with feeling.

Rosay, in his squatting concealment, froze in fascinated horror. Sir John? *Carmichael?* But where was Connel the gardener! His flabby eyes strained fruitlessly into the unyielding weed green.

'Then how did you overcome their opposition?'

'Ah, Elizabeth! There lies a lengthy tale, which would weary you, I fear.'

'Not at all, Sir John. My ears cry out to hear it.'

As did Rosay's, white-fleshed in the fury of their twitch.

'Well,' Carmichael drawled musively. 'Look you, my lady. As your basket overflows, and mine lags but a handful behind, what say you we labour no more awhile, but recline instead in the sun's caress? There would be pleasant, would it not? Upon the moss beneath the bluebells, where we both may lie atop my plaid.'

'Very well, Sir John. I do confess my back is aching.'

Rosay tensed frantically. The lilt of Elizabeth's voice and the heavy rustlings of laden movement were approaching! Surely they would not . . .

No! It seemed the mossy spot Carmichael had picked lay beyond the weedy thicket, up the slope to the snooper's right.

Who exhaled in ragged reprief and willed that the gargling of his crouching belly should subside.

'But we must not tarry long, Sir John,' Elizabeth went on. 'His Majesty arrives this night, and soon must I return to oversee the final preparations.'

Carmichael tutted in irritation. 'But there is the steward! The scullions. And the housekeeper! *And* Betty.'

'Yes, Sir John. But the visitors shall be numerous. And as it is my household, I wish not only that the King shall rest content, but that even the lower knights shall profit by every smallest crumb of comfort within my power to offer.'

Carmichael grunted his grudging plaudit, but wistfully added:

'While I lie scratching above the stables!'

'Oh come, sir!' Elizabeth's sweet fluency crystallized in rebuke. 'This we have been through: there just is no other way, else surely you shall be discovered!'

Carmichael sighed the sigh of a strong man lying back on his pillowed hands and frowning unfulfilment at the awning summer sky.

'Yes,' he tetched. 'And likewise must I cower like a baking rabbit within my wig, even here! So safely far from all society.'

'We are *not* safely far, Sir John.'

'Yet your husband is away up the Polmood Hill, a-barking with his hounds. I wonder, indeed, that the melody does not reach us here – a contrary breeze, I suppose, there must be upon the heights.'

'Quite so. But while Polmood is with the hounds we know not where young Thomas may be exercising with the horses. And what of my Lord Rosay?'

'Him!'

'Why do you sneer? The Duke of Rothesay is brother to the King!'

'And cousin to the Hornèd One!'

'Sir John!'

'Oh, Elizabeth! Surely you can see: the man is *evil*. Fornicator, adulterer, debaucher of helpless children – there is no scam he will not stoop to mine. The facts are well attested.'

'No, Sir John. I cannot and will not believe it. My Lord Rosay has his shortcomings – this cannot be denied.'

Filthy two-faced trollop! Rosay silently hissed within the captivity of his secrecy. *Stinking hypocritical slattern!* How *dare* she?

'To take a solid instance,' she blithely dared, 'he has no feeling for the humorous, as his Majesty so handsomely has, and yet imagines his wit to be consummate, and requires that one admire his every pleasantry, which can prove tiresome. But as it is a failing shared by the great preponderance of gentlemen – yourself not included, Sir John, of course – it surely cannot be held against my Lord Rosay in particular.'

Oooh, venomous slut!

'But as to those other allegations of iniquity, Sir John, I truly cannot entertain them, and entreat that you never more repeat them in my presence. Lest they offend my modesty, savouring more, as they do, of gentlemanly rivalship than truth.'

'As you command, my lady,' Carmichael grumbled. 'Though I fear you are perilously mistaken. But no more of that. The thought first to my mind when you did mention the Duke was: that we are in no danger of discovery by him.'

Elizabeth delicately yawned, in the graceful intonation of a beautiful lady sitting up in the afternoon and stretching her unclad arms and lightly draped shoulders in dainty pleasure.

Rosay, meanwhile, was aghast to perceive, hairy as his own bushy brows, with unblinking baleful eyes, the spinning descent of a large black spider not two inches from his nose.

'And how, Sir John, may you be so sure?'

'Ha!' scoffed Carmichael. 'The man rides his horse as it were a herd of swine. And is as like to *walk* out for his pleasure, forby, as a pregnant washerwife.' He indulged in a sardonic chuckle.

Elizabeth was doubtful, tightening in anxiety as the afternoon matured and the ordeal of hostessing drew nigh. 'But sure it is, in our situation, that timid caution is the wiser part of – what was that sound?'

'It was but the barking of a distant grouse, my lady! No more.'

But Carmichael was much mistaken.

Far from a distant grouse, the noise that had worried Elizabeth was the propinquitous Rosay's choked reaction to the assault of the thread-hanging spider upon his gaping lower lip. His melting terror of discovery cooled a shade when he heard:

'Anyway, Sir John, I now must betake me home.'

'But . . .'

'With the baskets, our mile shall take us a full half hour.'

'Not at all, my lady! I shall carry both with ease, at any pace you choose.'

But Elizabeth had resolved.

'Come, Sir John,' she chided, her voice informing Rosay that she was rising to her feet and smoothing out her dress.

Before Carmichael took up his basket load he solemnly urged:

'As, sweetest lady, it seems that no more may we tryst for several days, I beg you permit that I bestow the chastest token of my esteem.'

'Right gladly, sir!' Elizabeth sparkled in willing fun.

There followed the music of a briefly lingering kiss.

Which Rosay, writhing in his viewless impotence, perceived pulsating with the lust erect of tongues intertwining.

While in truth it merely pressed, in purest respect, on the back of the lady's hand.

Who then said:

'And as we walk, Sir John, you must divulge to me the story of your joining the Paris players.'

'Well ...' Carmichael pondered, his voice receding from the clandestine turmoil that throbbed to burst Rosay's every orifice. 'At first they gainsaid me. Owing to my less than tender years and my noble birth, which, they said, is the most cruel hardener of attitude and manner, like a noontime shadow that one never may cast aside.'

'But you were not disheartened?'

'Very much, my lady. Yet my need ordained that I persist. And on the day following I singled out their leader, in a tavern, and spilled to him my woes.

'"My love is wed to another man," said I.

'"*Ah bon!*" said he, and his interest was aroused.

'"And my life to me", I continued, "is but a broken quill, a cast-off shoe, all the while that I must shiver without the radiance of her beauty."'

'Truly, Sir John,' Elizabeth thrilled, 'your phrasing was wrought most winningly!'

'And all that I desired, I put it to him, was to dally a while in the wings of the troupe. To learn but a little of the arts of disguise, of the wiles of character, of concealment and portrayal.

'"For the privilege of which," I advised him, "I shall gladly pay my way. And more!"

'"*Ah bon!*" said he.

'And soon we were ...'

The saga dwindled beyond earshot, down the heath toward the Tweed, and Rosay's agony of fury and terror relaxed to a jittering tremble.

'Festering *sloven!*' he mouthed. 'For this you both shall *pay!*'

13
THE ROYAL HUNTING
PARTY ARRIVES

TRAUMA

'Oh, POLMOOD!'

Elizabeth's heart lurched in dread. It was after five and she was busy in her chamber, which she would vacate in deference to his Majesty, removing her feminine effects from view and re-re-arranging the roses in the vase by the bedside.

'GOOD EVEN TO YOU, MY LORD. AND HAD YOU A PLEASANT BELLYFUL OF GATHERING THE RASPS?'

'A WORD WITH YOU, POLMOOD. TO YOUR PROFIT, I TROW!'

'AS IT PLEASE YOU, MY LORD. I AM BUT BOUND FOR THE STABLES.'

Elizabeth rushed to the window.

Why should Rosay accost Polmood so? His voice intent with urgency?

'Oh, alack!' she wailed. For there on the lawn her direst trepidations all converged. Rosay was hastening, with the gait of a virtuous messenger, toward the waiting Polmood.

'WHAT?' the latter bellowed, when Rosay had embraced him in a conspiratorial huddle and whispered foul somethings in his ear.

Rosay nodded emphatically.

'CARMICHAEL!' Polmood thundered.

Rosay nodded again and muttered more.

'No!' Elizabeth prayed. Realizing that she might be seen, she stepped back from the lattice and nearly fell from the dissolving weakness that drained her every muscle. 'Mother of God . . .'

'THEN SHALL HE PERISH *WITHIN THE HOUR*!'

Elizabeth saw her husband transformed to a giant embodiment of jealousy, hatred, and open lust to kill. Sword drawn and glinting impatience in the sunlight, Polmood faced Rosay with a heat of berserk insanity that went far beyond the informer's anticipation, causing him, indeed, to retreat a prudent pace, as it looked as though Polmood were about to initiate his programme of slaughter with the summary beheading of the Duke of Rothesay himself!

But why?

Because Polmood was already a hopeless ruin (though this the quailing Duke and the stricken wife quite failed to see), wherein the rats had broken through, were running wild, and never again could be controlled, save by the total razing of the edifice they had colonized.

Elizabeth saw Rosay point defensively, intimating his hazard that Carmichael might be found engaged about the orchard.

'*Nnyurrr!*' Polmood howled, and charged across the south wing with his broadsword high.

Rosay, watching the avenger go, ran his tongue round lips that pursed from frighted relief to malicious satisfaction. Then he turned and strolled toward the Castle gate, shouting to some minion out of view:

'Hey, you! A flagon of wine to the parlour, and a chicken leg or so. At once!'

'Oh, Sir John!' Elizabeth sobbed. 'What madness . . . oooh!' But what would hysterical abandonment avail?

Bar the cost of Carmichael's head?

Full of the spunk that desperation spurs, she flew from her chamber, down the servants' stairs (to avoid the invidious Rosay on his way to the parlour), out of the Castle precinct, and along the river path to the Cleaker's Pool.

'There is a trout', Carmichael had earlier said, 'that lurks about that pool, full as huge . . . thus!' he had gestured, 'as ever the Tweed has yielded. And what a triumph for the kitchen, if we could take him while the King is here, and serve him whole upon a silver platter! Thus shall I deploy me, sweet Elizabeth, while you your noble guests receive.'

'Pray God he is still there!' Elizabeth gasped, holding high her trailing skirts and racing along the riverside as fast as a maiden may. 'And not . . .'

But there he was! Lying prone on the great grey stone, with two small fish already in his creel and the tip of his long cane rod playing gently against the still-moving water.

'Oh, Sir *John*!' she cried, rushing up to him.

'Elizabeth!' Carmichael exclaimed, leaping up and catching her heaving shoulders. 'Dearest lady! Whatever is the matter?'

'We are undone, Sir John! My Lord Rosay has . . . discovered us.'

'*What*?'

'And you must fly, Sir John. *Forthwith!*'

'Never – '

'My husband is beside himself with passion, and already is scouring the orchard with his blade unsheathed. In hope to find and . . . cleave your person!'

Carmichael's dismay protruded like a broken bone through the padded cheeks of his Connel disguise.

Elizabeth, flushed to fever hue, locked eyes with him.

And he despaired at her resolve. Saying:

'But Elizabeth!'

'No, Sir John! You must flee, and *now*! Heaven knows, in only minutes the King rides down the bridleway. And then where should we be, if Polmood came upon us too, at just that time? Lord knows if my honour may be saved at all, yet do you wish me doomed without a doubt? As surely shall I be if you do tarry!'

Carmichael mutely swallowed, his shoulders slumped.

'Therefore, *away*!'

'As you are in danger, my lady, so must I go.'

'Indeed!'

'But never shall I vacate this region, while I have life and strength to watch upon your own sweet self, from whatever lonely unseen distance I must keep.'

Elizabeth broke away from him. 'This only is further foolishness, Sir John,' she remonstrated with threatening tears, 'and must not be!'

'Indeed it must, my lady,' he objected, quiet now, and gravely resigned. 'Rosay may not be trusted, this I swear. And Polmood too, I cruelly fear, may take some violent step against your safety.'

'No . . .'

'Therefore shall I remove awhile to the mountains, and live in secrecy among the curlews and the stags, whence to keep a vigilance against danger to your welfare.'

Elizabeth took breath for further dissent, but then paused.

Certainly it was a bizarre proposal, but not without appeal. And besides: who could now deny that her own future *was* insecure in the extreme? King James would stay four days at most, and then? How would Polmood . . .

'But it is not possible, Sir John,' she suddenly observed, 'for a gentleman to live thus, like a beast of the heath.'

'Be assured, my lady, that I shall *make* it possible!'

'No!' she impatiently waved the thought away, and in a flurry of feminine practicality said:

'But *I* shall see you want not for provender!'

'But how?'

'That bed of moss, do you recall? Where in the sun we lay this afternoon, above the rasps?'

'Yes?'

'There shall I hollow out a cache, beneath the moss, and every day deposit food and news.'

'And wine, I pray.'

'And wine, of course. Tomorrow, in the morning, shall I first go there, when the hunt has ridden out, and mark the spot – what say you? – with . . . with a rose embedded in the turf. Like so.'

'Hark!' Carmichael stiffened.

Knight and lady strained their ears.

And heard, faint but approaching from the north, a drumming rumble as of –

'It is the King!' Elizabeth exclaimed. 'And all his nobles. Ooooh!' In panic she clapped pretty fingers to her lips. Then: 'I tell you, Sir John! Go that way; walk forward to meet them.'

'Huh?'

'Yes, yes! For they will see you as a peasant trudging north. And if my husband happens also along this way, then must he desist in his pursuit, to show his hostly courtesy to the King.'

'Truly, Elizabeth, you are a jewel!' Carmichael marvelled. 'Yes! Then, should Polmood disclose my guise to his Majesty, they all will suppose I am gone north, to Peebles or beyond.'

'Exactly so.'

'While I by night shall circle back, and find my furtive lair some distance south, among the hills of Herston.'

'Whereafter all shall fall out well, God willing.' Elizabeth drew a heartfelt cross upon her breast, and added: 'But you *must go now,*

Sir John! That the horsemen may not see us together, or even near!'

'I go, I go!' he moaned. 'Oh, Elizabeth!' In the giddy passion of hopeless proximity he swept her off her feet, clasped her to his bosom in a hugging tremble, and pressed a kiss of worship to her temple. 'Come whatever may, my fairest lady,' he vowed, 'I shall love you through all eternity! Farewell.'

Before she recovered her balance he was gone, scrambling up the bracken slope to the bridleway.

Without a backward glance.

'Farewell, Sir John!' she whispered, her feelings scattered as by a broken prism.

Nevertheless, before commencing her journey home (in expectation of being overtaken by the royal party), she cooled, and calmed, and collected wits sufficient to consign Carmichael's catch to the river's bed, with a boulder in its belly, and to break his rod in several, around the leverage of a sapling tree, and cast the pieces to the current.

THE NEXT SIX HOURS

The spot Carmichael chose for his hiding place is well known, and is still pointed out by the shepherds and farmers of *The Muir*, as the Tweedsmuir district is sometimes called. It is a little den near the top of the Herston Hill, where he could oversee all that passed about the Castle of Polmood, which lay northward down the valley by half an eagle's league. The vantage of Carmichael's retreat was such, its entrance baffled by the chance falling together thousands of years before of three enormous rocks, that no-one could approach closer to him than a mile without being seen – while, if danger did appear, he could withdraw from his lair and creep southward to the far side of the hill without risk of discovery.

Here we will leave him awhile, to linger out the day, to weary for the haven darkness of moonless night, and then to haunt the straggling lanes and boortree bush above the forbidden Castle, at whose every lit window he watches till his vision swims, in unrequited hope that his tragically mis-wed Elizabeth may there appear for a magic moment framed.

And what of the frantic husband?

No sooner had Rosay informed him of the staggering circumstance, that Connel the pliable gardener was none other than
young Carmichael of Hyndford in disguise, than? The outraged
forester was swept beyond all hope of reason by a conscience-
wiping deluge of vengeance-wreaking resolve which lashed not
only at Carmichael the heinous imposter, but at Rosay and
Elizabeth too. The truth of Rosay's ingratiating mumblenews he
could not doubt, as a thousand leaves of scattered detail at once
rose up and blew together in a cloud of condemnation, yet he
viewed the Duke of Rothesay's acrimonious divulgement as merely
the gall of a lecher's pique, and he no longer entertained any scrap
of doubt that Elizabeth had been criminal with both alike.

That embrace he had espied from the Nidpath parapet!

The brazen lust of Elizabeth's attempting to sleep Rosay in the
chamber next her own!

Then the countless recent frolics with Connel: orgasmic fornications by the dozen, in the name of plucking fruit!

Viewed from the narrow rat-hole that was now his only window
on the world, the situation appeared to Polmood to convict his wife
of the most shamefully flagitious infidelities. Hence it was that the
emotions of his swollen heart could not be concealed, when Rosay
came upon him to clipe, and, driven like a feather by a storm, he
sallied sword-drawn into the orchard to rend Carmichael lifeless.
And thence, finding the hated vermin nowhere among the apples
and the cherry trees, the demented Hunter, having no suspicions
of Carmichael's flight, continued his frenzied chase all through the
following hour: in the kitchens, the stables, the armoury, along
every leafy lane in the Castle locale where the gardener might
conceivably stray, there Polmood raged to no avail, the vilest
execrations streaming out like a trail of slime behind him.

Until, a quarter mile along the northbound bridleway, he came
upon his Guest.

Who rode serene.

With thirty nobles, twenty pages, and a dozen soldiers of horse
strung out two-abreast at his heels.

And Elizabeth riding demurely side-saddle on the same great
milky white stallion with a sinewy Avuncular arm about her waist.

'Ho, Polmood!' his Majesty Jovially saluted. 'And are you still in
pursuit of our dinner, man? To stick it with your blade!'

This tickled the gentleman behind to a venting chuckle. For was not Polmood more than ever the wild man of the mountains? In his thick soiled hides, his high thonged boots, and his brow deeply furrowed in the feral glare of the thwarted carnivore!

Elizabeth smiled painfully, though only Polmood saw. As the sun filtered through the trees to dapple her pretty face and dress in twisted shapes of chestnut leaves, she found her bosom torn between shame and apprehension. To be married to a man who could forget to abject before the King! Yet what appalling havoc might the same man spout, should his passion overwhelm his tongue!

Then Polmood recalled:

'Forgive me, Sire!' he blurted, and sank in the requisite genuflexion. 'I was but ... but ...'

'No matter, Polmood,' his Majesty breezed. 'You clearly have laboured hard this day! As has your beauteous spouse, we hear. And what sounder exculpation can any man call up, when the Judgement Day lists out his peccadillos, than that *he laboured hard? Umm?*'

The company did not know, it seemed.

Wherefore:

'Have the boys SEND UP A MOUNT!' King James decreed. 'That our host may ride us to his home.'

From then on all was hurry, noise, bustle and confusion. The numerous horses, hounds, hawks, and other hunting appurtenances were stalled and stowed in their various lodgings, the attendants scurried to vet their billets, the nobles strolled in garrulous clusters about the lawns, making much of the fragrant evening air and the slopping bumpers the servants plenished, and Elizabeth appeared to transcend the human in the vibrant bright-eyed energy she poured into entertaining her Guest and guests.

'And when is the baby due?' she asked the Lord James Douglas of Dalkeith, further to her first kind question as to the Lady Annabelle's health.

The Lord Douglas, drinking dwarfly alone at that moment, like a sheepish terrier in the presence of tolerant wolfhounds, mumbled wetly into his goblet that he believed the happy day was not far away though himself he was far from savant in the precise ins and outs of these affairs.

Overhearing this, the blondly languid Duke of Hamilton, in a crony gaggle ten paces distant, observed with a drawling grin that the Lord Douglas might safely repeat his confession countless times, as no man (nor woman, neither!) was like to contradict him.

The crony gaggle honked appreciatively.

'And the children?' Elizabeth asked of the blaze-haired Earl of Mar.

Fine, it seemed. All fine!

'And you, little one? Yourself. How are you keeping?' King James inquired in a lazy murmur, stroking the profusing ginger of his beard with his right hand, as he led the only lady in to dinner.

Elizabeth thanked his Majesty for his considerate concern, assured him she had never been fitter, and gave effusive thanks for her good fortune in finding the married state to suit her better every day.

But James was unconvinced. Norman of Polmood, he perceived, was a soul in the coils of some serious disturbance. How else at such a banquet of reconvened acquaintance, ostensibly high in the spirits of sportive anticipation, could the host comport himself so tersely sullen and inattentive to his guests?

And glower across the table at his beauteous lady in such prolonged and unveiled attacks of blackest loveless loathing!

While eating barely a turkey breast from the splendid feast.

Yet drinking like a drain.

And what foul poison had Polmood to lay at the Duke of Rothesay's door – he who prattled foppishly with the Duke of Hamilton and his spineless kith, while deftly feigning not to see the beaming shambles in the forester's regard?

'But Polmood has been indisposed of late, has he not?' his Majesty mildly probed, when the general hubbub round the table had reached that luxuriance of volume in which individual conversations may quietly nestle.

Elizabeth was sitting at his right hand, at the head of the table. 'No, my Lord!' she said in unconvincing wonder, as she smiled glancingly round the company in pleasure at their pleasure.

'Umm. You say so? Yet he is hardly himself tonight, it seems. Unless we are most strangely mistaken.'

Elizabeth pushed in nervous dismissal at her hardly touched platter of roast mutton in caper sauce. 'It appears, your Majesty,' she mumbled. 'That my husband is afflicted by . . . some passing gripe. Born, perhaps, of his excitement at your coming.' But her dress of turquoise lace was cut low enough for the worldly King to notice the shame of her disingenuous evasion flushing hotly on her breast.

'Very like. Very like,' he mused. 'Though when he excused himself a moment ago, and that right bluntly too, he looked to us rather more in a wrestle with some powerful passion, that he scarcely could control.'

'My Lord, I do not believe so!' Yet Elizabeth did believe so, as her quavering voice betrayed. 'Though painfully do I blush that my husband's manners . . .'

'Tush, tush!' the King made light. 'Not a bit. Most probably he has rushed away to relieve his belly of such gripe as you describe, my lady. The which let us dwell upon no longer, for fear it impair our own delight in this magnificent repast. More wine for you? No? Then alone we shall indulge.' A laconic length of Forefinger angled slightly and the royal steward stepped from behind the Polmood throne and charged his Master's goblet with the colour of heady rubies.

Down the table an animated dispute had developed over the question of the correct analysis of the foundations of the metaphysics of poetry, and this his Majesty latched upon to distract Elizabeth from whatever sombre trouble she was unwilling to confide.

'Has not Sir William turned out *well*?' he winningly enlisted the value of her opinion. 'He that only a year ago was but a gangling bumpkin!'

Elizabeth had to smile at the deadpan dryness of the *Bon Mot*. 'I fear, my Lord,' she said, brightening, 'that I have not found a moment yet to engage Sir William in conversation. But I have no doubt that beneath such excellent tutelage he only can have prospered.'

His Majesty chuckled appreciatively. 'But hark! And you shall hear him rout our brother, whatever their contention.' He dabbed absently at his mouth with the knuckled fold of a large linen napkin, and added:

'Which goes some way to show, think you not, that in letters and in learning at large there is no one class in our society which naturally excels, and that it therefore behoves us to institute equal schooling all across the nation, that he may profit best who best is able, regardless of his station?'

Elizabeth thrilled to be consulted on such a theme.

And modestly confessed:

'So far as I may follow your Majesty, this reasoning seems faultless. Yet must I also say: it is a matter I have not pondered previously.'

'Umm! Then hark: let us overhear together, and see if some timely moral may be drawn – like a broken tooth from an unwilling child, if you can pardon the devious trope! – from the gnashing of their rhetoric.'

Monarch and maiden then leant their ears to the mid-table debate.

In time to hear the Duke of Rothesay sneer:

'Your preaching then, sir, is that the poem is not *fashioned* by the poet, but rather *appears* within him? Like a *dream*!'

'Ay, my lord,' Sir William curtly nodded across the protein remains that heaped the table. Over the year his flinty eyes had evolved an even confidence that now projected calmly, through neither smile nor frown, upon the gesturing extravagance of his antagonist.

'In that case, dear sir, it is surely most perplexingly uncanny that we are not poets all! Mnyah? As we all of us certainly dream – man, woman, child, and stinking hound forby!' Rosay waved his non goblet hand in florid graciousness, like a musical conductor who strokes to silence the final note of some rendition beyond surpass, in intimation that Sir William might resume the exhibition of his callow absurdity.

'Ay, my lord,' the yellow-haired youth sniffed, picking disrespect-fully between two meat-bunged teeth. 'It is true we all dream, this I grant you . . .'

'Most gracious, sir! Most abundantly . . .'

'But yet never will claim, my lord, I dare say, that we all of us dream *the same*?'

'No. But what of that?'

'Or that we all are gifted alike with the power to communicate our dreams, in painting or what have you?'

'Well . . .'

'*Very* well, my lord! And will ye deny that what a man *dreams* grows out of what he *is*, of what he has *done*, and of what he has *become*?'

'Possibly, sir. I shall not deny it. Not least as its relevance fails utterly to strike me!' Rosay glanced for support from his nearest peers.

But was scantly rewarded.

'Relevance, my lord?' yawned the Duke of Hamilton, two seats down the table and beginning to slur. 'No! I do confess me quite unstruck by relevance of any kind. And you, Lamington! What shay you?' he nudged his lumbering neighbour in the ribs.

'Eh?'

'Are you struck . . .'

Sir William sat forward and fixed Rosay with a stare the temperature of the ocean freezing. Raising his voice to assure a general audience, he continued:

'Just as, my lord, his Majesty is like to dream through long hard nights of how our nation will be served when the throne of England passes on.'

'Yes?'

'While such concerns will rarely be found parading through the sleeping nights of the kitchen staff.'

'And what of that?' Rosay frowned, not seeing where he drifted.

'Just this, my lord.' Sir William redoubled the suspending interest he had attracted by pausing, taking a dilatory sip from his wine, and wiping his mouth and thickening beard on the back of his hand. Before saying:

'That as not even his Majesty may control his dreams, which yet grow out of the man he is and the life he leads, so neither may the poet control the coming of his songs, for all that they too spring from the man that he is. *And!* And from the time, the toil, and the tears that he has shed, to make his life a garden wherein such songs may flower.'

'But – '

'I am nearly done, my lord, if ye will permit me. And nothing would I presume to have *proved* by the foregoing remarks, but merely, my lord, from the bottomless humility befitting my age and rank, to have given some ground for suggesting that a *true* poem (by which, my lord, I do not encompass the myriad jumbles of sightless artifice that bunglers everywhere contrive) – that a true poem is indeed not unlike a dream – to utilize the aptness of my lord's own figure – in that the coming of neither may be precisely bidden, though arduous may be the labour that loves the soil wherein the whimsical seed may fall.'

Rosay inflated for a vehement riposte.

Sir William hurried on:

'To which, my lord, I would only add that the labour without the soil is fruitless ever, while the soil without the labour may yield a single peach, but never an opulent harvest. And all of this explains, my lord (indeed: your Majesty, my lords and my lady – for myself I throw upon your general judgement), why it is that for every *poet* in this world who truly has a song to sing, you may swiftly find a hundred *dabblers*, who in their time have scribbled down a single honest line but lacked the power to make it thrive. And a thousand worthless *praters* forby, my lord, who screen their lack of even that lonely solid line in a vapour of sapient snivel pertaining only to the works of others: bleating endlessly betwixt undeserved effusion over the baubles of their fellows, which they secretly gloat to despise, and the crafty spraying of their bilious envy over each and every work of worth that dares to raise its noble head and smile its smile of grace!'

It has to be confessed that the ensuing hush was not unrelated to the imperfect comprehension of certain persons present of the purpose of Sir William Moray's onslaught.

Then:

'YOU INSOLENT PUPPY, SIR!' Rosay roared. 'How *DARE* you . . .'

'BRAVO, Sir William!' King James adroitly interposed. 'A lofty sentiment, sir, and praiseworthy. Though perhaps a morsel over-stated toward the close? The hinting grind of a personal axe creeping in to vex the music, could it be, and thereby detracting from the gallery's admiration? Hmm? But enough of discursion for the moment. Else our heads shall prematurely spin! Therefore, a toast! A toast to the beauteous architect of our bountiful banquet – all rise!'

All rose, except Elizabeth.

Who becomingly blushed.

'To the lovely Dame Elizabeth of Polmood!' his Majesty proposed, when the glasses were charged. 'To the lovely Dame Elizabeth!'

'To the lovely Dame Elizabeth!' the baronial company echoed.

All drank.

Elizabeth wondered when she might withdraw.

'And to our valiant host!' the King enthused. 'To our honest Hunter of Polmood – may his belly gripe allow his imminent return to our society. To Hunter of Polmood!'

'To Hunter of Polmood!' the nobles agreed.

All drank again.

And again, and again, for the next three hours.

LESS GOOD

While the King and his knights caroused, swapped yarns and bragged their expectations of the morrow's chase, in their habitual alcoholic loosening of sense and cohesion, from which Elizabeth shortly excused herself and slipped away, their absent host lagged further and further behind their leading thoughts, rather as an upaid debt sheds importance in proportion to the length of the creditor's silence.

And this was well.

At least in a way.

For, had anyone gone searching for the missing laird, what would he have thought to stumble upon the hurricane fury that was Polmood that night? All about his environs and beyond he stormed again, sword bared, and slavering from the rage of his gibbers, from time to time howling out like a wounded stag from the driving pain of his craving to light upon the diabolical Carmichael.

But the villain was nowhere to be found.

Nor could the menials give the smallest account of him, save that no trace had been seen since earlier he had departed down-river with his fishing rod and creel.

Five miles downstream Polmood's torment then took him prowling.

To no avail.

'You, boy!' he snarled at Thomas the groom half an hour before midnight, when he rapped him blinking from his cottar's couch.

'Sire?' croaked Thomas.

'From now until dawn ye will get ye back to the stables for to stand watch there. Eh?'

'But Master!' the naked youth protested, knuckling his eyes as his manhood sank in disappointment from its blissful dreams of Betty. 'The King's men . . .'

'SHITE OF BOGGERY, SIR!' Polmood seized the terrified Thomas by the ear, twisted him against the doorpost and laid cold steel against his throat. 'As ye prize your gizzards ye will take them to the stables, *will ye not?*'

'Ay, Master!'

'To watch for yon filthy . . . Connel fellow.'

'As ye say, Master.'

'And if he returns, Thomas, for it seems he has gone missing, ye shall say to him *nothing,* but let him sleep, then creep to the Castle and inform myself alone.'

'Ay, Master.'

'Then get you there with no delay.'

Thomas flung on his clothes and scrambled in haste to obey, finding sorely the worse for drink in the stableyard two guards from his Majesty's cavalry platoon.

But no Connel.

Polmood, when he returned to the Castle, was informed by the less addled pair on duty at the gate (to guard the Presence within) that a message had been left for him by his lady.

'Uh?'

'She says, my lord,' ventured the spokesman, anonymous behind the haft of his pike and beneath the shadowing rim of his iron helmet, 'that we will please to request that you bed this night on a flock sack in the hall.'

'*What?*'

'That, my lord, is what the lady said. As the master chamber is given to the King, the second to the Duke of Rothesay, and all other closets on the third and second flats to the nobles of higher rank.'

Polmood turned abruptly away from the soldiers, that they should not see the ebullitions that ravaged his features. Across the terrace, over the lawns, and into the towering trees by the river his wild thoughts wandered where his eyes could not. Somewhere out there the cloudheavy night gave undeserved sanctuary to one of the two satanic souls in Polmood's universe for whom death by slow disembowelment would be too sweetly merciful.

Temporary sanctuary!

'While those of the rank of knight, my lord,' the spokesoldier ventured, 'are grouped together on flocks in the hall, where it be passing comfortable with the fire lit.'

Polmood turned slowly to face the speaker. Growling.

'And she?'

'My lord?'

'The lady herself, ye dullard shite! Where, did she say, would she bed herself this night?'

'She did not say, my lord.'

'And ye did not inquire?'

'Indeed not, my lord!'

Polmood groaned, and hissed, more to himself than to the guards: 'Then ferk ye to boggery for the vermin ye are!'

The soldiers stiffened in apprehension as the agitated laird shouldered past them, tore down one of the six oily torches lining the archway that tunnelled beneath the keep, and passed beyond their sight.

Right across the rectangular cobbled courtyard, the self-convinced cuckold half-strode and half-staggered, as though acutely drunk in only one half of his brain. To the kitchens he resorted, vaguely thinking he there might find some late domestic to tell him where his wife could be found.

But no.

In the freshly scrubbed spickness that Martha left ever behind her there was only the carcass of a sheep on the spit to suggest that so lavish a banquet had so recently been prepared.

And a strong smell of mint hanging sweetly in the air.

Polmood lodged his torch, hacked himself a hunk of meat, and slumped heavily on a wooden stool to debate with a flagon of wine.

His wife was where?

In bed with Rosay!

Of this Polmood had not the slightest doubt.

Lewdly and relentlessly disporting. They plainly were. Their hotly spurting adulterous secretions besmirching the very sheets that he, Polmood, had inhabited (chastely alone!) not eighteen hours previously!

But what could be done?

The chamber of the criminal cavorting, albeit that the door was round the corner of the wing, shared a wall with that wherein his Majesty slumbered! And certain it was that the King's door would be guarded. So where would that leave Polmood, if, going stealing that way with a naked weapon in his grasp, he should alarm the guard?

Who would then believe he had not schemed against his Sovereign's life?

But if . . .

For two hours and as many quarts of wine Polmood sat there brooding on the conspiracy against him, muttering a hundred schemes of mounting impracticality and incoherence. By the time his torch had begun to smoke its last reeky rite, his wits and will had ossified together in a deadlock of near catatonia. The nervous exhaustion of his hours of rampage, dulled by the mechanical immoderacy of his drinking, all in the shadow of the seemingly unscalable mountain of his woe, for a short time filled his throat with a mighty lump and squeezed wetness of self-pity to his eye.

In this broken spirit he lurched to the hall, resolved in the jaded weakness of no resolve to defer all resolution to the morning.

'Lord give me strength,' he lowly rasped, lying heavily on a free sack mattress, 'that I shall seek my enemies everywhere, *until I see them perish*!'

'Gnurr?' some sleepsozzled voice inquired. The dining table had been pushed against the west wall, and dormed about the floor, discernible by the cool smoulder of the ashing logs in the grate, were some dozen sleeping knights. Variously:

Snoring.

Grinding drunk-tense teeth.

Creaking as they tossed.

And collectively smelling like a rotting corpse steeped in vinegar.

'Gnurrr?' the same voice dreamt. 'Shat you, Hip barn?'

Polmood lay back and kept silent. Having removed his boots, doublet and sword belt, he now wished only for sleep to swoop down and spread protective wings across his soul till dawn, when he would rise recharged to execute his purposes.

But sleep, where had you flown?

Ever further from rest, in the agonizing immobility of not wishing to disturb his fellows recumbent, Polmood found that the smoulder-softened blackness of the hall came explosively alive with images beyond his power to bear. Elizabeth he saw, unclad, as never in the flesh he had. And Rosay too, with his broozler shuddering erect, burstingly massive and blacker than a stallion's. And Elizabeth kneeling in her eagerness, lips drawn back, tongue protruding stiffly, to . . .

'Nnnyeee!' Polmood moaned.

'Whuuurf?' Some shallow kipper surfaced for a moment, then turned and once more sank.

Polmood rolled into a silent crouch, paused to listen, rose to his bare feet and padded from the hall. Inaction he could endure no longer. Therefore would he steal upon the adulterers unarmed, to throttle them where they bucked. And if foul chance should first betray him to the officers that watched the King? Then was he sleepwalking, undressed and with no weapon, afflicted still by the same ague that earlier had driven him from dinner!

Up the narrow servants' stair he stepped in utter darkness, as only a lifetime inmate could, and met no let save the hollow heaving sound of a spewing cat in a loophole recess. When he cautiously pushed open the door to the third-floor landing, he saw, glimmering round the corner to his right, a patchy brightness that evidenced his Majesty's guard. Polmood paced intently toward the light, holding himself ready in the armstretched posture of somnambulance. Reaching the fateful door to iniquity, which opened off the corridor to the left, just before the corner leading round to the west wing, he pressed a hammering ear against it.

And for a lengthy minute listened.

Nothing.

Another minute.

Still no . . .

Around the corner a voice that dripped with boredom cleared its weary throat and said:

'Bogger me! How long is it now?'

'It is fully as long now, my young friend,' a sterner tone rejoined, 'as ever the Good Lord intended it to be. And never will grow a hairbreadth longer, whatever the potion peddlers say: it never can be done. Therefore rest you easy, learn patience, and grumble not about your task. For if his Majesty . . .'

All in one swiftflowing motion Polmood clicked the latch, swung the door inward, glided into the pregnant blackness of the chamber he knew so well.

And again paused to listen.

Hearing nothing, he pushed the door to but not latched, inched with toe-exploring care to the near side of the lust-ample bed.

And strained his hearing yet further.

No loin-grinding motion, but . . .

Yes!

Beneath the high-pitched rushing of the silence there breathed two different rhythms: one deep and fatly nasal, the other *softer and* . . .

Close to swooning from the effort of not howling in triumph, Polmood leaned over the bed, ran light fingers up the blanket covering the torso nearest, and found a hairy face atop it! 'Aaaaah!' the invisible avenger crowed deep within, taking breath to fuel his coming orgy of strangulation.

But what should freeze his throat-reaching hands more instantly than the most unexpected development?

The bearded body near him, which he itched to despatch as that of Rosay, turned suddenly in the bed and sharply elbowed the personage lying on the far side.

Who in a deeply drowsy voice appealed:

'Eeelizzabeth?'

Polmood stood dumbfounded.

For the voice was that of Rosay!

So where was Elizabeth?

And whose was this other bristly chin, that he had just touched?

Sluggishly Rosay's voice added:

'Elizabeth? What ails thee, Elizabeth, my jewel?'

There followed a few breathless seconds, during which the excruciation of Polmood's anguished amazement can hardly be imagined.

Then the nearer bedfellow stirred with a jolt, and rumbled:

'Whaat?'

'Be still, Elizabeth, my dearest one! Be still!' returned Rosay, in the slow, faraway monotone of speech-in-sleep. 'For all is well. And *I* . . . am here!'

'What the hornèd devil!' exclaimed the Duke of Hamilton, for he it was. 'Is my Lord of Rothesay thinking of? I suppose he imagines he is sleeping with Polmood's lady – ha! For the which he doubtless much would give. Eh?'

Rosay broadcast an adenoidal snore.

'Hey, hey, my lord!' Hamilton hounded him, together with unbashful nudging in his ribs. 'I charge, my lord, that you break your dream. For it seems you paddle in illusions most dishonourable.'

'Oh, oh, oh!' Rosay complained, in the wheedling fashion of one begging to be left in slumber. 'What, what?'

Hamilton conveyed his cynical amusement in a muciferous chuckle. 'This, this, my lord!' he mocked, and shook the other's shoulder. 'That I venture to intrude upon your kippering, as it seems you dream you are abed with Dame Polmood. And this, alas for you both, is not the case. Which is why I feel it meet, my lord, to parade the matter before your attention, lest your lordship's dream spill out in actions not conductive to the welfare of myself!'

Rosay's mouth made several short wet swallowing noises, suggestive of reluctant coming to. 'Oooh, alack!' he groaned. 'Your pardon, sir? I beg it of you.'

'My pardon, my lord? Yours, yours! As ever. But why should you wish it now?'

'As my chattering sleep, most unfortunately, has divulged to you the secret of my success with the superlative Lady Elizabeth.'

'No!'

'While it had been my design to keep the conquest chivalrously private, in defence to the lady's delicacy.'

'My lord, you are too noble!'

'There are times when I do fear so. However, sir, since the fact of this affaire has sailed unbidden from my lips and harboured in your ken, may I trust that it will not voyage further?'

'Already it is blockaded beyond pregnation! Which is well for you, my lord! For how soon might the jealous husband engineer the liberation of his lady's lover's soul, if he but knew?'

'Precisely, sir. My sentiments precisely.'

'But what of the lady herself, my lord?'

'Eh?'

'If her façade of innocence should crumble, and she you betray, as still she is so young?'

'Bah!' Rosay sourly scoffed. 'Of that there is no fear.'

'How not, my lord? It cannot be that Polmood ever talks with her as scant as he did this night?'

'Passing near, sir. A word or two at meals, no more.'

'But . . .'

'And plain it is as his own hog face,' Rosay retched, rolled over and spat on the floor, 'muckle muffin that he is, that he cannot service her with that she needs . . .'

'As can you, my lord!'

'As can I, indeed.'

'But how, my lord, may you be so certain? In the dead of night, perhaps, they come together in intimacies you never can know? And at this instant . . .'

'No, no, *no*!'

'Wherefore?'

'You have, sir, to observe them together for but an hour, to comprehend that the Lady Elizabeth feels no more desire for her husband than a rutting tender filly for a grunting greyhead he-swine.'

'You are rich, my lord, in comparison for your brother man!'

'From which it safely follows that we stand in no danger of a sudden womanish confession, by her to him, of the delectable transports she has learned to achieve with myself.'

'Heavenly ecstasies, my lord! I have no doubt.'

'And forby . . . you *dirty dog*, sir!'

'My lord?'

'You have broken a filthy wind, sir! A *filthy* wind!'

'Not I, my lord!'

'Eeuuugh!' Rosay snorted in disgust, and nosepinchedly expostulated: 'Such a fildy sdinking diff, sir, I dever would have bedieved – bore dauseating (treefold!) dan a keddle food of howds!'

The Duke of Hamilton made blowing and waving noises. 'It was not I, my lord,' he blew. 'And therefore: perhaps yourself?'

'Eeeeuuuugh! I charge you, sir, that your diet you must mend, before – ooh! ffoooo! – before you share my bed again.'

Hamilton sniggered in mock contrition. 'Oh, my lord, you are too cruelly stern! Yet, as the foremost of my life's desires is to lie beside you ever more, so shall I endure the pain this morn of breakfast without ale – what more may a gentleman sacrifice?' Then with his tonguetip reeding between obscening lips he produced a prolonged variation on that singularly impolite sound which is analogous to a minor explosion between the buttocks.

And the potential disaster was averted:

The buckpassing habits of the two bedding dukes being such that each was convinced the offensive odour had been generated by the other, who was pleased in his perversity to deny it.

Whereas in fact it was Polmood who had rifted.

Yes, what more transfixingly frightful for an eavesdropping gentleman than the betrayal of sudden anal seepage in the midst of overhearing the boasting confirmation of his wildest sexual paranoia? Polmood's initial panic at this leekage of his presence had impulsed him to fall upon the bedders in singlehanded executive pre-emption – for what further testimony did the case against them require? But how could he possibly attain this justifiably homicidal end before the King's guards were alarmed to the rescue? Was it then better to abandon his murderous intent for the time being, and flee this sinful chamber in a headlong blundering charge: blowing the secrecy of his intrusion for the sake of avoiding identification and capture? If only . . .

'You were saying, my lord?' the Duke of Hamilton reverted.

Polmood remained rooted, newly fearful of being given away by the pounding of his pulse, or the scent of sly poison in his squeezing sweat. If only he could . . .

'Mnyah?'

'Concerning the heavenly ecstasies, my lord, that the incomparably fortunate Dame Polmood has achieved with yourself – though not, it seems, with her grunting he-swine husband – you said . . .'

'Regarding my possible danger of sudden exposure through some unforeseen hysteria of female fidelity?'

'Yes?'

'I was merely about to remark upon the multiple unlikelihood of any such event.'

'How so?'

'Hmmm,' Rosay deliberated, as though debating the wisdom of

acquainting his companion with the sequel. 'You see, sir, the lady is – was! – altogether less chaste than you imagine.'

'Whaaat?'

'As forby myself, though only this very day have I chanced to learn it, she has kept a second secret paramour.'

'Never!'

'Yes, and it wounds me not a little to confess it. So expertly did the craven wench dissimulate the affaire that not even myself had the slightest notion of it, until this afternoon my strolling ears were pricked by the stridency of a lustful moan, that scraped their trysting nest.'

'Then why, my lord, did not you rush upon them, and fell the villain at a stroke?'

'Because, sir, because . . . to do so was beneath my dignity.'

'How possible?'

'As he that the lady chose for secondary service was barely animal. A bumbling peasant loon, no more, not capable of thought. And therefore: what would the shedding of his blood avail, bar the staining of my sword? No! Beyond a doubt it was the lady herself, in licentious insatiety following naturally on Polmood's impotence, that led the fellow on. Further spurred, it could well be, by her hankering for a champion broozler – for the gardener was certainly a prodigy in size.'

'The *gardener*!'

'Indeed. Thereby do we see the pain of the lady's unbroozled frustration hitherto.'

'And is she slack, my lord? That she needs a champion broozler?'

'Slack, sir? Slack! How dare you so impugn a lady whom myself has favoured?'

'Your pardon, my lord!' the Duke of Hamilton faintly murmured.

'On the contrary,' Rosay warmed to the despicable enlargement of his falsehood. 'A towdie more neatly small and firmly juicy you never could wish for. That honeys at a single touch, and has the power to grip at will, like a mouth about a straw. Aaaah!'

'The moving poesy of your lordship's evocation has conjured me quite stiff with envy. Shall it please you feel?'

'No, sir!' Rosay tartly snapped. 'It certainly shall not, and therefore tarry where you are, be advised, lest you drive me to doubt the normalcy of your proclivities.'

Hamilton snickered nastily. 'My lord, I intended only tribute.'

'Ha!'

'But does it not trouble you, my lord, that even now your beauteous lady may lie embedded by another? Disporting with a menial!'

'Ah!' Rosay crowed. 'No. And herein lies the charm of it all: the flesh of the jest, you may say.'

'The flesh of the jest, my lord!'

'Very droll, sir. Killingly so. Truly do I tremble for the power of my sides to survive your wit. But let me tell you.'

'Yes?'

'The perfection that crowns the lark is this. That since I have informed Polmood of his lady's dissembled frolic with the clod-delver, the laird has gone deranged with jealousy and passion to hew the culprit's head (as witness his outrageous comportment at dinner this night), the latter has somehow got the wind up and fled, and hence in the days that follow Polmood without a doubt will range abroad in pursuit of his vengeance.'

'Leaving you, my lord, in sole possession of the coveted lady!'

'Precisely, sir. You have me in a nutshell.'

'The cunning of the rustling fox is nothing, beside the elegance of your lordship's guile!'

'There are many, indeed, who have said so.' Rosay yawned again and bedturned away from his professing admirer.

Who fished:

'And shall you . . .'

'Indeed I shall, sir!' the retort came blanketmuffled. 'When I choose and where I choose, until my fancy wearies. And weary it shall all the sooner, I fear, if I catch no further rest this night, before the tedious sports of the morrow. Wherefore return you to slumber, I urge you, as hardly an hour can remain until the rally horn.'

'But . . .'

'Goodnight to you, sir!'

'Goodnight, my noble lord!' the Duke of Hamilton undertoned, then rummaged in the bed, to better his sleeping comfort.

While Polmood stood stock still his long arm's length away.

And scarcely breathed.

14

THE POLMOOD HUNT

THE COURSE OF THE DAY

Is there any man so apt to brag of the favours bestowed on him by some outstanding beauty of the fairer sex than the libertine who in fact has received naught but disappointment?

Surely not.

And few will disagree that it was the nagging of such frustration, reinforced by his vile conviction that Elizabeth had committed clandestine adultery with Carmichael, that moved the Duke of Rothesay to unleash such a detestable pack of howling lies that night, for the warped diversion of the Duke of Hamilton, who, though cynically incredulous at first, was latterly won to credit Rosay's yarn by the spinner's uncharacteristic admission of having had to share the conquered lady with a second lover – of low degree! From which the aspirant purveyor of deceit may draw this moral: that it is through the meticulous depiction of the entirely unexpected that even the staunchest scepticism is eventually overcome.

Then what of lurking Polmood, who was already convinced?

For a further twenty minutes he stood in that room, his animation as suspended as could be, until the resuming rhythms and discords of sleep and snores persuaded him that his creeping egress might now be effected undetected by the ducal vermin in the bed. The window of that chamber faced out to the south, and through its wooden shutters the grey dawn was chinking as the mightily deluded forester enlatched the door in silence behind him, and stole to the stair and downwards, away from immediate danger.

There was a cold and curious calm about his bearing as he strode first to the hall, to retrieve his boots and leathers from amid the knightly bodies, some of them beginning to turn and mumble in protest against the cool clean light that angled through the unshuttered windows of the east wall, ever brighter on their dreaming eyelids. Then at a clattering pace across the courtyard cobbles to the armoury, emerging minutes later with a newly strung bow (the stoutest from the rack) and a quiver of his own special arrows: as long again by half as any normal man could draw, and finely fletched from herongull wings by the patience of his own thick fingers. Firm was the jut of his whiskery chin and cloud-masked the savagery in his eye as he barked a morning greeting to the nodding soldiers at the Castle gate.

Then to the stables.

'So ye have not set sight on yon Connel fellow, Thomas?' he inquired.

'No, Master,' the apprehensive youth chattered, rubbing his arms against the lingering chill of dawn. 'Neither glimpse nor whisper.'

'Ach, well,' said Polmood, nonchalantly distant. 'He has but filched a sabre from the armoury, and it is little worth our trouble to raise a hue and cry for that.'

'No, Master.'

'Though, if the foolish fellow does return, ye will mention nothing of the sabre, mind? But inform myself without his ken.'

'Ay, Master!' Thomas enthused, much boosted by this man-to-man enlistment of his discretion.

'But leave off here for the by, and get you rouse the other lads to saddle the beasts within the hour. For myself ye will groom the red mare.'

Thomas nodded in pleased importance.

'Then get off with you now.'

And off Thomas got, marvelling at the novel mildness of his Master's manner.

Polmood watched him go, then slowly followed, out of the stableyard. Turning right, across the brilliant dewy yellow of the dandelion-clumped bridleway, he headed pensively toward the river.

All around the morning was rubbing its eyes as the first warmth of sunlight shafted down from the east through the valley of the Polmood Burn. Invisible behind their damp green camouflage, a hundred sparrows were hard at their bickering, while a single starling mocked them from a tall greenboled beech tree, and in the sky a pair of larks like doubtful motes upon a gazing eye rose ever higher in their song.

But to Polmood these impressions came filtered through dullness, as though already diluted by the passing of much time. The birdy sounds that circled all around him (for there lilled too the purring low of a ringdove coo) were as they might rehearse in the recollection of a prisoner in a dungeon: a man doomed to the gallows but with the grim satisfaction of knowing that his executioner cannot realize what bliss his peace in death will be.

If death brings peace!

Polmood did not accomplish this cogitation in so many words, but such was the spirit that gripped his simple soul that morning. His ascending derangement had brought him to a plateau of near serenity, at the far side of which his goal was plainly marked, like a blazing beacon on a dark horizon, so that all he had to do was march in patience towards it, unwavered by fruitless doubts as to what lay beyond, and vengeance would be his.

Vengeance!

How sweet the sound.

'Vengeance will be . . .' he deeply breathed. *'Mine!'* Pushing through the brambling roses that battled with their cruel backcurling claws against the subtler grasp of the elegant windowlace weeds for dominance of the riverbank, he glanced southward and saw two swans some fifty paces upstream.

Drifting down the current.

Their hostile black eyes like mouths, yawning their lordly contempt.

'"Honeys at a touch", eh?' Polmood muttered, swinging his longbow off his shoulder and reaching to his quiver. '"Like a mouth about a straw". Uh?'

Ten seconds later the starling had flown, the sparrows were rising like startled flies from a corpse, and the world by the river was all a screech of terror, blood, and death. Crazed with raging pain and astonishment, the great white birds spread wide their wings and fell on one another with wild sweeping stabs of their shrieking mouths. Each seeing its mate as author of the burning suffocation that pierced through the base of its neck, they flapped madly above the water in the hatred of combat already mortal, then fell back in heavy splashes of weakness growing.

Flapping up.
Falling back.
Screaming.
Croaking.
Flapping.
Falling.
Dark blood spurting all the while, down their milky breasts, to nourish the million mouths beneath the Tweed.

And Polmood said:

'So shall we see.'

When he returned to his Castle he found chaos commoving rapidly into readiness for the day's chase. Breakfast of oatcake and goatmilk cheese, with fresh fruit and brown ale, was being had by the King and nobles in the hall, while the grooms led the saddled horses down from the stables to await their masters in the courtyard. Elizabeth, who had passed the night in restful innocence, sharing a bed with Betty in the servants' quarters, flitted busily here and cheerfully there: seeing that every lord had what necessaries he required, inquiring if his Majesty had found sufficient comfort for his sleep, and running to the kitchens to hasten the lunches – for as the party would likely be broken by the various fortunes and enthusiasms of the hunt, she had decided that each rider must be given his own pack of food.

'Else some of you might starve, my Lord!' she explained to the King.

'To death?' he joked. 'Truly, my lady, we do doubt it. Not a few among us, indeed, might profit by the loss!'

'My Lord?'

'His Majesty means, my lady,' explained Sir William Moray, pausing in his nearby struggle to tighten his horse's girth, 'that there are bellies enough in the company whose stoutness could well survive the loss of feeding for a day.'

'Not excluding his own!' cried the King. Already mounted, and tingling with zeal to enjoy the day, he beamed down at Sir William in benevolent aggression. 'For he himself is a stouter fellow by half, is he not, than he was a year ago? Ah! Polmood! How do you, sir, this morning? In better fettle, may we hope, than we found you yesterday?'

Polmood responded to the King's good wishes with stolid courtesy, allowing that he was much improved, though regrettably still a way below his normal health. And all the time he spoke he never once looked at his wife.

Who never once looked at him.

Perceiving this, King James felt a dent in his zest. For who more than he had pivoted the wedding of this woman to that man? Polmood should not be cast down, he bade. The ardour of the chase would soon restore his accustomed condition.

Polmood nodded politely, and hoped that might be so. Ten minutes later he partnered his Sovereign at the head of their two-abreast troupe as they clopped through the Castle portals to the terrace, where the hounds had been brought and were yowling for release.

South they then trotted, in their crocodile of noise and colours.

And no man looked round to return Elizabeth's wave.

The tinckell (a line of men with beating sticks to drive the deer) had congregated the previous evening, according to Polmood's instructions, in the vicinity of the forest of Frood. The place of rendezvous, where the deer were to be driven, was a height called the Quarter Hill, which rises above the north end of where the Talla Reservoir lies today.

However, the tinckell was but thin for the wide and rugged terrain to be covered, and the deer seemed uncannily shy that day, as though some eerie warning had reached them through the freshing breeze. The consequence was that, when the hunting paltry arrived near the summit of the Quarter Hill and unleashed the dogs, they found that the beaters had there circumscribed a paltry dozen head of beasts for them to slaughter. Of these, the King shot one fine stag as it bounded to escape, and two others were later run down by the hounds at a place called Carterhope, but the greater number fled back down the southeast shoulder of the Quarter Hill, broke through the straggling tinckell, and ran to seek rocky sanctuary of the steep and craggy mountain named the Ericle, where for the moment they left both dogs and riders far behind.

'Well, Polmood!' James exclaimed, as King and forester led the snorting plod up the long sloping back of the Muckle Knowe, in the direction of the towering Ericle.

'Sire?'

'We could hardly feed the nation on our kill thus far!'

'No, Sire,' grunted Polmood. 'But truly, in the few days that your Majesty allowed me, I had not time to get more men. Nor get them better versed.'

'No, no, Polmood. Of course you had not, and we mean no innuendo. Yet how feel you regarding the remainder of the day?'

'Your Majesty may be assured that I shall furnish him with double the sport he has already got. And more!'

'Indeed, Polmood. That you *can* is beyond question. But our thinking runs more to whether you *should*, for the sky is closing, is it not, and there is a breathlessness of storm about the air?'

Polmood rested his reins on the pommel of his saddle, and sagely surveyed the heavens above him and the earth beneath. Far below on either side the winding burns of Gameshope and Menzion glistened white in the sunlight, like filmy spider threads lying motionless between the infinite shades of brown and green that lined the long narrow valleys. These bleak uncompromising intricacies that the rains and snows of countless years had etched upon the block of nature: how well he knew them all. Each waterfall and stilling pool, each hidden gulley and lonely . . .

'And while, Polmood,' the King elaborated with the acerbity of some impatience, 'it is clear that all the men are high in mettle this day, and will chase until dusk with their vigour unbated, we must bear in mind that few are at home in this terrain, and that some of our number might therefore lose their way, should the weather severely worsen. What think you?'

'Ay, Sire,' Polmood nodded, looking up at the banking cloud wall of sullied pink that was closing all around them like the rim of a shrinking well. 'It looks very like that we shall have a passing squall.'

'No more?' queried James, hopeful but realistically cautious, knowing well the tales of death by misadventure that abounded in these hills, and that even a King might vanish over a precipice in a mist! 'No following fog?' he therefore demanded. 'To spoil our sport and confound our journey home?'

Polmood pulled low over his eyes the long pointed peak of his featherless leather cap, and for the first and second-last time in his life he dared to tell his Sovereign a direct and premeditated lie:

'Indeed not, Sire. A mite wet we surely shall get, but this will happen whether we turn back or no.'

'Yes?' drawled his Majesty, looking down on his companion from the vantage of several white stallion hands. 'And?'

'But there will be no mist to talk of, Sire, before the night. On this I would gladly stake my Castle and all my . . .'

'Hardly necessary, Polmood! A man must be desperate indeed before he wagers on the weather in such a realm as this!'

'Then, so please your Majesty, I would suggest, just in case the day disappoints my expectation, that each man minds to bide constantly with one particular fellow, however the hunt may break.'

'So that none shall go astray alone! Excellent, Polmood. A capital plan!' Restored to his champing zest by the forester's climatic reassurance, James caracoled in his saddle, pushed back his bonnet brim, and regarded the noble train flanked out behind him in slow negotiation of the boulders and peat hags that pocked the slope.

And what a wealth of manliness was there!

Among them:

The Earl of Mar and Sir William Moray, apparently deep in the heat of some learned disputation, with the Lord James Douglas of Dalkeith contributing odd remarks.

Then Sir Partrick Hepburn and Donald of Lamington, together in their customary conspiracy of complementary insipidity: merging their individual mediocrities in a polarized partnership of the snidely reedy and the boisterously large.

After them, the slow-witted Duke of Dumfries and the characterless Lord Solway.

While the tip of that strung-out equestrian tail was made up, predictably, by the Duke of Hamilton in concert with his Majesty's own brother: Rosay declaiming to Hamilton with a lavishness of gesture that proclaimed his effeting detestation of the entire expedition.

Which the King grinned to see. Trumpeting his hands, he called:

'GENTLEMEN! We look to have a drenching not far off. Let us therefore ensure, should the company fragment, that each man remain always within hailing of at least one other. Yes? That solitary mishap may thereby gain no purchase upon our ankles! What say you?'

Meanwhile, what could be further from Elizabeth's mind than the fermenting weather overhead? It was just afternoon when she made her tremulous return to that bed of moss beside the Herston Burn, where she and Carmichael had lain upon his plaid to rest from their picking of wild raspberries.

Where Rosay had discovered them.

And where, she later had vowed to Carmichael, she would dig a secret cache below the turf, to harbour food and drink for his survival.

'And mark it with a rose!' she reminded herself as she skirted the foot of the Great Hill and turned east along the burn. 'But what if he is hiding there to greet me? What shall I say?'

What indeed?

From her right hand swung a capacious osier basket containing a large oatmeal bannock, a pound of cheese, the greater part of a leg of mutton, fresh fruit galore, a quart flask of red wine, a whole comb of honey, and a sharp-bladed trowel to delve the hiding place.

All packed beneath the concealing weight of a thick woollen blanket.

Small wonder, then, that the slender maiden panted as she hurried, her heavy basket handle chafing a sore spot on her palm that later would rise in a ridge of angry blister.

But for the moment such discomforts were as far from her thoughts as the brewing of the sky.

'Truly, Sir John,' she rehearsed, 'though it is most gallant of you to linger thus – no! To *tarry* thus! To tarry thus in watch upon my safety, I yet do fell the greater wisdom lies in . . . oh!' she gasped.

There was the bank of bluebells.

And below it the trysted spread of moss. Yellow, soft and dry.

But with this difference!

That, where Elizabeth herself had come to dig and demark, a blood-red rose already stood: glaringly unnatural on its planted ten-inch stem.

'He has already been!' she exclaimed between relief and dismay.

'But . . .' Laying her basket on the ground, she knelt by the rose and found a halfpace square cut subtly in the turf, betrayed only to a close inspection by droppings of crumbly brown soil about its edges. Lifting with impatient effort, heedless of damage to her fingernails, Elizabeth discovered a neatly scraped recess in the ground.

And in it?

Nothing!

Nothing, that is, but a length of bark from a desiccated tree of great diameter, on which she found inscribed, as by a dagger point:

Dearest, dearest lady!

For the infiniteness of your merciful bounty my gratitude knows no bounds; doubt not that *all will soon be well*; this I swear!

Your devoted and adoring servant,
J.C.

'But how?' the dearest lady fretted, the fine dark lines of her eyebrows narrowing in perturbation. 'How so?'

All will soon be well!

What could that *mean*?

She looked about her in alarm, suddenly fearful of observers lurking. Seeing none, she hastily wrapped Carmichael's wine and victuals in the blanket, pressed the lumpy parcel flat in the hiding place and relaid the turf atop it. The piece of bark with the vexing missive she took with her when she stood up, collected her basket, and set off home at an anxious pace.

All will soon be well!

At least twenty times she rescrutinized that ominous vow, before she snapped the bark into small pieces and threw them to the river. What did he mean? How could he seriously say such a thing? Unless . . .

'No!' she murmured plaintively, as she rejoined the bridleway. 'He cannot so propose. He *cannot*!'

Yet:

This I swear!

But how could he swear such a thing if he did not intend some imminent action? And what action could he possibly take that would not multiply a hundredfold the peril in which they both now stood? If he . . .

'Never!' she tried to assure herself, crossing the little wooden footbridge twenty paces upstream from the bridleway ford across the Polmood Burn.

As the pioneering raindrops fell.

Like a plague of blemishing moles upon the pale lavender fabric of her dress.

'Never! Sir John Carmichael is an honourable man!'

But was he?

Was he *really*?

During the remainder of that day the weather raged through spectral vicissitudes of a violence quite exceptional, even for those most mountainous parts of the Scottish border country. First it rained gently, though with droplets big and heavy. Then came an hour of stifling sultry heat, while the pink sky descended to a heavier redness, like a gigantic overhanging belly slashed in a welter of hideous wounds, which rapidly gangrened into an ever lowering menace of blackest grey.

The thunder storm, when eventually it bolted down the valley, came rather as a spasm of cathartic relief, at least to those safely housed. When the lightning passed over, leaving behind it the feeling that bodies of gargantuan gods deposed had been hurled in rage from the heavens to reshape the contours of the earth, the rain that followed was so torrential as to elicit only gaping awe from those who gave no hoot as to the fortunes of the King and his nobles out hunting in the hills.

Such as Thomas the groom.

And Betty the maid.

Together they pressed in the scullery doorway to gaze in silence upon the sheeting rods of water that lashed from the lowhanging sky like a million beams of metallic light that smashed like arrowheads of flint against the cobbles of the courtyard and bounced everywhere in fragments of crazy foam before settling in dirty rivulets and sloshing through the cracks between the stones, to join the overloaded swirling of the gutters.

'Oh, Thomas!' exclaimed Betty.

'Yes, Betty,' Thomas hesitated, 'my dear?'

'I feel this surely cannot last.'

'Why ever not? My dear?'

'It is too extreme, I fear. It is of a violence that touches the unnatural, and hence it cannot last.'

'Why so, my dear?'

'Because, Thomas, the world we live in is the world of nature!'

'Ay?'

'Therefore,' Betty elaborated, slowly, with the lingering excitement of a mind expanding, 'something which is *not* natural may not endure very long in our world, which *is* natural, because if it did it . . . would *not* be natural! Our world, I mean.'

'Oh, Betty!' cried Thomas in a frenzy of adulation that seemed to fall upon its knees before her reasoning, though his mind was anchored to matters less intangible. 'It is such a pleasure talking to you that I . . . I know not what to say – except that,' he suddenly plunged in an unplanned fervour of commitment, 'except that: is *love* unnatural, Betty, my dear, if it be as violent as yon rain? Love!'

'Goodness now, Thomas!' Betty blushed, intently regarding the growing puddles in the yard. 'Since whensoever have you been a one to talk of love?'

'But now I am.'

'Yes, but love is never unnatural, Thomas!'

'But . . .'

'Yet also: love can never be violent.'

'Why so?'

'For if love be violent, it is not love! But some other thing.'

There followed a pause long enough for the river in the distance to tumesce by a thousand gallons.

Then Thomas croaked:

'*My* love is violent! Betty.'

'Oh!'

'For you, my dear!'

'But Thomas!'

'Feel here: my heart!' he urged, his pimply shyness lying flattened by the juggernauting species. Taking her trembling hand, gently, pressing it sacredly between his own, he laid it in communion of wonder against the shirted thudding that drummed against his breast with almost the impossible fury of the rain on the courtyard stones.

Pit-pat-pit-pat-pit-patpatpat . . .

'Oh, Thomas!'

A moment later the rain had served its purpose, nudging the reticent sweethearts into each other's arms by bonding them with awe to share:

Thin pimples against plump smoothness.

Stubbly cheeks nuzzling rosy.

Lips hard and bristly kissing greedily into lips full and soft, moist and yielding.

Breast flat and bony against breasts warmly rounded, large, yet stimulatingly firm.

Loins . . .

'BETTY?' the strident irritation of a housekeeperly voice broke out within, echoing harsh and dry off the cold grey mortared walls. 'BETTEEEE? Are you THERE?'

'Yes, Martha,' gasped Betty, pulling her lips away from Thomas's all-embrace. 'YES, MARTHA! I'M COMING.'

'WHAT ARE YOU *DOING* DOWN THERE?'

'NOTHING, MARTHA.'

'*WHAT?*'

'WATCHING THE RAIN, I MEAN. Stop that, Thomas!'

'Ooooh!' moaned the immaculate selfishness of the young man's passion.

'WHAT DO YOU MEAN "WATCHING THE RAIN"?' Martha's yell rose an octave in trebled indignation. 'YOU LAZY YOUNG BESOM, *GET UP HERE!*'

'YES, MARTHA!'

'*NOW!*'

'I'M COMING!'

'Oh, Betty!' Thomas whispered in the hollow between her jaw and the flesh of her neck. 'I wish you were!'

'What?'

'Nothing!'

'I DON'T KNOW WHERE THIS WORLD WILL END!' raged Martha. 'WHEN A STURDY YOUNG HUSSY LIKE YOU CAN LEAVE A FEEBLE OLD SOUL LIKE MYSELF TO SLAVE HER POOR OLD BONES *TO DEATH* IN THE KITCHEN, *TO WATCH THE RAIN*! LORD SAVE US! BETTY?'

'I'M . . .'

'AND WHAT ABOUT THAT YOUNG SCOUNDREL THOMAS?'

294

'WHAT ABOUT HIM, MARTHA?'

'WHERE IS HE?'

'I DO NOT KNOW.'

'Oh, my treasure!' Thomas groaned. 'What a treasure you are.'

'WELL YOU JUST *FIND* HIM THEN! AND TELL HIM TO FETCH SOME WATER UP HERE TO WARM FOR THE GENTLEMEN'S BATHS. FOR WHAT WILL HIS MAJESTY SAY, EH? WHEN HE COMES DRIPPING OFF THE HILL, AND FINDS NO WATER HEATED? TO BATHE HIS FEET? EH?'

'YES, MARTHA.'

'LORD SAVE US FROM THE YOUTH WE HAVE BORNE, FOR I DON'T KNOW. TRULY I DON'T.' Then the merciful respite of bustling footsteps receding.

'And what would the old sow say,' murmured Thomas, venturing a fumbling hand upon the rotundity of an affable buttock, 'if she knew about *this?*' Lovingly he squeezed.

'No, Thomas!'

'Just a wee – '

'No!' Betty insisted sharply, pushing him away. 'You heard what Martha said, and now you must fetch the water.'

'But I *love* you!' he pleaded.

'Not now. Later.'

AN EVENING OF THICKENING MISTS AND APPREHENSIONS

It was about six o'clock when the Duke of Rothesay splashed back through the Castle portals – the first of the hunting party to return. Sodden and revealingly hatless, with odd lank locks of temple hair clinging like windblown worms across his pasty pate, he abandoned his reins in a gesture of ineffable loathing, swung off his spongy saddle, and landed with ungainly sloshing weight in a two-inch pool of water backlogging across the courtyard behind the overburdened drains.

'Hey, BOY!' he bellowed at no particular person.

And no particular person duly appeared.

'Damn you for a shitesucker, sir! BOY!'

Thomas's pimply visage appeared nervously in the scullery archway.

'Hey, you!' Rosay snapped, glaring at him in black myopia.

'My lord?'

'Take you my horse to the stables. Rub him down and all, and see him fitly tended for the night.'

'But my lord . . .'

'And do it *now*, filthy churl. Before your idle erse shall sunder by the breadth of my booted toe. *Now!*'

'Ay, my lord,' mumbled Thomas. Abandoning his prior duties, he picked the reins from where they floated in the puddle lagoon and led the shivering foamflecked horse away.

'And a pocks upon your progeny to the thousandth generation!' the heir to Scotland's throne cursed after him.

'My Lord Rosay!'

'Uh?' Rosay blinked about him. The rain was now spent except for the occasional giant droplet falling slow yet heavy, as from the lowermost leaves of a tree.

'Here, my lord. Up . . .'

'Ah! My Lady Elizabeth. How do you?' Rosay squinted vaguely at the first-floor window in which Elizabeth's anxiously smiling face appeared framed.

'Myself I am well, my lord,' she called. 'But for you and for his Majesty and . . . the others I have been feeling much concern.'

'Tchuu!' Rosay scorned, eloquently conveying his absolute disgust at the arduous soggy discomforts to which the zeals of others had subjected him. 'For my own part, my lady, I am yet alive – Lord be praised! And as to the others, I warrant they too shall survive in the main, whenever it shall please them to abandon their madness and re-assemble hither.'

'But they surely are not still in the chase, my lord!'

'I know not whither they gambol *now*, my lady,' Rosay barked, running an irate fat hand around his neck, to save it from the stranglous tightening of his wringing velvet ruff. 'Yet certainly, when I did remove from their society they still were so engaged. Some three hours since.'

'Oh, dear God!' Elizabeth gasped, having some idea of what treacherous deathtraps the mountains could become when swollen with inclemency. 'But yourself, my lord! Your damp attire you must shed this instant! Else your death shall be upon us.'

'I thank you, my lady,' drawled Rosay, squeezing trickles from the cuffs of his sleeves.

'In your chamber, my lord, you shall find dry garments laid out.'

'Most consummately considerate!'

'And in the parlour a handsome fire is lit, and a tub of water will be heated for your feet.'

'Exquisite!' Rosay enthused, his dander dwindling as comforts loomed. 'And a jug of hot wine, could we have?'

'My lord, it is already by the fire.'

'Then shall I be with you, my lady, in a veritable trice!'

And so he was.

If a trice lasts twenty minutes.

'But why, my lord,' Elizabeth asked him, 'did not you return all together?'

'Ah, dear lady!' Rosay returned, 'to know this you must inquire of your estimable husband.'

'My lord?'

'I mean . . .' gobble, swallow, 'that when once the rain had set in, we gathered us together in a sheltered gulley to take our luncheon and debate the option to pursue.' He paused to take a sluicing draught from the goblet in his right hand. Comfortably seated by the crackling parlour fire, in soft and colourful courtly finery and a velvet cap once more, in his eating hand he grasped a hefty joint of honeybaked pork – and while his ankles dangled luxuriously in a shallow metal bath of water still steaming and consecrated with various arcane herbs that Martha swore were surety against all sneezing ills, his pudgy knees and naked calves splayed shamelessly at Elizabeth.

Who sat on her heels on a rug on the floor.

And betrayed no glimpse of the fascinated repugnance aroused in her by the blackly bestial hairiness of this gentleman's short thick legs. Brushing from her awareness a buzzing of curiosities both alarmingly improper and unsuited to the situation, she said:

'And what option, my lord, did you finally elect?'

'Aha! Well. By this time the deluge was quite diabolical, as clearly it also was here.'

'Indeed.'

'And moreover, up the wild and uncouth glen whereinto the deer had long since vanished, we now espied a solid mass of mist descending – thick as ever I have seen, like a cloud that cut the heights away from view as sheerly as a razor.'

'And my husband, my lord? You mentioned some matter of which I must inquire of him?'

'Verily so!' Rosay sniffed contemptuously and drank deeply to the health of his narrative. 'For when his Majesty said: "And what, Polmood, say you now?", the laird replied:

'"I regret, Sire, that your Majesty should receive such a muckle wetting for his sport. But be assured, Sire, that the rain shall have pissed its heart out within the hour." Your pardon I beg, my lady!' Rosay interjected, warming with relish to his mocking rendition of Polmood's vernacular crudity. 'But such were your husband's words.'

Elizabeth expressed with a frowning nod her ability to survive such language.

'Whereat the King said: "And the mist, Polmood? It is yonder fog that bodes us direr than the rain, we fear. Think you not?"

'"Not at all, Sire! If I may be so bold," said Polmood. "It is but a belt around the bellies of the hills, that will vanish when the rain falls off, and we could walk through it now to daylight at the summits, should we so please."

'"And *should* we so please, Polmood? Vouchsafe us, sir, your soundest judgement."

'"It is not my place, Sire, to say what we *should* do, but this can I guarantee. That if we have patience and continue up to the head of Gameshope, we shall find us a dozen more stags this day."

'"But Sire!" protested I, essaying mildness I did not feel, in hope that reason might prevail. "This surely would be madness beyond compare! These mists will never lift this day."

'Then yapped the Earl of Mar, insolent rednecked puppy that he is: "In any event, your Majesty, this is Polmood's country, is it not? And he can lead us home whatever. Yet how can we there repair, with our heads held high, while our bag is all but empty?"

'"Very well, very well," said the King at length, almost pleased, so it seemed to me, that his decision might discountenance myself! "As we value Polmood's expertise (and as we are valiant warriors all!), so shall we press on a while. But mark you all what we earlier did say: that each man bide always within purview of at least one fellow."'

'You have a fine way with a tale, my lord,' Elizabeth murmured.

'You are too kind, sweet lady.'

'And was it then, my lord, that you absented from their reckless company?'

'Not quite, I now regret to say – in view of the abortionate sequel. No. For a further half hour, it must have been, though it seemed ten times as long, I continued with their folly. Upward, ever upward, till the mists grew so thick and wet that we seemingly rode through the midst of the rainclouds themselves: nose to tail, in single file we trudged, as each of us could see no further than two mounts before him.

'Through peat hags by the thousand, round about the blueberry bogs – on and on, up and up. With nothing for the hounds to chase bar the flushing of a few frighted whaups. When suddenly . . . Rosay paused to enhance the suspense that might be expected of one who had a fine way with a tale, and took a slurp of wine that over-reached the corners of his mouth and dribbled in his beard.

'Yes, my lord?' Elizabeth urged. 'Suddenly?'

'There came a great cry from the front: "Now we have the boggers, Sire!"

'In Polmood's voice, without a doubt, though it came very muffled through the fog. And then we heard a rising rushing noise, as one might hear when riding hard toward a waterfall. Then all was bedlam. Horses rearing, hounds a-yowling, and four dozen head of deer, at least, came bounding through our ranks from above us to the right.

'"Follow now, my lords! And we shall have them pinned against the Raven Craig," came Polmood's yell. Whereupon all the gentlemen in the party wheeled their chargers about and spurred them in pursuit. Excepting the Duke of Hamilton and myself.

'"It is lunatic, sir," I opined, "to gallop in this blindness! They shall break their necks, beyond a doubt."

'"Very like. Very like," my Lord Hamilton agreed. Yet argued: "But if we follow soft behind them, my lord, we may permit the necks in the van to break the trail for us, and thereby preserve our own!"

'"As you please, sir," said I. "Though myself I am returning home forthwith."

'"Alone, my lord?"

'"Thus it seems!" said I with acerbity. "Unless it please you, sir, to accompany me."

'"I know not the way, my lord."

'"Come, sir!" I rebuked him. "It is not the way that troubles you, for you have but to follow down the gulleys to the water, and follow then the water till it joins the Tweed. With patient care."

'"If you say so, my lord," said he. "And yet I feel a certain obligation to myself, to fell at least one stag this day, if only to recompense the trials of the trek."

'"Piffle, sir!" I told him. For I know his mind right well, my lady, and that he hankers for the hunt not a jot more than I. "It is not to the felling of stags that you are drawn," I charged. "But to the felling of your comrades by the mountains!"'

'No!'

'My lady, I do fear so. The Duke of Hamilton has his graces, but times there are (and truly I do trepidate to burden thus a tender lady's confidence) when the gravest malformities are manifest, in the lurchings of his soul.'

Elizabeth daintily cleared her throat, in substitute for comment. 'And then did you part, my lord?'

'We did indeed. "Farewell, sir," said I.

'"Farewell, my lord!" saluted he me, with a jeer.

'"His Majesty you may inform of my superior wisdom," I called after him, "if Fate be so miraculous that you rediscover him this day." But before I had shed my final words he was gone: swallowed beyond a shadow in the wet grey gloom.'

Elizabeth shivered, taut with worry.

'And here I now am!' Rosay expansively indicated, with his hands of pork and wine. 'Having followed my own counsel to the letter, restored to these splendid appurtenances of civilized life, and primely rewarded by the company of your charming self!'

'But what think you of the others, my lord?' Elizabeth pressed. 'Shall they too return unharmed?'

'Ummmm . . .' If Rosay's disinterest in the welfare of the others was commensurate with the mouthful of meat he now tore from his joint, then pity Scotland's children if the throne should fall to him. 'I see not why not,' he cloggily mumbled. 'An ankle turned or two, perhaps. A twisted knee . . .' He looked round as the parlour door opened.

There stood Martha, blinking like a nervous owl in the presence of such high nobility.

'Yes, Martha?' Elizabeth asked.

'There are more riders, mum,' the old lady warbled. 'Just returned.'

'You see!' crowed Rosay.

'And is his Majesty among them?'

'No, mum.'

'Or the Master?'

'No, mum!' Martha's dithering agitation showed plainly in her wringing red fingers. 'I know not who the gentlemen are, mum, and I . . .'

'Thank you, Martha,' said Elizabeth, rising. 'I shall come down to greet the gentlemen myself.'

'Very good, mum.' Martha's grateful visage withdrew.

'If you will excuse me, my lord?' Elizabeth said to Rosay. 'I shall return ere long.'

'As you please, my lady!' said he tersely, still voraciously chewing, and frowning in displeasure at this loss of his lovely audience.

The hostess smiled politely, courtesied briefly, and rushed away to lavish succour on the unknown others.

These, it soon transpired, were the Earl of Mar, the Lord Solway, and the Duke of Dumfries – dripping, sneezing, and muttering in an incoherence of shivers and curses about the lunatic escapade into which they had been led. Long had the party endeavoured to regroup, according to the garbled account of these three drookit gentlemen. And great had been the confusion of bugles blowing, whistlers whistling, and lone voices roaring hoarsely for kindred souls to gather round and relieve their isolation. But the issue, Elizabeth in due course discovered, when the nobles had dried out, changed, and convened to dilute the Duke of Rothesay's ascendancy in the parlour, had ultimately obliged each man to find his own way back to Polmood – with one or two companions if his luck was in, though many there were who found no fellow to clip the wings of their solitary darknightly fears.

This, then, was the manner in which the shattered hunting party continued to dribble back to the Castle in ones, twos and occasional threes, until close on midnight.

While others did not appear at all that night.

And some were never to return again.

It was past ten o'clock when King James sloshed back into the torchlit courtyard, with Sir William Moray trotting exhaustedly yet jubilantly after – as if to say: 'Here am I with He who is Infallible!'

For the King had somehow managed to bring down another fine stag despite the impossibility of the conditions, and carried the fallen pride of its sturdy red body on the back of his mighty horse, behind its saddle.

All who had not already retired to bed (as Rosay long since had) exclaimed in wonder at his Majesty's ingenuity, and it was even conjectured that here, in this crowning killing feat, combined with the Providence manifest in his safe return, was further conclusive proof that the sovereignty of the House of Stuart was upheld by the Hand of Heaven.

'Either that,' the King agreed, 'or a stroke of good fortune that the beast took a turn towards the Craig, and was almost spent from running forby. Eh, Sir William? Or both, mark you! For ill-advised is he who disputes that Providence is all-present in even the fall of a fledgeling sparrow from its nest.' Declaiming from the parlour chair vacated by his brother, James glanced about the rumpled lords who sprawled around the room, drying shaggy manes and toasting hairy toes in the heat of the fire, while wolfing the tender meats and the heated wine that Elizabeth kept circulating all through the evening despite (and as a sedative to) her mounting distress.

Where was Polmood?

It was natural that some of the knights, being strangers to those parts, would founder in the fog and lose their way, but what of Polmood? He who knew every ford and pass in the forest as well as the walks in his gardens? His conversancy with the mountains was every inch as intimate as the familiarity of a formerly beautiful lady with the contours of her body!

So what could have happened?

'Well, gentlemen,' said the King, accepting one of each from the bowl of apples and pears that Elizabeth was offering round. 'What think you? It is gone midnight, and here we are; a handful short of our complement still. Accordingly, let us enumerate a muster, including the lords already abed, and the rest of you then take away your weary limbs likewise, and gratify them in repose. Our penitent self, stung wakeful by the blame of having led you all to the shambles of this day, shall maintain our vigilance perhaps a further hour, and with our welcome warm the drooping cockles of any stragglers yet to come.'

'But, Sire!' the Earl of Mar protested, though with eyelids fast closing. 'It is not meet that you should watch alone.'

'Doubtless not, sir. Yet selfishly we dare to scheme that Mistress Polmood may share our wake a while. My lady?'

'My Lord . . . why yes!'

'Capital! Capital!' his Majesty jovially chuckled, fingering damp strands of long red hair away from his neck, shrugging deeper into the fluffy yellow blanket that shawled about his shoulders, and adding:

'So shall the rubbing of this, our sackcloth, go not unsoothed by congenial balm! Now, let us list off the gentlemen already asleep. The Duke of Rothesay, of course. And . . .'

It was soon established that five of the huntsmen were still wanting: the Duke of Hamilton, the Lord James Douglas of Dalkeith, Sir Patrick Hepburn and Donald of Lamington, and Polmood himself.

The resident laird.

The conversant host.

Whom none could believe had mistaken his route.

Hence it was in a spirit of doubt and perplexity that the drowsy nobles bid a bowing goodnight to the King and their comely hostess, and shuffled away to their slumbers.

'Come, little one,' said James, when they had departed. 'Let us sit a little and freely talk, that you with your beauty may cheer our gaze as the flames here warm our flesh. You are anxious, are you not?' he gently asked, when Elizabeth had gratefully pulled across an amberdyed sheepskin rug and snuggled by his feet.

'Yes, my Lord,' she admitted, tensely quiet, the strain of the day showing faintly blue in the crescents beneath her eyes.

Which she turned to the dancing fire.

Away from the comforting King.

Who stroked her silky head with all the mellow sexual disinterest of a fondling father, and said:

'Why so?'

'I know not, my Lord. It is only a vague and groundless feeling, you may say, a worry born only of my womanly weakness, and yet . . .'

'Mmmmm?' through a Yawn.

'It is most ominous, my Lord!'

'Yes?'

'That my husband should be last to return.'

'*Among* the last, little one! Let us never be blown from the ground of fact, however stiff the gusts that bend us.'

'Very well, my Lord. Yet still it bodes ill, I fear. For Polmood is at home in the hills!'

'Importing?'

'Like the great old trout in the Cleaker's Pool! He knows the country as a dogfox knows its march, and therefore he surely cannot have lost his way. He *cannot*!'

'Umm. And?'

'Oh, my Lord,' Elizabeth poured in a rapid monotone wail, 'it follows that he has met with some terrible mishap!'

'Ah, Elizabeth! How smooth and lovely the touch of your burnished locks against the wrinkles of these old fingers – would that your reasoning were as sleek! But then again: not so. No! We wish it not. For when ever did icy logic sit as pretty on a maiden's mind as the ripples of her unfathomable intuition?'

'The most gallant gentleman in the land', Elizabeth said with a hint of petulance, 'your Majesty has always been. Yet here I fear his chivalry bypasses my humble understanding!'

'Alack-alack, humble lady!' King James apologized and mocked together, reaching his stroking fingers down to tickle the pouting softness beneath Elizabeth's chin. 'Pardons without number if we did offend! Intending but to share our observation that it follows not at all from what you said that Polmood has fallen victim to some misadventure.'

'No?'

'By no means! Is it not possible that his delay is due to difficulties experienced by the *other* missing gentlemen? Whom he, as sure-footed host, has located in distress and dallied to assist?'

'And yet . . .'

'Or that his pony has cast a shoe and only may be led home, limping like a snail?'

Elizabeth looked up at her former Ward, to thank him with a smile for the patient confidence of his reassurance.

Which he then unwittingly ruined, as a sudden hysterical scream may shatter a crystal wineglass, by saying:

'And since some such harmless cause is most likely the reason of Polmood's continued absence, we urge, Mistress Polmood, that you join with us in trusting that all will soon prove well.'

Elizabeth glanced away to conceal the triggered panic in her eyes.

All will soon be well!

What *had* Carmichael intended?

There could not, could there, be any link between . . .

'Yes, my Lord,' she faintly whispered. 'Your Majesty is kind as ever.'

'Though perhaps a few grains less so than a year ago,' he joked. 'For Time is unkind, is he not, and rubs abrasive on our souls? But that is not the matter.' He paused to mark a change of tack.

Elizabeth's curiosity pierced her panic. 'My Lord?' she said.

'It is gratifying beyond expression, little one, to see you fret so for your husband. You, who are yet so very, very young – though your birthday is not long, as we do recall?'

'Five weeks, my Lord.'

'And you will be?'

'Sixteen.'

'Y . . . e . . . s. A perfect age for a winsome lady! And we have a wee token in our baggage to salute the occasion, and a second from her majesty, which we must lodge in Polmood's custody ere we leave.'

'My lord, you are the most generous gentleman in all the land.'

'Most generous?' James bantered, disturbed by the lack of enthusiasm in Elizabeth's mechanical compliment. 'Kindest? Most gallant? What a wondrous gentleman is this!'

'Wondrous as God pleases, my Lord.'

'Hmm. But neither is our wondrousness the matter of our drift. Nor gifts for birthdays, neither. Rather is it this. That you now are arrived at the fullest state of womanhood, are you not?'

'My Lord, I am bound to suppose so.'

'You never could deny it but your ripened charms would belie you.'

Elizabeth bowed her eyes.

As in a modest blush.

And the King went on:

'Yet still you do not *know* your husband?'

She did not reply.

'In the *deepest* sense?'

'No, my Lord,' she whispermumbled. 'Polmood has been most nobly . . . deferent. To my delicacy and youth.'

'And much is he to be commended for it!'

Elizabeth nodded.

'However, no body can there be more aware than yourself that such restraint on his part is barely longer warrantable.'

Mute assent.

'Polmood is by no means young, forby, and yet has no sons, nor daughters neither, to carry hope into the future, for the seeds of his blood and the banner of his line.'

'Quite so, my Lord.'

'Your concern for his safety is great. That is plain.'

'Yes, my Lord. Of course!'

'And many a greyhead dame now abiding in Scotland's castles would pale in crying shame beside such sleepless duty.'

A tiny sniff broke free like a bothersome lamb from Elizabeth's penning self-control.

'Elizabeth?' the King cajoled gently.

'Yes, my . . . *Lord?*' she sobbed.

And the whole flock followed.

A dozen fleecy sobs. Perhaps a score.

'Little one. Will you not vouchsafe these tiring eyes the favour of a meeting?'

She obeyed with slow fearfulness, her eyes like melting glass.

'There! For where is comfort to be drawn, if not through the gaze of friends?'

'I know not, my Lord.'

'Then be instructed. And pray you now instruct ourself in this, as we have held your welfare in our heart these four years past: whether, Elizabeth, your yearning for your husband's safe return is balanced by your passion to bear his child hereafter?'

Polmood's *child?*

A monster cub sucking being from her entrails, to bloat her

belly like a melon, make grained and coarse her satin skin, and puff her willowy limbs to the hideous bulge of leeches sated. Then the labour, the straining, the howling: the screaming of the utmost agony she oft had heard attend the births of others.

For Polmood?

Then the same distortive defilement all over again, as soon as she could stand the strain: grinding every ounce of beauty from her exquisite body until it no more would catch the eye of the world than the hulk of an ageing ferry boat that knows no respite in the carrying of its cargo until its timbers grew too feeble and its final load goes down.

And who then cares if the boat sinks too?

All this?

For Polmood!

Thoughts such as these, though minced in the fury of their crowding, so treed Elizabeth's awareness with the snapping of their ugly fangs as to raise her of a sudden to an elevation wherefrom she perceived with stark clarity an uncertainty of a grotesqueness seemingly infinite, which she never could share with another living soul:

Was her distress over Polmood's absence mere wifely concern to have her husband home? Or was it the pain of suppressing her fiendish excitement at the possibility of freedom through untimely widowhood?

Which was the true explanation?

If Elizabeth did not know, then how may we?

It is however beyond dispute that this recognition of her graceless state of doubt so appalled and shamed the troubled maiden that not for another instant could she dare to bask in the avuncular affection that beamed upon her from the King's kindly eyes like morning sunlight on a trembling orchid.

'Oh, my *Lord*!' she cried, throwing herself forward and burying her tears in his lap. 'Of course I wish to bear his child! Of *course* I do. He is my *husband*! Oh-oh-oh-oooh!'

His Majesty softly matched the desperate falsehood: 'Of course you do, Elizabeth. And forgive us now, will you not, for the temerity of our asking?'

Muffled nodding in the King's loins.

James massaged the bunching muscles beneath her slender neck.

The fire burned low.

A candle guttered on the wooden branches of the low chandelier, singing a smoky swansong to its seven more thrifty brethren.

'The gift of life', his Majesty reflected, deliberately rambling, 'is a benison of the utmost glory!'

An elm log smouldered with the rustling sound of light rain on dry leaves.

'Like gold, we may say. Since that which is most precious at the same time constitutes the burden most onerous, and the greater our trove of gold in this life, the stouter must we build our shoulders. But with this difference: that in the guarding and the portage of the gold of life the shoulders are bestowed by Nature: to woman, not to man! A most perspicuous assignation! Mmmm? For where in a thousand men would we find a dozen willing to . . .'

'Let me pass, let me *pass*!' a voice of reedy anguish sounded through the parlour door.

His interrupted Majesty cocked an Ear.

And heard, in his guard's guttural bass:

'In good time, my friend. And if his Majesty please. But first ye must state your case.'

'I *cannot*!' Thomas squeaked frantically. 'Except to my lady and the King. I *must* . . .'

'ALL IS WELL, SERGEANT!' commanded James, grinning at the thought of what the soldier must imagine he was about with Elizabeth. 'LET THE FELLOW PASS.'

A moment later Thomas was in the parlour and jibbering on his knees. 'Su – Sire!' he jabbered, so white that his pimples stood out like angry measles.

'Be calm, boy!' the King advised. 'Rise up and speak clearly.'

'It is the Master, Sire!' said Thomas, stepping forward and clasping his hands to tame their trembling.

'What is it, Thomas?' asked Elizabeth. Loth to appear hysterical before a male menial, she sat back and dabbed as at the eyes of a streaming cold.

'Sire! My lady! His pony is returned!'

'Yes?' said James, a Frown gathering.

'Without the Master, Sire! Alone. Oh, your Majesty, and Lord knows what a state the beast is in!'

'Then tell us, lad. What is the trouble?'

'Sire, she is quite mad with fright – like as if she had come face to face with the Evil One himself. And there is *blood*, Sire! Everywhere. All across her back. And a wound in her neck, forby. Like as if she had been struck by a blade!'

'Oh, dear God!' Elizabeth lowmoaned.

All will soon be well!

'Not *this*!' she prayed.

King James rose up in a resumption of high regality, cast the shawling blanket off his shoulders, and said:

'Lady Elizabeth, fear never the worst. This matter may be lighter than it seems. Tarry here awhile, we pray you, and we shall investigate. You, lad!'

'Ay, Sire? Yes, I mean!'

'Lead us where the beast is stabled.'

'Yes, Sire.'

15
COMPRESSION OF EVENTS

The day following the Polmood hunt was the first Friday in August, and oh what a grey and dismal day it was. No mist. No rain. Just an endless sullen blanket of grey that was thwarted in its leaden ache to fall and smother the world below by nothing but the intense humidity that buffered like a sandwich-filling between the joyless lumpy crusts of the heavens and the land. Likewise the collective mind, which awoke that morning in a Castle dankly seething with doubt, perplexity, and direst foreboding.

What could have happened to the gentlemen still missing?

Why had Polmood's mount returned alone?

And what had sunny optimism to say concerning the sword gash in the pony's neck and the copious crimson gules upon its back?

No-one knew.

Yet how could anyone but fear the worst?

As many a pair of furtive mutters surmised.

By an hour before noon a considerable number of local people had arrived at the Castle – shepherds of the region, crofting cottars and the like – to offer their services to his Majesty in assisting with the driving of the deer for his sport, for the news was now well spread that the King was hereabout holidaying and that the previous day's tinckell had been overly meagre for his proper entertainment.

King James ordained that these wellwishing commoners assemble on the terrace, and there, when refreshments had been served them, he in due course appeared, thanked them for the supererogatory warmth of their willing fealty, and explained that due to his concern over the fates of those not returned from the previous day's chase he was regretfully obliged to cancel all further sport until the safety of the absent gentlemen be ascertained.

In this quest, however, his Majesty went on, the motley multitude that here had so generously gathered could do him an even greater service, for it was necessary that every house and shelter in the country adjacent, every trail in the forest and valley in the mountains, should be combed with the greatest possible diligence by the greatest possible number.

Would the hale and trusty folks of Tweedsmuir win their Sovereign's eternal gratitude in this matter?

Certainly they would, they loudly affirmed, with ringing hurrahs reiterating their recommendation that the Deity's watch over his Majesty be continued.

Small search parties, led by the nobles who had taken part in the fated hunt and by the leashmen (who had the additional task of looking out for the many hounds still missing), were duly formed and sent off in every direction. Two of the feared-for five were soon discovered: the Lord James Douglas of Dalkeith and the Duke of Hamilton. Thrown together by the fortunes of the fog, this unlikely pair, it transpired, had ended up in entirely the wrong valley (riding down the Fruid Water, which is next west to the Menzion Burn, where they should have been), and had eventually found looming before them the Castle of Hackshaw, on the border of the forest, where they had received a grudgingly bare entertainment from an elderly curmudgeon knight named Hugh Porteous.

But what of Polmood, Hepburn and Donald of Lamington?

The Lords Douglas and Hamilton had no clue.

So the search went on.

Niggling fruitless across the sultry hump of the scowling day.

And it was not until late in the cooler, darker greys of the evening that the Earl of Mar galloped back along the Castle terrace and whinnied to a foaming halt in the courtyard with redolence of evil tidings oozing hotly from his every pore.

King James, who had remained at Polmood, to stand at the hub of all incoming intelligence and to cushion Elizabeth's anxiety with his Presence, then heard it reported between spent pants that the Earl of Mar's party, while journeying wearily homeward, had happened upon Sir Patrick Hepburn's horse – a young dun gelding – grazing alone by the bank of the tiny Gameshope Loch, and that their subsequent exhaustive examination of the vicinity had eventually discovered, in a slimy gulch in the narrowest and most impassable ford of Gameshope, the murdered bodies of Hepburn himself and of Norman of Polmood.

With their heads and necks roughly severed from their shoulders, and so disposed of that further effort had been unable to find them.

This was tragic news indeed, his Majesty remarked, his tone and frown severely sombre, and then inquired whether Donald of Lamington had also come to light.

Unfortunately not, the Lord Mar replied, and excused himself for having to convey the additionally fiendish detail that not only had the heads been hacked off the bodies, but the corpses had been horribly butchered – chopped at, slashed, and repeatedly run through – such that portions of Polmood's entrails, for example, had spilled out through the shreds of his jerkin like the ruins of a haggis exploded under pressure and since had been substantially devoured by a wake of gloating crows.

'Lord save us!' his Majesty grimaced, and fingered his pennant chain.

'Indeed, Sire. And the body of his hound, forby, was prone beside his own, with a death wound in its gullet.'

'The great wild beast that was much like a wolf?'

'Sire, the very same.'

'Oh, good Mar! What a dastardly abomination!'

'None more so, Sire. In all my experience.'

'And was there no evidence of combat? For Polmood was a doughty foe, was he not?'

'Indeed, Sire. And evidence there was. Polmood's blade we found drawn and in his hand, and grasped so firm in a bloody vice of death, despite the mangled tendons of his wrist, that it scarce could be forced free. And when it was, Sire, we found it argued, by the scarlet smirches and flakes of splintered bone upon it, that some deadly blows had very like been thereby given.'

'Then mayhap Lamington too lies slain not leagues away?'

'Possibly, Sire. Though not a glimpse we yet have found.'

'For plain it seems that it must be he has authored this heinous atrocity?'

'I am driven, Sire, to believe so. For though we have no proof as yet, all circumstance cries out against him.'

Still, his Majesty reflected, the whole affair stank foully of the unaccountably incredible, as Lamington and Hepburn were not only longstanding cronies but distant blood relations too, while between Lamington and Polmood no previous contention had existed, or at least was known to exist – excepting perhaps the consummate ease of the defeat of the former by the latter in the semi-finals of the Crawmelt wrestle a year before, which surely seemed insufficient grudge to have actuated such a gruesomely belated revenge.

By all that was holy!

King James then inquired if the bodies were expected back that night.

The Earl of Mar informed him to the contrary: in view of the late hour at which the grisly discovery was made he had instructed his henchmen, most of them unmounted, to bear the headless cadavers to the farmhouse at Talla Linnfoot for the night, thence to fetch them back to Polmood Castle with all expedition the following morning.

This had been a commendable decision, said his Majesty, for it allowed some bridging hours during which the demise of the hapless Polmood could be broken to his lady, without the risk that she might impetuously rush to wail her bereavement in the presence of the maimed remains. Such a macabre spectacle would prove irreparably injurious to the fragile sensibilities of so tender a lady, and therefore, King James observed, the Earl of Mar could consolidate into impregnability the already formidable vantage he held in his Sovereign's affections, if he would but tactfully assist in shielding the youthful widow from the full spurting grotesqueness of carnage and decapitation in which her husband had expired.

'That he has been murdered we cannot conceal, as a great hue and cry must howl across the land until the villain shall be cornered – alive or dead, it matters not.'

'Indeed, Sire.'

'But we shall not have the lady's dreams infected with the pus of putrefaction and the stench of disembowelment.'

'Your Majesty, you have my solemn oath.'

'And you, sir, our heartfelt thanks. However she shall receive the news, we must and shall frustrate her any wish to examine her dear departed.'

But Elizabeth, much to his Majesty's unexpressed surprise and relief, received the Expurgated version of the morbid news in a quietly pale spirit of apparent resignation, for which she begged pardon, lest it seem callous, and adduced that though her feelings went beyond the power of the spoken word to tell, yet this ghastly upshot was no more than she had been expecting, as she had intuited it with indubitable vividness in that moment when Thomas had burst in and informed them of the return of the bloodsoaked pony. Might the Good Lord have mercy upon Polmood's soul, she petitioned, and grant forgiveness that her meagre and ungrateful store of tears had been squandered in the selfish privacy of the night and was now unable to flow seemly moist in the eye of her desolation.

Later, King James found occasion to guardedly inquire whether Elizabeth had knowledge of any smouldering animosity between her husband and the Laird of Lamington, as it seemed beyond doubt that it was the latter that had perpetrated the appalling assassination.

Elizabeth appeared markedly more shaken by this suggestion than by the account of Polmood's death itself, and, replying in the negative, asked his Majesty in turn whether the accuracy of this attribution of blame were established unassailably.

The King allowed that the proof was certainly not absolute, as the evidence was wholly circumstantial.

Elizabeth despondently supposed that total certitude could only be achieved through location of the vanished Lamington.

This caused his Majesty to lavish praise on her astuteness and impartiality.

Praise, however, that was radically misplaced.

For Elizabeth's despondent supposal was a feigned red herring.

As the inner walls of her mind rang painfully to the echoing yells of an utterly alternative conviction.

Sir John Carmichael!

All will soon be well!

Who else?

So he had vowed, and thus he quite clearly had acted, imagining, no doubt, that by slicing her bondage to the husband she did not love and who never could give her true happiness, he would win to his caitiff self her devoted gratitude and adoration!

Well, she resolved, just as she had been so foolishly callow as to miss the grainy specks and sooty streaks that lurked between the scripted lines of Carmichael's outward character (though he was a gifted mummer, was he not, and had everyone deceived in his Connel-the-gardener guise?), so would he discover with a vengeance how signally *he* had mistaken *her*!

Condone the slaughter of her husband?

Notwithstanding the purgatorial shortcomings of the match?

Never! No, by the Grace of the Holy Virgin, *never*!

So determined, and bolstered by righteous outrage, Elizabeth arose at dawn on the Saturday, slipped from the Castle unnoticed except by a drowsy guard, hastened along the riverbank to the mossy patch by the Herston Burn where Carmichael had delved his survival cache.

And there she left the following note:

Wretch!
You have slain my husband; deny it not. Let me never see your face again; oh murdering fiend! Fly now this place as you value your unworthy life; for though I have not told His Majesty of your guise the Duke of Rothesay surely will; and then shall you be pursued to the death; if you have no wit to flee. I cannot bear to point my finger to you; frail woman and forlorn widow that I am. Yet know that I do wish you haunted by the curses of Heaven; as you shall be by those of them you have wronged.
Therefore be gone!

Her conjecture concerning the Duke of Rothesay proved correct, though it was some time before she learned as much. Rosay's heart sang hymns of secret praise on hearing from his judgement that Carmichael it surely was that had done the horrid deed – for how could his guilt-ridden rival now stir except to abandon the country with all possible speed, or end upon the axeman's block?

In either case, all obstruction to Rosay's own designs upon Elizabeth were removed: with her husband murdered and her lover either banished or executed, how could her resistance to his own courtly charms outlive the decency of her mourning by a day? Moreover, in the longer term, the winning of Elizabeth's love was now an affair of property at which not even a royally landed Duke could lightly sniff, as till she remarried she would retain sole title to the extensive lands of Polmood, in addition to the valuable estates of Fingland, Glenbreck and Kingledores, which King James had given as her dowry.

In Rosay's vision, therefore, Elizabeth's timely widowhood made her a peach of double succulence, in that successful plucking of the fruit would endow the plucker with possession of the orchard.

But what if the peach were blemished in reputation?

With her husband out of the way, no-one living was aware of Carmichael's having lurked there in disguise save Rosay himself. Therefore, he reasoned, in order not to affront Elizabeth and alienate the affections he had no doubt his suasory company would in due course wheedle from her, and likewise that his intended conquest should retain the high value of her virtuous respectability in the eyes of the world, it was only proper to keep Carmichael's imposting from becoming public knowledge. However, since Justice required that the King's vengeance point aright, and in case Carmichael might dare to remain somewhere within the borders of the nation, the Duke of Rothesay concluded that it was his bounden duty to disclose the whole affair to his Majesty in confidence.

And this he did while strolling gravely on the lawns, on the afternoon of the hotly disconsolate Saturday.

Minus only the slatternly detail of Elizabeth's eager entwinement with Carmichael!

'Indeed, sir?' said the King, looking sideways down his nose at the unaccustomed earnestness of his shorter fatter brother. 'The particulars of this singularly distasteful episode being so, we must conceive with you that Carmichael is the assassin. Yet still we have much unexplained.'

'Sire?'

'If Carmichael it truly was that mauled yon miserable gentlemen, then what has become of the final absentee: the Laird of Lamington?'

'Possibly, Sire . . .'

'And is it not puzzling that all the searches have uncovered neither a feather from his bonnet nor a snort from his mount forby?'

'Myself, Sire,' Rosay deprecated, while wrinkling his nose and sidestepping the remnants of a cat-savaged blackbird mouldering buzzily in the anklehigh lushness of the unsickled grass, 'I positively see no puzzle. Are not the mountains vast, the valleys interminable? That a *hundred* men might thereamong go lost without a trace!'

'You are hyperbolic, sir. As ever. Though consider you this. That the vastness of the mountains and the interminability of the valleys is in opposite proportion to the enthusiasm of he who traverses them.'

'Unquestionably, Sire,' Rosay smarmed, 'there is much in what you say! Yet I persist in finding it not at all mysterious that *one* man might vanish irretrievably in the conditions of two days ago. Over a precipice in that fog he might easily have cantered, might he not? And lie spattered now, and his pony beside him, upon the rocks beneath?'

'Hmmm.'

'Or thrown by a stream, concussed, and drowned in but a shallow pool? The possibilities . . .'

'Are endless, sir. As is time, but not life. Or patience!'

'Sire?'

'Nothing, sir. Nothing!' King James glanced again, his liking scant, at this his present heir, and pictured how his brother's mask of grave concern would crumple were its wearer to learn that he himself had been listed in his Majesty's suspicions. The relationship between Rosay and Polmood had been so clearly poisonous, at dinner on the evening of the hunt's arrival, and the King's awareness of his sibling's lack of scruple so acute, that his first response to the report of Polmood's despatch had been to suspect that Rosay was the culprit: that he had felled the obstructive husband to clear his path to the lovely wife. That Rosay was capable of such intent his Majesty had no doubt. But of the physical execution? Hardly. And in any case, Rosay had returned to the Castle much too early to have been involved in such foul play upon the moors. Hence . . .

'And forby, Sire,' that Duke now urged, 'the search goes on, and before this day is out the men may return with all the facts, concerning the fate of Lamington. Who knows?'

'Who, indeed?' James wearily murmured. When the bodies had been borne in, shortly after eleven in the morning, he had undertaken a brief inspection to glean whatever might be deduced from the nature of their mutilation – but the sight had been so sickening and the stench so warmly nauseous that even his hardened gorge and battletempered eyes were quickly tested to the limit. And now there was the memory: the reek of it still swilling in his belly, polluting his luncheon like the carcass of a bloated trout in a stagnant pool. 'Yeurk!' he exclaimed, and about-turned suddenly in his walk, to dislodge the thought.

'And tomorrow too they will search,' he added, as they headed back towards the Castle. 'If need be. While we attend the burial. But on Monday a halt must be called, if nothing emerges in the time between, as our business in Edinburgh shall countenance no delay thereafter – not least the King of Denmark's importunate ambassador: bah! "A thousand soldiers, Majesty!" he whines. "A thousand would be *ample,* and *two* thousand so *lavishly* handsome!" There, sir, is a gentleman whose acquaintance you must not neglect to make.'

'I, Sire?'

'For wherever else are you like to meet a man with a waterfall of oil where his mouth should be! Eh? But enough of that. And concerning the delicate secret you have vouchsafed us, our resolution is this. That if no light is cast upon Lamington's disappearance ere we leave, it shall be publicly proclaimed that it is *he* has wrought the deaths of Polmood and Hepburn, and therefore must be hunted – yet meanwhile shall we discreetly circulate to the sheriffs across the nation that it is Carmichael they must pursue.'

'A sterling resolution, Sire! And now, if I may, I would crave of you a boon?'

'Mmmm?'

'Regarding the lady, sire. The woe-smitten widow.'

'Y . . . e . . . s?'

Rosay scratched nervously at his breast through his blouse of green silk. 'You said, Sire, that the party shall vacate these premises on the Monday – that is two days hence?'

'That is so.'

Then, to cut a bush-skirting gale of hot air to a lukewarm puff, Rosay beseeched to be suffered to remain at Polmood and keep Elizabeth company during the harshest first months of her bereavement, representing that she had many household and proprietary responsibilities to shoulder, for which she was patently ill-fitted and would be much the better for a friend and protector to advise and assist her.

King James was at first exceedingly reluctant to assent to this request, as he instantly saw through the logicizing solicitude to the real motives rooting beneath. On the other hand, who was he, even He, to deprive Elizabeth of any chance of happiness? Rosay was a contemptible crawler, that was true – yet were not the best marriages devised by the angels of Heaven, rather than the lords, even Kings, of the earth?

Moreover, the Duke of Rothesay, in rank, property and wealth, was Scotland's premier noble at that time: why, therefore, if truly he did covet Elizabeth's hand, should that beauteous, cultivated and now well-landed maiden be obliged to settle for less? If Rosay could woo her fancy to blow his way? Then there was the consideration that (whatever a spirited lady might sometimes pretend) the female soul and bodily constitution could never know true joy in the absence of the master sex, and that without men, indeed, they need not be said to exist at all.

'Very well, sir,' James accordingly said, before dinner on that Saturday, having mused at morose leisure through the several pros and cons. 'As you hereby shall swear to us upon your oath that your intentions toward the lady are wholly honourable and maritally inclined, we shall grant you this request.'

'My gratitude, Sire . . .'

'Your *oath*, sir!'

'Sire, I do swear it! Upon my honour and the Cross, most solemnly!'

'And there is, of course, a cardinal condition.'

'Sire?'

'Come, sir. Come! It is obvious, is it not? That you must broach the matter with the lady, and that she must freely approve – nay, *welcome*! – your proposal.'

'Naturally, Sire. I shall – '

'But not until the morrow!' his Majesty softly warned. 'Eh? Some short pause of decency past the hour when she must see her husband laid away. Mmmm?'

All in favour of Elizabeth's virtue remaining intact will be relieved to learn that King James had up his voluminous blue bell sleeve a second condition with which to qualify the prolongation of Rosay's stay at Polmood, should he manage to elicit the lady's blessing.

However, his Majesty being somewhat dubious that this blessing would forthcome, he kept his rider to himself until that time should ripen.

And Rosay?

Though obliged to postpone the putting of his project to Elizabeth until the Sunday evening, he lost no time in the opening of his campaign. Had there ever been a history of ghosts in the Castle of Polmood, he inquired of the elderly housekeeper in the kitchens, late on the night of the Saturday.

Ghosts!?

Yes, ghosts.

Or perhaps a single ghost: it was difficult to tell – but he, Rosay, had certainly had his slumbers ravaged, in the smallest darkest hours of the previous morning, by the wildest and most eldritch cacophony of creakings, creepings and unearthly groanings that ever had set his teeth on edge and his pelt to icy hackling!

'*Ghosts*, my lord?' old Martha gaped again. 'No, never! Never in all my days, my lord, have I ever heard or even heard *tale* . . .'

'No, no. Indeed!' Rosay nodded reassuringly. Doubtless it had been but the aftermath of some unusually disturbing dream, which just went to show, did it not, how even the soberest and most rational of gentlemen, such as himself, could allow themselves to become superstitiously deluded at times?

In the weakness of their unlit nights alone!

Amongst the unfamiliar echoes and stony whispers of old castles such as this!

Thus was the seed sewn.

And behold!

Although the Duke of Rothesay survived the Saturday night unmolested by further spectral manifesta, it was not so with Martha. She had not slept a wink, Rosay was dismayed to hear after breakfast next morning, and distinctly had detected a far-off minatory shuffle, as of cold and weightless feet, flecked at petrifying intervals by an eerie vocal garble of undead moans.

'No!' Rosay disbelievingly exclaimed.

'Oh, yes, my lord!' Martha blabbed. 'And what with the poor Master so recently . . .'

'Peace, woman!' Rosay scolded, but in conspiratorial kindness. 'The man's unfortunate body is *not yet buried*!'

Martha pressed her hands to the large wooden crucifix betwixt her desiccated breasts, and shook her head in twitching fright, like a tabbycat with a cankerous ear.

'Yet they say his *head* was missing when they found the bodies,' Rosay debated in ominous puzzlement. 'Could it then be . . .'

'AAAAAHHHH!' screamed Martha, whose crabby palms sprang up from their oaken cross and pressed violently against her ears. 'AAAA . . .'

'*Silence!*' hissed Rosay. 'Else you may affright the menials, and then where shall the rumour end? Which has no ground, woman, I yet am convinced, but the rattlings of some draught in the cooling night. Wherefore keep you our converse to yourself, and spread it not – you hear me?'

'Yee-yee-yes, my lord.'

But an old and long unmanned soul such as Martha was perfectly incapable of keeping any such thing to herself.

As Rosay had accurately anticipated.

With the result, by the Sunday evening, that all of the resident lower echelons in the Castle, together with many of the visiting scullions, pageboys, grooms, leashmen and the like, were gripped in varying degrees of exulting horror by the conviction that the headless spirit (or worse: the bodiless headspirit!) of the murdered Laird had risen already from gory death and returned in the fury of his purgatorial agony to crucify the sleep of all who had wronged him in life.

And who among the domestic staff could say they had not?

As Thomas warned Betty, when pointing out that never again should she dare to sleep alone.

Elizabeth, however, was forged of less volatile mettle.

'A *ghost*, my lord?' she wearily scepticized, when Rosay intercepted her route to bed, close to midnight on the Sunday, and begged her to return with him to the parlour awhile as he had a proposition of the utmost exigence to lay before her.

'Indeed, my lady!' the suitor pressed. 'This is what the menials bleat – though Heaven save us from their passion for fabrication!'

'Quite so, my lord,' sighed Elizabeth, as tautly sombre as her garb was flatly black. Her golden hair was hidden away beneath the severity of a chimneypot head-dress, again plain black, from whose rim a cone-shaped veil of black gauze hung down to her shoulders. Thus did she dress for the funeral, which had taken place in the blistering heat of the day, in the tiny graveyard of the chapel of Drumelzier ten miles to the north, and thus she had remained clad ever since – deriving a curiously ascetic satisfaction from the sweltering discomfort of the attire, which screened between her disfiguring misery and the harshly bright external world. 'And I am not sure, my lord,' she added faintly, 'that ghosts are to be believed in. For never have I seen one.'

'Nor I, dearest lady! Nor I. And very like it is all but a chorus of yokeling havers. The which being so, why should it be too lonely and frightsome for you to be left here by yourself, in a place where such abominable assassinations have lately been perpetrated?'

Elizabeth averted her headgear and politely blew her nose beneath her veil.

'Nevertheless,' Rosay urged, 'though the pratings of the phantasm may be hogwash, consider what lowering morale and rife indiscipline they may wreak upon your gullible retainers!'

'My lord?'

'Disobedience, dear lady, you may be faced with. And rank defection forby! If these insidious rumblings are not sternly checked and given the imminent lie.'

'Oh! This, my lord, I . . . had not thought upon.'

'But how could you?' Rosay engagingly took for granted. 'Here in your hour and robes of grief! And possibly these spineless desertions will be of little consequence: depending on your plans.'

'Plans, my lord?'

'Whether it is your intention to linger here, within the cheerless site and memory of your tragedy, or rather close up house and betake you to more amiable walls?'

Elizabeth shivered inside the chilling seal of her day's perspiration. The parlour fire had not been lit, as the night was warm and the season looked set for a spell of harvest heat. But she felt cold as winter moonlight through frozen trees; and twice as pale. What now? As joyful as a sinking stone, so her marriage to Polmood had seemed while he lived – yet was her plight not worsened by his death? And confounded by this: that when at dawn she had stolen again to the spot where yesterday she left her note of banishment for Carmichael, she had found to her immeasurable horror that it was gone! Which meant that on the Saturday at least, Carmichael was still skulking in the region. And with what desperate purpose?

Oooh! How she had hoped to find her note still there, untouched, implying that the assassin had fled upon the freshness of his bloody guilt and never would trouble her thoughts again, except through the etiolating torment of the memory of the atrocity he had committed. For love of her! This was the cruellest barb of all: that had she not suffered Carmichael to stay, concealed as Connel, her crude but scarcely evil husband would never have met with such a dismal doom! But then he would be breathing still, with her chained in wedlock to him. And that . . .

'You are weeping, dearest lady?' Rosay softly sympathized.

'No!' she smothered a sob.

'And the blame is mine. Solely mine. Though it was not my aim to wring you with odious reflections, and the likelihood of future difficulties and complications – absolutely the contrary! My desire is merely to paint to you that even should you soon decide to remove from these fateful whereabouts, it shall take you several months to order your late husband's affairs – and his many dependents – in such a posture as to enable you to leave them with your conscience unharassed. And therefore my offer is: that since there is no decorum or etiquette which forbids you the presence of a friend and protector with experience in such matters, I beg you accept my company and service, at least in the weeks most urgently ahead.'

What now?

Elizabeth took a deep unsteady breath, and looking up, regarded Rosay through her veil with a gaze moistly blank.

'And thereafter,' he concluded, his sincerity appearing to bore still deeper, 'a very great privilege shall I esteem it to lead you back to your rightful place amid the colour and the music of the court. Either as Dame Elizabeth Hunter, widow to Norman of Polmood, or else, if all goes well, and if you should please, as the honourable Lady Elizabeth, Duchess of Rothesay and Countess of Argyll.'

'Truly you are kind, my lord,' Elizabeth sobbed, tears streaming from her eyes as she rose to retire. 'And profoundly am I grateful though yet I know not what to say and fear I must hurry me away to sleep before I swoon. Therefore goodnight, my lord!'

'But my lady!' Rosay protested, blinking peevishly as Elizabeth stood in the doorway. 'I fain would know . . .'

'In the morning, my lord!' she blurted through the closing door. 'My answer shall be yours in the morning.'

16

THE NEXT EIGHT DAYS

A SMELLY VISITATION

'More to the left, Betty, if you please,' said Elizabeth. 'My left. So the table runs a perfect line between the stag's head and the fireplace. Ready?'

'Yes, my lady.'

'Then: one, two, heave! Perfect, Betty. Thank you. And now could you look to the kitchens, and help Martha with the lunches?'

'Yes, my lady. My lord!' Betty courtesied uncertainly to Rosay, who was lounging irately by the door, then passed him and departed.

'Truly, my lady,' he plainted, 'it is simply *too* bad!'

'Pray what is too bad, my lord?' asked Elizabeth, assiduously polishing the dining table with a soft leather cloth and a knob of fresh beeswax. It was an hour past Monday breakfast, before which she had wanly agreed to Rosay's proposal to stay on as her guardian, companion and administrative adviser. How else could she choose, she had concluded at the end of a sleepless night, when her predicament was so desolate and her heart so vacant of attachment? And of hope.

'This impossible pronouncement by his Majesty!' Rosay spluttered. 'It is both glaringly unnecessary and conspicuously insulting.'

'To whom, my lord?'

'Why, my myself!'

For when the King had learned at the breakfast table of Elizabeth's consent to Rosay's request, he had smoothly unsleeved his hidden card: that while it was indeed exceedingly desirable that Elizabeth should profit by the Duke of Rothesay's most gracious offer, the presumptuous wagging of malicious and propriety-bound tongues must also be guarded against, lest either the lady or the gentleman ('or both, by the Lord!') should suffer the slur of any slanderously disseminating misconstrual of their arrangement, wherefore both parties would be delighted to discover, would they not, that the day had already been saved by the bounty of Sir William Moray, who had undertaken to tarry at Polmood conterminously with Rosay, that the latter's presence be thereby chaperoned against degradation at the uniquitously anonymous hands of salacious mumblers?

'But *Sire*!' Sir William had boyishly yelped in thunderstruck dismay, while choking on his oatcake.

'Silence, sir!' his Majesty had sternly boomed. 'Else the reiteration of your willingness shall milk the gesture of its magnanimous spontaneity! And it shall also serve well yourself, we trow, to dally a spell in the quiet of the country, reflect and commune with the glorious mysteries of Nature awhile, as all true poets rhythmically must – and fashion up a novel batch of verses too, to cheer us when the nights again turn cold and long. Eh? Wherefore we desire to hear no further word on the matter: all is settled.'

'It may be insulting, my lord,' Elizabeth rejoined, 'though myself I see not how.' Still draped in unrelenting black from neck to toe, her grief had softened the length of exchanging the unbecoming bonnet and veil of yesterday's funeral low for a slender bow of black velvet ribbon, which, perched in the place of her wonted gay rose, now bobbed and shook precariously as she rubbed with therapeutic vigour at a cheese smudge on the old oak table. 'But', she added, 'it plainly is not impossible.'

'Uh?'

'I mean, my lord, that, as the King has ordained it so, it plainly must be possible. Must it not?'

Rosay glowered at her, suspecting goating.

Though the literality of Elizabeth's logic was no more than an unintended coping device: a grapnel thrown out blindly by the unconscious mind, eager to hook on to normality at any point.

'I take the strictness of your reasoning, my lady,' the Duke coldly said, pacing in agitation beneath the great stag's baleful head. 'Yet I ask me: must it really be?'

'My lord?'

'If you will allow the harsh economy of my bluntness, my lady, for my own part I desire the yapping of that insolent puppy about my heels as little as the plague! No more, I dare warrant, than you do wish the encumbrance of his person and effects about your house and stables, and the drain of his gluttonous appetite upon your kitchen.'

'Oh no, my lord! If Sir William is pleased to be our guest . . .'

'But he is *not* pleased! Do not you see? Which magnifies the folly a hundredfold: that he is no more eager to linger here than I am keen to suffer the penance of his lurking – it is madness! Madness all!'

'Oh!' Elizabeth lamely said. The tickle of this subtlety had previously failed to penetrate her numbness.

Rosay paused to allow his hostess to reflect on the lunacy of his Majesty's imposition.

Through the open east windows bright sunlight angled from the south, casting pools of glassy brown across the table and ricocheting upward to dazzle the faded and forgotten eyes of several Polmood forebears hanging portraited upon the wester wall.

As no more Hunter of Polmood ever would, except by the grace of some artist's fancy.

And with the sunbeams came the clattering courtyard sounds of readiness being made: noble commands and scullion whines, the creaking of saddles, the jingle of bridles, and the stamping snorts of horses impatient for motion.

'Ffoff!' Rosay angrily snapped, and slapped a furious fat hand up and down before his nose, with which a speeding bluebottle had collided. 'Dah! No, my lady,' his argument raged, 'the situation is preposterous utterly, to everyone except his Majesty. Who remains headstrongly adamant . . .'

'And therefore – '

'And therefore, dearest lady, the only person in all the world to procure us remedy is yourself!'

'Me, my lord?' Elizabeth looked up in wide-eyed startlement.

'Yes, my lady. You!'

'My lord, I see not how.'

'This is your household, is it not?'

'But – '

'And the honour in name for which his Majesty fears – or might I say: *appears* to fear – is yours alone!'

'And warmly thankful am I, my lord, that my widowhood sees my interests yet remembered!'

'Quite so. But since the fangs of his concern are bared to no good purpose, as your honour is in no wise imperilled by my sojourn, and since neither you nor I nor the invidious Sir William himself deem expedient his further presence here, nor desire it a measly whit, I put it to you, my very dearest lady, that if *you* approach his Majesty *now*, before the party leaves, and speak in person against this odiously impracticable scheme – well! How could he but comply with your whim in grief?'

'I do not know, my lord,' Elizabeth doubted, slowly, the energy of her polishing sagging like the buzzing of a bee on a cool autumn evening. 'For I am not agin Sir William's residence.'

'But *he* is agin it!' Rosay frantically barked, swishing his floppy yellow-sleeved arms through the moteful air in Latinesque despair. 'Doltish blockhead that he is, he has yet the grain of wit to perceive – '

'No, my lord,' Elizabeth regretted wearily. 'I should esteem myself guilty of an unforgivable ingratitude to plead thus against his Majesty's good judgement on my – oh! Good day to you, Sir William.'

'Good day to you, my lady,' returned Sir William, stepping into the hall and nodding a minimal bow. 'My lord.'

'How do you, sir!' snapped Rosay, his eyes bulging with loathing. 'Is there something ails you, pray, within our power to appease?'

'Doltish blockhead that I am,' Sir William pokerfaced, acidly charged by what his moment's loitering had overheard, 'there is much invidious ails within me, my lord. Yet I fear it lies beyond the notious lengths of your lordship's own appeasements.'

'You are a slinking scoundrel, sir!' Rosay fumed. 'And have been overlistening us!'

'Only, my lord, so please you, the fleeting and edifying snatch that my ear had not the time to barricade against, as my fist rose up to knock – for the which, as your lordship may imagine, my sentence already is fitly meted. And now, my lady,' he addressed Elizabeth, his tone chameleonizing from tightlipped banter to prosaic courtesy. 'There is a matter just arisen that begs your attention.'

'Yes, my lord?' Elizabeth inquiringly murmured.

Rosay bristled:

'He is *not* your lord, my lady! He is but a paltry *knight* – no more! A fortune-seeking – '

'Cowering in the courtyard at this moment, my lady,' Sir William cut in with loudness-slicing coolness, 'there is a wandering friar has happened by and seems to covet shelter for a time.'

'Oh!'

'And what is his order, pray?' yacked Rosay, as though suspecting Sir William of some sneaking attempt to smuggle his ragamuffin relatives into free board and lodging.

'I know not precisely, my lord,' Sir William drawled.

'Then . . .'

'But it plainly is one of those vowed to mutery, as the fellow will only mime if he can, and grunts in last resort. Saint John of Jerusalem, I dare say – though your lordship's acquaintance with the orders is unquestionably more catholic than my own.'

'And what is he like?' asked Elizabeth.

'He is old, my lady. Near to ancient, one might say. Large and fat, with a hump on his back like a malformed toad. And he crouches within his cassock and brooding cowl like as if they were his only hole and he a timorous whitebeard mole.'

'Ravishingly picturesque, sir! But is he *real*?'

'Real, my lord? I confess I had not thought to debate the issue. My bonnet here is real, is it not? The plumage too? My colours? Scarlet and silver my doublet really is, or so it really seems. And my hair is truly golden, is it not? When clean, you may say! Wherefore forgive me, my lord, if I ask of you: when is a pilgrim palmer really real, and when is he really not?'

'You are an insolent slavermonger, sir! As one day it may cost you to repent. But for the present you shall oblige me by opining merely whether the man is genuinely of the cloth, and not a filching hunks in borrowed robes, bent only on slothful scavenge.'

'There is no question, my lord, but that he is truly what he seems. For never have I espied such fanatical melancholy and distempered gloom outside of some monkish devotion. Most like he hails from far away, and wishes but to break his journey to the shrine of his reverenced saint.'

Elizabeth smiled in relief. 'Then shelter he must have!' she exclaimed. 'And shelter we shall give him.'

'Hoy, HUP!' cried in from the noiseful courtyard.

'It sounds, my lady,' Rosay urged, 'that his Majesty and his nobles approach their departure. Therefore I *pray* that you reconsider!'

'Already have I said, my lord! That I cannot undertake what you would have me.'

Sir William allowed his deadpan features to crinkle in a grin of sour pleasure at the Duke of Rothesay's frustration. He too was galled to his roots by this latest and most perverse of the King's velleities, but he knew better than to hope for revocation. So he said:

'There is one minor problem, my lady.'

'Yes, my lord?'

Rosay winced, but managed not to interrupt.

'Concerning the pilgrim friar, my lady . . . well, two things there are, it is said, that stink of fish – ye have me, my lord? – and he stinks of both!'

'Oh!'

'Ay, my lady! "Oh!" And: "Yeeek!", and all that. For never, I pray, shall you nose a smellier fellow: that could fley a polecat from fifty paces!'

'THEN SEE THE MAN AWAY, SIR!' roared Rosay. 'And clutter not our hours with baubles!'

Sir William turned to Elizabeth for confirmation.

She pouted in effortful indecision.

Rosay advised:

'Rest assuaged, dear lady, of any sense that the Lord obliges us to hospice a reeky prelate that will not even speak to give us mass – for it is not so. And therefore let us bid the fellow gone.'

But the reign of James IV was as much renowned for its devotion as for its gaiety, and pilgrimages to holy places were as frequent as they were highly valued – the King himself setting an annual example by his homage to the shrine of St Duthac in Tain – and Elizabeth too was extremely devout in her own quiet way, following the courtly orthodoxy of the time at least in strength of faith, if not always in extravagance of overt worship.

And how could strength of faith be better tried than by a fetid friar?

'No, my lords!' she said. 'If we find no charity in our hearts, it yet may profit us to feign it in our doings – so his Majesty once did advise me. For habits, he expounded, are just as apt to form the habitual as he his habits. I did not fully comprehend his notion at the time, I do confess, but here believe we have a chance to groom our impulse for the better. Therefore, Sir William?'

'My lady?'

'There is a corridor of tiny closets in the north wing, up the stairway from the armoury.'

'Ay, my lady?'

'They are bare and musty and long unused, excepting by the leashmen in the few days past. Yet they are dry and not unhabitable, and one of them shall provide a fit asylum for our passing man of God, while keeping him at such distance as will shield our sensibilities from what . . . frowsty habits he may have. Could you, Sir William, tell him this?'

'Ay, by dady!' the young knight chuckled, holding closed his nostrils in the conventional prophylactic pinch. 'Ay hab it!'

'Hold your tongue, sir!' barked Rosay.

'Dod by dose, by dord?'

Elizabeth ignored the clowning. 'And tell him also,' she pondered, 'that a tray of food . . .'

'OH, QUICKLY MUM! COME QUICKLY!'

'That a tray of food shall be placed for him by the stairway foot, at breakfast and at dinner – as we wish him not to break his vows of silence by begging in the kitchen. Yes, Martha?'

'Oh, mum! Come quick, you must!' the panicked old lady panted in the doorway. 'His Majesty is set to leave!'

'Very – '

'They are mounted on the terrace, mum, and *the King is asking for you*!'

'Very well, Martha. Thank you. We are coming now without delay, to bid them all farewell.'

HEAT-HAZE DAYS

As frequently happens after a particularly severe winter, the August of 1507 turned out uncommonly hot – unnaturally so, according to the common folk who laboured through it and swore they had never experienced its baking like before. By the Wednesday, two days after the departure of the hunting party, Elizabeth was forced to bow to the fact that she either must forsake the black stifle of

330

her mourning weeds or succumb to heatstroke. Not through frivolous insouciance, then, but rather due to burning necessity did she so quickly return to her becoming array of light summer sandals and elegant dresses in thin and colourful lawns and muslins.

The black ribbons in her hair, however, she continued to wear.

Partly as grieving token.

And partly as warning to Rosay.

Who nonetheless persisted in the most strenuous endeavours to banish from her mind any posthumous fidelity to her former spouse, to seduce her maiden morals and gain physical possession of her person. After all, as Rosay perfectly appreciated, if Elizabeth would not yield in the quiet solitudes of Polmood, where no other suitor clamoured, how could he hope to achieve his end with her elsewhere – back at court, perhaps, where new admirers would fly to try her like wasps to a freshly unsealed jar of cherry jam?

And moreover!

Nothing had transpired to rattle Rosay's conviction that Elizabeth had already been unchaste with Carmichael. The longer and more charmingly she deflected his own breathy advances, therefore, the most uncomprehendingly piqued and boilingly exasperated his presumptuous familiarities became.

Much to the sardonic amusement of Sir William Moray.

Although his ostensible brief was to guard the good *names* of the widow and the royal duke by the potential testimony of his witness presence, Sir William was sufficiently conversant with the King's obliquities to understand the equal importance of his ulterior role: to act as a sobering brake upon Rosay's sotting lust.

However, as King James had naturally not informed Sir William of the continuing survival of Elizabeth's virginity, and since the youthful poet-knight was quietly furious with his Master for forcing him to fester in this arid bumpkin outpost for an indefinite term, as good as infinitely far from the tauntalizing Lady Ann, we may forgive him a degree of his cynical indifference to the increasingly crude and blatant siege by which Rosay strove to pound Elizabeth's defences down.

'A stroll by the river, my lady?' the Duke might propose at breakfast. 'Before the insufferable scorch of noon?'

'While the morning is yet but pleasantly warm!' Elizabeth might consider. 'Why yes, my lord. Sir William? If you would join us we should be honoured.'

'Thank you, no, my lady,' Sir William would decline. 'I have a verse requires completion, and must regretfully prefer the company of my horse and hawk among the whispers of the hills.'

'Then do we understand, sir, that we are once more deprived of your society until the evening?'

'Ay, my lord, though it shames me to confess it!'

At which, Rosay would struggle through his gloating with:

'Tch, tch! But perhaps tomorrow?'

'Indeed, my lord. Perhaps.'

Thus the days passed, with Sir William riding off on long solo flights of bardic mystery (taking only his falcon or fishing tackle, to nourish his interminable musing exhilarations with the occasional bloody game of earthly joys) and abandoning his vulnerable hostess to his fellow guest's devices.

Still, it cannot be denied that Elizabeth allowed freedoms and accepted intimacies from Rosay that never could clear the hurdles of mature reflective wisdom. Little by little, under the covering barrage of his glittering compliments, he sneaked into the practice of toying with her – of administering childish tickles, playful little pinches and brotherly embraces – and of kissing her hand (first the back, then the palm, and soon the pale soft flesh of her inner wrist and forearm) in respectful greeting in the morning and as passionately sad goodnight. And of course it was not long before the tickles ceased to be childish, the embraces became far from brotherly, and the kisses fell like rain throughout the day, at the slightest lame excuse.

Oh *foolish* Elizabeth, we may again incline to scold! Oh fanciful and *reckless* maid! How can you fail to apprehend the rank defilement whereto his vile carnalities tend? That all his sparkling blandishments and allusions to the untold bliss that lavish remarriage will surely bring (as soon as decency permits!) are but a specious gilt: a tinsel carrot that will vanish like a snowflake on a stove in the very moment of your transporting him to his grunting destination – *cannot you see*?

But who are we to judge?

Who of us, unhusbanded by hideous murder and emotionally marooned within a hateful home, would not waver before such sophistically ardent wooing by the brother of our King? Even with his legs unpleasantly whitely fat, beneath their thick matting of black brutish hair?

So let us withhold harshness from our censure of Elizabeth when she does not immediately cry out in protest as, on the night of the second Friday in August, the incorrigible Duke of Rothesay slips uninvited into her chamber, clad only in his kneelength thin white nightshirt, its falling folds distorted by the protrusive form of his priapic excitement.

And a skullcap of purple velvet.

Elizabeth gasped and pulled her single covering sheet up to her chin.

Causing her abandoned bible to roll from her bed to the floor.

'My lord!' she exclaimed. 'What can this mean?'

'Oh, dearest lady! No wink of sleep shall come my way this night . . .'

'But I am *undressed*, my lord!'

For so she completely was, save only the filigree gold chain and crucifix about her neck.

'But what is that, my lady, against the throbbing adoration that bars my rest until I have declared it to you?'

Elizabeth regarded him with heartfluttering scepticism as he posed by her bedside with his right hand clasped against his bosom, beneath the hairsprouting V of his nightshirt neck, and his left hand wide aloft, bearing the silver-holdered candle he had brought to illumine his suit.

'So please you, my lord,' she remarked, 'but you have declared it to me a hundred times this day, and again just an hour ago, as we did say goodnight.' Lying back on her readingpiled pillows, she grasped her sheet in two smallclenching fists and pulled it prohibitively tight across her throat.

Rosay's maleness wagged.

Elizabeth's pupils swelled in horror.

'Yes, my lady,' he complacently concurred. 'But never have you answered me, wherefore: my sleepless state!'

'I beg you, my lord, to muster patience. For how may I countenance such proposals, who am but a week in widowhood?'

Rosay lodged his candle beside its partner on Elizabeth's bedside cabinet. Then eased his uninvited hunkers down upon the mattress whereupon the willowy damsel helpless lay.

So he thought.

As languorously he leaned over her, posted hands like pudgy sentinels on either side of her captive head, beamed intense significance into her eyeing alarm, and coaxed:

'But the dead are dead! And care no more what days or years may ornament the obsequies of we who survive them.'

'Not so, my lord!' Elizabeth shrank from his liquorfumet mouth. 'Our lamentations for the dead grow surely from the sanctity of Life!'

'I see it not. Ooooh!'

'Yes, my lord – I pray you that you *do not*!'

'As you wish, my lady: sweetest Elizabeth! But do you *truly* wish it so?'

'In*deed*, my lord!'

'Very well, very well. Though deeply do I question that your lips obey your heart. But oh, what lips! Elizabeth. Like slices of the rosiest peach, that – '

'My lord, our neglect in the matter of the former cannot but infect our appreciation for the latter!' Elizabeth spoke in growing desperation, for Rosay's cruel nostrils twitched a bare hand above her own, and he had squeezed the meaty bulk of his torso down upon her breast.

'Eh?' he blinked in bafflement.

'Our lamentations for the dead, my lord. And the sanctity – '

'Nyah! What are such womanish cavils to us? We! Who are here alive and ripe . . . for *love*!'

'*No*, my lord!' Elizabeth cried. 'I shall *scream*!'

For Rosay's left hand had begun to explicitly explore where a gentleman's left hand should never explicitly explore in the absence of a lady's encouragement.

'Then scream, my lady,' he rumbled as she struggled. 'But I will not believe your cries to speak your deepest wishes, and forby they shall not stir a soul beyond my passion, which thereby shall be exquisitely fanned: as a bonfire by a lilting breeze. Mmmmmuh!' he throated in anticipation as he rolled his total weight on top of her.

Elizabeth went suddenly limp.

Rosay nuzzled back endearments to her neck, jockeying his stiffness against her thinly sheeted thighs.

Elizabeth shuddered.

Which Rosay sensed as a shiver of arousal.

'Oh let us become one single flesh of ecstasy!' he moaned. 'Dearest lady! This night is destined for our union – do not you feel it in your soul?'

'Very well, my lord.'

'Uh?'

'As my cries would go unheard, and besides would gender much embarrassment were they heeded, I shall not drown my dignity in screams.'

'Well . . .'

'Nor wrestle against the flattery of your passion.'

'Well *said*, fairest lady! And with great pleasure shall I reward you for this obedience to your heart!'

'My lord, I thank you for it in advance. And ask that you release me for one moment, that I may slide free from this hamperment of my coverlet, and thus rejoice your gaze with such appeal as my modest charms possess.'

'Oh, Elizabeth!' Rosay exulted. 'Right *gladly* will I: as the honeybee that sniffs the perfume of his flower, before he sips of her nectar within.' He twisted back and reclined on the right-hand third of the large fourposter bed.

Elizabeth wriggled across to the left-hand edge.

And in one darting movement emerged denuded of her drape.

And for a fleeting instant stood unabashed, regarding her oppressor.

Who squinnied in his incredulous delight.

'Aaaah!' he crowed, gorging his weak black eyes on all the pink and bushy nodes of a lady's person that men most treasure. 'What a diadem you are! Come to me now!'

Elizabeth did.

Though not exactly as Rosay expected.

Reaching to the floor, she took hold of the trailing hem of the sheet, lifted it above her head, jumped back on the bed, and scampered across both it and the bewildered Rosay, bundling the sheet in her arms as she went. Down she jumped again on the right side of the bed, heaved on the coverlet with all her might, and in that manner contrived to deposit the spluttering Duke of Rothesay in a helpless white cocoon upon the flagstone floor.

Dividing him from his risible cap, which rolled beneath the bed like the peeling off a purple fruit.

'Forgive me, my lord!' Elizabeth panted, as she snatched a gown from the stool by her dressing table. 'But truly you did leave me no option. Goodnight, my lord!' she flashed him, flitting still naked from the room, to pass the remainder of that night in the company of Betty, with whom she had cheerfully bedded while lending her own fine chamber to the King.

'Teasing *trollop!*' Rosay spat, tearing out of his foolmaking wrapping. 'For this shall you ere long *suffer!*'

THE AGILITY OF THE POLMOOD GHOST

What an industrious gadabout it had become.

All up and down the valley it nightly walked, from dusk till the brink of dawn. Midnight would find it: howling havoc about the farmsteading at Talla Linnfoot, where the murdered corpses had spent their second night of headlessness; scratching with fingernails of malevolence against the windows of shuttered virgins in the Tweedsmuir village; distantly prowling through creaking doors and shuffling corridors in the Castle of Polmood: and at the same time groaning its gory grievances about the graveyard at Drumelzier, where the bodies had been buried.

And all these unrestful perturbations would take place absolutely simultaneously, if the many breathless accounts were to be collated with credulity.

Yet Drumelzier lies fully twelve miles north from Talla, or nine as wings might fly.

What a poser, then, for philosophy. If not theology.

And what a pleasant bonus for the eligible young lusties of those parts. For the young women were so dreadfully alarmed that scarcely one durst sleep a night by herself for twenty miles around, and, as they rapidly found precedented in the region's spiritlore, there was scant security to be had in such perilous circumstances from the company of their own frail sex.

As Betty had by now been convinced by Thomas.

So thoroughly that, on the night of Rosay's thwarted intrusion, when Elizabeth fled her own chamber and ran to seek sanctuary in

Betty's little room above the scullery, she found her maid engaged with loud enthusiasm in precisely those exertions which she herself had just escaped by the skin of her sharp young wits. This was very embarrassing at the time, and had boiled Elizabeth's moral stance on such matters into a flux of confusion.

It had also obliged her to seek an alternative billet with Martha, which had the indirect effect of further promulgating the stranglehold of the Polmood Ghost on the local imagination – since, because Elizabeth could not confide to the housekeeper that she was in fact a fugitive from the Duke of Rothesay's rutting, she was forced to allow that fearfully receptive old lady to believe that her craving for company that night derived from anxieties stirred by the knockings, rustlings and indecipherable moanings of the undead ghoul's agitations.

'Oooooh, mum! Dear Lord, watch over us till day – did I not *tell* you?'

'Indeed you did, Martha. Yet rest assured, I pray you. For what have we, in our innocence of crime and strength of faith, to fear from such a thing? Therefore, fret not.'

'Ooo . . .'

Thus did Elizabeth unwillingly reinforce the rumour, concerning which her own private scepticism remained undented.

And again the following day.

For, while there were no locks in Polmood Castle at that time, there were two massive bolts at head and ankle height on the inside of Elizabeth's chamber door, which, in view of Rosay's preposterous overtures, she deemed it prudent to awaken from their long disuse. Accordingly, the following afternoon, she had Thomas report with a hammer and chisel and a jar of bacon lard, to chip the bolts free of their sluggishness of rust and render smooth their sliding.

'You are wise, my lady, if I so may say,' panted Thomas, as crouching he scraped at the lower bolt. Fusing the blush of his lingering sheepishness with the hot flush of strenuous labour.

Elizabeth sat gazing from her window, caressing the pregnancy of the air with the spread of a goosefeather fan.

'Wise, Thomas?' she inquired. 'Why wise?'

'To guard yourself so, my lady. Against the . . . spirit.'

'Ah. So you too, Thomas, believe there is some presence that hereabout disturbs our nights?'

'Why yes, my lady! And sure as the sweat here tickles on my brow have I heard it mutter!'

'And *what*, pray, did it mutter?'

'I . . . know not, my lady.'

'You know not!'

'Its words were not clear, my lady. Yet muttering it surely was!'

'And tell me, Thomas, if you will: when you heard these sounds you were alone, were you not?'

'Ay, my lady! But how could my lady know? So please you.'

'And you heard it here? In the Castle?'

'No, my lady. It was someways in the trees behind the stable.'

'With the noise of movement, Thomas? Like the breaking of twigs, perhaps?'

'Ay, my lady.' Thomas paused in his metallic scratching and looked in puzzlement at the young mistress who was quizzing him more sternly than was her custom.

Elizabeth fanned a breath of coolness down the bosom of her dress and continued to feign interest in the distance across the lawns.

'So it could have been a foraging stag you heard,' she reasoned. 'Come to tine his antlers on a tree?'

'No, my lady! As God is my judge, I swear by Heaven: it had a human voice!'

'A *human*, voice, Thomas?'

'A sound uncanny *like* a human voice, my lady.'

'And did you recognize this voice?'

Thomas busied himself in smearing lard on the lower bolt and shoogling it in its fixture.

'Well, Thomas?'

'It could have been the Master's voice, my lady.'

'*Could* have been! And will you also swear to this, Thomas, as God is your judge: that it *was* the Master's voice?'

'No, my lady, I cannot swear!' Thomas mumbleblurted. 'The clickets here, my lady, are fine and easy now, and will give you no trouble.'

'One moment, Thomas! You cannot *swear* you heard the Master's voice – that is to say: the *ghost* of the Master's voice – but did you convey this doubt to Betty?'

'No, my lady.'

'Why so?'

Thomas stood up, and plucked uncomfortably at the clinging of his saturated smock to his heated torso.

'My lady,' he urged, 'it *was* a mortally unnatural sound that I did hear. And I *do* believe . . . and that is why . . . last night . . .'

'That will do, Thomas!' Elizabeth frowned a warning.

But his propitiations were already in free fall:

'Truly, my lady, we are both of us most ashamed of what did happen last night!'

'Thank you, Thomas! That – '

'But we had no notion, my lady – how could we know? – that you . . . that *anyone* would come upon us so!'

Elizabeth glanced at the fraught youth's headbent writhing.

And took pity:

'Enough, Thomas. You must not take on so. The fault was mine – I should not have entered as I did: it was but my . . . fright that spurred me to it.'

'So you *do* believe in the ghost, my lady?'

'I thank you for greasing the clickets, Thomas. And now you may go.'

'Very good, my lady.' He stooped to retrieve his tools.

'And remember, Thomas!'

'My lady?'

'The matter of last night is closed.'

'Ay, my lady!'

But the matter was *not* closed.

It continued to bang like an unfastened door in a gale at the back of Elizabeth's mind throughout the roasting stifle of the long days following. What was it that Betty, so simple and ample, with her rosy cheeks and broad peasant shoulders, could enjoy with such eulogistic abandon that she, Elizabeth, could not?

Was it the crowning flower on true love's stem?

If so, it seemed forbidden her for ever.

Or was it a mere physical pleasure, to be enjoyed like eating?

But that would make it odiously bestial! No nobler than the yowling couplings of promiscuous pussycats at night, and hence by definition beyond the possible experience of a genteel and cultivated lady!

While such issueless broodings went flapping like ineradicable bats around the darkest passages and mazing cloisters that proliferated in the perspiring halfsleep of those sultry nights, Elizabeth was further alarmed to discover new and ambivalent sensations mushrooming within the innermost being of her physical person and around the outermost outposts of her lonely unstroked flesh. Perhaps it was largely an irritation spawned by the abnormal heat of that month. Possibly it was all symptomatic of more fundamental transmutations taking place in her personal alchemy – in which case, how cruel that one so young and pure in heart should suffer such disturbing ebullitions in a state of unguided widowhood! The sudden unheralded ripenings of the yearning body, the conscience-shuddering images of glowing fulfilment that cram the startling mind . . . oh where was the knowing sister, the kindly elder friend, to tell Elizabeth how normal these developments were, how gladly they should be embraced, and that not for a moment must they shake her faith and her sense of innocence and grace?

Yes!

While Sir William kept himself poetically aloof, Rosay scrabbled and gushed with great vigour and loquaciousness to mollify his hostess and glue back together the pieces of the pretence he had let fall to no avail, the minions and menials continued to tremble and fornicate by night (up to six in a bed in one particular house in Tweedsmuir, so it was said but never certified), and to indulge by day in the novel sport of taunting Friar Fish (as the newly employed Andrew Stoddart had dubbed the mute reclusive whitebeard then boarding in the north wing): 'Come down, Friar Fish! Quick, quick!' might be shouted up at his tiny slit window above the armoury, 'For the cats are hungry and must be fed!' – while all this was taking place, Elizabeth paid less and less attention to the struttings of Rosay and the ghost-rabid pratings of the domestics and devoted more and more torment to the contamination that seemed to climb her soul like dirty rainwater up the hem of a spotless gown.

And what of the consequences on the eligibility of that soul for Salvation?

On the Sunday following the morbid funeral she made a private pilgrimage back to the chapel at Drumelzier, once more draped from top to toe in unmitigated black and with only Thomas to attend her, and there she made confession, attended mass, lit candles to King James and Queen Margaret and to the memory of her husband, then knelt in the tiny graveyard to lay a wreath of roses on Polmood's resting place – white and yellow they were, with a sole crimson giant in the centre, shedding petals like tears of blood.

That night she knelt again.

In self-punitive prayer.

From midnight until dawn.

And was so exhausted next morning that after breakfast she had to return to bed and fell into the deepest and richest sleep she had enjoyed for almost a fortnight.

Then, later that same Monday, something was to happen that would begin the erosion of her sceptical attitude to the supposedly ubiquitous ghost and thereby diminish the insidious purchase of her lurid introvertings.

For what better than a threat without, to lull a cankerous dubiety within?

'Then why does he linger?' asked Betty, concerning the resistible Friar Fish, whose movements were under review.

'I know not, Betty, my dear,' said Thomas. 'Except perhaps that these days are so uncommonly warm, and he is so old and fat, that he wishes not to continue his journey until the hot spell passes.'

'Yet never does he stir from his thick and hairy habit! Which must be like a boiling cauldron to abide inside, in weather like today.'

'Ay, my dear. Although he seldom seems to venture from his closet through the day, but waits for the sun to wane a way before he goes abroad.'

'Waits for yon wicked Andrew Stoddart to be off home to Kingledores, more like!'

'Importing?' drawled Thomas, who had scavenged the idiosyncrasy from Sir William.

'I mean that since he has been over to tend the gardens – which he does not a quarter as well as yon gawky Connel fellow! – yon Andrew Stoddart has been *at* the poor father every day.'

'How *at* him, my dear?'

'Oh, you know.'

'No, Betty! I do not – as my own work is now multiplied three times and more, with all the Duke of Rothesay's strange commands.'

'Well – shouts foul jibes at the poor father's window, does Andrew. And creeps along behind him when he sees him and loudly shouts: "Miaow, miaow!" With his fingers holding closed his nose. And other things the same.'

'I know not, Betty,' Thomas seriously debated, 'that it may not in the long run be as well.'

'Thomas! He is a man of *God*!'

'But a very smelly fellow all the same. And who can say that he is not an idler forby, and tarries here because he knows he will be fortunate indeed to light upon a hospitality the equal of what he gets from us, where next he begs for shelter?'

'*Thomas*!'

'No, Betty, my dear. You must not "Thomas!" me so, for there is reason in what I say, and it is folly to aye be overgenerous in this life.'

Betty sniffed indignantly.

'And forby: yon Andrew Stoddart is truly a genial fellow underneath, and means no serious mischief.'

'Huh!'

'Importing?'

'Importing, my dear man, that for all that Andrew Stoddart may be a genial fellow underneath, it did not stop him tweaking my erse in the kitchen just this morning!'

'Eh?'

'Yes!'

Thomas puffed. 'Then shall I bleed the impudent bogger's nose for him tomorrow!'

'Oh, Thomas!'

'What mean you: "Oh, Thomas!"?'

'Of course you shall not bleed his nose.'

'That I *shall*!'

'While he has muscles like a horse, and you are like a foal beside him?'

There followed a pauseful of diverse significance, during which

Betty adoringly stroked the forelock from Thomas's eyes and snuggled closer to him, while he huffed over the baldness with which his inability to bleed Andrew Stoddart's nose had been flaunted.

It was afterdinner evening, and the servant lovers at the close of their long day's travail had repaired to the nest they had borrowed of late from nature – a half-circular dell about a mile up the Polmood Burn, on the east side of its lowest tributary hope, where they might lie amidst the sweetscented seclusion of a rising riot of yellow broom and gaze between endearments at the daylight just hanging with a dying languishment over the verge of the Oliver Dod Hill three miles due west.

'It is a sad thing that I cannot give over dreaming, Thomas,' murmured Betty, tugging his huffing hand to her warmbeating breast.

'Ay!'

'Thomas?'

'Ay?'

'Be not unkind to me, Thomas. I meant no ill.'

'Ay.'

'Do not you think, Thomas, that there can be no other person so much troubled with his dreams as I?'

'Oh, Betty!' the ruffled young rustic relented. 'Your dreams must always be good and sweet . . . like yourself!'

'Oh, Thomas!'

'No, Betty – I mean it truly.'

'My dreams *are* ever delightful and sweet when I dream about *you*, Thomas!'

'Truly?'

'Yes, truly! Yet too have I had some fearsome dreams of late. Heavy, heavy dreams. Ah! Such dreams as I have had – I fear they can bode no good to us.'

'Hush now, my dear.'

'No, Thomas. I must *not* hush!'

'But – '

'For with whom else may I share my troubled thoughts, Thomas? That if unspoken may disease my mind!'

'Very well, my dear. Then speak them now.'

Betty hesitated.

Then, coyly:

'What is it, Thomas, to dream of . . . the *dead*?'

'It generally betokens good to the dreamer, Betty. Or to those who are dreamed of.'

'Oh, Thomas!'

'What?'

'This is but manly kindness to reassure me! And I fear it is not true.'

'Betty, my dear! How so?'

'I once did hear my poor old mother say there was one general rule in dreaming.'

'Ay?'

'Which always might be depended upon.'

'Aaah?'

'It was that dreams never can bode good that do not leave grateful and pleasing impressions on the mind! And therefore my dreams *must* be bad – very bad indeed!'

Thomas deployed his pitchfork-blistered fingers about some delicate preambles.

'And how comes it, Thomas,' Betty pressed, 'that whenever we dream of the dead they are always living?'

'God knows, Betty!' Thomas averred, as he stroked her bosom beneath her dress. 'It is the most curious reality in the nature of dreaming, is it not? That we often dream of the living as being dead, but whenever we dream of those that are dead . . . they are always alive and well!'

'And we never then remember that they are now departed this life – never once recollect that the grave separates us from them!'

'Indeed, my dear. All these things have a mysterious language of their own, to them, at least, that understand them. But they are above the comprehension of the likes of us, Betty, my dear. And therefore we ought not to think of them, nor talk of them.'

'But Thomas . . .'

'For thinking of them leads us into error, while talking of them makes us sad – and to obviate both of these I will reave a kiss from your sweet lips, my dear, and compel you thus to change our subject.'

Betty's sweet lips pulled back.

'No, Thomas! Do not – not yet. For I love to talk of these

things. For I am much concerned about them. And whatever concerns me, I love to talk of to you, Thomas.'

'And what, pray,' sighed he, 'may those dreams have been, which have given my Betty so much concern?'

'I have been dreaming of our late Master, Thomas!'

'Ah!'

'And such dreams have I had! That I fear there has been foul play afoot!'

'Hush now, Betty. *Hush*! We must not say what we think concerning yon dreadful incident. Although, for my part, I know not what to think.'

'Listen to me, Thomas. But be not angry, nor laugh, I pray.'

'My dear! When ever have I laughed at you?'

'I believe, Thomas, that Martha's tale about the spirit speaking to her is *every word of it true*!'

'My dear Betty, you must *not* believe it!' Thomas scolded, earnestly, beginning to rummage and probe as young men will.

'But I do! I do! And Martha says the spirit said: "Oh, *wicked* Elizabeth!", when it lurked without her door and groaned!'

'Believe me, Betty. This is nothing more than the workings of an old and distempered imagination.'

'No, Thomas – it is not. And neither would you say so to Martha's face!'

'That I – '

'Be careful, Thomas!'

'I am sorry, my dear. Did you say you liked . . .'

'I do, Thomas. I do. But gently. You must go softly, with your hands so rough and ragged.'

'Like so?'

'Yes, Thomas. That is indeed most pleasant and befitting of a kindly man.'

Thomas therefore continued to do it.

While he harked:

'But seriously, Betty. These babblings of Martha's you must discount. Because the late events are wrapt in mystery and horror, the minds of individuals are oppressed by vague conjectures and by surmises of . . . dark infamous deeds! And hence in sleep and lonely darkness the fancy turns to these images, and thereby becomes frighted by fantasies of its own creation.'

'Thomas! I do believe your words are borrowed of Sir William!'

'Not so!' said he with rumbled heat. 'And even if they were, what matters that, so long as they are true?'

'But they are not true, Thomas.'

'Indeed they are! And therefore I will not have you, my dear, nor any woman, to believe in the existence of ghosts.'

'Thomas!'

'What?'

'This is far, is it not, from what you did believe when saying to me that no more must I sleep alone?'

'That was – '

'Unless, Thomas, it was your purpose to deceive me?'

'Betty, my dear! Not at all! I – '

'You did say to me that you yourself did hear the spirit making noises near the stable. Did you not?'

'I did say, my dear, that I did hear *noises*, that is true. But I never – '

'Ah, Thomas, but it matters not.'

'Huh?'

'I mean that even if it were not true then, it certainly is true now that I never more must sleep alone – yes, Thomas, do not stop! And on the question of the being of ghosts I fear we might dispute for ever, as I must and will always believe in them. As that belief gives us a pleasing idea of an over-ruling Providence, of a just God, who will not suffer the guilty and the murderer to escape – nor those of His creatures who are innocent to be destroyed.'

'Betty, my dear!'

'Yes, Thomas?'

'Who now is guilty of the borrowing of words?'

'Not I, Thomas.'

'Indeed, Betty, but you are. For these notions are lifted straight from Father Wylie's sermons, are they not?'

'Yet do I *believe* them, Thomas! And therefore the owner of the phrasing matters not. As you yourself did say!'

Thomas expressively grunted.

'And forby, Thomas, I now will tell you what I would not any other!'

'Ay?'

'That also did I *hear* the spirit of our Master a-moaning and lamenting, while you did snore beside me!'

'But that was only in your sleep!' Thomas hoarsely protested. 'My dear Betty! It was *only in your dream.*'

'No, Thomas. I was awake.'

'And what did you hear this . . . voice to say?'

'Oh, Thomas! It was so low, so deep – so infinitely mournful!'

'Importing, my dear, that what you did hear was but a distant and shapeless sound. Without the sense of words!'

'Thomas, it was *the Master's voice*!'

'No, my dear! It is not possible to recognize a voice so surely, if one cannot catch the words it speaks. And I dare wager it was but the call of some restless beast you did hear: a hunting owl, perhaps.'

'An owl, Thomas? The cry of an owl is shrill and – '

'Or the throating of a lowstraying stag – hold still!'

Betty froze.

Thomas freed a hand from within her garments and caught the thread of a tiny red money-spider that was hanging in the curls of her hair. 'You see?' he said, holding up the omen insect before depositing it on a sprig of tinderdry and pollendusty heather. 'Our future fortune is assured!'

'Oh, Thomas!'

He leaned over her, and the two humble sweethearts exchanged a gaze of fondness still shy with wonder at the forces that bound them – she with her cheeks a blaze of supernatural excitements, happiness, and womanly arousal; he with his great jug ears afire in matching hues, and his pimples much improved in recent days.

With heartbeats in their mouths they kissed.

'No more let us hear', breathed Thomas, as he mounted her with growing assurance, 'of your fey apparitions and ghostly grumblings in the night.'

'Gently, Thomas!'

For several minutes they made love with passionate simplicity. The last faint fringe of molten golds and crimsons had faded behind the rolling hills of the western horizon, and overhead the deep dark blue of cloudless summer night stretched all across the world, yellowed only dimly by the rising crescent moon.

While a halo of silence shone round the lovers' crying sighs, their urgency blinding them to the background sounds of the hillside's nocturnal routine: the high toothy yelps of far-up foxcubs squabbling, and the leisurely tinkle of the drought-thin stream below.

Where Thomas shortly made his way.

Gingerly barefoot in his descent of the slope steeply sharp with bracken stalks baked spiky.

To dampen his kerchief in the cool clear water.

To polish the tender altar of their bodily sacrifice.

However!

Just as Thomas was stooping over a pool some forty paces downhill from the broomscreened dell, he was petrified in a long moment's horror by a terrified scream that issued therefrom and continued for several seconds in a staggered shimmer of spinechilling echoes.

'Betty?' he croaked. '*Betty?*' He leapt to rush back to her side.

But so unnerved was he that his first leap at the bank above the burn failed utterly, landing him back in the pool with a haunch-drenching splash. Wet moments later he thrust through the yellow-flower wall of the love-nest and found his lady in the choking convulsions of an asthmatic attack. Throwing himself down beside her, he inquired what the matter was, but received no answer, bar the helpless goggling of eyes superlarge with fright and respiratory distress.

He sponged her brow with his dripping kerchief.

Still breathing eluded her, as was testified by a rasping lungless wheeze.

'Oh, Betty!' Thomas desperately cried, then slapped her face repeatedly and pummelled her midriff.

This produced some promising gasping.

'Whatever is *wrong?*' he wailed, pulling her to her feet and embracing her sob-wracked form.

But not a word would she say in that place.

Only when they had limped near to home, with Thomas supporting her as though she were a legless drunkard, did Betty gather her demented backwardglancing trembles sufficiently to explain, in disconnected chatters, that:

She had again heard the ghost!

No!

Yes! No doubt about it. Lurking someways up the hill from their sunken den it had been, and must have witnessed all the motions of their loving – oh, horrible! Most horrible!

And what had it said?

It had said: "Yes, yes! It was she! It was she! Oh, wicked, *wicked* Elizabeth!"

Not possible!

Yes, indeed. It had spoken those very words, and in tones so rending and threatening that they would follow Betty's memory like a shadow to her grave, though hopefully not thereafter.

And was it . . .

Yes! The voice of the Master – to this she would solemnly swear.

On the Cross?

On the Cross, and by the Blessed Virgin!

And when Betty had screamed?

The Spirit had paused, though apparently not in surprise, and then moaned: "Oh, wicked, *wicked* woman! The torments of Hell are slight . . . compared to . . . *this*!"

Then it had vanished, had it?

So it seemed, although she had become numb with the violence of her attack, and for all she could say it might have ascended on burnished wings into the upper air, or melted into the earth beneath – or else be following them still in its cloak of cold and dire invisibility!

'Great God of Heaven!' muttered Thomas, crossing himself fervently as they lurched through the sycamore trees around the orchard.

'But Thomas – this is *wonderful*! Do not you see?'

Thomas was unusually eloquent in confessing his failure so to perceive, and in expressing the depth of his concern at this intimation that his sweetheart's mental hinges had been stressed to sheering by the trauma they had undergone.

'No, Thomas! Though my mind is greatly confounded yet it is not harmed, I swear!' she babbled. 'But only bowed in wonderment at this further demonstration of the Good Lord's Glory!'

'Uh?'

'Oh, yes, Thomas – yes! For did we not all see him nailed in his coffin, and lowered to his grave?'

'Ay, my dear. That we did.'

'And you, with his Majesty . . . you did see his piteous body, lying butchered into a lifeless, headless trunk?'

'Ay!'

'With the streams of blood', Betty almost enthused, 'all crusted black upon his ravaged limbs and breast?'

Thomas shuddered.

'Yet here he is again, Thomas! Walking among us in his own real form and manner, and speaking in his own gruff voice!'

'Now listen here to me, my dear!' warned he in a manly tone. 'You must not say you saw what you did not – '

'Oww*woooof*!' sobbed Betty with a frantic gasp. As the gaudy horrors of her own reflections and fankled reasonings combined to overwhelm her, she sank to her knees on the path with a moan, pulling Thomas down with her, and proceeded to dissolve the worst of her ghastly fears and fantasies in a long roaring flood of hysterical tears.

The return home of the servant lovers that night was very late and dramatically picturesque, with Thomas (his swoonweak damsel cradled in his arms) making heavy going of the last few hundred paces through the orchard. His attempt to sneak his weepy burden unnoticed to bed was thwarted by Martha, who was struck quite speechless (though only for a moment) by the ashen spectacle of the young man limping wearily into the Castle, seemingly laden with a corpse.

All of which appeared to confirm the most dreadful of the housekeeper's prognoses.

With the consequence that Thomas was sharply obliged to render up a meticulously detailed (if goadedly hyperbolic) account of the eerie experience that he and Betty had undergone.

So that by the following morning the rumour was circulating outward from Polmood Castle, like a ripple of infectious disease, that the ghost of the laird had appeared to the courting domestics in his own natural form and attire, that he had conversed familiarly with them, told them he was condemned to the infinite tortures and agonies of Hell and that his intolerable torments were further excruciated by the fact that Elizabeth, his own fair lady, had murdered him!

That Norman of Polmood should be consigned to Hell surprised the natives somewhat, and alarmed a few of them exceedingly. For, while none would claim that the laird had been angelic in his moral stature, he had been just (in his own crude way) to his vassals and minions, and was unflaggingly staunch and true to his King and country – at least if appearances could be relied upon. And if such a man could not escape the Everlasting Fires, what hopes of Heaven might the rest of them seriously entertain?

However, as was gloomly remarked, the Spirit himself had the best means of information on the matter, and could not possibly be mistaken.

At the same time, and as might be expected, more scepticism was occasioned by the claim that the Lady Elizabeth had been guilty of the foul assassination of her husband. Was it not well known, after all, that she had remained at home all the day of the illfated hunt, to ensure the quality of hospitality that would greet the huntsmen upon their return in the evening? But no! It shortly emerged that the lady had in fact been espied (by two young lads stealing grouse eggs far across the valley) walking down the river – with a large osier basket in her hand! Which could have been the means of carrying away the hacked-off heads from the scene of the filthy deed! But that had been in the morning, had it not? Whereas the murders could not have taken place until much later in the day, when the Lady Elizabeth was known for a certainty to have been busy within her household.

Ah!

Then the ghost's accusation might imply that the lady had *initiated* the crime, by suborning the vanished Laird of Lamington into carrying out the actual act!

Some there were (as there always are) who went along with this witching conjecture, but the majority opinion among the stolid country folk went against the bruited culpability of their fair young mistress, arguing that no previous relationship was known to have existed between the lady and Lamington and that, indeed, she had hardly ever exchanged even words with that gentleman, providing that courteous salutations and hospitable greetings were discounted. And besides: what profit could she reap from such a scheme? When Lamington, if ever he should reappear, could never last a week before his head would roll? Accordingly, although it would be close on blasphemy to suggest that the ghost might be *lying*, there was a general feeling, noddingly hinted at rather than clearly avowed, that it must somehow have got its information wrong.

This, at any rate, was the state of the story when the Duke of Rothesay barkingly extracted it from an unwilling gaggle of villagers in Tweedsmuir. It was about noon and Rosay was slowly and sweatily trotting home from an unsuccessful attempt to locate some part of the valley where a breath of cool breeze might be found to freshen up one's boiling irritation. The sky was as cloudless as it had been for days, but the heat was so opaquely heavy, itchy with a plague of drifting greenfly, that the precise position of the sun was hard to ascertain – except by reference to the shadows cast by such interposing objects as the thatchroof well on the village green, where Rosay came across and duly upbraided the yattering locals for their loafing.

So please his lordship, they said, but the heat was simply impossible to work in – although, pray God, there would be a storm, right enough, to clear the air and drown the flies before the day was out – and forby they were all temporarily stunned by this awful tale they had got from Andrew Stoddart, who had idled by an hour previously to collect provisions for the Castle, and whose final winking pronouncement had been that anyone wishing to secure his physical person most surely against molestments by the ghost had best seduce the Friar Fish with his caustic stench, as not even the Goblins of the Nethermost Regions were like to risk the inhalations of his vile effluvia at close quarters!

But nevertheless, so the locals cannily ridered, and so please his lordship further, though they were flabbergasted and chilled to the cores of their humble marrows by the apparition of Polmood's ghost, yet they found themselves respectfully unable to accept its extraordinary theory that the blame for the murders attached primarily to the Lady Elizabeth, whose honesty, goodness and exemplary devotion were greatly admired by them all!

'Quite so, my lord!' Elizabeth unsmilingly commented down the luncheon table, when Rosay had finished relaying the now colour-fully embroidered tale.

'And there is no question, my lady,' he added, 'but that *I* – '

'Of course, my lord.' Elizabeth cut him almost rudely short. It was the kind of day when even the lightest exertion beyond the basic movements of existence and relaxation will spark off flashing niggles of vituperation over trifles, and since a matter much weightier than a trifle was preying on her mind with the insistence of a needlessly barking dog, Elizabeth may be forgiven a measure of her impatience with Rosay's voluminous drawling.

'Forgive me, my lord!' she apologized. 'I did not intend – my thoughts . . .'

'Not at all, dear lady! We are all of us affected similarly, I fear. And none more gracefully than yourself!'

'I thank you, my lord.'

There followed a taut but listless lull, during which Elizabeth sipped at her glass of watered wine, glanced in distaste at the excellent venison steak topped with baked gooseliver paté that languished untouched upon her platter, and wondered with a twinge of disgust how the Duke of Rothesay could wolf his food with such houndlike voraciousness when it obviously gave him no pleasure at the time and would afflict him with bilious discomfort within the hour.

Men!

Not to mention wafty flatulence by dinnertime.

Yeuch!

The tension between Rosay and herself had reached the pitch of the screamingly intolerable – with the gap ever widening between the rapturous and lyrically nuptial profusions of his speech, on the one hand, and the narrowing carnal lustings of his unloving eyes, on the other – yet what was she to do? She had no other company of any cultivation (as Sir William was constantly away by day, and in any case appeared not to care for her society: holding her responsible, no doubt, for the compulsory prolongation of his absence from Lady Ann, to whom he was occasionally unable not to allude in tones most wistful), and besides: she had not the means to rid herself of Rosay's presence. Save, perhaps, by writing secretly to the King – which would be a very drastic step indeed, and one she was therefore loath to take. And now there was the additional complication that . . .

'I wonder, my lord?' she murmured.

'Gnyah?'

'Do you believe there *is* . . . some manifestation? As the people say?'

'Ha!'

'My lord, I am serious.'

'I wager a thousand merks, my lady, that there is no ghost, in this world or any other, that would not fall to the ground and bleed himself to death, when run through by my rapier!'

Elizabeth was silently thoughtful.

'But tell me, my lady: why do you ask?'

'I tended much to the same opinion as yourself, my lord. Until last night.'

'Indeed? And then?'

'Very late it happened – in the darkest hour before the dawn. I could not sleep – I know not why – and was reading in my bible, by a single candle, when of a sudden . . .'

'Yes, yes?' Rosay gaped at her eagerly, his unchewed mouthful half-exposed.

'I heard a sound . . .' Her eyes took flickering refuge in her wineglass.

'A *human* sound?'

'Like the shuffling of tired and heavy feet. Approaching to my door from the direction of your own.'

'No!'

'I therefore called out, my lord, for I thought it possible that you yourself had come – '

'Indeed not, dearest lady! Rest assured that never again shall I allow myself to be so overcome by the strength of my admiration. My regrets – '

'Are much appreciated, my lord. And in fact I was soon to learn that the author of the sounds was not yourself. For when I softly called: "My lord? My Lord Rosay?", there came a deep and hideous growl that froze me instantly twice as chill as ever I was in the winter past – as though some dreadfully tortured soul were crying out in rage and pain.'

'Dearest lady!'

'And worse was to come.'

'Heaven be merciful!'

'For when I then cried out: "Sir William? Is that you?", thinking myself perhaps the victim of one of his humorous charades, I was answered by the most savage and inhuman howl of fury imaginable.'

'I heard it not,' Rosay pondered.

'I dare say, my lord. But then you do sleep deeply, do you not?'

'Ah, my lady! Indeed. Whenever I am not bound wakeful by my loving thoughts of you! However, was this all?'

'No, my lord. Before the echo of that horrid howl had stilled, my latch flew up and a blow so mighty fell upon the door as to shudder the heavy lintel in its fixture.'

'And did not you yell for succour?'

'My lord, the door now is bolted right firmly of nights, top and bottom. So strongly, I do believe, that any being with the power to smash it open would render ineffectual any aid my cries should have summoned.'

'Pah!'

'My lord?'

'Had you, dear Lady Elizabeth, in your besieged distress, called out to *me*, your impertinent assailant, whatever the matter of his constitution would soon have taken to his heels. Or met his end upon the spot!'

'I feel, my lord, that hardly would you have heard the screams of woe, if first you were not stirred by the creature's ghastly howl.'

'The voice of a lady – '

'Was frozen in her throat, my lord – it shames me to confess.'

'No doubt in wordless terror? Such as even a *man* might be forgiven: an *ordinary* man!'

'I am not sure, my lord, how far it was rank terror did afflict me, and how far pure dumbfoundment.'

Courtly ladies might say that Elizabeth's coolness of response to her dread ordeal was symptomatic of nothing so much as a certain streak of insensitivity in her nature.

But Rosay said:

'Aah, Elizabeth! It is an old maxim among the mountain people that "He who is unconscious of any crime is incapable of terror". And the truth of this must surely here apply.'

'How so, my lord?'

'In that you, being conscious of no guilt, were enabled thereby to fear no evil!'

Elizabeth primly disagreed:

'My lord, you are too kind. But the fact is more that the incident transpired too quickly for my trepidation to develop. And had the ogre got its access to my chamber, I doubtless should have swooned away.'

'Then it did not?'

Elizabeth's nose wrinkled delicately in puzzlement.

'This . . . *thing*? It did not overcome the door?'

'No, my lord. Upon the failure of its first attempt it gave another curdling growl, in which I fancy I discerned the word "Again!", and then it slunk away where it came.'

'Very like, my lady, in anxiety lest the din of its antics arouse myself.'

'Possibly so, my lord.'

Rosay wiped his mouth, drained his wine, impatiently banged the handle of his knife on the table to summon service, and peeringly eulogized:

'Oh, sweet lady! I see it all. There you were, lying in such an attitude (when your extraordinary personal beauty is considered) as to make the heart of the most savage fiend relent. Your exquisite face was turned toward the door, the bedclothes flung a little back, so your fair neck and bosom, like the most beautiful polished ivory, were partly to be seen, while one of your arms outstretched lay pale above the coverlet, and the other turned back prettily, in support of your dimpled cheek!'

On that dimpled cheek a flush of pleasure faintly rose.

Quickly followed by a hotter flush of annoyance at the pleasure.

Rosay beamed fatly.

Elizabeth said:

'It may have been as you depict, my lord. Though my attention was overly engulfed by the disturbance itself to give notice to the pose I might present should the spectre force an entry!'

Rosay repeated his knifebanging on the table, and shouted over his shoulder, through the hall's open doors:

'COME HITHER, WOMAN, damn you! We are WAITING!'

'Have a care, my lord, I pray!' Elizabeth mildly remonstrated. 'For Martha is old, and the heat is crueller to the servants than to ourselves.'

'I see not why!' Rosay grouched. 'For they are coarser born than we, and duller in sensibility. And forby: I desire more wine, and am hungry for my cheese.'

'Then forgive me for remarking, my lord, that if your desires overween you, you have only to reach out your hand and you shall obtain their objects.'

Rosay's eyes and mouth blinked together at this expression of what, for Elizabeth, was close to indignant temper.

'Ah, Martha!' Elizabeth hailed, as the old retainer panted in, lines of perspiration falling from her rheumy eyes on either side of her prominent nose, like glistening rivulets of tears.

'Yes, mum?'

'The Duke of Rothesay is ready for his cheese, Martha. And would like more wine.'

'Very good, mum. And yourself, mum?'

'Just a peach, Martha. Thank you.'

'Thank you, mum.'

'Oh! One thing, Martha?'

'Yes, mum?'

'I understand that Betty had a strange experience last night? While walking out with Thomas?'

'Oooh, mum! She – '

'Then ask her, Martha, to visit me in my chamber. Directly after luncheon.'

'As you wish, mum.' Martha's starchly white kitchencap bobbed nervously on her stragglygrey head. 'Although . . .'

'Although?'

'She is still very shaken, mum. From her upset.'

'So it would appear, if truly she is overly indisposed to serve us up our luncheon.'

'Indeed, mum!'

'And *that is why* I wish to speak with her!' Elizabeth's tone was imperatively cool.

'Yes, mum.'

'Thank you, Martha.'

The housekeeper bowed, gathered up the meat platters, and scurried away with the soft flustered steps of a professional worrier.

Elizabeth took a dainty bite of her peach.

Rosay put the finishing touches to a large wedge of bread and chivelaced goatcheese.

Then tetchily scratched behind his ear, where a greenfly had alighted.

Outside the insect plague continued to sit across the valley in a freakish limegreen haze, and now and again a cluster of them would float in through the west windows like a breathless puff of feathery rain.

Filling the parching air with the colours of baby leaves.

Getting behind ears.

Up nostrils.

And . . .

'A pocks on the boggers!' grumbled Rosay.

Elizabeth would have grinned.

Had her heart not been so heavy.

'My lord?' she said seriously.

'Yuh?'

'What think you concerning this untoward occurrence, that robbed me of all sleep last night?'

Rosay, chewing again, debated with himself. Though privately convinced that the events Elizabeth had described had taken place nowhere except in (that most fertile of theatres!) the world of hysterical nightmare, and quietly tickled to learn that the ghost germ originally hatched and planted by himself had bred with such successful virulence as to infect the dreams of even his educated and previously sceptical hostess, the Duke of Rothesay and his lustful cunnings were quick to see in Elizabeth's profound disquiet the makings of a promising plan.

So he gravely lied:

'I clearly perceive, my lady, that these evidences that so have spoiled your rest are far indeed from the spectral creakings and demoniac dramas of a vulgar woman's dream.'

'Absolutely.'

'Yet what think you, dear lady, I wonder, concerning the *essential nature* of a ghost?'

Elizabeth napkinned her peachy mouth and fingers. 'How mean you, my lord?'

'Is a ghost *material*, in the manner of a corpse risen physically from its coffin? Or is it of the *spirit* only, and not impinged by doors and walls?'

'The thing – '

'And has it the faculty of *intellect*, to reason like ourselves? Or is it bovine like a beast, and tethered for ever to the purgatorial tedium of a crass routine?'

Elizabeth's eyebrows arched the surprised extent of her relief that Rosay should take her revelation seriously.

'Our nation abounds', he rambled on, 'with legends of eldritch spirits from death returned to hound the peace of their mortal transgressors – with their moans and shrieks and moribund wailing, and the vaunted creaks and rattling of their fleshless bones, and all suchlike paraphernalia of the countless traditions. Yet never have I heard tell of a ghost endowed with the means to wreak physical ill upon the living. Have you, my lady?'

'I know not, my lord. Such things were not encompassed within my firm beliefs until last night. And now I find some similar emanation has touched my maid, inflaming the poor girl's wits with turmoil and with slanders against my own good name.'

'Preposterous haverings, of course!'

'I suppose, my lord, that I now must accept the counsel vouchsafed me by the good Father Wylie, last Sunday when I did make confession.'

'Being?'

'That the manifestation of the dead to the living, and the reality of occasional communications betwixt the two, must not only not be doubted – they must be welcomed.'

'Huh?'

'Yes, my lord! As, so the good Father has it, our conception is thereby confirmed of the Justice of the Providence that over-rules us: that He is all-seeing, all-knowing, that He will not let the guilty soul go free, nor tolerate that the innocent should suffer – at least in the life that awaits us after this.'

'Ah!' Rosay chewed at thoughtful lips, eructed sibilantly, and made the heroic gesture of stretching to pour himself more wine. The mellowing effect of his midday alcohol had not yet yielded to the jagged aggravations of its fading, and he was exhilarated by the gelling appeal of his scheme. Hence was he transiently able to regard Elizabeth with a bright enthusiasm that a stranger might mistake for brotherly fondness.

Elizabeth blinked at his unaccustomed verve.

'Doubtless', he boomed, 'there is much in what the good Father says. However, I will observe that in all the tales of revisiting apparitions that ever have reached my ears, one constant theme runs through!'

'I pray you will inform me, my lord!'

'That they are, without exception, *habit-bound*! Like ancient hounds awaiting peace to ease the aching of their limbs. And once their schedule and itinerary are laid down, it seems, they are not free to deviate therefrom.'

Elizabeth nodded warily. Beneath her cultivated composure she felt wretched with perplexity and weariness, compounded by the tantalizing tickles of greenfly in her hair and bodice, which it was not possible for her to alleviate in full view of a gentleman.

'And herein, my lady, our course of action surely lies implicit!'

'I see not how, my lord.'

'Well! If some nocturnal phantom there truly is, and if it once has rattled at your door, we may be sure its visitation will recur. Until it obtain the satisfaction it desires.'

'And how, my lord, does this leave me?'

'Why, my very dear lady! It leaves your surety of safety and precious peace of mind in the willingly offered hands of myself – your truest – '

'No.'

'I *beg*, my lady, that you *consider*! Allow me to wait up this night within your chamber – why should you not? I shall be armed, and your mortal safety thus assured.'

Elizabeth was silent.

Oh, for a Shoulder to cry on!

Rosay pressed:

'And if some spirit comes whose substance is intangible, you may face it with the courage of stout company. Oh, Elizabeth! Yes, yes! This is our only course. And if it speak! United shall we be in our reply: to query its presumptions, rebuke the impertinence of its uninvited coming, and – who can tell? – mayhap allay for ever the grisly delusion that is its banishment from rest.'

Elizabeth scolded her thoughts together for a long hot moment.

Then aloofly said:

'Very well, my lord.'

'Good – '

'Provided that Sir William shall agree, upon his return, to keep watch with us. That our testimony may receive corroboration.'

Rosay was furious at the insinuation but confident that the budding bard would refuse to wait up with them, and hence that his illicit designs might still prevail. So he forced a smile, and gushed:

'Of course, dearest lady. Whatever is your wish.'

Elizabeth, rising, had to clutch at the table to ride out a wave of giddy nausea that rushed her from all sides.

'But for now, my lord,' she managed to say. 'If you will excuse me?'

WAITING FOR???

Midnight found the ghost watch in its second hour.

Consisting of:

Rosay, lounging in the easy chair, with a rapier at his belt, a goblet in his hand and a yawn of disgusted unbelief about his mouth.

Elizabeth, primly perched on the doorward side of her fourposter bed, desperately tired (having failed to sleep through the afternoon), but quietly sewing a square of tapestry upon her knee – determined to discipline the nodding hours to come.

And Betty: poor Betty! Trembling on the dressingtable stool she cowered, between the bedhead and the outer wall: as far as possible from the dreaded door. At which she peered in fascinated apprehension several times each minute, as a nervous chicken clucks.

But no Sir William.

'It is most gracious of you to invite me, my lady,' he had curtly grunted at dinner. 'And I regret most deeply that my exhaustion obliges me to decline.'

The afternoon had stewed the world even hotter and drier than the morning, and while the snowing greenfly had continued to thrive a rival cloud of thunderbugs brewed up and burst about the hour of three, falling so heavily that a dish of freshly turned milk put out by Martha was blackened into undrinkability before the insatiable Castle cats had time to touch it, and clarting the poring complexions of all panting persons with the irritation of a thousand dirty smudges. Meanwhile, high on the slopes of the Hunt Law

Hill, to the east, Sir William had nearly broken his heart, his neck and his pony's wind, in the eventually unsuccessful pursuit of his much-prized falcon. The bird had been stunned, it seemed, following a misjudged plummet on a basking hare, and had soared erratically to an almost invisible height before drifting limply on currents of southbound air toward the horizon humps of the Crawmelt Craig and the great Broad Law.

Two of the three highest mountains in the south of Scotland.

Where the frantic young knight could not hope to follow in time. But had tried.

And failed.

Hence his disgruntlement at dinner, for which he had arrived twenty minutes late, too delirious with disappointment and fatigue to eat more than a token.

Sir William's refusal had occasioned the enlistment of Betty as third member of the spectre vigil. This met with pitiful pleas that she be excused, from the maid herself, and with equally vehement pontifications from the Duke of Rothesay as to the superfluousness of the girl's inclusion.

What, he had required to know, was to be gained from the additional presence of some hysterical hussy whose credulity was already so notorious as to vitiate the value of her any subsequent testimomy? Elizabeth herself had questioned the girl that very afternoon, had she not, and found her story about the woeful spirit of Polmood's voice to be full of inconsistent holes?

That was so, Elizabeth sweetly allowed, but a third witness was necessary notwithstanding. They might have to sit until dawn, after all, and what if one of only two of them should doze off and miss the vital moments of whatever might occur? While to the fearful Betty she pointed out that if it really was that ghost that had startled her in the hillside dell (though personally she doubted it) then obviously she, Betty, had nothing to fear from it. Why? Because any grudge it bore against her would clearly have been requited there and then, when it had her defenceless and alone!

Whether there may have been a trace of feminine vindictiveness in Elizabeth's insisting on Betty's taking part (bearing in mind the lingering disquiet that had troubled Elizabeth since her bursting in upon the loud buckings of Thomas on Betty in the latter's closet and the fact that it was the maid who had put about the slanderous rumour that she, Elizabeth, was responsible for the murder of her husband) is difficult to say at this remove. But one thing is indisputable: that the burden of any sensible reasoning that night would fall upon the lady, not her petrified maid or her ulteriorly motivated gentleman protector.

For example:

Both Rosay and Betty, for reasons embarrassingly similar, had been in favour of flooding the chamber with the light of candle clusters burning cheerily in every corner.

Leaving it to Elizabeth to argue that any visitant, perceiving such effulgence escaping beneath the door, might thereby be deterred from entering. Which would undermine the object of their exercise, if truly that object was to challenge any comer to its face.

Similarly over the mode of the door.

Rosay had been unaccountably obtuse in failing to see why it should not be bolted, as it had been the previous night. After all, he expostulated, where was the merit in positively inviting trouble to enter in?

Elizabeth reminded him with vigour of his lunchtime protestations: that an insubstantial apparition could do them no physical harm, while their protection against any more material manifestation resided precisely in himself – in his strength of arm and martial prowess. 'Seeing which, my lord,' she had added, glancing pointedly at his oftdrained goblet, 'it does us well to remember how beholden we are to yourself remaining steady, to take our helm should evil strike us.'

Rosay had taken snapping offence at the innuendo, but was unable to refute the case for leaving the door unbolted, given that their purpose was to entice the putative phantom within their presence, the better to inspect the authenticity of its credentials and listen to its grouse.

So picture the scene now. The door is latched but not snibbed, as Betty's popping eyes have bewailed a thousand times.

On the night-table by Elizabeth's bedside a single candle burns, throwing just sufficient light for Elizabeth to sew and for the pouring of Rosay's liquor (who has switched from the coarse red wine to smaller measures of a stronger courage brought from France – an oily thick concoction of sweet green viscosity, which he dispenses from a flask pouched at his hip).

While the room swells up with the dark life of shadows.

And with the ephemeral fluttering life of moths, which enter and depart through the three open windows in a hundred unknown varieties of intricate mystery and tapestry colour.

Outside the sky is abnormally low and bulbous with instability, like a ceiling black with rotting damp, impatiently awaiting some shock to trigger its collapse.

Add to this the high tension between the principals:

Rosay, as his postprandial intoxication dissipates, finds it increasingly difficult to conceal his fury at this further thwarting of his seduction of Elizabeth. While she more artfully disguises her seething indignation that he should drink himself dopy when the circumstances cry out for him to abstain and remain capably alert. And who can blame her for not yet forgiving his recent brutish attempt (in this very room, on this very bed!) to plunder her delicate virginity?

Thus the time passes in slow discomfort between the hours of twelve and one.

Thomas, to his enormous consternation, has been despatched to the keep above the Castle gate, there to measure out the night (by an hourglass set earlier according to the sundial on the terrace) and toll its hourly numbers on the great brass alarm bell so long and dustily unused.

Rosay's sporadic remarks grow dull, duller, and die away.

Pallor rises up his face; his eyelids drip.

One o'clock chimes: a single deep and hollow dong.

Rosay twitches but does not awake.

Betty cannot contain a little scream of muted startlement.

Elizabeth scolds:

'Hush, Betty. It behoves us to be *still*!' Then repents: 'Take comfort in your beads, can you not? If your nerves will not lie down.'

'Yes, my lady.'

Twenty minutes elapse.

The first grumble of thunder coughs in the distance.

Rolls its way nearer.

Rosay snores as if in sympathy.

Suddenly there is panic: a frantic staccato rapping noise breaks out like the drumming of epileptically frenzied fingers in the corner to Elizabeth's left, behind her dressing screen.

Betty emits a second soprano squeal.

Even Elizabeth rises up in deathly trepidation.

The Duke of Rothesay stirs and groggily slurs: 'Gwaa?'

But it is a false alarm. A giant moth, the size and weight of a baby swallow and the colour of ripe corn overrun by red ants, has flapped in unnoticed and got caught between two sections of the dressing screen.

Elizabeth sets it free and forces a laugh that is shallow above the pounding of her heart.

Betty returns to the muttering popping of her rosary.

Rosay sits up; rubs his eyes. Glares at Elizabeth. Slouches back in his seat. No longer inebriated, he is greyly leaden with the poison in his blood, yet milked of the brash bravado it earlier afforded him. His heart too is rough with fear as he straightens his feathered bonnet and gruffs:

'Dearest lady!'

'Yes, my lord?'

'It surely is established now that your . . . visitor shall not come this night. Wherefore . . .'

'The hour of two, my lord, has not yet rung!'

'Has it not?'

'No.'

'Ah.'

In this mood their wake goes on, individually unwilling but corporately determined.

The solemn peals of two resound but are almost drowned by the thunder encroaching overhead.

The lightning begins:

Ten seconds away – yellow.

Five seconds away – sheeting white.

Three seconds away – so intense in its streaking brilliance that it registered only upon their eyes in afterimages of dazzled blue.

While the lowburning candle guttered.

The soul of the earth cried out for the teasing heavens to cease their ceremonial overtures and simply, softly, generously rain.

And Elizabeth exclaimed in a whisper:

'Hark!'

'At what, pray, my lady?'

'It comes!'

'Eh?'

'Oh yes – the Thing! It comes. I hear its shuffle.'

In the rolling troughs between the thunder claps they strained their ears all six.

And sure enough!

A low and regular dragging sound was heard.

Growing nearer.

And nearer.

And all at once as Betty moaned and Elizabeth's trembling needle pricked her fingers and the Duke of Rothesay's milky blood turned jellysour there came a deafening and sightsearing blast of thunder and lightning all directly overhead and the latch flew up and the door flew open as though driven by a battering ram and the Polmood phantom was among them in the chamber.

17
CLIMAXES

BOOTED BOOBLES

It all happened with blinding rapidity.

'AAAAAH!' screamed Betty, who fell in a slumping dive beneath the bed and continued to scream: 'OWOWOOEEE . . .'

'Holy Mother have mercy upon our undeserving souls, we pray!' Elizabeth cried in a high split monotone. Powerless as a snaketrapped rabbit, she sat rigid on the edge of her bed, motionless except for trembles and the groping of her fingers for the crucifix at her breast. Yet managed, in tremulous desperation:

'There it is, my lord – look, look! *Arise and give it challenge!*'

Rosay drew no comfort from what he saw. The prominent chin of his pugnacious beard sagged several inches as his pallor hued green and a wet gurgle of terror was kindled at the back of his throat and blazed loudly out through the cavernous O of his musclefrozen mouth.

'Oh, my LORD!' Elizabeth wailed.

Rosay lurched to his feet like a drunken somnambulist, grabbed at his rapier with a hand so shaking that he nearly skewered his belly before he had the blade aloft. Then took a wobbling pace toward the Thing, and croaked.

'Hold off, foul f-f-fiend!'

It was, so the Duke was later to allege, at least a head taller than the tallest man – this could be deduced from its having had to duck the lintel (though Elizabeth would object that this was a detail her memory could not confirm). Draped from top to toe in funeral-shroudlike white, it was capped (unspeakably grotesquely, such was the violence of the incongruity) by the very leather bonnet that had gone missing with Polmood's head, while all about its own head and torso (and dripping from its crimson hands, Elizabeth later claimed), in stains the size of dinner platters, was *blood freshly shed*!

To judge by the shining red richness of its texture.

In the tension of the pendulum swings between the stabbing lightning and the faltering candle.

Its presence throbbed with the asphyxiating stench of burning brimstone.

Its arm held out a gigantic sword, drenched along its blade with a tacky new spillage of arterial blood.

Pointing at the Duke of Rothesay's throat.

Which was all a shade too much for *any* man to bear (by Rosay's subsequent account). 'I c-c-com*mand* you . . .' he bleated octaves higher than his wonted confidence, then buckled at the knees like a slaughtered ox and fell senseless to the floor.

'. . . EEYOWEEE . . .'

Elizabeth watched, transfixed in flashing timedilation.

The monstrous apparition stepped forward one heavy swaying pace, bent over the fallen gentleman and laid its abnormal blade against his unconscious neck.

Then raised it high to hack.

Elizabeth's piercing horror surpassed even Betty's ceaseless yelling:

'OH NO, DEAR *GOD*! HE MERITS NOT *THIS*!'

Another stoneshuddering crack of thunder was followed instantly by a flurry of lightning and rumbling sky which lasted perhaps five seconds. During this elongated moment, Elizabeth afterwards recounted, the deathlusting phantom appeared to pause in mid-swing at the defenceless Rosay and still holding high its ghastly weapon, turned and flowed towards herself.

Or rather towards her bed, she was to decide in retrospect.

When she recalled the chilling detail of its hatefilled scarlet eyes.

Rolling several times across the spotless testimony of her unrumpled coverlet and pillows.

Followed by a ghoulish growl of the most hellish frustration, so bassly throttled and grindingly evil that one felt it could only have emanated through some orifice neither mouthly nor mortal.

Of course, there is much in the foregoing that can never be objectively established. As Elizabeth was the first to admit, it may be that the details she thought to have witnessed were actually hallucinated in a fleeting lapse from consciousness, for the next thing she could recall was that the spectre had retreated from herself and once more stooped over the prone form of Rosay, who had contrived to fall with his buttocks angled in her direction.

All of a sudden the Thing stood straight to its superhuman height. A further gruesome gargle peristalsied from the lips of its whatever sphincter, a swishing motion began around the belly of its shroud, rippled to the floor, and culminated in the Duke of Rothesay's groin.

Lifting that hapless noncombatant several inches into the air.

Heaving his podgy body several paces across the floor.

Causing one of his flailing arms to thud against the bedside table.

Which upset the candle.

Which spluttered for a second before drowning in its own hot puddling.

Allowing the disruptive Presence to exit unobserved save for the slow dragging weight of its shuffle, which in any case was doubtfully audible below the hoarsening screech of Betty's clamour.

A minute later, possibly two, Sir William Moray arrived upon the scene. Barefoot, and clad only in his leather hawking breeches, he rushed in with a fuming torch in his left hand and a sabre in his right.

And a resolute scowl contracting his steely eyes and tightlipped mouth.

What had been the matter, he inquired of Elizabeth.

Who continued paralysed by her bewildered astonishment.

While Betty viewlessly persisted beneath the bed:

'HOOO, EEEEE . . .'

'Hold your TONGUE, WOMAN!' roared Sir William, who detested unnecessary noise.

'AAAAH . . .'

'*SILENCE*! THERE IS NOWT MORE TO FEAR, WITLESS BESOM! Therefore come you out from there.'

Betty's howling broke off, but she did not move.

'All is now well!' Sir William attempted to persuade her, then switched his attention to Elizabeth's unseeing immobility. 'My lady?'

Elizabeth's unblinking gaze was bound by chains of apprehension to the open yawning of her chamber door.

Perceiving this, Sir William padded to the door, latched and bolted it, lodged his torch in a holder on the wall between the door and dressing table, then returned to Elizabeth.

Kneeling on one knee before her, he said:

'I was waked, my lady, by the storm. And looking from my window at the heavenly flames did hear your woman wauling – hence: here I am.' He laid his sabre flat upon the fleecy rug of stitched sheepskins that stretched the length of Elizabeth's bedside. Seeing the lady's stare still magnetized, he moved himself between her eyes and the doorway. Took her hands from their crucifix clasp, rubbed them gently between his own, and urged:

'My lady, my lady! This is myself – Sir William! Come to succour you from your affright, which is now over. See there? The door is made fast. The rage of the storm has passed away down the valley, and there now is nowt without your windows but welcome rain that falls to slake the shrivelled earth. Wherefore, my lady, I pray you share a word with my understanding. Pertaining to the source of all this shambles?'

Elizabeth blinked, and blinked again, slowly refocusing on the naked nearness of Sir William's tawny shoulders.

'There, there!' said he. 'All is *well*! Yourself and your woman are guarded against further harm by the presence of myself. Therefore apprise me, will you not, of what befalls his lordship? Is he killed?'

Betty's towsy curls, popping eyes and jibbering cheekchubs rose above the far side of the bed like the face of a lady clown in a travelling puppet show.

Elizabeth allowed the waking wavering of her gaze to be drawn by the cool grey steadiness of Sir William's inquisition.

Then the word 'killed' flew into her mind like a boulder through a plate of coloured glass.

'Uuuuuh!' she moaned, as her pretty vacancy of expression screwed into the common lines of grief.

'My lady! You must not – '

But Sir William was wrong: she must.

And did.

Throwing herself forward into his arms, gripping him tightly around the neck, and weeping deliriously upon his shoulder for the next quarter of an hour.

When a hundred tears had sluiced their sheendulling way into the shoulderlength wavy blondness of Sir William's hair, Elizabeth was able to communicate the salient gists of what had taken place, and this despite her crowding doubts as to the veridicality of her own perceptions during the lightstarved handful of instants involved, and notwithstanding the hyperbolized ejaculations of Betty in the background, who had not witnessed anything at all, apart from that single horrific moment of the phantom's entrance.

Sir William was dubious at first that anything more harmful had transpired than the scarifying antics of some eidolon sparked from the hysterical expectations of the watching persons by the sudden violent explosions of the storm, but soon he had to solemnize his scepticism, when, upon inspection of the Duke of Rothesay's inert body, he found his face, beard, throat and breast all sticky with coagulated blood – while along his neck ran a distinctly skinbroken line, where the ogre's sword had ostensibly measured for a chop.

However, it was not long before Sir William found a hopeful pulse, beating erratically some way beneath the fleshy insides of Rosay's wrists. Very well, if the gentleman had not yet bounced beyond the mortal pale then it behoved his fellows to haul him back from the prickly brink and deposit him again within conscious view of earthly living. This Sir William achieved by taking Elizabeth's washjug from the dressing table, upending its tepid content all over Rosay's face and neck, and slapping his lordly jowls with vim while shouting in his ear:

'Awake, my lord! Awake, AWAKE! YOU ARE NOT KILLED!'

This procedure he maintained with great vigour for upward of a minute, occasionally casting such asides to Elizabeth as:

'His lordship is barely so comely, my lady, what think you – if ye will pardon the licence of a rhymer's view – with his bonnet off his bonce?'

Although Elizabeth could hardly be expected to pronounce upon such a matter, the regaining of her own composure, and of Betty's, was much catalysed by concern at Rosay's condition. When he eventually did revive, and had his head raised up upon Sir William's knee, and saw the wealth of gore that smirched his doublet, he catapulted straightway into a dismal blabbering panic that here were the last drops of his lifeblood ebbing away for ever, and it was only through Sir William's administering further beefy smacks about his chops (and roaring in his ear that there was little amiss save that he had been bleeding prodigiously at the nose) that his hysteria was gradually disabused of its maudlin misapprehension.

Thereafter, having scraped a few scraps of dignity's semblances back together, mainly in the form of reinstating his bonnet atop his pate, he diverted attention from his previous exhibition by discovering and complaining of agonies about his loins. But, as Elizabeth had neglected to relate to Sir William the manner in which the malevolent sprite had so brutally projected Rosay across the floor, and since she now considered it unseemly to depict the humiliation in the victim's presence, it was left to Sir William to impress upon the groaning Duke the likelihood that his crural, scrotal and abdominal anguishes were due to nothing more wounding than mortal terror. After all, the former were a very well known and widespread (not to say *healthy*!) symptom and consequence of the latter, were they not?

This sop Rosay was pleased to accept.

And in due course he limped away to his own chamber, leaning for support upon Sir William Moray's arm.

Yapping with resurgent turgidity about the impotence of mere valiant mortals in the face of Supernatural Malice.

And calling back, to the lady he had so nobly risked his life to champion, of the wisdom of shooting all her bolts till dawn.

Wisdom which she had already anticipated.

While through the outside night the rain fell down.

Down, down;

Down.

AN UNCLIMATIC WEEK

It was discovered the following morning, on the Wednesday, that the Duke of Rothesay had got enough of watching for ghosts – a great deal more than he approved of, he affirmed at length, and would be damned if he cared who knew it. His loins were still afire with crippling pain, and in view of this and other circumstances he gravely announced his regret that Elizabeth should be incommoded by his decision that it was against the interests of the nation for the Castle of Polmood to lodge himself within its walls for even one night more – the Queen had still to produce a healthy heir, and this must be borne in mind!

Elizabeth rallied him a little here.

Saying:

'But *what* other circumstances, pray? Oh, my Lord Rosay, surely!'

'Surely *what*, my lady?' snapped he.

'Surely you will not abandon me here in such an unheard-of dilemma, but shall continue to sleep in the Castle as heretofore?'

'Would, dearest lady, that it might be possible! But seeing that Scotland's present heir is me, and admitting that the Evil Manifestation appears to bear a particular malevolence against myself, you must appreciate why I *cannot* risk a further encounter.'

'But my lord!'

'Nyuh?' Grunting his discomfort, Rosay winced from the mounting block in the courtyard to his departure-ready saddle.

Elizabeth could not resist adding, through a mask of perfect seriousness:

'I, my lord, for my own part, am entirely willing – forby that I am *obliged*! – to sleep in my own chamber still. For all that has come and gone. And therefore, my lord, why may not you adhere to yours? In which you never have been disturbed!'

'No, my – '

'And it is now demonstrated, my lord, is it not, that the Thing has not the power to sunder massy bolts. Wherefore – '

But Elizabeth might as well have offered an abstract carrot to a donkey bent on a heating she. Rosay's personal safety was uniquely high among his priorities, and from that time forth he mounted his horse every evening after dinner (brought forward to the hour of six for his special convenience) and cantered ten miles up the bridleway to safety through the night within the ghostless castle of John Tweedie of Drumelzier.

And did Rosay inform his new host of the reasons underlying his sudden switch of sleeping quarters? On the contrary: he said it was due to his conscience representing that it was not consistent with decency for him to stay under the same roof with the young and beautiful Elizabeth every night, now that she had no husband to protect her – not for a moment, as Tweedie would of course understand, that Elizabeth's virtue would be endangered in truth. No! It was just that the tireless and unanswerable tongue of scandal might suddenly leer out to blast the lady's reputation and future fortune, and he, Rosay, was unable to live with the prospect that any such invidious infamy should fall about her shoulders on his account!

Tweedie of Drumelzier was privately much astonished at this profession of Rosay's altruism, in the first instance because it parted consistency with those oating traits for which the Duke was nationally notorious, and then yet more dubiety was to be cast back from the vantage of his cynical hindsight – when it emerged that of Tweedie's three eldest daughters (aged thirteen, fifteen and eighteen) the younger two had contracted nasty chancres from their father's guest's attentions, while the elder pair conceived, bore and had to rear in shame the King of Scotland's brother's bastards. These details are attested in that passage of the *Records of Financial Accounts of the Lord High Treasurer of Scotland* which relates that in the following year (June 1508) a generous life pension was bestowed upon John Tweedie in compensation for the specified wrongs inflicted upon his family by a certain unnamed personage of the Royal Household.

But that is by the way, and it is not our remaining purpose to portray the squalid minutiae of Rosay's debauched seduction of helpless girls within the walls of Tweedie, who in any case appears to have acted extremely dishonourably in the matter: actually egging his visitor on to sample of his daughters' charms, no doubt desiring to curry favour with one of such exalted rank, and possibly in the outside hope of vastly increasing his own worldly fortune by the procuration of a match between the house of Tweedie and the Crown.

But this was not to be.

As shortly shall be explained.

Suffice it to say, in the meantime, that Rosay persisted in his plan of sleeping the night at Drumelzier and riding south in the (progressively later) morning to take luncheon at Polmood and resume his glitteringly flattering, plaintively protesting, and touchingly presumptuous wooing of Elizabeth.

Meanwhile:

After the post-thunder rain left off around breakfast on that Wednesday, bequeathing the damp leafy scents of grateful greenery to the flowers and trees and the pride of springs replenished to the river and its thousand tributary streams, and weather returned to its apogee dry beating heat – sizzling yellow and burning brown the grass of the Castle lawns, baking into chalky dust the turf beneath, yet bearing fruitful compensation in the orchard, where the cherry trees sagged beneath a weight of red ripeness that almost split their limbs.

But the cast was now more acclimatized.

Elizabeth took her breakfast in the laconic company of Sir William, who appeared to hoard his daily language ration for the feeding of his ditties, which (with his falcon defected) he continued to spawn, rear, polish and rehearse in the endless lonely hours he spent away on endless lonely hillsides in the skintoasting hair-bleaching sunshine.

'Will it not please you recite me just a verse or two, Sir William,' Elizabeth requested with a little petulance one morning, 'of the ballads you lately have fashioned?'

'No, my lady.'

'Why so, I pray? Does it not weigh with you that I should be much enchanted to listen?'

'No, my lady.'

Elizabeth nearly choked.

Sir William explained:

'The motives wherefore a bard will compose and perform, my lady, are roughly three.'

'Yes?'

'In the beginning, he will write and sing for his own pure pleasure (providing that his destiny removes him from the dabbling dilettante dribblings of the likes of the Duke of Rothesay, whose limiting delight is the mutual parading and applauding of their own occasional hackneyed baubles, to the deliberate and despicable exclusion of any works that have true merit!), though it will not take him long to find that his pleasure's purity is sullied – that it is become tainted with a soiling streak of *need*.'

Elizabeth did not entirely follow.

'I mean, my lady, that when a rhyming man outgrows the

frolicsome freedoms of his puppyhood he will discover himself not a little enchained, by the crafting of his talent. As a sheepdog cannot abide to live without the practice of his skills.'

'And the second motive?'

'Is to entertain his patron and his patron's company, if Fate has smiled to bring him to a handsome patron's notice.'

'Who in your case is the King?'

Sir William nodded curtly, regretful of having launched into such an exposition.

But Elizabeth was avid:

'And what, Sir William, of the third motive that you did mention?'

'It is', he wisted grudgefully, 'to taste of the heavenly sweetness that flows angelic from his loved one's eye, when his creations have brought her joy.'

'Oh, Sir William! You are talking in truth of the Lady Ann Gray, are you not?'

'Begging your pardon, my lady,' said he from table rising, 'but I must be off and yapping now at the heels of my errant ewes.'

And away he went.

Leaving Elizabeth to tend her household and otherwise amuse herself till luncheon.

When the resumption of Rosay's campaign of loquacious lechery would seem almost welcome!

Which the dogfox in the Duke was quick to sense.

'Well, well, my lady!' he might jovially boom between mouthfuls made more gluttonous than ever by the unaccustomed exercise of his riding. 'And has our Spectre walked again?'

'No, my lord. It has not. So far, at least, as I may tell. I am sleeping now with Martha and Betty both for company, on flock beds on my chamber floor. And since this arrangement was begun we none of us have heard a squeak nor seen a shadow beyond the norm. Though we keep the door fast, of course.'

'Yes, yes.'

'The servants say, my lord, that the Thing is to be heard a-prowling nightly around the woods at Stanhope Farm. But myself I am far from persuaded that its being is not mythical after all, nor that we three that watched that night may not have fallen dupes in our state of terror to the frightful commotions and suggestings of the storm.'

'No, no, *no*, dear lady! Be you persuaded by my suffering! Never has any man been dealt such injuries by a fancy.'

Whereupon Elizabeth would rail him anew (with a hint of neglected peevery behind her banter) over the excessive caution underlying his daily prophylactic measure. Which in any case would be unavailing, would it not, if truly there were a vengeful fiend with a personal axe to grind against himself? For how could any such griping spirit be thwarted by the short ten miles to Drumelzier? Where in any event it had been overheard mooching about the graveyard after midnight, if you went by the local grapevine.

'And so, my lord, I simply cannot see why you will not favour Polmood with the restoration of your undivided company.'

'You are kind, dearest lady – so very gracious! – to request it. Yet wisdom counsels otherwise.'

And thus the week progressed.

DOWN BY THE RIVERSIDE

The morning of the following Tuesday gave early promise that this would be the hottest day of all. Before breakfast, in the trees and bushes and under the stable eaves, the umpteen sparrows bickered more furiously than ever, as if sensing the urgency of chattering out their insults *now*, before the blazing maturity of the day should beat down like a stifling bludgeon to quell their twittering chorusing into a slow and lazy yawning air of individual tweets.

Tweet. Tweet, tweet. Twcce . . . eeet!

By nine o'clock the Castle cats had all resorted to their favourite shades and were practising their panting. All, that is, except Polly and Moody, the matriarchs of purewhitetabby moulting that had been Martha's scolded darlings for fifteen years.

For they had recently gone missing.

It was the wicked heat, said Thomas, that was enough to drive any self-respecting elder pussy to slink off and long lie low in some cool and unmolested cranny.

Nothing of the sort, said Andrew Stoddart. It was the wucked Father Fish that had lured them away to his stinking cell by niftering promises of trout, with the secret dastardly motive of picking off the poor pussies' countless leeching fleas, therewith to restore to his diet the balance of red meat that Martha lately had cut back!

Well, she said, he must go sometime! Already he had long outstayed the Mistress's overgenerous welcome, yet still he showed no sign of moving on. How else, therefore, was he to be persuaded, if discourse was forbidden him, except through the lowering bread level in his privileged beggar's bowl?

'Ye are a cruel and vindictive uld wumun!' jeered Andrew Stoddart, whose enormous warty nose and deep-pocked face made him famously the most ugly person in the Tweedsmuir district.

'That I am not! And get you away from my oatcakes there! Else shall I tell the Mistress what a good-for-nothing scavenger she has employed in Andrew Stoddart.'

'My, my! Madam Housekeeper. My, my, *my*!'

'Get you *away* from me!'

'As ye wish, madam. Forby that you are the single exception in a thousand wumun that would shrink from such a wonderful opporteeyounitty! But seriousleee! Ye will find that Father Fish goes with the sun.'

'And what, my man, am I to understand by that?'

'*Your* man, eh? Well, ye are to understand just this, *my* gud wumun, that when yesterday I put it to the Good Father – or rather, ye might say, to the back of his retreating habit – that his pulgrumage would be like to take him quite an age if it wuz his purpose to maintain his present rate of progress very long, he wuz pleased to advise me that it only wants this wucked weather to cool off a mite and then he will be off. Not, in my view, that he is not sufficiently off already – ha!'

Martha ignored the crude pun in her amazement.

'He *spoke* to you?' she questioned.

'Ay, madam.'

'But he never has . . .'

'That is to say he spoke to my handsome proboscis with his eloquent pungency, while with his arm he gestured at the sun above – which is where the sun chanced to be at that moment – doubtless having gleaned from his previous encounters with my wit that such would be sufficient to cast the shadow of his intended meaning upon my understanding. And now, madam, I must away, if ye can find it in your warm uld cruel vindictive heart to pardon me, for the Duke of Rothesay will have my head, he assures me, if I have not the butterfly bower groomed by noon. "*Immaculately!*" Therefore, good day. And I thank you for your choice comestibles!'

'Oi!'

But Martha's protest came too late, and Andrew Stoddart chortled off with a cheery grin distending his perspiring features into even wider homeliness, and with several oatcakes on their way to fuel his sweaty labours.

The unlost pussycats slumberpanted on.

In the paddock between the stables and the river, the half-dozen ponies and Elizabeth's dappled mare with her gangling newborn foal were soon all gathered in the shadow of the single central oak tree, morosely whisking with their dry dusty tails and blinking in futility against the clouds of thirsty clegs that humming sucked the moisture from the corners of their helpless eyes.

And Elizabeth herself went out for a stroll.

Considering that by afternoon the heat would be prohibitive, she set off alone at about ten o'clock.

In her lightest, whitest, lownecked houppelande of finest soft lawn, loosely girdled around her waist and flowing to whisper about her ankles.

With her cool stargold hair cut freshly pageboy short beneath a light butterfly head-dress of translucent lemon-coloured gauze, which she pulled low over her forehead as she crossed the north lawn, to shield the smoothness of her brow against direct inspection by the sun.

Then north up the bridleway.

Into the murmuring shelter of the awning trees.

The lime trees.

Their tacky spittle lay copious along the path, puddling thick between the dandelion clumps and the clover patches, oozing their cloying seepage in sticky discomfort between the bare toes of the lady's sandalled feet.

The chestnut trees.

Their screening away the shimmering azure heavens was so complete that when she gazed up at the lighter green undersides of the deeply layered leaves Elizabeth felt like a seagull, floating in a dream above an emerald sea below.

The beech trees . . .

'Oh!' Suddenly she paused, a hundred paces before the Cleaker's Pool.

There it was again.

A foliagemuffled splashing sound, as of a heavy bird flapping clumsily upon the surface of the river.

Then a distinctly manly grunt.

Followed immediately by a prolonged purposive burst of swishing and thrashing.

Who could it be?

Elizabeth continued along the bridleway in cautious silence, not sure that she wished to know. For while (though not fully aware of it herself) she was undernourished companywise, the splashing and grunting evidence of wilful human striving had arrested her on the threshold of a glorious childish reverie, will all its timeless gliding freedoms and endless elidings of novel entertainments and sparkling yet harmless excitements. And who, when arrested so upon that brink, will not guard jealously her slightest chance of marking time to take the magic plunge when wilfulness has passed?

Nevertheless.

Elizabeth's urge to soar without reality sank.

As she rounded the bend into view of the Cleaker's Stone.

And glimpsed the tawnytanned litheness of his body gleaming brilliantly through the sunshine, as it rose from the Stone in a diving arc.

She exclaimed:

'Oh! Sir William!'

Though neither loud nor particularly close, this unexpected advertisement of another's presence was enough to spoil the poet's rhythm.

And he landed flat upon the water with a bellysmarting splat and a tersely gargled curse.

'I pray you will forgive me, Sir William!' Elizabeth called down when the swimmer's head resurfaced. 'I had not meant to startle you.'

'Trouble yourself not, my lady!' the knight called up with a little acidity, as his clearing head shook fleeting rainbow curves of waterdrops from the tips of his wetdark locks. 'I was in any case conducting explorations upon novel modes of entry.'

'I see,' said Elizabeth, not sure that she did. The sun was behind, to her left, and she could feel its growing power chop down upon her neck in echo times to the flustered throbbing of her own protesting pulse. Or was it the other way about? This, she decided irritably, did not really matter. But what was undeniable was that the cool aquatic manner in which Sir William had elected to drown his hour of the day's discomforts looked extremely inviting – not to say unbearably enviable.

But had he not at breakfast said . . .

'You surely did announce, Sir William, that you were bound for the Crawmelt mountains today; in search of kestrel chicks?'

'Ay, my lady. And there shall I head ere long. But I thought when I saw the clouds already burned away that I should have myself a peaceful dip before departing for the heights. While his lordship lies still abed at Drumelzier and cannot tax my patience with his slavers!'

'Sir William! He is the King's own brother!'

'Indeed, my lady. And a slaverer forby. Or would you murder truth?' Sir William bobbed gently against the slow northward drag of the current, bouncing the balls of his feet off the large smooth boulders of the riverbed.

This gave the glimmering surface of the water the appearance of a faint tidal pulsing, licking suggestively from the young man's navel to his hinterland of loins.

Which Elizabeth found strangely fasinating, she was strangely fascinated to find.

Then flushingly embarrassed.

So it was looking at the rusty desiccation of the bracken slope down to the riverbank that she coyly inquired:

'Is not the water somewhat cold, Sir William? On even such a day?'

'Indeed, my lady!' he retorted, his right hand blinkering his gaze against the glare. 'And is not the itching air a trifle warm?'

Elizabeth sighed a sort of short impatience.

'Indeed it is, Sir William. And growing more so by the moment.'

He squinted at her thoughtfully.

Through thirty paces of bugdotted shimmer.

Then said with a neutral shrug:

'You are welcome, my lady, to join me. If the prospect should please you.'

'Oh Sir William I could not!' Elizabeth gasped in a rush.

'*Could* not?'

'It would not be seemly!'

'*Seemly?*'

'I . . . but you are *unclad*, Sir William!'

'Ay, my lady!' he chuckled sardonically. 'Yet your delicacy is protected from the polarities of my shame by the deep discretion of the pool!'

'Y . . . e . . . s. But . . .'

'But you are right, my lady!'

'What?'

'It would in sooth be less than seemly for yourself to join me in the water.'

'Why so?'

'Aaah, my lady! For that the deep discretion of the pool is but a decoy mask, a snare laid out in deceiving calm to lure you into rash disclosures!'

He spoke ominously.

Elizabeth was taken in.

'How so?' she seriously asked.

'As while the water veils you modestly from the land, a hundred lurking eyes will ravage your privacy down below!'

'I do not . . .'

'The trout, the mouthing pike and the diving duck, my lady: they will ogle you without mercy – hey, hey! But I must keep moving.'

Elizabeth blinked as he turned in a buttockflashing lunge and thrashed toward the further bank. When he came to rest again, a distant bob of golden brown against a backdrop green with showering weepingwillow tears, she shouted out to him:

'SIR WILLIAM?'

'MY LADY?'

'IT IS FULLY A YEAR, SIR WILLIAM. SINCE I HAVE HAD A BATHE.'

'A YEAR, MY LADY? SINCE YOU HAVE HAD A BATH!'

'A *BATHE*, SIR WILLIAM!'

'AH!'

'AND SORELY AM I COVETOUS, IF THE TRUTH BE TOLD, OF

SHARING BRIEFLY WITH YOU THE COOL REFRESHMENT OF THE WATER.'

'THEN HONOUR TRUTH, MY LADY! AS YOUTH AND BEAUTY SHOULD!'

'BUT YOU MUST NOT *LOOK*, SIR WILLIAM!'

'EH?'

'YOU MUST NOT LOOK AT ME. WHILE I UNDRESS AND . . .'

'AS IT PLEASE YOU, MY LADY. IN HOMAGE TO DECORUM SHALL I BURY MY PEEPERS IN THE MURK OF THE WEEDY SLIME, AND ROUST THE SKULKING BREAM!'

Elizabeth watched as he snatched a great gulp of air, flipped like a jumping salmon, and submerged into invisibility betrayed only by a trail of rising bubbles. Should she? Or should she not? If . . .

SKWAAAG! SKWAG, SKWAG, SKWAAAG!

She started in fright as a pair of loudly joking ducks zoomed down, an arm's length above her head, and skwagged to a cheeky halt upon the near side of the pool. And somehow this decided it. Annoyed at her prudish wavering, she scrambled down the short steep slope, raising a cloud of reddish mud-dust behind her, kicked off her limesapped sandals and in half a minute was out of her flimsy garments and swimming in the river.

Gasping with shock at its penetrating chill.

'Good . . . day to you, Mistress . . . Polmood!' Sir William hailed when he resurfaced six paces to her west, snorting for breath like an agitated seal.

'Really, Sir William!'

'Uh?'

'You did not tell me that the water was so v-very *cold*!'

'That I did!'

'Sir William, you d-d-did *not*!'

'"Is not the water somewhat cold, Sir William?" you inquired of me. "On even such a day?" And I replied: "Indeed, my lady!" Did I not?'

Elizabeth said nothing through her chattering teeth. To speak to Sir William she had ceased her breaststroke and now, in order to keep a neckline decency of river, was having to hold her body bent in a bottom-treading squat.

Sir William scoffed:

'But truly, my lady, you must not stay still. Else shall you perish!'

'Indeed, Sir William. But I p-p-pray you forgive my bashfulness, and allow . . .'

He grinned his bard's derision.

'But of course, my lady. I now shall take me off again yonder, by the willow. And yourself shall have such spacious solitude in which to splash as our newly borrowed proprieties dictate. For the immeasurable benefits of which it is my nightly practice to offer up a prayer of thanks to the Court of England and the endless refinements of its fashions. However!'

'Yes?'

'I counsel you, my lady, that you shall not wish to swim near to yon rushes by the bend.'

'Why so?'

'There is a powerful reek of rotting death among them.'

Elizabeth would have paled if she could.

'Dear Lord!' she dreaded. 'Not . . .'

'No, my lady. It is but the putrefaction of a swan. A murdered swan, for all that. With an arrow through its throat.'

Elizabeth was indignantly horrified.

Sir William was stoically cynical.

'There is a great majority of men, my lady,' he opined, 'that get more pleasure from greeting beauty with a violent extinction than from bowing to the glory of her thriving.'

'But you, Sir William! You yourself go hawking!'

'Certain it is that I *did* go hawking!'

'And fishing.'

'Which is a world apart, my lady, from the wanton shooting of a swan! When the effort of its being receives not even the salute of finishing roasted on a hungry dinner table! But now, my lady, we both must flail our limbs about – else we soon shall join yon bird's decay.'

Before Elizabeth could reply, Sir William lurched into an energetic backstroke and was windmilling away from her.

Leaving her to exercise a slow but bracing breaststroke up and down the east bank of the long wide pool.

After which she called:

'SIR WILLIAM?'

'GLUUR?'

'I AM GOING OUT NOW.'

'SO SOON?'

'YOU WILL NOT . . .'

'NO, MY LADY! OF COURSE I SHALL NOT LOOK — SEE HERE! MY GAZE IS FASTENED TO THE WELKIN!'

Confirming this through a glance quick with guilt, Elizabeth clambered out.

But:

When Sir William followed her out, some ten minutes later, expecting to find the lady dressed and perhaps departed, he was appreciatively surprised to find her still unclad.

Stretched out.

Demurely face down.

On the lush green grass of the riverbank turf.

Her head, pillowed on folded arms, pointing out towards the water.

Her eyes closed.

Too tightly twitching, however, to signify sleep.

He thought.

As with sweeping hands he brushed river droplets off the lean and sinewy body concerning which he felt anything but shame.

His eyes roved in pleasure up and down the beautiful nudity of Elizabeth's demure recumbency. The spot where she lay was on the edge of the ragged shadow of a sycamore tree, its outermost member playing shadily across her brilliant white thighs as the sun crept south.

'How do you, my lady?' he jovially breezed, throwing himself down beside her, on his front, taking care to leave a pace of prudence between their elbows.

Elizabeth's silence was intense.

Sir William suddenly enquired:

'And is this rebellion?'

She stirred as from shallow dozing. And without opening her eyes responded:

'Rebellion, my lord?'

'Against the English fashion?'

'I . . . no, Sir William. It is not. It is just that I . . . had no cloth to dry myself, and . . .'

'What better cloth than the rubbing sun! Quite so, my lady. Very wise. And best it is to bask, I feel, before his rubbing turns impossibly abrasive. Wherefore, my lady, I am anxious lest you find it irksome, to have me join you here?'

'Not at all, Sir William. Why should I?'

'Then I thank you, my lady,' said he, and closed his eyes.

A short time elapsed.

Silent but for drowsy birdy murmurs, and the deep subliminal rolling of the river.

The bathers lay acutely tense within their posing relaxation, with lurid hoards of images in pantomine upon their flooding eyelid screens.

Until Sir William heard a stifled gasp.

And saw a that a large sycamore seedpod had fallen from the tree above and landed in the small of Elizabeth's back.

Causing the surrounding smooth paleness of skin to shiver furiously.

The poet grinned.

'Mistress Polmood?'

'Yes, Sir William?'

'There is a great winged beastie has landed upon your spine!'

'Oh!'

'Will you not therefore turn, my lady, and swipe him off?'

'I . . . may not move, Sir William! Without . . .'

'Or will you rather, my lady, that myself shall pick the impertinent fellow from your person?'

'Oh, Sir William! I should be so grateful!'

'Very good, my lady. The pleasure is mine!' This was very true, he thought, as he caressingly lifted the botanical dropping from the grateful lady's flesh. Twirling it by rubbing the stalk between his right thumb and forefinger, he held it slowly closer to Elizabeth's face, until the tiny wind from its fanning wings fluttered cool against her lashes.

'Neee!' she exclaimed, flinching in alarm.

'See here, my lady.' He chuckled. 'Will it not please you examine your tormentor?'

'Really, Sir William!' Elizabeth tutted. 'You have been gadding me!'

'Not so, not so! For herein resides an extraordinary menace to any lady!'

Elizabeth laid her cheek on her forearm and regarded her companion with doubtful solemnity.

His glinting gaze inscrutable with mischief.

He urged:

'My lady, it is *true*!'

'How so?'

'Among the simple folk of Peebles it is well known: that the sycamore pod is Nature's emblem for the Spirit of Copulation.'

Elizabeth swallowed to clear her throat.

But found it dry.

'Here', the loremonger expounded, holding the pod at a suggestive angle, 'is the upright stalk: his quhillelillie. Standing straight, and stiff with his desire. And here his podding boobles, big and bulging green with spunk . . . but my lady! You blush!'

'And why should I not, Sir William? Truly, sir! It is lewd indeed of you to address a lady so.'

'Then your pardon, my lady, I most humbly beg of you – and shall desist forthwith.'

Which he did.

Continuing to twirl the seedpod before his nose.

And lapsing into a pensive muse.

Shortly broken by Elizabeth coyly asking:

'But what of the wings?'

'Uh?'

'If the other parts of the pod are . . . as you say, then what role is left for the wings to play? According to this legend?'

'Ah! The wings! They are most beautiful, are they not? My lady? See here: how delicately wrinkled they are, and coloured like the pages of an ancient tome.'

'Yes?'

'But their role! Their role, my lady, is devilish indeed.'

Elizabeth's expression made it plain that her desire for enlightenment on the matter had not diminished.

'It is to speed the quihillelillie through time and space into nuzzling nearness with his own appointed towdie. And they also say, though of course it is all but an old woman's tattle, that if the seedpod fall upon a lady in the hours preceding noon, then shall she receive the broozling of her heart's desire before the day is out.'

'Oh!'

'But it is all nonsense. I suppose.'

'Yes, indeed! But tell me, Sir William?' said Elizabeth, disengaging in her embarrassed anxiety to change the subject.

'Ayee?'

'There is something you did say to me two days ago that preys upon my mind.'

'Um-huh?'

'When you spoke of the motives wherefore a bard will compose and recite, you numbered to me: his own pure pleasure . . .'

'With a smirching streak of *need*!'

'And then the entertainment of his patron . . .'

'And his patron's company – you have a most notable memory, my lady!'

'And finally the motive of desire to bring his loved one joy.'

'Ay.'

'Well!'

'Well?'

'But may the man with such a gift not also wish *to lift the souls of all the world?* Outwith his patron's retinue?'

'Indeed he may.'

'But Sir William!' Elizabeth exclaimed accusingly.

'He will sing his heart out for the meanest wretch in the tolbooth death cell, given only that the prisoner truly wish it.'

'Yet you did say his motives were *three*!'

'I said they are *roughly* three, my lady. And forby I was being – shall we say? – somewhat liberally extempore.'

Elizabeth's indignation mounted:

'Then why had you to decline my invitation to recite a verse for me?'

'Simply, my lady, as I did not wish it.'

'You did not wish it! And am I not the hostess whose table has fed you handsomely for many a day?'

'Indubitably you are, my lady. None other!'

'Then would it not be courteous of you, Sir William, to invest a moment of consideration into that which *I* might wish?'

'Ay, my lady. And I dare to say I have.'

'Yet . . .'

'Forby it is never my own desire to lodge at Polmood a single day – though that is not the matter. Yet will I say this, my lady, since you press me . . .'

'I pray you do!'

'That the reason of my not reciting lines for you was this: that the motive of your asking was not pure.'

'Sir, you are forward!'

'Very like, my lady. The remark has been previously ventured. Yet my forwardness is true. For you did not purely wish to hear my songs, but rather to dig in any clay that would fill the hours of emptiness occasioned by his lordship's caitiff absence. Did you not?'

Elizabeth's eyes filmed glassily: windows of liquid crystal dropping to shield her cerulean radiance from the glare of further harshness.

But Sir William ignored this moist rebuke to his needless pertinence.

'However, my lady,' he offered, 'if it please you to audience a cheeky wee rhyme that fell together between my ears as I did walk this way this morn . . .'

Elizabeth's doubtful sniff left the offer in limbo.

'But then again, if it please you not . . .'

'Oh no, Sir William! I pray you do!'

'You are *sure*, my lady?' he flirted. 'For it is hardly a masterpiece.'

She nodded impatiently.

He took an inflative breath and barked his throat in a clear parody of Rosay.

But did not see the curl of amusement play on Elizabeth's lips.

As he boomed across the river:

> There once was a Friar called Fish
> Who only had one wish . . .

'Are you surpassing certain, my lady, that you desire me to go on? For the ending . . .'

'Yes, yes! I *urge* you!'

'Then shall I commence afresh, that I sunder not the integral unity of the work!' And louder than before he Dukely boomed:

> There once was a Friar called Fish
> Who only had one wish.
> That his filthy habits
> Could smell more like rabbits
> And a wee bit less like *pish*!

A shock of silence vibrated between their hotting bodies.

Then Elizabeth exclaimed:

'Sir William, that is *cruel*!'

'But – '

'Cruel and vindictive, sir. And impiously, unspeakably . . . *vulgar*!'

'Did not I *warn* you – '

'You spoke only, sir, of a "cheeky wee rhyme". But gave no intimation that your recitation would be rife with vile obscenity.'

'I am rent with remorse, my lady, if I have given you irreparable offence.'

'And rightly so, sir!'

'But would plead that though it was an unpardonable error of taste to give it utterance within your hearing, as now I see as clear as today's blue sky, yet yon wee doddle cannot be attributed to malice active in my awareness. As you did imply.'

'But you did compose it!'

'Not so, my lady.'

'I fear, Sir William,' Elizabeth said, with the sternness of affronted youth, 'that I follow you not at all.'

'I said, my lady, and truly mean, that the rhyme fell together between my ears already complete – that it sprang upon my mind already whole, and would not go away! Like a phrase of melody that haunts the memory like a thirsty leech.'

Disapproval and perplexity did battle in the lady's frown.

Which stung the rhymer to unaccustomed earnestness.

'Ever is it so, my lady!' he proclaimed. 'Like wild and violent dreams to the sleeping head do couplets come unbidden. Sometimes welcome, sometimes not. Yet who will hang the man that does a murder in his dream? And would not the population thereby perish?'

'I do not see . . .'

'Then am I cruel, to whom odd cruel thoughts do come? And I say: No! That the cruel thought to the human race is like the toothache.'

Perplexity ascended.

Sincerity argued:

'For while the fortunate few may voyage from womb to tomb unbuffeted by either – unscarred by cruel thoughts and unwracked by spasms in the teeth, I mean – yet must the great majority suffer!'

Elizabeth nodded without meaning to, more swayed by the fervour of his delivery than the force of his reasoning. Never before had she known his discourse so unpeppered by sarky barbs, and did not the mantle of plain vehemence wear handsomely upon him! To his becomingly narrowed brows and exigent voice, she assentingly said:

'And therefore, my lord?'

'And therefore, my lady, I suggest to you this. That the cruel man is never he that maims his brother in a nightmare. Or he that comes on wounding ditties in his head, like myself. For the cruelty is in the *witting deed*, and the cruel and evil man is he that maims his brother in the living flesh, and that right wilfully. And cruel would I be, in my own regard (which is not to claim that never in my life have I so sinned!), if I were to render yon fishy doddle in the hearing of the unfortunate Friar himself. As yon Stoddart fellow doubtless would, if I should speak it to him.'

'Which you will not, Sir William!' Elizabeth hoped.

Of course not!

She rewarded him with pleased relief.

But he required a richer balm to ease his smart.

So he said:

'And now allow me, my lady, to lay my head upon a block whereof yourself shall bid the swinging or the sheathing of the sword. Permit me, that is, to render up a deeper song for your appraisal – which I may call my own in that it came to *me*, and also *not* my own: in that I found it ready formed within my mind, like a fountain in a forest glade.'

Permission was graciously granted.

Whereupon Sir William came over shy, plucking at the weedy grass with nervous fingers, and seeming to retreat within himself as though repenting rashness.

'And you may be assured, Sir William,' Elizabeth encouraged him, admiring the halo waves of his hair fluffing dry, 'that my wish to audience a verse has never been more pure than now.'

He did not acknowledge this, but a moment later began to recite in an otherworldly plainsong chant:

I move without motion
In a line without time,
Effortlessly,
For I am the art work
Evolving.

I build my own monsters,
I people my hell,
And for those that make good
I make heaven as well,
For these are the wages
Of striving.

I give you a cipher,
The key to my gaze;
Mark it well,
For such is a lesson
In dying.

An unworded hush ensued.

Which rapidly became unbearable to the volunteer upon the block.

'Of course, my lady,' he huskily deprecated, 'there is no denying that the piece is a mite abstruse and – '

'No, no, Sir William!' Elizabeth exclaimed in precipitated rapture. 'It is quite, quite . . . beautiful!'

'Truly, my lady?'

'Indeed!' she averred, examing his bowed muttering countenance with eyes that shone a warmer shade of blue – shimmering with the energy of a new and unexpected interest. Prompting:

'One of the most beautiful and deeply moving songs, I swear to Heaven . . .'

'I am not myself sure, my lady,' Sir William diffidently confessed, 'that "beauty" is a class in which the piece may study.'

'Oh yes, Sir William! It is. It has a subtle beauty of its own, profoundly stirring. Even – may I say – *disturbing*!'

The flattered poet nodded thoughtfully.

To himself.

Which piqued the flattered lady into ridering:

'Although, so modest is my womanly understanding, I fear there must be great treasures of import within the verse that are vaulted from my grasp. And therefore, Sir William, I should be most glad to have your prose account of what it signifies.'

'Aha, my lady! You wish me to unroll the meaning of my song before you, like a rug of stitched skins?'

'If you please.'

'Yet this I cannot do.'

'Why so?'

'I know its meaning little better than yourself – the skins are all intangible, outwith my reach, still bounding about the mountains upon the backs of living stags.'

Elizabeth was unsure that this aesthetic should be condoned.

'And is the practice rife among the bards', she inquired, 'of fashioning up ballads profound in sound yet questionable in meaning – mercy, but my neck is afire!' So saying, she wriggled without cautionary deliberation and rolled over on her back.

Bringing her naked nubile body into elbow and ankle contact with Sir William.

Who winced as if scalded.

But lay his ground.

While struggling not to ogle round and follow Elizabeth's hands as they smoothed odd scraps of grass and dust off her silky bosom, her unseen thighs, her . . .

'My lady,' he steadfastly resumed, 'if I could say what it meant, I would not think it worth the bother of singing. It is enough for me that the song *does mean*.'

Elizabeth ceased her body grooming and folded her arms in a dazzle baffle across her eyes, pulling tautly high her pertly pointed breasts. Though she was only umbrally aware of the fact, the dynamics playing between Sir William and herself had been revised by a rising restlessness and provocative curiosity in her own state of mind, and in her physical and vocal expressions.

He was more conscious of the shift, feeling the claws of his natural goating truculence retracting without his willing, as though some instinct tide were turning.

'I suppose, Sir William,' Elizabeth murmured, 'that you sing your songs often to Lady Ann?'

He grunted reservedly.

'And that you write many songs uniquely in her honour?'

'Ay, my lady.'

'Then might it please you, Sir William, to sing such a song to myself?'

'No, my lady.'

'Why so?'

'It would be false, my lady, for me so to do. And vicarious, forby, for you to hear.'

'Your love is for Lady Ann, you mean?'

'Ay.'

'And not for myself?'

'Indeed not. With respect.'

'Is she a very wonderful lady, Sir William, to . . . to broozle?'

Sir William found himself both shocked and excited.

But managed to keep both motions from showing in his cold reply:

'My lady! What a question to put to a gentleman!'

But Elizabeth's blood was up and her prudence floundering amid the same swellings and wellings of wholly healthy arousal that had so crucified her rest in the two weeks past. Except that now in the heat of the day and the throes of stimulating company she neither reflected nor felt shame.

Asking:

'And would you never wish, Sir William, to broozle myself?'

'Thank you, my lady. But . . . no!'

This was the answer Elizabeth had been expecting, but it nonetheless swept her with a shiver of hurt frustration.

'Why so, I pray?' her smallest voice insisted.

'It is one of my few immovable resolutions in this life that never shall I broozle . . .' he paused for effect, 'where the Duke of Rothesay had broozled before.'

She gasped in horror. Then sobbed.

'How dare you, sir! How *dare* you!'

'How dare I what, my lady?'

'To suggest that I should have allowed – that – to suggest, sir, that *hideousness* which you did!'

Sir William fought to play down his amazement.

'I cannot hope, my lady,' he sleepily drawled, 'that you shall pardon me if my presumption has done you wrong. Yet . . . truly! Do not all the circumstances point that way?'

Elizabeth's breathing fury disagreed.

'Ay, my lady! It may be an unjust notion – yet consider! He is with you every moment of the day, when his yellow belly is not cowering at Drumelzier. He walks with you, talks with you, constantly. Incessantly. He takes your arm, he pats your shoulder, showers kisses upon your wrist and fingers ... while his pocksy donkey's eyes undress your body and ravish you for all to see. And forby his chamber is distant from your own by just the thickness of a wall! Wherefore, my lady, my judgement lies in abject shame if it has erred. Yet the selfsame error is bandied as established gospel among the common folk for miles about.'

'Oooh!'

'Ay!'

Elizabeth sank back from the neck-craning instability into which she had twisted to glare her indignation at Sir William's unabashedly eyesealed nonchalance. Again she folded her arms protectively across her eyes, and there was a desponding quaver in her saying:

'Well you can take it, sir, as sworn upon the Cross, that an error it most certainly is. And shall remain!'

'Very well, my lady. Your promise is the quill that writes correction upon the page of my belief – bogger a tup, but this heat indeed is fierce!'

Elizabeth tensed in humiliated disappointment as she felt him turning over.

Moving away from her.

Outwith the bounds of extremities accidentally touching.

While above to her right a ringdove loudly purred in the heart of the sycamore leafage.

And immediately a reply purled faintly across the water from the weeping willow on the far bank.

'Therefore what say you now, Sir William?' Elizabeth prayed her voice would not betray the turmoil of her feelings.

'My lady?'

'I asked – before we ... did digress – if you could never wish to broozle myself?'

'Ah, my lady! I regret, though with the greatest of respect and admiration, that the answer must remain: No.'

'I see,' said she, a salty pricking in the corner of her eye. 'And why, if it please you to tell?'

'My lady, were I to broozle you (in the absence, let us say, of yourself directly requesting it), I would thereby run the highest risk of losing for ever my patronage, not to mention my head forby. As you, my lady, are the rosiest of all the apples in the orchard of his Majesty's affections.'

'Oh. And am I still, do you believe?'

'Indeed, my lady. Any stranger might conclude, to hear the King wax lyrical upon your virtues, that here he spoke of his only daughter. Were it not so known across the world that in fact he continues childless.'

'But the Queen . . .'

'Ay. And the birth may already have been. Yet not a soul among the court would stake a merk that Queen Margaret shall ever produce a child to outlive the passing of a year. For all that she is a splendid lady and a truly noble queen.'

'Indeed.'

And no reference was made to the many thriving natural children that already had stemmed from his Majesty's amorous escapades (and that he was not ashamed to acknowledge, support and honour where merit was deserving – as in the case of his illegitimate son, Alexander, who was made Archbishop of Saint Andrews at an early age and subsequently sent to Siena to study under Erasmus of Rotterdam).

Sir William emitted a sound that Elizabeth felt was alarmingly close to the prelude of a snore.

Hastily she returned to her preoccupation:

'But suppose, Sir William, that I were . . .'

A tremendous row of beaten leaves and snapped twigs erupted overhead, spraying into the flapping flight of the purring dove and the arrival on Elizabeth's knee of a large hot globule of freshly evacuated dovedung. 'Tchuh!' she tutted, sitting up with a jolt and pulling a handful of grass to wipe the desecration off.

When she had done this, and casually glanced to see if Sir William were indeed slumbering, her mouth fell open in fascinated disbelief.

For there he lay.

Lean, pleasingly muscled and evenly bronzed.

With his manhood erect: swollen rigid and held aloft at the rearing angle she never before had seen.

Or even imagined.

Like a little cannon aimed across the river.

'Ooh, Sir William!' she exclaimed, doubtful fingers across her marvelling lips.

'Hmmn?'

'Your quhillelillie is *large*!'

'No, my lady,' he demurred. 'Not large. Though it may now be at its largest.'

'And there is a bead of moisture upon its tip!'

'Ay, my lady. A love tear. But surely you have seen a tear of love before?'

'I . . . why, yes! Of course. But – look, Sir William. Look!'

'Eh?'

An enormous peacock butterfly flitted madly around the river side of the sycamore tree and hovered over Sir William's body, the circular painted eyes on its fluttering wings flashing brilliant in the sun.

Suddenly it alighted on the bulb of his straining member.

And dipped in his tear of love with its long thin proboscis delicately twitching.

'Aaah!' he startled, blinking his eyes open to investigate.

'No, Sir William!' Elizabeth urged. 'I pray you, do not move. It is but sipping . . .'

But it was too late: the nectar tippler took fright and flitted off.

'It was but a butterfly, Sir William, a perching upon your quhillelillie.'

'Indeed?' said he, pushing up and resting on his elbows.

Causing his manhood to twag.

Then for several long moments the young woman and the young man surveyed each other intimately.

And Elizabeth murmured:

'Sir William?'

'Ay, my lady?'

'Shall it please you allow myself to touch where the butterfly sat?'

'Certainly, my lady, if it pleases you it shall also please myself.'

Only slightly did she tremble as she reached to gently feel.

Then wonderingly grasped.

Flexing her pale slender figures around the thrilling hardness of his unyielding pulsing mystery.

Eliciting a gurgle of raw desire from deep within his throat.

'Would you like me to tell you something, Sir William?' she coyly invited.

He nodded through a moan.

'That I should *like* you to broozle me! If it please you. *Truly* I should.'

'*Truly* truly, my lady? Upon the Cross?'

'Yes, yes!' she tugged impatiently. 'Come!' she commanded, suppling into the blatantly receptive posture that the lewd Lady Annabelle had demonstrated to her horror a year before.

For an instant Sir William was unable to believe his gaping eyes. But then he overcame this disability.

And groaning with primal anticipation was upon her.

And in a trice Elizabeth's virginity was at an end.

IN THE ORCHARD SUN BOWER

When the Duke of Rothesay arrived from Drumelzier for luncheon that day he was agitated almost to delirium. Everything on his principal dish was left untouched except the meat and he refused both cheese and fruit, meanwhile wining himself yet more royally than usual as he raged grandiloquently against the obligations attaching to mighty birth and office.

Asked by a distantly attentive Elizabeth which regal duty in particular had aroused his present ire, Rosay explained that the previous evening had witnessed the arrival at Drumelzier of a messenger from the King in Edinburgh. Bearing no bad news, Elizabeth trusted. Quite the contrary, Rosay snorted bitterly. For the sweatsodden rascal's tidings were that the Queen had two days since been delivered of a bouncing baby boy. But that was absolutely wonderful, Elizabeth exclaimed. Indeed it was, the displaced heir to Scotland concurred grimly, except that himself had been summoned back to Holyrood to homage at the christening. Forthwith? Well, the following day at the latest, according to his Majesty's instruction, for celebrations began on Thursday, for the christening on the Saturday.

And was it . . . did it seem a *healthy* babe?

Pah!

But why did Rosay appear so dismayed? Herein was ground for great joy. Not so?

Oh, indeed! For the nation, at least, the birth was unadulterately capital.

But?

But upon the Duke of Rothesay personally it imposed much sorrow – sorrow beyond the power of a noble heart to bear!

Yet how? Had not Rosay (on the very afternoon of his arrival here at Polmood, as doubtless he would recall) confided to Elizabeth that he would repudiate the succession a thousand times, given only that her majesty manage to present the King with a lasting heir?

Yes, yes, *yes*! But that was not the matter.

Then what was?

That this demand for his presence in Edinburgh must remove him from Elizabeth's delightful society – from her charming conversation, and from the enriching glow of her peerless beauty.

But . . .

Prolongedly, without a doubt. And, he foreboded, perhaps for ever!

Elizabeth was visibly jolted by this dire prognosis.

Oh yes, Rosay assured her. He feared King James would forbid his return to Polmood and the wooing of its widow, when he learned that the lady continued obdurate in her refusal of his, Rosay's, tenderly offered hand in marriage.

Oh! This was a possibility Elizabeth had not foreseen.

Ah, but that was the way of the world, Rosay broodily gloomed. And if it was truly no part of Elizabeth's desire to return to court in a resumptuous blaze of fashionable glory (as Elizabeth, Duchess of Rothesay, the nation's leading lady in beauty, costume, taste, cultivation . . .) then probably it would be for the best, after all, if the smitten suitor were to cut his hopeless losses before the agony of his unrequited desolation grew to crush his soul beyond repair. But that was Life, that was Life! And what were the loving woes of one rejected gentleman beside the mountainous miseries of all mankind throughout the ages?

But surely . . .

And the final insulting touch to the whole injurious scene was that he, Rosay (Scotland's premier noble, he stressed, as if Elizabeth might have forgotten), should have to ride on the morrow with the insufferable Sir William in attendance – blighting the air, as he surely would, with his supercilious mouthings.

Then Sir William's stay was also over?

But of course, Rosay sneered. Of course! For his doggerel pretensions were now required at court, to enshrine the memory of the Little One's arrival in a swaddle of vacant stanzas.

Elizabeth paled.

Her vision misted.

So *both* her gentlemen guests were to leave?

Leave her alone! With no future in prospect. Here at Polmood. Their presence had been largely thrust upon her, that was true. Yet she had grown by imperceptible degrees more dependent on Rosay's lascivious attentions, Sir William's cool cynicism, and perhaps most of all upon her own role as adroitly feminine mediator of the flaring dinnertime hostilities between the two.

Who tomorrow would be gone!

The implications crept into her marrow like chill from damp garments.

Especially now that Sir William had . . .

'A pear, my lord?' she faintly asked. 'Some cherries, perhaps?'

'Thank you, no, my lady,' Rosay effusively declined. 'Of *material* nourishment I have had me sufficient for the time!' Seeing that Elizabeth had not grasped his ponderous insinuation, he added:

'But, ooh! My starving heart!'

'Your heart, my lord?'

'Dear lady, yes! The unhappiest heart in all the world have I this day, who now must beg for scraps to solace the ordeal of my coming fast!'

Elizabeth felt suddenly undulatingly queasy in her viscera, as once she had during a turbulent ferryboat voyage from Edinburgh across the Firth of Forth to Fife. Would she survive the afternoon without fainting from the heat? She wondered with a lurch, and gave her eyes a visionclearing rub.

Which Rosay construed as encouragement.

'And therefore, dearest Elizabeth, paragon effulgence of all womanhood that never may be mine to cherish (alas, *alas*!), I crave of you this one last boon.'

She nodded wearily.

'That I may escort you everywhere on this our final afternoon. To take your arm, should you please to stroll. To recite you verses, if it please you to rest. Even, dear lady, to recline at your feet in the pose of a doting hound! As you may wish to ply your needlework in silence.'

'But it is so very *hot*, my lord!'

'Yet the weather boils us of a muchness everywhere, does it not? Indoors, outdoors? North, south – east, west?'

Elizabeth could not deny it.

'Hence what say you we resort awhile to the butterfly bower, which I have had the warty fellow put in order for our pleasure? There to pass a precious hour in the fragrant shade, and seal the memory of our times together with impressions warm and pleasing? Hmmn?'

'Very well, my lord,' said Elizabeth.

Whose thoughts were elsewhere.

The arbour in the centre of the orchard was a triumph of sculpted flora. Snuggling in the midst of the pear trees, cherry trees, gooseberry bushes and their fruity like, it was encompassed by an oval hawthorn hedge some seven feet high, and it measured about twenty paces by thirty along its approximate axes, the longer of which pointed west towards the Castle and east to the rear of the orchard, with the Polmood Hill and the Birkside Law looming humpily in the background. The one entrance was through the south side of the thicket wall and had been freshly hacked clear of obstructive entwinements and dress-rending thorns by the now vanished Andrew Stoddart, whose labours evidenced on the ground all around in spiky splinters that lay almost white against the darker deader yellows of the sun-sered grass.

Inside the suntrap grotto presided a single apple tree, of elder vintage with heavy green strangling ivy creeping ever higher up its trunk, and a circular wooden seat (still functional, though precariously warped and cracked) built around its shady base. There one could sit at any hour of any day and contrive cool seclusion from the sun, or shelter from a freshening breeze, by shifting round the endless bench until one's comfort optimized. Alternatively, one could bask from breakfast until dinner in such sunshine as there was, always beyond the edge of the apple-tree shadow yet shielded against unwelcome draughts by the stalwart hawthorn, and subtled in spirit by the blending sweetness of the orchid scents (violet, carmine, marigold) that wafted in shifts through spring to autumn from the small heartshaped flowerbed that lay as far west of the hedge-gap as the apple tree was to the east.

This, then, was the cloistral haven, the resurrected idyll.

Where the desperate Rosay enticed Elizabeth at three o'clock on that breathtaking afternoon.

When the dominant flower was the butterfly bush, with its long curving stems as tall as a man, and the memorywaking bouquet of its pot-pourri perfume lilting an irresistible invitation from the tiny petals on its phallus-like deep-purple heads swaying a lazy dance in bending time to its arriving and departing guests: the guzzling bumble bees and the prettily sipping brimstone butterflies, their gorgeous yellow wings a halftone darker than Elizabeth's dress and those dainty crimson spots like . . . like *stains of bleeding shame*!

This suddenly struck her as she watched the butterflies flit in their dozens from head to head of the silently ecstatic bush. And she panicked anew that stinking beneath the shallow satin skin of her superficial pulchritudes there festered the hideousness of waxing evil, of the irredeemably fallen soul of a wanton woman steeped wilfully in sin and rotten with lust.

Yes, Elizabeth was well below her guarded best – how else could Rosay have duped her with his puerile farewell gambit?

There was the alertness-dulling heat.

There was the prospect of further loneliness so abruptly announced.

And, above all, the alloyed aftermath of her adventure with Sir William on the riverbank.

What had he exclaimed, perceiving the stigma of her erstwhile maidenhood? 'Bogger me, my lady, but *why*? For I am *doomed* if this comes out!' She had been badly shaken by the pitch of his indignant anger, especially in view of the roaring pleasure he seemed to have derived only moments earlier from pounding upon her with a vigour that she found alarmingly uncomfortable.

But when she had sworn upon the Cross that the incident would remain for ever a secret between them two, and said she was most regretful if she had misled him, though truly she had not meant to, and explained that actually her fanciful yen to be broozled owed more than a little to curiosity (tinged with envy, though it pained her to confess it) aroused by her accidentally stumbling upon the belling ecstasies that the same exertions stimulated in her maid, Sir William soon calmed sufficiently to suggest in his inimitably laconic style that it might be both sensibly refreshing and cosmetically expedient for Elizabeth and himself to share a second dip in the cool cleansing waters of the Cleaker's Pool.

This they duly did, with the evaporation of Elizabeth's former reserve much enhancing the thrilling exhilaration of their intimate nudgings, playful duckings and splashing teasings.

Then Sir William had broozled her again.

But it was imperative that he did not get her in a family way, she had this time thought to insist. A laudable sentiment, he allowed, then explained in cheery detail that she need not fear conception at either encounter, as a gentleman's generative secretions were widely known to remain infertile for several hours following immersion of the boobles in waters of chill degree. Truly? Ay! Indeed, it was one of the very few reliably preventive measures available to the common man.

Reassured thus, Elizabeth had allowed (if not actively encouraged) him to set to anew. And this time, toward the culmination of his more protracted endeavours, she had begun to glimpse why such pursuits might come to be valued (by ladies, that is) and to feel a tingling dawning in her flesh of the firmament joys that Thomas so clearly set blazing in Betty.

But Sir William had desisted before she herself reached that Heaven. Time was getting on, he remarked, and himself he must be off.

Why so? She had pouted. Whatever was his need to hurry?

The Duke of Rothesay would soon come trotting his fat erse along the bridleway, Sir William explained. And forby he must shake a leg back to the Castle and saddle up, or he never would get to the Crawmelt mountains and back before nightfall. *Must* he go? Most certainly he must! Why? Would not Elizabeth join him in a final douse before he left? In a moment she would, she said. Then, timorously, as he laced his breeches:

'Did it *pleasure* you to broozle me, Sir William?'

'Ay, my lady. To tell ye true, yon second go was one of the very best broozles that ever I have had. Not *the* best, mark you! But coming parlous close. And if truly ye never have had a man before this day, as my eyes oblige my amazement to accept, then verily, my lady, ye are possessed of a bonny braw talent for broozling. As the Peebles folk would say. And it lifts my heart to the height of song to picture the murder in His Lordship's face, if he should learn what he has missed and I have had.'

'But he shall not!'

'Indeed not, my lady,' Sir William chuckled. 'As my discretion is your muted slave! Farewell.' And away he had marched.

Abandoning her to the miseries and panging doubts that ever crowd the hours of deflowered solitude.

Possessed of a bonny braw talent for broozling!

Yet not once had he kissed her – *not once!*

Ooooh, dear Lord! Where, oh where, was the beauty, the spiritual poetry in this?

What he has missed and I have had!

This was the abominable reality!

While the firmament joys were no more than the luring flashes of a cheap deception: a painted artifice on a tawdry puppet-theatre sky. And oh it was so true, too true, what the Blessed Saint had said. That woman was a temple erected upon a sewer – yes, yes! And all her life the temple had apparently immovably and immaculately prevailed, but now that she in a single weak and wanton moment had cast the holy sacrament away the surging sewer had risen up and broken through and slapped at the coloured windows from within, its mounding excrements all set to smash the brittle tinted panes and shower their foetid proclamation in a rain of stinking slime upon the unforgiving world.

Ooooh, lubricious jaded wretch that she surely was, *why had she done it?*

It was horny recollections and harsh reflections such as these, strumming relentless on her mind that day, that blinded Elizabeth to Rosay's lower motive: to exact her physical surrender by force, if necessary, on this his ultimate afternoon.

In the calculate privacy of the orchard bower.

Where, in the shady comfort of the old apple-tree seat, he could eulogize:

'Oh, what bliss, what *bliss*, my lady! What a glorious plenitude of harmony in the air – though I see yon lumpy varlet has neglected to prune the nettles beneath the bench. While here am I, the happiest of saddest men, with you, dearest Elizabeth, my benison of perfect loveliness – if only for this fragile hour!'

Which was harmless enough (if somewhat tedious) while it lasted.

Not fifteen minutes later, however, his arm was pawing blatantly around her waist, his black furry lips were nuzzling in her cringing neck, while his rankly alcoholic breath inflamed her ear with proposals ever lewder.

'I *beg* you, my lord!' she implored. 'You *must* not!'

But it was no use.

'Oh, Elizabeth, why so? Why so?' he manically crooned, his fingers affronting her bosom with a crude caress.

Elizabeth wriggled.

Struggled.

But Rosay was implacable.

And shortly had her on the ground, rolling on the rich dark twiggy soil beneath the tree – he in the rampant heat of an ardour quite deranged, she in quietly protesting desperation.

'My lord!' she cried. 'You have torn my dress! I shall call . . . I pray you, my lord, that you *desist*. Else shall I call out!'

'Then call, contrary lady!' crowed Rosay. 'Call all you will, and who shall bring your succour? Ha? The cuckoo boy? But he is miles away, is he not? Then shall some menial come, perhaps? And find his mistress rutting with a Royal Duke! And what then say but "hem!", or do but squirm and blush? No, no, Mistress Polmood! Sly vixen that you are, you owe me this: the debt is overdue and shall be promptly paid. For I . . . aha! But you are ripely moist, I feel, in the mouth that never lies!'

'Noooo!' she tearfully pleaded.

'Yeeee-es!' he exulted, pinning her arms to the ground with his hands and holding her body captive with his weight. He was dressed in a loose-sleeved bell-legged suit of white silk, topped by a green velvet cap with a rubycrusted ornament affixed to the forehead of its turned-up brim.

And through the thin fabric of his pantaloons Elizabeth could feel his swollen lust prodding.

As once she had before.

'Hark, my lord!' she suddenly hissed. 'What was that?'

But Rosay fancied he had got enough of Elizabeth's devious ruses the last time, when she had rolled him in a sheet and bundled him to the floor.

Therefore:

'It was nothing!' he opined, with nasty liplicking relish.

'No, my lord,' she urgently assured him, straining to squint at the hawthorn hedge, 'it was *not* nothing! I heard – '

'A tabbycat a-pouncing on a finch, or something like. If at all, cunning lady . . . aha! No, you do not, madam! I vow. Yes, that was all you heard, if aught. But now! Now shall you see and feel and harbour that which soon shall have you mewling like a *hundred* cats in heat!' So saying, Rosay arched his body upward, supporting himself on his toes and left arm, thus freeing his right hand to unfasten his pantaloons and the phenomenon of which he appeared so proud.

Giving Elizabeth a moment of precious respite.

On the level of fighting instinct now, convinced that she had nothing left to lose except her life, she bucked with all her might at Rosay's groin.

Bringing her united knees into hammering contact with the genitals he had left uncodded in anticipation.

(As the Lady Elinor Hume had one rainy day advised her was expeditious in such put-upon conditions.)

'RAAAAAH!' Rosay bellowed in unbalanced agony.

Elizabeth thrust at his chest with her free hand and twisted sideways as he collapsed in a doubled-up cursing heap. Then, smoothing down the crumpled grass-soiled skirts that he had so rudely lifted, she scurried round the apple tree, ran through the gap in the hedge and away into the orchard.

Only instants later Rosay was up and limping after her.

Screaming in hateful sobs:

'Madam, it is no use to flee! For I shall tell all Scotland WHAT A STRUMPET MISTRESS POLMOOD IS! That JUICES AT A . . .' The vilification aborted when Rosay saw that his exit from the bower was obstructed.

By a darkly hulking mass.

Standing squarely in the hawthorn gap.

The brownly-habited odorous form of the lodging palmer: the cowlcoy Friar Fish.

'Get you aside, old monk!' Rosay hissed, poking imperiously at the great sacked chest. 'Make . . .'

What happened next struck the Duke of Rothesay dumb with terror.

The eyehooding cowl flicked back.

The stooped figure stiffened to a towering height.

The dirty white beard came away in a giant hand.

And there stood:

'P-P-Polmood?' Rosay gabbled. Recoiling. 'B-b-b . . .'

Norman Hunter, Laird of Polmood, stepped into the pollensweet arbour. His countenance was horribly gaunt, yet contorted with unmistakably slaughterous intent.

Rosay was too stricken to run. Begging:

'N-no, Polmood! N-NAAH!' he howled, as he realized.

And the monstrous fury of Polmood's huge bunched fist lashed through the air, crunched Rosay's nose into a pulp that never again would twitch pugnacious, and felled him senseless to the ground.

Meanwhile Elizabeth was still weaving west through the cherry trees, tripping and gasping in frantic flight from the pursuit she had no doubt the royal rapist would quickly mount, and clutching tight across her breasts the flaps of yellow dress that he had sundered.

'Oh, dear Lord,' she mounted as she ran, stumbled, recovered, and ran again, 'make fleet my legs this . . .'

Imagine the agony of her despair when she heard a thunder of heavy feet racing up behind her at the insane pace of a stampeding bull.

'HELP!' she yelled, lifting her skirts and sprinting for the orchard gate. 'THOMAS! SOMEBODY . . . *HELP ME!*' But then she made the fateful mistake of glancing round.

And was so appalled by what she saw that her footing faltered, her advancing right toe caught against her left heel, and she dropped to the ground with a winding thud.

'H . . . e . . . l . . . p!' was all her puffstunned voice could croak.

Then Polmood was upon her.

'But you are *dead*!' she whimpered, staring up at the rageblack pallor of his hellish visage in astonishment that transcended terror.

Polmood said not a word.

Only gnashing his foul grey gums and coated yellow stumps together and jibbering the chorus of a frenzy that was at once gloating and dementedly anguished.

As he commenced the execution of his diabolical purpose.

Standing over Elizabeth, between her fallen figure and the gate, he hauled off his cumbersome fishrancid habit and was revealed naked above a stout pair of ankle-length buskin boots and tattered faded-beige hose held up by a belt of thick leather, from which hung a short but heavy double-edged broadsword.

While his grizzled barrel chest heaved in passion.

Elizabeth's appreciation of her peril now filled her lungs with breath to scream.

Polmood saw this and kicked her violently in the belly.

Leaving her retching for air in soundless spasms.

He rummaged in the false hump of his monk's attire and produced a large coil of rope. From this he cut three short lengths, then bound Elizabeth's wrists and ankles, stuffed a single twist between her teeth and tied it viciously tight at the back of her head. With the savage glee of a terrier snapping the neck of a rat, he threw his wife's trussed body over his right shoulder, anchored his rope coil upon his left, and back to the butterfly bower he hastily bore his helpless prey.

(All, however, is not yet lost for Elizabeth. For the chase between the cherry trees and the assault upon her by the transmogrified Friar Fish have been observed. High on the shoulder of the Birkside Law, two miles to the east, an interested party has been watching, and now is racing to attempt a rescue.)

Inside the hawthorn pallisade, a glimmering of bloody consciousness was returning to the prostrate Rosay.

Polmood dumped Elizabeth by the flowerbed, where the delicate yellow fluttering of the brimstone butterflies and the lazy guzzling of the bumble bees continued to move the long waving heads of the purple orchids to delight.

While the heroine's cheeks turned puce and her eyes bulged unbecomingly from the futile effort of straining at her skincutting bonds, and the glotted choking that was all she could emit past the bit of hairy rope that gagged her mouth was so dreadfully hoarse and piteous as to render impossible its transposition into dialogue.

But Polmood was long past pity.

Silent except for a constant humming whinny, as of unbearable ecstasy and terminal agony combined, he strode to the apple tree, looked up at its branches, then jumped and caught hold of a limb that ran almost parallel to the ground, some ten feet up.

The whole tree swayed and groaned.

A flurry of apples broke from their stems and showered down.

But the branch withstood the giant weight.

'Oooh, my *fashe*!' Rosay's bloodswamped voice lamented.

'*Nyaah*!' Polmood exulted, leapt across to the groggily rousing lamenter, turned him flat upon his front as though he were a fish to fillet, and bound him as he had Elizabeth.

And moulded him almost tenderly, into a posture from which his eyes must perceive the lady by the flowerbed. Inquiring in a guttural perversion of joy:

'Honies at a touch, eh? My *lord*? *No shall we see*!' The lunatic laird returned to his hapless wife, and there were tears in his burning green eyes when he said:

'Honey at a touch, madam, do you? Then HONEY NOW!'

And he raped her.

Ripping her garments like flimsy parchment.

Producing from the cod of his hose a genital engine that was abnormally gargantuan even allowing for the vast bulk of the man himself.

Having to masturbate it into stiffness sufficient to perpetrate the violation.

He cut the lashing from her ankles.

Spread wide her legs with his huge brutish hands.

And entered her with the tenderness of a battering ram.

All the while slobbering pathetically – defiling the air as he defiled his wife with a streaming mishmash of obscenity and deformed endearment.

But brief indeed was the sweetness of his putative revenge, for he ejaculated only moments later, and in the further salting shame of his premature detumescence he heard Elizabeth (herself delirious with pain from the massive savagery of his attack) croak feebly through her gag of rope:

'Ooh, why . . . do you . . . this?'

To which he replied, withdrawing, rising, and blinking brine:

'And why, madam, *did you me wrong*?'

'Ne . . . ver . . .'

'You LIE!' he howled. 'And for it SHALL YOU HANG!' So vowing, he trussed her legs again, and added: 'But first shall you witness the courage of your paramour IN DEATH!'

Rosay by this time had managed to writhe to within feet of the arbour exit. Blood vessels like knotted cords laced his baldness, the delicate snowdrop silk of his chemise and pantaloons was blotched with spurted blood, and as he struggled to worm away he snivelled in muffled soprano hysteria.

Polmood now remarked the misery of this bid for freedom.

'HAAA!' he roared, pranced over to Rosay, and urinated upon his head.

Rosay jerked rabidly.

But failed to dodge the blinding flow.

'Come now, *my lord*!' Polmood muttered, seized his victim by the temple hair and dragged him across to the apple tree. There he cut his remaining rope in two, looped the end of one half into a noose and tucked it tight around Rosay's neck. The other end he tossed over the tested bough and hauled with his superior weight until Rosay's feet dangled unsupported about fifteen inches above the ground.

Meanwhile Rosay and Elizabeth continued to gurgle and rasp as loudly as their gagging would permit.

Polmood braked the rope in a doublehitch around the gallows branch and anchored its end to a leg of the circular bench round the trunk.

'Wish you now to converse on the matter? My *lord*?' he quietly raved.

As Rosay's hopeless buckings only sped his own strangulation.

Polmood held the edge of his sword against the side of Rosay's face and sliced through the rope that snaffled him.

And into his ear.

The volume of rage, pain, terror, and suddenly pious beseechment with which the Duke of Rothesay commenced the singing of his swansong was so bloodcurdlingly tremendous that (as afterwards was established) it carried all the way to Tweedsmuir.

'Hark here, madam?' the executioner invited his wife. 'Your paramour repents! But let us see. Hey?' He tapped with the rounded tip of his broadsword at Rosay's swinging loins. Then cut away the fine silverbossed belt from the dukely midriff, and with it the slender Italian dagger that was Rosay's only weapon that day – so complete had his confidence been.

And tore the silken pantaloons down.

And bellowed in revulsion:

'But the reptile HAS THE POCKS, FORBY! Of all ... and you, madam, you have it too! *Aaaach*! And now have given it to me. Eh? To pus my corpus, as long since you have pussed my soul! Well, sir,' he turned again to the throttling Rosay, leering obsessedly at the brownchancred penis that lifted halfgorged with noose-squeezed blood, 'for the damnation that you have assured my spirit in the Everlasting Fires of Hell, my final payments is ... *this*!' He pressed his sword flat against Rosay's hairily fat thighs.

And slowly, in leisurely scything strokes, sawed upward into his scrotum.

Rosay's throat rattle was like the falling of dried peas on a wet stone floor.

His severed genitals slithered down his legs and slopped to the ground.

His lifeblood urinated out as from the bursting of a scarlet bladder.

And Elizabeth's bludgeoned mind gave up and sank to rest in a catatonic coma.

Two minutes later, when Sir John Carmichael hurtled into the bower affray, he did not notice the sumptuous purple fragrance of the butterflybush or hear the intoxicate rejoicing of the bumbles, for he saw that Polmood had Elizabeth noosed and strung up alongside Rosay and was fussing around her like an agitated mother: patting her lolling cheeks in the hope of restoring her to consciousness, while weeping with the uncaring abandon of a deserted bride.

Carmichael blanched in the split second of his taking in the macabre scene.

Then:

'What in the name of ... POLMOOD!' he roared.

And charged.

With his sabre at the ready.

Polmood whirled in offguard surprise. Seeing but not recognizing his fast-closing antagonist, he stooped to snatch his sword from where it lay propped against the apple-tree seat, and with the speed of second nature backed off several paces to size up the opposition.

Who was this tall intruder in shepherd's garb?

With long lank hair the colour of haystacks after rain?

Carmichael used Polmood's retreat to slash at the rope from which Elizabeth hung.

She fell to the ground in an awkward folding heap.

Like a disjointed doll dropped out of a petulant cradle.

'What ails you, fellow?' Polmood snarled. 'What business have ye here?'

Carmichael's left hand reached warily and removed his haystack wig.

Polmood saw.

And the valley rang with his unhinged delight:

'CARMIIIICHAEL!'

For was not this an unforeseen dessert, to make his feast of retribution total?

Carmichael stepped sideways, away from the tree. Though all his body ached terribly from the effort of his two-mile sprint downhill from the Birkside Law, his large dark eyes narrowed in glinting alertness, and (while the sweat beaded off him like droplets from a cloudburst) the voice was soft that said:

'Polmood, sir. You have become possessed – you know not what you do. Lay down your blade, therefore. Surrender unto me, and forgiveness . . .'

Polmood's thrilling anticipation was sexual in its growl.

As he sprang.

And beat at Carmichael with a windmill blur of cold flashing steel, berserkly superhuman in its lightning power and accuracy.

The galahad baron gave ground – how could he not? He could not reciprocate Polmood's monomaniac craving to dispense death, his leg muscles were closer to spent from his running than he had realized, and he simply was not gifted with the same unique endowment of weapon power and force of arm.

So back he went.

Defensive all the way.

Able only to parry (and that right desperately) as Polmood cut, thrust, flailed and slashed.

Lunge, parry: hiss, clang.

Even in swords Carmichael was disadvantaged, for while Polmood's was no longer it was double-edged and heavier than his own (the hunting sabre that Polmood himself had given him in his Connel role).

Hack, block: swish, clash.

Leaving Carmichael's right wrist ever more numb.

Backwards he circled the sweltering arena enclosed by the apple tree, the flowerbed and the sides of the hawthorn hedge.

'Come, Polmood!' he panted, passing the butterflies for the second time. 'Leave off . . . sir. Will you not? This is *madness*! When ever . . . have I . . . done you wrong? And you me neither, Polmood? Sir! I pray you, let reason . . .'

'Haa!' Polmood feinted a Herculean swing at Carmichael's neck but dropped immediately into a crouch, so that the arc of his swipe would certainly have cut Carmichael's knees from under him if it had struck home.

Barely in the nick of time did Carmichael contrive to ward it off.

Twisting his sabre desperately to shield his left side.

Holding it parallel to his body by twisting his wrist.

So that when Polmood's blow connected it not only snapped the tip off Carmichael's blade but the force of it juddered his hand so severely as to dislocate his right thumb.

Feral joy drooled in Polmood's mouth when he perceived the other's handicap.

And the ferocity of his onslaught redoubled.

Lunge, clang – hack, clash – hack, clash.

Driving Carmichael back to the apple tree, towards the bough wherefrom Rosay's mutilated cadaver limply depended.

Carmichael ground between his teeth:

'Polmood, I *beg* you . . .'

But it was no use.

Polmood dealt a two-handed chop at Carmichael's head, from above, that would have split him near to the waist.

Carmichael dodged right and with his crippled sword deflected certain death by a hair's breadth.

But his wielding now was perilously weak.

And Polmood's power knocked the sabre from his grasp.

Twirling through the air it flew, and was lost in the thicket hawthorn.

Carmichael sobbed in exhausted defeat, sank to his knees in the shade of the apples, and pleaded:

'Polmood, *why* . . .'

The forester sucked lips that were tart with the taste of victory. 'NOW!' he bellowed, and raised his sword to lop off the vanquished head.

When out of the blue.

'Merciful Saviour, it is the Master RISEN!'

Polmood was distracted the fractional moment necessary to glance back and observe, peering round the hawthorn gap, the alarm-sick faces of Thomas, Betty and Martha.

Carmichael saw a slight chance glimmer. Throwing himself backwards, he rolled underneath Rosay's dangling body and scooped up the elegant stiletto that lay forgot beside the dead Duke's sundered genitals.

'Uuuung!' Polmood raged.

And rushed.

And hacked.

Carmichael danced round the corpse of Rosay, then pushed it in Polmood's path, causing the latter's sideways-slicing weapon to miss himself but completely sever Rosay's right arm above the elbow and cleave its way several inches into his lifeless torso.

Polmood cursed and hauled mightily to dislodge the blade.

And had it free in the blink of an eye.

But the eye was too slow.

Carmichael already had the slender stiletto plunged fully to its crafted hit between the giant's ribs.

And through his heart.

And thus the Laird of Polmood fell dying.

Mouthing disbelief as his blood seeped away and his pulse began to dim and grow erratic.

Seeing the danger past, Carmichael hurled himself down where Elizabeth lay inert, her yellow dress and undergarments all in ravaged shreds.

He leant his fearful ear against her breast.

Then cried:

'Oh, Holy Mother, *she lives*! Hey, you!' he commanded, regarding with dark sternness the three menials still whitely poised for flight. 'Come hither now and attend the lady. For yet she lives.'

Martha and Betty and Thomas (despite the poleaxe he had brought along) were hesitant at first, but soon obeyed when Carmichael angrily assured them that King James would see their persons broken upon the rack if ever he learned that Dame Polmood's distress had been exacerbated by the cowardly negligence of her servants. And forby, the threat was vanished – could not they see? For the aggressor lay mortally wounded, and never would harm a soul again. Martha and Betty flustered round and arranged Elizabeth's attire as decently as they were able. Thomas was then called to bear her slender form back to the Castle (with infinite care, as he valued his life!), where her womenfolk alone should remedy her disarray and minister to her injuries.

Meanwhile, Carmichael tarried in the bower and shared with Norman Hunter of Polmood the final few minutes of his tragic life, eking from him in broken and disconnected sentences the circumstances of his demented behaviour in the several weeks preceding.

And as Polmood's breathing faltered and his moments flew away, while the red blood seeped and oozed and welled down his matgrey chest, the pillar of insanely jealous hatred that had built up beneath him collapsed: he grew calm, resigned, like a tired old hound that sniffs the scent of death upon the breeze.

And when, having teased such details from him as he could, Carmichael endeavoured to convince the dying man of the injustice of his nesting suspicions with regard to Elizabeth, whose virtue was undoubtedly as spotless as any woman's in all the world, Polmood sighed faintly and in a wheezing whisper said:

'If truly . . . she be innocent, then let her . . . be happier, henceforth, than . . . ever I . . .' But that was all. His body arched and cramped in the last long shiver of death, and the soul (if souls there are) of the piteously misguided Laird of Polmood forsook for ever its earthly tenement, and left his giant mould a pale disfigured corpse in the rustic peace of the hawthorn bower that had so lately been his own.

Baron John Carmichael then followed the domestics back to the Castle. For the next three hours, while waiting for Elizabeth to recover consciousness, he interrogated all the staff, retrieving fragments of the story from odd warps of jumbled memories and doing his best to reconcile them all in the coherent unity of a single picture – the possession of which was a matter of great importance to him, as will soon emerge. When Elizabeth did come round he was aghast to find that she did not recognize him at all. Totally bemused, it seemed, she lay immobile in her bed, fixed her gaze upon the ceiling, and gave voice to nothing but a few words of unintelligible baby-talk.

Shortly after seven o'clock Sir William Moray returned, boggered, he said, from his day's exertions, but triumphantly bearing a brace of likely kestrel chicks. Carmichael explained the situation over a tense and tasteless dinner and entreated Sir William to remain in command at Polmood: to supervise the disposal of the orchard corpses, and, above all, to oversee the proper tending of the languished lady.

While he himself rode through the night.

To Edinburgh.

To throw himself upon the mercy of King James.

18
DEBRIEFING

UP ARTHUR'S SEAT

'In other words, Carmichael, you entirely disobeyed our express command!'

'Sire, this can I not deny. But – '

'Which was, sir?'

'You ordered, Sire, that I must quit, for three full years, the society of which – as it pleased your Majesty to pronounce – I had proved myself unworthy. The sentence, Sire, is burned upon my memory like a brand upon an ox.'

'And is your memory brand enciphered also with our warning that were you to loiter within a score of miles from our present residence, within those said three years, your life should answer for it? Hmmmmn?'

'With respect, Sire, your Majesty's precise condition pertained to my *being found* within the twenty miles. The which, Sire, I submit in all humility, has not occurred.'

'Has it not, by Heaven?'

'No, Sire.'

'Then will you say, sir, that you are not walking here upon this hill beside us? That the porters found you not without the Palace gate, and on a cruelly broken nag forby, at gone the stroke of four? Huh? Will you say, sir, in a word, that we are ourself in cuckoo land, with you a wispy figment?' King James allowed Carmichael to feel for a moment the inscrutable penetration of his sharp sad eyes – eyes that seemed, on this mournful morning, to match the icy bleakness of the distant sea.

His Majesty's attire was black, without ornament, except for the chain of iron remorse about his waist.

In lamentation of the cradle death, the previous morning, of his newborn son: a defective heart, the physicians supposed, that had not evidenced at first but had snapped of a sudden from the strain of his lusty bawling.

Carmichael, also darkly sombre, in borrowed garb, felt a pang of panic that his trust in the King's mercy had been misplaced. It was a grievous tragedy indeed that the infant prince had died, but could not Heaven have picked a better time to call him up? Masking his pangs with a serious frown, he said:

'Nothing is further from my wish, Sire, than to impinge with flippant quibbles upon the gravity of your bereavement.'

His Majesty grunted, and plodded on up the slope.

Carmichael followed. Arguing:

'Yet my feeling and my sole defence is this. That it may not fairly be said that I *was found*, when to the Palace I came and surrendered up of my own free will.'

'Free Will?' the King questioned in a faraway murmur. 'What a glorious notion!'

'If, however, it please ...'

'Aaah, Carmichael! There is nothing can please us on such a day. Nothing can, and nothing should. But that is not the matter.' He sighed heavily through lips pursed with sleepless sorrow. 'Wherefore, we pray you, rehearse again the cardinal details of these dastardly events at Polmood. For it is imperative that we have the facts aright, and our thoughts were bent by other winds when first you were announced. And you were wanting in coherence. And while we talk let us continue on to the summit, shall we not? That we may quell our ravenous woes awhile, by breakfasting upon our nation's peerless beauty.'

'As it please you, Sire.'

It did.

And the two men began at a leisurely pace to contour up the steep and narrow valley between the Craw Hill, on their left, and the peak of Arthur's Seat itself, to the right.

With Carmichael weaponless, as befitted his unsure future.

While King James was lightly rapiered.

With a half-dozen sergeants of the Palace Guard marching after, protectively near yet respectfully out of earshot.

'So it was in fact Polmood that butchered up poor Lamington and Hepburn?' James recapped.

'Yes, Sire. Though without so intending.'

'As it was our brother he wished to do away, and the Duke of Hamilton with him?'

'Indeed. And it was they he followed in the blinding confusion of yon mists that spoiled the hunt.'

'But lost them?'

'So we must conclude, Sire. For when he espied two figures again it was to Lamington and Hepburn that they belonged.'

'Who easily might, in size and shape along, be taken for the dukes.'

'Yes, Sire.'

'And Polmood slew them then in error?'

'According to his dying confession, Sire. In the rage of his passion he shot the both of them through the neck from a distance, and never realized his blunder till he rode up close and found them choking past repair.'

'May the Lord have mercy upon his simple, tortured soul! And thereafter?'

'He despatched the unfortunate victims beyond their mortal pains, exchanged the garments of Lamington for his own – as the two of them were alike in bulk – then struck off their heads and hacked their bodies into strips, to hamper recognition. And slaughtered his own hound, forby, to aid that purpose.'

'In which he did succeed! As even we ourself were foiled, imagining at first that Lamington was to blame, but then concluding that you, Carmichael, had done the filthy deed.'

'Me, Sire?'

'Indeed. For when our brother apprised us of your lurking, and of your trysting illicitly with the lady – that is true, is it not?'

'Yes, Sire. But . . .'

'Well, Sir! There were you in breach of the law already, with every reason to wish the lady's husband dead.'

Carmichael was silent.

The King went on:

'However. What did he with the severed heads?'

'He carried them away to Loch Skeen, Sire, that feeds the fall they call the Gray Mare's Tail. And cast them to its depths.'

'No wonder, then, that they were never found. Dah! A hellish affair, Carmichael. Most hellish. And thereafter, did you say, came Polmood slinking back in a monkish masquerade, to crave asylum within his very walls? Yes? To terrorize the household through the nights with his fabricated ghosting?'

'The former part of that is so, Sire. But the latter detail appears yet partial.'

'Importing?'

'It is true, Sire, that he returned in the guise of a palmer, the scheme for which, he acknowledged to me as his life dripped out, he borrowed from myself – from my sojourning as a gardener.'

'Very like. Very like. Never could it be said that Polmood, poor fellow, had much of a power for novelty. But how, in Heaven's name, could he hope to go undetected?'

'Ah. There, Sire, I believe a glimpse of novelty may be descried. As forby his voluminous cowl and habit – that he slew an authentic friar to obtain . . .'

'Tchah!'

'Forby that cloaking, which he wore always hooded down, he affected vows of muteness, as the inmates surely would not question, and did contrive an obnoxious stench to reek out from his person, and give accosters pause to keep their distance.'

'An obnoxious stench?'

'Indeed yes! And later yester afternoon, when my inquiry took me back about the orchard (and truly, Sire, it all but cost me the content of my stomach so to do) a long dead trout secreted in a pocket of his habit.'

Disgust was echoed by Nostrils sniffing.

'And later, Sire, beneath the cot bed in his closet, did I unearth the gralloched and decomposing carcasses of two white cats! It seems . . .'

'It is plain as noon, sir, that the miserable wretch had long since hocked his soul beyond redemption, with his judgement as the first deposit. But tell us of the partial detail.'

'Sire?'

'Come, come, Carmichael! The hours speed by like the clouds above and the funeral of our son requires attending. Wherefore, sir, try not our patience! You spoke . . .'

'I have it, Sire! And do crave pardon of your Majesty for the billowing of my unslept brains. It was the matter of the bogus ghost.'

'Yes?'

'And he claimed, Sire – and why should he dissemble, I could not but wonder, with his doom only minutes away? – that never was it any part of his outset design to mount a haunting. But the conception came to him a few days on, when he did discern the legend with which the region was already rife.'

King James was perplexed by this, and murmured, half to himself:

'Then the phantom was not of Polmood's instigation?'

'No, Sire. The rumour was about even before his furtive return! Which was on the Monday that your Majesty and the hunters did depart – indeed, it was under cover of the furore of your leaving that he came.'

'A cunning enough ruse, that. Yes. But what of the apparition? Precisely when was its manifestation first reported?'

'The housekeeper, Sirc, who never will be disabused of the conviction that Polmood's revisitation was a resurrection from the grave, avows that the first disturbances to rend her sleep were through the Sunday night. But . . .'

'Well?' the King prompted, irritated by Carmichael's reticence.

'She also does swear, Sire, that the Duke of Rothesay had approached her on the evening of the Sunday, and had given out that he had noted some ghostly doings *through the night of the Saturday*! Before the bodies were even laid to rest.'

His Majesty thought for a moment, than exclaimed:

'Dah! Then doubtless it all began as a vicious hoax.'

'And I have a theory, Sire, though never can it be tested until – pray God! – the lady does revive to sanity. But all accounts report the ardour of your Majesty's brother to linger at Polmood as the lady's guest.'

'Ahm.'

'Yet did not you oblige him, Sire, that first he get her free approval?'

'We did indeed.'

'I therefore diffidently conjecture, Sire, assuming a certain reluctance on the part of the lady who believed herself so lately widowed, that the . . . suitor, Sire, may he not have *invented* the apparition? To kindle fear in her defenceless breast, and anxiety for the presence of a gentleman protector?'

King James did not reply.

Carmichael fretted:

'It is merely a supposal. Sire. And I repent me of the slur . . .'

'No, no, Carmichael! You are very like right, sir – it fits upon his character as does his chain about our belly: he ever was a one to mingle malice in his yarns. But why, Carmichael? *Why?*'

'Sire?'

'The motive of it all? Every deliberate action has its sufficient reason, has it not? Sane and unsane alike. And therefore would we know where any due cause resides, in all you have imparted, why Polmood should abominate our brother so atrociously. Eh?'

'It seems that Polmood was sorely galled, Sire, in the days of his honeymoon at Nidpath, by the lavish attentions showered upon his bride from the Duke of Rothesay's gallantry.'

'But what of that? It was but gossamer frippery, and seen to be innocent by all the court!'

'Indeed, Sire. But may not proofs of innocence slip unseen past the dark blinds of jealousy? And then . . . but it is a particular, Sire, that I fear shall cause offence.'

'Then cause it, sir!'

The voice was desert dry that said:

'On the eve of the hunt, Sire, Polmood, already persuaded – though wrongly, there is no doubt! – of his wife's adultery with Rosay, went creeping to the latter's chamber in hopes of finding them in sin.'

'But did not?'

'No, Sire. Yet did he overhear the Duke of Rothesay depict to the Duke of Hamilton the intimate fashion in which the former *claimed* to have made amatory conquest of their hostess! Whereat Polmood . . .'

'Ooooh!' cried James, as if in physical pain. 'Malignant facile braggart that he was: the nation doubly lacks an heir for *this*?'

Carmichael hung back in awe as his Sovereign sank to his knees on the dry red soil of the turfscuffed hillside, some forty paces from the summit.

'OH, BLESSED LORD,' his upturned Voice addressed the scudding skies, 'IS THIS THY JUDGEMENT ON MY SINS? THAT MY NATION SHALL BE PORTIONED WHEN I DIE? THEN CRUCIFY MY SOUL, DEAR LORD, I BESEECH THEE. BUT SPARE MY PEOPLE THE TORTURES OF DIVISION.' The silverstreaked red head then bowed beneath its plain black cap, and King James, forehead pressed against tight-clasped hands, spent several minutes in silent prayer.

Carmichael turned away and fixed his gaze upon the rising peaks of Pentland, to the south – his breast volcanic with embarrassment, confusion, and trepidation. What if the griefsmitten King should prohibit his . . .

'Come, sir!'

The bewildered baron looked round again, and in silent obedience followed James to the jagged rocky tip of the ancient height.

It was a restless contrary day: pleasantly warm on the plain of the city a thousand feet below, but cool and blustery here on the highest point for miles. And, while rain banked heavy and sullen across the Pentland horizon, the clouds that flocked west along the line of the Forth estuary were fresh and light and jumbly white, like a snowball fight of newly laundered rabbit tails.

His Majesty's gaze was stoically melancholy as it revolved around the visible realm – the tears in his eyes could well have been stung there by the salt breeze gusting off the eastern sea.

'You know, Carmichael,' he reflected, 'the world is more vast than has long been supposed.'

'Sire?'

'The King of Spain has a captain, sir, that has found the Indies by sailing *west*! And many fantastic isles forby, where the sun shines ever, the natives go naked and know no care, and the drinking cup of the humblest man is moulded of purest gold. What think you on that?'

'Why, truly, Sire! The sound of it smacks of roving fancy, does it not? Though, as your Majesty takes it for a fact, it must be true.'

'You are kind, sir, to say so. And if we assured you it were proved that the earth rotates about the sun?'

Carmichael had no reply to this preposterous proposal.

'But our deeper query is:' the King mused on, 'shall ever the King of Spain discover and subdue a land more beauteous than his own?'

'Beauty is . . .'

'And is there anywhere, in all the vastness of the world, more beauty to be found than here? Mmm? Look west, to the lush green woodlands of Corstorphine. North, to the tireless yawning of the river mouth, and the dreamy brown and purple hills of Fife beyond.

Then east, to the cornfield yellows of Lothian – while the sheep dot the southward grazing lands like seagulls a-floating on a many-coloured pond . . . where-ever else could such magnificent diversity of prospect exhibit harmony within a single horizon?'

'Sire, not anywhere!'

'So think you? Yet shall the King of Spain not say the same of *his* horizon?'

Carmichael, torn between honest puzzlement and courteous fealty, uneasily supposed that the King of Spain probably should.

'No, sir! He shall not. Unless he truly loves his people. For a king that cannot love his people loves not himself, and he that cannot love himself may savour beauty nowhere. But you are foxed, Carmichael! By our meandering discursus?'

'I should lie, Sire, if I denied it.'

'Down in yonder Palace, sir, the Queen of Scotland lies prostrate with desolation at her further failure to present a surviving heir.'

'Very natural, Sire,' Carmichael murmured gravely.

'We love our Queen, Carmichael.'

'Of course, Sire.'

'Not with the passionate urgency of youth, perhaps. Yet also do we love our people.'

'And all the nation loves your Majesty in return!'

'Not all, sir. To be exact. But the major part: yes.' Fretfully James stroked his beard. Then his anguish tumbled from its pinnacle isolation with:

'And would you not say, Carmichael, that there is many a king across the world that easily would sacrifice a barren queen?'

Carmichael's romantic loyalty sprang forward:

'But never your Majesty!'

'Oh? Would we not?'

'Never, Sire! Nor seriously debate the option for an instant. And consider, Sire, that the Queen is yet young and *far* from barren! She has . . .'

'Yes, yes. She has tried before and shall try again. And all – God willing! – shall be well.' A flourish of Fingers dismissed the King's lapse from poise. 'And you, Carmichael, by the generous wealth of your trust in ourself, have done your cause great service.'

'Sire?'

'We have got ourself enough, for the while, of this tragedy at

Polmood. The details, however, shall you record – and hence will there return this day, when the burial of our son is done.'

Carmichael bowed in willing assent.

'Sir William Moray's final duty there, you may inform him, shall be to write down fairly the full report that you shall gather and dictate: as posterity must have access to the truth.'

'Indeed, Sire.'

'Yet prudence oft requires that liquor so heady be served to the present somewhat watered, that weaker heads get not too addled, and therefore shall we put it out, for now, that our brother's neck was simply broke in a riding misadventure. Yes?'

Carmichael nodded.

'When the documentation is complete, Sir William shall convey it hither and be restored to our society. And you, Sir John, may deem your banishment revoked and go freely where you will. To resume command of your house and lands, and mingle with the courtiers as it please you – who all shall be advised of your reinstatement in our favour.'

'Your Majesty is surpassing gracious.'

'Yet not gracious enough, we see! Wherefore, sir: what ails you?'

'My thoughts are drawn to the lady, Sire. And with them my heart. To Eliz – Mistress Polmood.'

'Ah! Dear, sweet, unfortunate Elizabeth. And?'

'Shall it please you, Sire, to approve that I court her when she mends?'

'But *shall* she mend, Carmichael?'

'If she does not, Sire, then shall I die!'

'You love the girl so dearly?'

'As dearly, Sire, as you the nation. More dearly than my life itself!'

King James smiled wistfully at the truthsodden cliché. Then sternly recalled:

'But it seems, from what you earlier did say, that the lady is a maid no more!'

'That is so, Sire. Her womenfolk . . . in short, there is no doubt but that she was . . . desecrated before the slaughter began.'

'And therefore may be with child!'

'Yes, Sire.'

'And?'

'If it so should prove, I shall take it to my heart as it were my own, and raise it as my son.'

'Or daughter!'

'Or daughter.'

'Very well, Carmichael. If and when the lady's health shall decently permit, as never, it seems, can she hope for a suitor more steadfast in concern and pure in love, you may woo her with our blessing.'

Carmichael's eyes shone wet with joy.

His gratitude gulped wordlessly.

The King said:

'But now we must descend, sir. There toll the funeral bells.'

TIME LAPSES

1507	August	25th	Sir John Carmichael returns to Polmood.
			The remains of Norman of Polmood and Alexander, Duke of Rothesay, are buried at Drumelzier.
	September	1st	Sir William Moray rides back to Edinburgh to deliver a detailed testament to King James. On the evening of the same day Carmichael returns to his home at Hyndford, but visits Polmood every day for the next fortnight, to ask after Mistress Polmood's continuing recovery and to pay his most cordial respects.
		7th	Elizabeth's 16th birthday passes without ceremony.
		16th	Elizabeth Hunter of Polmood agrees to marry John Carmichael of Hyndford.
		23rd	They are quietly wed by Father Wylie at Drumelzier.

1508	May		Lady Elizabeth presents Sir John Carmichael with her firstborn: John James Hunter Carmichael. In the next five years she produces two more children, both daughters.
1509	April		Henry VII of England dies and is succeeded by his son, the youthful Henry VIII. Relations between Scotland and England are not at first affected.
1511			Relations between Henry VIII and James IV have begun to deteriorate drastically, largely as a result of the Barton affair. James is preparing for war.
1512	April		Queen Margaret at last gives birth to the son who will live to becomes James V of Scotland.
1513	September	9th	The Battle of Flodden Field, disastrous for Scotland, in which James IV and the flower of the nation's manhood (including Baron John Carmichael) are tragically slain. The dead King's body 'was taken to London and Henry (who perhaps envisaged himself as chief mourner in appropriate magnificence) designed a splendid funeral. This did not take place. The royal corpse lay in its lead at Sheen until the house was despoiled after the Reformation, and eventually the embalmed head was hacked off by Queen Elizabeth's master-glazier who

	used it as a sort of *pot-pourri* until he tired of it.' (*A History of Scotland*, by J.D. Mackie, Pelican, p.132.)
November	Lady Ann Gray, fallen from favour in Scotland, returns to England, where three months later she is married to the Earl of Huntingdon.
1514 April	At Hyndford the widowed Lady Elizabeth Carmichael receives a visit from Sir William Moray of Crookston, the celebrated poet and dramatist.
May	Lady Elizabeth takes Sir William for her third and final husband, thereafter bearing him three children, all sons.
1521 July	Publication in Edinburgh of Sir William Moray's dramatic masterpiece: *The Fourth Estate (A Satyre)*.
1528	The sixteen-year-old James V escapes the paternalistic clutches of the Douglas family and is vested in full regal power and dignity. A new era begins.

MORALITIES?

Tease them, if you please, from the following outstanding facts.

That when Elizabeth convalesced from the physical injuries and spiritual gashes inflicted on her that fatal afternoon, the return of her reflecting reason plunged her deep in a pessimistic melancholy. She wept bitterly for hours at a time, and her ponderings at length concluded that (though no particular action could fairly be denominated heinous) the general tenor of her life till then had

428

been manifestly wrong – that though her lifeline did not appear deformed, yet she had allowed it to stretch in an ill direction.

Her marriage to Polmood, she decided, had largely stemmed from overweening desire for certain gratifications which she now perceived as transient and all but worthless: the envious admiration of her sisters, the crowding gallantries of many gentlemen, and the ceremonial glories of a single day – beside the appalling consequences she had suffered? What trifling bubbles they all had been!

Meanwhile, as Elizabeth's thinking matured in this this way, Sir John Carmichael was visiting her every day, patiently, considerately, imposing great discipline on his champing passion, until she mended well enough to bear its weight. And then it was unnecessary for him even to mention love, for gratitude had already so softened up her heart and knit her to him that he was surprised to find, when eventually he proposed, that she accepted without a murmur, having taken it for granted for some time that their ultimate union was both natural and inevitable.

That the marriage of Elizabeth and Carmichael was nonetheless far from an unqualified success.

That he came in time to resent his firstborn, which he took for Polmood's son.

That Elizabeth never disclosed to Carmichael the possibility (indeed, *probability*, when you looked at his yellow hair and bright blue eyes) of the boy's having been sired by Sir William Moray.

That by the time of his honourable death on the battlefield of Flodden, Carmichael was spending tersely blatant periods away from home, and Elizabeth was obliged to lean for company and entertainment on her three demanding children.

And that only at the age of twenty-two, in her final marriage, to the radically reformed Sir William, did our heroine lastingly come to enjoy, amid a blooming offspring, as much of peace and happiness as this fleeting and imperfect scene of existence can ever be expected to confer – even to the point where Sir William could confess to her (as is deducible from his marvellously touching and evocative *Epitaph to the Lyrical Life*) that never once, in all the yearning years of his poetic attempting, had he managed to lay even a fingernail on the luxurious Lady Ann.

Fiction in Paladin

In the Shadow of the Wind   £2.95   ☐
Anne Hébert
Winner of the Prix Femina
'A bewitching and savage novel . . . there is constant magic in it'
Le Matin

'Beautifully written with great simplicity and originality . . . an
unusual and haunting novel'
London Standard

Love is a Durable Fire   £2.95   ☐
Brian Burland
'Burland has the power to evoke time and place with total authority
. . . compelling . . . the stuff of which real literature is made'
Irish Times

To order direct from the publisher just tick the titles you want
and fill in the order form.   **PF3**

All these books are available at your local bookshop or newsagent, or can be ordered direct from the publisher.

To order direct from the publishers just tick the titles you want and fill in the form below.

Name _____

Address _____

_____

Send to:
Paladin Cash Sales
PO Box 11, Falmouth, Cornwall TR10 9EN.

Please enclose remittance to the value of the cover price plus:

UK 60p for the first book, 25p for the second book plus 15p per copy for each additional book ordered to a maximum charge of £1.90.

BFPO 60p for the first book, 25p for the second book plus 15p per copy for the next 7 books, thereafter 9p per book.

Overseas including Eire £1.25 for the first book, 75p for second book and 28p for each additional book.